"The knockout fir̲ s̲ t̲ ̲e̲n̲t̲ry in Kageyama's detective series starring Kats Takemoto… Arresting plotting and suspense, Hunters Point becomes a vital vessel to illuminate the past and those who lived there. This stellar San Francisco noir novel boasts rich characterization and a vital connection to the past."
Editors Pick, Booklife by Publishers Weekly

"Well researched… immersive setting… striking cameos. A fun and captivating historical noir."
Kirkus Reviews

"City politics rules in Peter Kageyama's debut mystery featuring a fully realized Japanese American detective, Kats Takemoto, during the height of the Cold War era. San Francisco, the center of the arts, naval history, and Asian American communities, is the perfect setting for P.I. Takemoto to encounter sharp turns and dangerous inclines in his investigations. A very intriguing beginning of a promising series."
Naomi Hirahara, author of the 2022 Mary Higgins Clark Award winner, *Clark and Division*, **a Japantown Mystery**

"Navigate a thrilling noir San Francisco world as Kageyama weaves fact and fiction into a story packed with social awareness and mysterious wonder."
Justin Eisinger, Co-author New York Times bestseller,
They Called Us Enemy

"To the long line of memorable private eyes who work the mean streets of fictional San Francisco, add a very cool newcomer: Kats Takemoto... Kageyama has done his San Francisco homework, and some of the city's legendary places and characters make wonderful cameo appearances here. You've got to love a novel in which Jack Kerouac and Neal Cassady barrel out of a Beat poetry reading and kick some bad-guy ass, and the heroes use the off-menu delicacies of Chinatown to fight the forces of evil. Hunters Point is a fun, well-plotted page-turner that lovers of San Francisco, and good detective yarns, will enjoy."
Gary Kamiya, bestselling author, *Cool Gray City of Love: 49 Views of San Francisco* **and** *Spirits of San Francisco: Voyages Through the Unknown City*

"In his debut novel, Peter Kagayama conjures up 1950s San Francisco and packs it with famous names from the era, including two beat icons who deliver an actual beating, but the magic of this compelling tale is his fictional creation, Kats Takemoto, a wily detective who combines a little ninja, a little Marlow, and even a little MacGyver. He's a character worthy of a dozen sequels."
Paul Wilborn, author of *Florida Hustle* **and** *Cigar City: Tales from a 1980's Creative Ghetto*

"Well-crafted, carefully researched, and written with insight and understanding of the lives of the people and the world they live in, this is a strong debut novel."
Judy Alter, award-winning author, Kelly O'Connell Mysteries

Published by St. Petersburg Press
St. Petersburg, FL
www.stpetersburgpress.com

Design and composition by St. Petersburg Press
Cover design by Justin Groom
Illustrations by Lisa Wannemacher

Paperback ISBN: 978-1-940300-63-4
eBook ISBN: 978-1-940300-64-1

First Edition

HUNTERS POINT

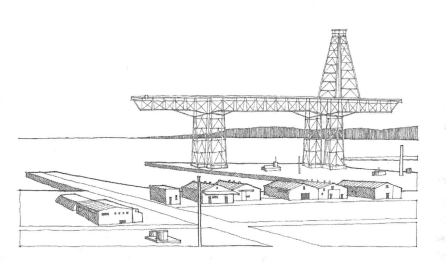

A NOVEL OF SAN FRANCISCO
BY PETER KAGEYAMA

For my father and mother, the original Kats and Molly.

And for Lisa, who believed every step of the way.

Acknowledgments

Although this isn't my first book, it's my first work of fiction, and it feels very different from previous journeys down this path. I must acknowledge the book *Facing the Mountain*, written by Daniel James Brown, as a huge inspiration. Like many of his generation, my father, Paul Kageyama, didn't talk about his internment during World War II. He'd mention "camp" occasionally, but he never shared those stories or his feelings about the experience with me. So reading Brown's book filled in the gaps in my own cultural and familial history and formed the idea of Kats. Writing this story connected me with my father in a way that we never had during his life.

I must thank San Francisco City Guides (sfcityguides. org) for their amazing love and knowledge of that great city. Thank you also to Rory O'Connor, Lisa Ryers, Joyce Kurtz, and especially Rodney Paul, who took me through Bayview Heights and Hunters Point. And speaking of great guides, thank you to Gary Kamiya, author and lover of all things San Francisco, for the insight into your city.

Thank you, Grace Lim, for your feedback and encouragement. You're a great reader. Amy Dann and Dominque Thuriere, I appreciate your insightful and thorough notes. Dave Bloch, thank you for the encouragement and "hazel eyes" suggestion! Thank you to Katherine Kamiya, Mark Kamiya, and Asaye Takagi for the insight into our family histories.

And my biggest thanks to my "first reader" in all things, Lisa Wannemacher, for all the love and support on our journey.

CHAPTER 1

K atsuhiro Takemoto watched the man who was watching the woman. Voyeurism wasn't unusual for Kats. As a private detective, he spent too much time quietly observing the lives of others. Today was different. Today he knew the man he was watching.

Fort Point, under the Golden Gate Bridge, was where tourists, lovers, and even the locals came for the spectacular view of the bridge and the bay. It was unusually empty today, but Kats wasn't looking at the scenery. The tall man in the dapper gray suit and brown hat kept his distance as he watched the woman walk toward the embankment's edge. He didn't need to conceal himself, as the woman was focused on the bouquet of flowers she held in her white, gloved hands. Even at this distance, Kats knew she was beautiful. Her hair was platinum blond and swept up, and she wore a dark blue dress that flattered her high-heeled walk.

She stopped at the elevated edge and began to slowly pick apart her bouquet, throwing the flowers one at a time into the cold water below. The gray-suited man shifted back and forth as if he was trying to puzzle out the meaning of this gesture. As the last of the flowers fell from the woman's hands, she purposefully turned toward the bay and jumped into the water.

The man stood stunned for a moment but then rushed forward to where she had stood. Throwing off his coat and hat, he approached the water and prepared to leap.

"Cut!" came the voice over Kats's shoulder. Instantly the empty park was filled with activity. Production assistants rushed forward, the stuntmen and stunt women crawled back up the embankment, and costumers grabbed the coat and hat as the park transformed into a Hollywood movie set.

Kats turned his attention to the gray-suited man who had turned and was walking back toward the camera and the large presence sitting there. Alfred Hitchcock, the acclaimed film director, sat talking with his cameraman and his assistants. "That was fine, James. I believe we have what we need," Hitchcock said in his unmistakable voice. Never one to lavish praise on even the finest actors, everyone knew that was Hitch's way, especially the man in the gray suit who was an old hand at dealing with the demanding director.

Jimmy Stewart, America's favorite male actor for over a decade, smiled as he approached the director. Even though the reshoot of this scene could probably have been done with a stand-in, Stewart was happy to reprise the scene and the character he had inhabited since late summer. "How about some b-roll of me swimming in the bay?" quipped the actor with a smile.

Hitch elongated his already elongated face, "Thank you, James. We are quite done with San Francisco." Production delays and these reshoots had put Hitchcock behind schedule, and everyone knew he was feeling pressure from the studio. He was anxious to return to the controlled confines of Paramount Studios in Hollywood to finish his film.

Kats quietly stood back as several folks approached the actor and attended to various bits of business. Eventually Stewart broke away and, turning to Kats, smiled and said, "What do you think?"

"I thought I was going to have to jump in after you." Stewart laughed, and Kats smiled at the face familiar to everyone in America. Kats was still amazed that he and this American icon had become friends over the past several months. The movie had brought them together.

"From Among the Dead" was the working title of the film that had come to San Francisco several months before. The city was the setting of the film, and the producers had sent word out that they were looking for a local private detective to help the then-unnamed film star act like a local private detective. Some friends of Kats, knowing he was a huge movie fan as well as an accomplished private eye, got him an interview that turned out to be more of an audition.

Back in June, Kats had been told to report to the Fairmont Hotel on Nob Hill to meet with the production team. When he arrived at the Casablanca suite on the sixth floor, he was ushered into the beautiful, sunlit room with half a dozen people busily working at the desk and tables. The production director introduced himself as Frank. "That's Ralph, our assistant director," Frank explained, pointing to a disheveled-looking man with glasses and two clipboards. "And this is our star," he turned and gestured toward the man sitting in the corner, quietly smoking a cigarette. Jimmy Stewart smiled and gave an affable nod toward Kats, who suddenly felt his heart accelerate, though experience and discipline allowed him to play it cool as he nodded hello to them all.

"I'll get right to it," Frank said. "We are looking for someone who can help Jimmy play the role of a San Francisco private detective. Someone who knows the lingo, the profession, the 'moves' as it were."

"Yeah, and someone who knows the city," added the assistant director. Kats nodded and gave them his resume highlights. Born in San Francisco in 1924 to first-generation Japanese immigrant parents, Kats was a Nisei, a second-generation Japanese American. He had been a licensed PI since 1952. Frank and Ralph looked over their notes, nodding their heads, but Kats felt they were only half listening.

From the back of the room, "Were you interned?" Stewart asked.

Kats sat for a moment, feeling his muscles tense as an old, familiar anger blossomed like an ember being blown upon. That anger was an old companion he had spent years trying to leave behind. Keeping his voice level and calm, he said, "Yes, my family was interned at Minidoka in Idaho." The sentence seemed to hang there as the room held its breath.

"And did you serve in the military?" Stewart continued.

"Yes, sir. I was in the army and served in Europe." Stewart sat forward in his chair, staring pointedly at Kats.

"What was your unit?"

"I was with the 100th Infantry Battalion and then the 442nd Infantry Regiment."

Stewart stared at Kats. The two men held each other's gaze in some silent dialogue that the others didn't seem to comprehend. Rising from his chair, Stewart approached Kats, who unconsciously stood before the taller man. Stewart extended his hand, and they exchanged a long handshake. "Thank you for your service," Stewart said.

Kats looked back at the man and replied, "And thank you for yours."

Stewart nodded and smiled warmly at Kats. Turning toward the production director, "Hire him," he said.

As the set began to efficiently breakdown around them, Stewart asked, "Still joining us for dinner tonight?"

"Yes. Tonga Room, eight o'clock."

With a nod and a wave, Stewart turned and made his way through the set. Kats took a last look around, thinking his Hollywood turn was quietly ending. It had been a fun and new challenge when he started back in August. It began with driving Stewart and the location scout around town, playing more tour guide than private detective. Stewart asked Kats about his practice and any interesting cases he'd worked on.

"Well, Mr. Stewart," began Kats.

"Call me Jim."

"Jim it is," Kats said. So began America's favorite actor's crash course into being a private detective and all things San Francisco. Kats explained that the job was mostly about patience and observation. Sitting, waiting for the story to reveal itself.

"Sounds like my last movie with Hitch, *Rear Window*,"

Stewart chuckled.

"I loved that movie, but a good PI wouldn't let himself be seen as he watches. You needed to be more in the shadows."

"Maybe next time," Stewart smiled. "Do you carry a gun?"

"Not since the war," Kats replied in a somewhat clipped tone. "Everyone thinks we're like Sam Spade or Phillip Marlowe, with strange, beautiful women showing up at our office, searching for lost artifacts and missing treasures. Usually we're looking for a stray husband or wife or trying to track down a long-lost relative. I spend more time in the library than I do in seedy bars."

After a week of 'teaching' Stewart, Kats thought his work would be done. But the studio informed him that they'd be retaining him for the duration of the shoot. Mr. Stewart needed security and a driver while he was in town and said he wanted Kats. So for the next several weeks, Kats got a crash course in Hollywood filmmaking. Much like being a private detective, he learned it involved a lot of waiting, punctuated by moments that demanded everyone's total focus and professionalism. After wrap each day, Stewart got to partake in San Francisco's culture and nightlife.

Kats took him to see jazz at the many clubs that had popped up across the city. They saw Miles Davis at Club Alabam and Chet Baker at The Blue Mirror. And Stewart's celebrity status got them in to see Ella Fitzgerald at The Long Bar. But it was Kats's local knowledge that took them to Jimbo's Bop City on Post near Kats's home. Jimbo's was at the intersection of the Black community and Japantown. It was where the jazz musicians came to hang out, drink, and jam after their official gigs were over. Open from 2 am till dawn, the proprietor, Jimbo, was famous for ensuring that no prejudice or racism was allowed through the front door.

Everyone was welcome, so long as you were cool. When they rolled up that evening with Jimmy Stewart in tow, Jimbo himself welcomed them. And cool as his reputation, Jimbo made Jimmy feel like just another regular, even charging him the customary $1 cover for nonmusicians, much to the star's delight.

One evening Stewart asked Kats what he knew about the Beat scene in the city. "Well, there's quite a lot of activity in the North Beach neighborhood. They call it the San Francisco Renaissance, and I do know a few folks in the scene. The obscenity trial involving the City Lights Bookstore owner from earlier this year brought a lot of attention to them, not all of it good."

"Yeah, I read about that. Some book of poetry caused all the uproar?"

"Words got some folks pretty riled up," Kats said in his most nonpartisan voice.

"Well, I'm glad that free speech won out. I've seen too much of that crap in Hollywood with the Red Scare and that bastard McCarthy."

Kats looked at Stewart, who noticed the raised eyebrow. "Hey, I'm a Republican and a military man, but I believe in art and free expression. We're big enough and strong enough to handle an unpopular idea or two." Kats nodded, wondering what the average American moviegoer would think of the surprisingly progressive ideas Stewart held.

That night Kats took Stewart to The Cellar off Columbus on Green. There, poets read their work and were accompanied by jazz musicians. Kats thought it a gentler entry to the scene than taking him directly to The Six Gallery, where Allen Ginsberg had first read his poem "Howl" and seemed to ignite the entire movement. Stewart clapped politely, but

Kats could tell it wasn't his scene. They were both impressed, though, when one of the young cocktail waitresses jumped on stage to perform her poetry to the beat of the musicians.

As Kats returned to town from Fort Point, he had one errand to run before dinner that night. Heading to the North Beach neighborhood, Kats parked on Columbus and entered the recently famous City Lights Bookstore. The bookstore was one of the centers of the Beat movement and had attracted artists, agitators, and outsiders since it had opened in 1953. Earlier that summer, the owner, Lawrence Ferlinghetti, had been acquitted of obscenity charges for selling copies of Allen Ginsberg's book *Howl.* The trial attracted national attention for Ginsberg, Ferlinghetti, and City Lights. Ultimately, art won out with the judge ruling that the poem *Howl* had some "redeeming social importance."

There, as Kats entered the store, was the book itself, prominently featured in its own display. Grabbing a copy, he headed toward the counter.

"Takemoto-san!" came the voice from across the store. Turning, Kats saw the smiling face of his friend, Shigeyoshi Murao, the store manager. Shig, a couple of years younger than Kats, looked a few years older with a wispy beard and longer hair. The two had known each other since camp. Both of their families had been sent to the Minidoka Relocation Center in Idaho in 1942.

The two men shook hands, and Shig noticed the copy of *Howl* in Kats's hand. "That little troublemaker," he snorted. "Not your usual taste."

"Going-away present for a friend," Kats said.

"I've got a few signed copies behind the counter. Let me get you one of those."

"Thanks."

Kats knew that the book really was a troublemaker for Shig. In fact, it was Shig who had sold a copy of the book to an undercover police officer and started the whole criminal procedure. Shig was arrested along with Ferlinghetti. Larry was able to use the trial to promote his store and his own book of poetry. Can't blame him for that, thought Kats. Even though the charges against him were eventually dropped, Shig was standing up for an idea, for a principle, and that made him brave in Kats's eyes.

People told Kats all the time that he was brave. For his service, for his unit's actions, for the Silver Star in the back of his sock drawer. But they didn't understand what so many of the "brave" ones knew—that they didn't do it because they were brave. They did it because they were young and didn't know what they didn't know. They didn't know what they could lose. They were brave because they were in a terrible place together and they loved their brothers and friends. If they'd had time to think about it, they'd have run screaming for a foxhole.

Kats knew that Shig was brave. Brave because he had been alone. When the law and the federal government had come down on him, it was his alone to bear. He didn't have a platoon to support him, and he wasn't standing up to an existential evil like Hitler. Shig was standing up for an ideal, an abstraction that many would never understand or even support.

To Kats, that made him a hero.

"Hey, man. I'm glad you stopped by. I was going to call you about a friend of mine who could use your help."

"My calendar has freed up a bit. Tomorrow?"

"Yeah, I think tomorrow night would work. How about

Vesuvio next door around 7 pm? My friend's got a day job but will be up here in the evening. He's reading at the up-and-comers night over at The Six Gallery."

"A poet?" Kats said, trying not to sound judgmental.

"Yeah, man, and a good one, too."

"Thought you would have had enough of that scene after getting busted."

"Nah, that was fun," Shig said, smiling.

Kats returned to his office at 1664 Post between Webster and Laguna, in the area known as Japantown. Prior to the war, the neighborhood had been the heart of the Japanese American community with restaurants, shops, and schools that made it one of the largest enclaves of Japanese outside of Japan. That changed with the attack on Pearl Harbor and the subsequent removal and internment of over 110,000 Japanese Americans, including Kats and his family.

Most of the Issei, first generation, and Nisei, second generation like Kats, had been forced to liquidate their businesses and sell their homes and possessions. Kats's family was able to transfer the deed to their home to Kats, who as a natural-born American citizen, was more protected than his Japan-born parents. So the family home was there when they finally returned after the war. It was full of squatters, but it was there.

The following year, Kats enrolled at the University of San Francisco using the GI Bill, eventually getting his degree in business. His older sisters had taken jobs in Chicago and Washington, DC during the war and didn't return to California. That left Kats alone with his parents. His mother, Yaeko, tried to make the best of their return. She reconnected with some of their original neighbors, who had returned and made a particular effort to welcome new arrivals to Japan-town. His father was another case. He was unable to return to his job as a salesman, in part because the company was no longer there, but also because most companies wouldn't hire Japanese Americans. The wounds, the resentments, were too fresh and too deep for many to accept. His proud father was forced to take a job in a candy factory to support his family.

For his parents' generation, especially for the men, there was a loss of station and of dignity that was hard to bear. His father was a quiet, reserved man and not one to complain, but Kats could see that the love that he once held for his adopted country was being stripped away, layer by layer. Even Kats, a decorated veteran, wasn't immune to the daily prejudices and slights that came with the color of his skin and the shape of his eyes. This environment was the deciding factor in his parents' decision to return to Japan in 1953.

Kats pulled into the alley, parking his car behind the office. His residence was upstairs in the narrow, three-story Victorian building that had once housed his entire family. As he entered, he knew immediately someone was in the office.

"*Irrashaimasse*," came the woman's voice from the office. Welcome indeed, Kats thought as he opened the door to the front room and saw the small, elderly Japanese woman busily tidying his office.

"Hello, Mrs. Harada," Kats said as Naoko Harada came over to him with a smile. Ever since his parents had returned to Japan, Mrs. Harada had made it her mission to look after him. She cleaned his place, did his laundry, and even occasionally cooked for him. Although he repeatedly told her it wasn't necessary, she continued to mother him. He had to admit, her musubi was delicious.

"How are you today, *O-bachan*?" Kats asked. Grandmother.

He had come to think of her like a grandmother figure over the years. The Haradas had been friends of the family as long as he could remember. They were in camp together. Their oldest son, Seiji, was a year older than Kats, and they had gone to the same school. Their daughter, Emiko, was three years younger than Kats and lived with her mother up the street.

"Oh, I'm fine, Katsuhiro-kun," she said, but Kats could hear a bit of worry in her voice. He knew better than to directly ask her about what was bothering her. It was considered rude, and one had to maneuver around the question before getting to the real issue.

"How is Seiji? Is he coming home for Christmas?"

"Unfortunately, no. His law practice in Chicago has him very busy. But I hope to see my grandson in the spring when they come out again."

"It's hard to imagine Seiji as a father. Seems like we were just kids ourselves," Kats offered. "And Emiko is well?"

"Oh," stuttered Mrs. Harada, "she's... she's well."

Kats reached over and took Mrs. Harada's hand and simply waited.

"I'm sorry, Katsuhiro. I'm worried about her." He nodded and let her continue.

"She's become so... so American. She insists on being called 'Amy,' and every time I talk to her about getting married, she gets angry. She goes out most every weekend but won't tell me where she goes. I worry about her. She's getting older, and I don't want her to be alone."

Emiko was three years younger than Kats, making her thirty. But he knew it was different for girls.

"And she's such a pretty girl, too," Mrs. Harada continued. "You think so, don't you Katsuhiro?" she asked as she

squeezed his hand. It was an open secret among the Haradas and the Takemotos that they had hoped Katsuhiro and
Emiko might end up together. The two had been friends
since childhood, and Kats cared deeply for her. But the one
time they had kissed as teenagers, it was both awkward and
comical, and they'd both laughed so hard it became clear that
they were meant to be more like brother and sister.

"Emiko is beautiful," Kats assured her. "But you can't force
love."

"But what's she doing when she goes out? I worry so
much."

"Well…," Kats began.

"Could you investigate her for me?"

"You mean follow her?"

"Yes. That's what you do, correct?"

"I'm not sure that following a friend is a good idea."

"Katsuhiro-kun, she's my daughter, and you're like a son
to me. It's perfectly fine for a mother to know what her child
is doing. Your parents would agree with me."

There it was, thought Kats. The familial obligation card.
As much as he didn't like the idea of following Emiko, he
knew that his parents would be ashamed of him for not
helping Mrs. Harada.

"OK. I will follow her on the weekend to find out where
she's going."

Mrs. Harada nodded firmly as if Kats was finally making
sense.

Stepping outside his office, Kats took in the cool night
air. He decided to walk to the Fairmont, just over a mile
away on Nob Hill.

Gliding into the opulent lobby, the hotel was outfitted

for Christmas, including fake snow on the Christmas trees. It reminded him that the first place he'd ever seen snow was in Idaho over a decade ago. White snow on black, tar paper rooftops was strangely beautiful. The barbed wire and armed guards made it less so, but he did recall how his family had all been together, and that made him smile inwardly.

Kats strode through the lobby with its high ceiling and marbled columns. He took the elevator down to the famous Tonga Room. Once it had been an indoor swimming pool, but after the war it had been transformed into a south sea's lagoon, including a floating island where the band would play. The food was good, the drinks had parasols, and it was a local landmark.

Stewart and a small group of people were at a large, reserved table facing the lagoon. Approaching the table, Kats recognized the director of photography, the location manager, a couple of men from the set that he could never quite tell what their exact job was, and actor Ray Bailey, who had played the coroner in this latest film and was another Hitchcock veteran. Kats greeted all of them and sat down.

"Sorry to keep you all waiting," he said.

"Well, we're waiting on one more," Stewart said, raising his drink to Kats. "And we know she likes to make an entrance."

Almost on cue, Stewart and seemingly the entire restaurant's eyes shifted to the entrance. Kats turned and saw Kim Novak, the female lead in the film, walk toward the table escorted by the maître d'. Several men at the bar openly gaped. 'Cool' was the word that came to Kats's mind. Novak knew every eye was on her but acted as nonchalant as if this were normal and happened every day. In fact, it did. One thing that Kats still marveled at was the effect that Hollywood actresses had on people. To say they were beautiful was a huge understatement. Novak was another in the long list of beautiful blond "ice queens" that Hitchcock seemed to prefer. The other female lead, Barbara Bel Geddes, despite being made into Stewart's bespeckled, somewhat frumpy pal, was also stunning. There's a reason they're *in* the movies, and the rest of us *go* to the movies, Kats thought.

The table stood as Novak joined them, and Stewart held out a seat for her. Despite the onscreen romance and clear affection Jim had for her, Kats had been impressed with Stewart's complete professionalism and propriety. Once he'd been known as America's most eligible bachelor, but Stewart had married almost ten years prior and now had four children—two adopted sons, and twin daughters born to him and his wife Gloria. Many times, on their nighttime adventures, beautiful and not so beautiful but remarkably confident women had approached Stewart with offers that would make a sailor blush. He always smiled, chatted with them, thanked them for the offer, and bought them a drink.

The waiter came around, drinks and food were ordered, and the group settled into what they knew was their last night in San Francisco together and likely with this particular group of friends. Movies were like that—a short, intense period of partnership and camaraderie until the project was done, and then everyone went on to the next mission. A lot like the military, Kats thought, but with less dire consequences.

Stewart went around the table and thanked everyone and, coming to Kats, proposed a toast. "To Kats, for making me look like a real private detective and keeping me out of trouble!" "Cheers," said the table, and Kats felt his face flush.

"And I have a gift for you," Stewart said, pulling a long box from under the table.

"I have one for you too," Kats replied. Passing the packages up and down the table, Kats motioned for Stewart to open his first.

Tearing the wrapping paper, Stewart laughed out loud. "*Howl and Other Poems* by Allen Ginsberg!" The table erupted in laughter.

"It's authentically San Francisco, and I know you're a bit of a Beat[1] at heart," Kats said.

Next, Kats hefted the heavy box, undid the string, and revealed a camera with a long telephoto lens attached to it.

"Is this…" began Kats.

"Yes. It's the Exakta 35mm camera and lens we used in *Rear Window*. I thought it would be perfect for a private detective."

"Or a voyeur," quipped Novak with a smile.

Kats, rarely at a loss for words, was dumbfounded by the gift. First of all, it was a great camera and lens for the type of work he did. But more importantly, it was the tool, the key prop from *Rear Window*, one of the best films ever made.

"Quite an artifact, Jim," Bailey said. "Do you have the Maltese Falcon back at your home, too?"

"Stuff collects at my house, and my wife wants me to declutter," Stewart replied.

"Thank you, Jim. This is amazing."

Around the time dessert arrived, so too did two rather drunken admirers. The two men had been sitting at the bar for a while, Kats had noted. They kept looking over at the table, back and forth from Stewart to Novak, though mostly at the actress. Approaching the table, they loudly proclaimed their fandom and offered to buy the table a round of drinks if Novak would join them for "just one drink." Stewart, the natural leader of the group, spoke up.

"Thank you, gentlemen, but we're celebrating here tonight. How about I buy you guys a round instead?" Stewart gestured toward the bar, but the two men were too drunk or too intent to be dissuaded. Kats noted that they were both reasonably well dressed, late thirties, and big. Big the way that once athletic men get as they grow a little older—thicker of waist and thinner of hair. The blond one spoke for the darker haired one, "Come on, Jimmy. Share her for just one drink."

By this time the waiter had arrived and was looking anxiously at the situation before him. "Please, gentlemen," he said and placed a hand on the large, blond man's arm.

With a sudden, violent shrug, the man said, "Don't fucking touch me!" The waiter stumbled back, and Kats rose gracefully to catch him.

Stewart rose from his chair, "OK, that's enough," he declared as the others slid backward in their chairs. Kats smoothly glided forward and stepped between the actor and the "fans" and raised his hands, palms forward in a gesture to calm the bulls before they got further riled up.

Blond sneered down at Kats, alcohol streaming from his breath, "Fucking slant. I chewed up guys like you all over the Pacific." And I chewed up guys like you all over Europe, Kats thought but didn't vocalize. Just then the big man's hand came forward like an exclamation point aimed at Kats's chest. In one seamless motion, Kats twisted to his right, disappearing from the man's thrust as his left hand caught the bigger man's hand and pulled him forward. The man seemed to lurch forward, but then suddenly Kats pivoted backward and to his left. The blond man screamed in pain as his wrist, then arm, bent in ways they should not, which forced him to fall onto his back.

His partner looked shocked at first but then bared his teeth and charged forward toward Kats as if to tackle him. Kats stepped inside his bearlike grasp, and with a pivot followed by an audible gasp, the second big man was suddenly rising up, feet over head as he was flipped over the railing into the lagoon.

Everyone's eyes followed the man into the pool, but Kats heard Stewart exclaim, "Behind you!" as he felt two large arms encircle his head and neck. Kats reached up and found the man's right hand, grasped his thumb, and applied surprising pressure, causing the man's grip to weaken. In that moment, Kats twisted, dropped his shoulder, and was free. An open-handed *atemi waza* strike found the man's kidney, and he grunted in pain. Kats placed his foot behind the man's leg as he swept an arm across his chest. The man seemed to fly into the floor, landing flat on his back. He lay semi-motionless, groaning.

Several of the wait staff then appeared, along with the manager and hotel security, who quickly escorted the two men away. As the restaurant returned to normal, the group marveled at what they'd seen. Novak kissed Kats on the cheek and thanked him for his chivalry, causing him to blush.

"So, what was that?" Stewart asked. "Karate? Judo?"

"Bit of both," Kats replied.

"Well, we should have you doing fight scenes in my next movie," Stewart laughed.

"Deal."

The rest of the evening was pleasantly uneventful, and when they parted late that night, Stewart and Kats shook hands. "Truly a pleasure getting to know you," Stewart said. "I hope our paths cross again. And I'm glad I got to see you in action. I knew you were a tough guy!"

CHAPTER 2

Vesuvio was a well-known watering hole in the North Beach neighborhood, directly across the alley from City Lights Bookstore. The bar had become a favorite of the arts community, especially the so-called Beats. The two floors were covered in art, and the vibe was bohemian but friendly. As Kats entered that evening, he immediately saw Shig in the back with a sandy-haired young White man.

Kats wasn't exactly surprised; he had white clients. But his main clientele were immigrants, the Black community, and of course Asians (except for the Korean community, whose enmity for the Japanese went back centuries). These folks weren't usually taken seriously by white private investigators. Kats never advertised. He just treated them all with respect, and he listened. Soon he had become *the* guy that certain communities went to see when they needed a certain kind of help.

Waving him over, Shig pushed out a seat for Kats to join. He sat next to a young, olive-skinned man. He was handsome, with high cheekbones and hazel, worried eyes.

"Hey, Kats. Meet Anton Vello."

"Hello, Mr. Vello."

"*Hajimemashite Takemoto-san,*" Anton said. Kats was impressed. Most people stumbled over rudimentary Japanese and how to pronounce his name, but Anton said it in a practiced way with a hint of an accent that to Kats's ear sounded Italian.

"Anton is an up-and-coming poet with an amazing ear for languages of all kinds," Shig said.

Nodding, Vello pursed his lips into a compressed line that only underscored the worry that Kats had noted before.

"Thank you, Shig. I wish I had more time for my words and for art, but right now I'm worried about my father."

Kats nodded and gestured for Vello to continue.

"This is about my family. My father, Carlo, came here from Malta in 1927."

Malta, thought Kats. That's why the accent sounded vaguely Italian. He'd heard it when he was in Sicily and Italy during the war. The tiny island in the Mediterranean was a crossroads of European and North African culture.

"He came alone, in the hope of making a better life and sending home money to his family still in Valletta," Vello continued. "He was the son of the son of a ship builder. My family has been making sailboats for four generations. My father came here and worked on the docks for local shipbuilders at first but soon saved enough money to start his own small business down in Bayview Heights."

Bayview Heights was in the south bay area and known for its cheap land and waterfront access to the bay. The dirtiest businesses located there, along with Hunters Point Shipyard, a huge navy repair station. Over 15,000 people worked at the shipyard, and one could regularly see destroyers, cruisers, and even battleships moving in and out of the shipyard. Good location for a boat-building business, Kats thought.

"My father is very good at what he does. He built the business from a one-man operation to having over a dozen craftsmen working for him today. My father is more than a craftsman Mr. Takemoto -"

"Please call me Kats."

"And call me Anton. Yes, my father is an artist, from his earliest, most basic boats to what he does today. He makes sailboats that are floating works of art. The smallest detail to the longest keel. He shapes wood and canvas like a potter shapes clay or a sculptor shapes marble."

"Sounds amazing," Kats said.

"Yes," Anton said, "it was."

Kats cocked his head at that, and Vello continued.

"You see, Kats, my father is dying. Cancer. He doesn't have much time left. He wants to ensure that my brother and I inherit the business and keep the 'Vello & Sons' name going. But about six months ago, someone started buying up large pieces of land in Bayview Heights. Many of the locals jumped at the chance to sell, but for long-standing businesses like my father's, no way would they sell."

"My father told me that a lawyer and an 'associate' had come knocking last spring. They said they represented an east coast ship builder that was looking to expand to California, but Dad said that it quickly became obvious they didn't know anything about ship building and were fishing for something else. They offered a more than fair price for the business and my father's land. But of course he said no."

"How much land are we talking about?"

"We have four acres in the South Basin on Armstrong. It's on what's called the Yosemite Slough. You can see Double Rock from our dock."

Kats knew the area. It was an industrial waterfront, with lots of businesses that cared more about their work than their appearance. It was near the naval shipyard, and Double Rock was a local navigation landmark that was literally two large rock outcroppings that stuck out of the water adjacent to the opening of the basin.

"It was around that time that my father finally went to see a doctor after we noticed how much weight he'd lost and how much pain he always seemed to be in. Cancer, in his bones, in his organs. Nothing to be done except manage the pain."

Anton paused, and Kats and Shig gave him a moment to collect himself.

"You know, my father went back to work the same day he received diagnosis. Still is in the shop every day. In fact, he seems more intent than ever. And more adamant than ever not to sell."

Kats quietly wondered what it was Anton wanted him to do, but experience told him to let the man talk and to just listen.

"My older brother Gianni is the true successor of my father. He loves ship building and has become a master craftsman. Second sons have more freedom, so when I had the chance to go to college, I jumped at it. I thought I was going to study business to improve the family trade. Freshman year at the University of San Francisco, I made the mistake of taking a creative writing class. Four years later, I could do a little accounting, read a profit and loss sheet, and had been published in half a dozen literary journals."

"But you still work in the ship-building business?" Kats asked.

"I'd been trying to leave, but with my father's illness, all those plans got put on hold. I manage the books, pay the bills, and let the craftspeople do what they do best."

"So, what is it you need a guy like me for?" Kats finally pressed.

"In the past couple of months, the offers became not-so-veiled threats. The same couple of guys came back talking about how the government was going to come in and force us all to sell using eminent domain and that we should sell to them to get a better price. Then they said people could get hurt if we didn't sell."

"Did you call the police?"

"No, the police don't help in communities like ours."

"What about your neighbors, the other business owners?"

"Bayview Heights was where immigrants like my father came when they couldn't afford land elsewhere, or even if they could, people wouldn't sell to them. The Italians, Maltese, and Chinese have been coming there for years. The Blacks have been coming since the end of the war because of the jobs at the naval yard and because there were no other places they could buy or even rent homes."

"Most of the folks like my dad, who came and bought land, are staying put. Their businesses and their homes are there. But there has been trouble. A couple of stores were broken into, and the boats of one Chinese shrimping company had all their nets cut one night last month. And last week there was a fire in an old warehouse that destroyed the entire building. Someone is putting more pressure on our community to sell and get out. I'm hoping you can help us figure out who's behind this and stop them before someone really gets hurt."

Kats took in the story. He'd heard nothing about any of this, but that wasn't surprising. The Bayview Heights neighborhood was so isolated and remote that it didn't feel like part of the San Francisco he knew. That was certainly one of the reasons the navy liked it.

Shig looked at Kats. "I don't like the idea of anyone forcing people out of their homes and their livelihoods," he said flatly.

Kats nodded in agreement, remembering how he'd met Shigeyoshi Murao for the first time. They were neighbors of a sort at the Minidoka War Relocation Center in south-central Idaho. Arriving in May 1942, they were housed in adjacent tar paper barracks. Shig's family with five children and Kats's family with three children, all about the same age. The bookish Shig, fifteen at the time, and the athletic Kats, then seventeen, made for an odd pair, but they were the youngest boys with strong older sisters and naturally gravitated to each other.

For their parents, long prevented from gaining citizenship, the camp represented their total loss of identity, economic status, and dignity. Some became bitter, but many others went in the other direction and loudly proclaimed their patriotism to the United States. Kats's father Shuzo initially insisted that the war would be over soon and they would be freed. He outwardly had faith in his adopted country. Kats's mother, Yaeko, would officially support his father, but Kats and his sisters knew that she didn't feel the same way. She knew that a massive injustice had been done to them, and it was maternal concern for her children that made her much more protective of the family.

For the young people in camp, especially the young men like Kats and Shig, the experience was strangely liberating. No longer under the strict discipline of their parents and pressures of normal education followed by jobs, the young folks had a strange bit of freedom. Kats joined one of several baseball teams that formed and quickly became a standout player as he had been in high school. Shig worked in the camp library and helped his father in the camp commissary preparing meals for the over 9,000 internees.

Kats, Shig, and 110,000 other Japanese Americans knew far too well about being forced out of their homes, and both knew that they wanted to help Anton Vello. They just weren't sure how to do it.

Across town in the Financial District, a small gray man in a gray suit and coat entered the thirty-two-story Russ Building on Montgomery. It was the tallest building in San Francisco and a prestigious address. On a Friday evening, the building was mostly quiet. A few people made their way out of the lobby as the cleaning crews began their nightly journey through the many offices and hallways. The gray man took the stairs, as the elevator operators had long since gone home. Arriving on the fourth floor, he proceeded down the hallway to suite 455, the unlisted office of H. W. Charles Construction, and entered.

Despite the late hour, there were three people in the outer office. Two men in cheap suits, and a woman who sat behind the secretary's desk. All eyes turned to him as he entered, but no one was surprised. He was expected.

The gray man removed his hat, revealing a bland face and

hair that was technically brown, but again, hard to define. He might have been thirty. He might have been fifty. Everything about the man was forgettable except his eyes. Behind his wire-rimmed glasses, his eyes were pale blue and sharp. They moved quickly from face to face, alighting on the once-pretty secretary. She drew in her breath and buzzed the intercom. Raising the phone to her ear, she said, "He's here." A moment later the door to the adjoining office buzzed and clicked open.

"Come on in, John," the booming voice said from inside. "John" entered. That wasn't his real name, but his business card read "John Sand—Emerald City Investments." The office was surprisingly opulent in contrast to the spare outer room. Behind a large desk sat a large man with rolled up shirtsleeves, an open shirt collar, and loosened tie. Harold Wallace Charles, forty-nine years old, and "Harry" to most, was a bull of a man. Just over six feet tall, his short, cropped dark hair was salt and pepper, as was his bushy mustache. At first glance, one might think he was a fat middle-aged man, but Harry was solid. Broad shouldered and barrel chested, he had thick forearms and ham-sized hands. Hands that Sand knew had killed many men in Europe during the war. Harry knew he intimidated most people just by walking into a room, and he used that to his personal and professional advantage. The fact that Sand seemed impervious to Harry's typical intimidation had at first made him angry. Then it made him curious.

H. W. Charles Construction had started out as a mostly legitimate construction business after the war. Harry had used his military experience with the Army Corps of Engineers to form the company and win some important early contracts. But Harry's hard-charging, take-no-prisoners style that had served him well in western Europe soon ran him afoul of city hall, local inspectors, and even the unions. So Harry turned to the tactic that had served him well his entire life: brute force and a willingness to get dirty using it. Harry hired former platoon mates and other ex-military types who appreciated his military-style leadership, his loyalty to them and the rewards of victory. They roughed up competitors, they sabotaged rival construction sites, they "liberated" shipments of building materials. Within five years, they more than tripled in size and increased revenue tenfold.

They learned to play the other side of the game as well. Paying off building inspectors allowed them to cut corners and save money on materials. Paying off cops kept him one step ahead of any possible raid. He paid for information from city hall and had his own underground of informants who told him when land was coming onto the market or had recently been sold. Harry learned how to deal with local politicians as well. He wined and dined them, made sure their re-election campaigns were well financed and, when necessary, used embarrassing information or photographs he acquired through his network of operatives. He ran his company like an occupying military operation in a hostile foreign land, which is exactly why John Sand had approached him twelve months ago.

"Good evening, Harry," Sand said as he sat and folded himself neatly in the plush chair facing Charles. Harry stood and poured them both a generous tumbler of scotch from the credenza behind his desk. Not the really good stuff. His sixteen-year-old Lagavulin was locked away inside the credenza. Harry wouldn't waste the good stuff on Sand, who never actually drank. Harry used the offer of a drink to take in the measure of men and watch them.

Setting the crystal tumbler to the side, Sand focused on

Harry and came right to the point. "We need to accelerate the South Basin operation. My partners are getting anxious to move, and you assured me this wouldn't take too long."

Harry took a swallow of the scotch and began pacing behind his desk. He'd been waiting for this meeting. His network of informants had turned up bits and pieces of interesting, seemingly unrelated information over the past several weeks. A few land purchases, a permit issued, businesses hiring, businesses closing, materials being ordered on a huge scale. Harry had told his men to slow down, to make things look like they were progressing as Harry tried to make sense of the situation, the apparent opportunity that was maddeningly in front of him, but somehow just out of focus. Then came the piece of information from the mayor's office that made it all click for Harry. So now, he finally had the pieces in place and was ready to attack.

"Yes, your partners," Harry said. "Emerald City Investments. I always liked that name. Loved the *Wizard of Oz*. You know I looked into you guys, right?"

Sand gave a thin smile and replied, "Of course, but my partners value their privacy, Harry. You should understand that. We needed a local proxy to front those land purchases lest we create a bidding war."

"Of course, of course. Makes sense for a local like me to buy land who could maybe start an industrial park. And you certainly paid well for securing those businesses and their land in Bayview. I appreciate that."

Sand nodded as Harry continued. "But acquiring all that land in that shitty part of town makes ya wonder. These guys must be planning something big. Another shipyard? A factory? Something related to the navy?"

Sand sat impassively, letting the accusations wash over

him.

"So, me bein' a smart guy, I thought maybe I should buy some of that land down there. Not just for you guys, but for me. Maybe I should really start a quarry or some industrial development—be in the mix as it were."

Sand's eyes narrowed as he looked up at Harry. "We had a deal. You were to acquire the land around the basin for us. We paid you a lot of money, Harry, and did not ask questions about how you got the land."

"Yeah, but that was before I looked behind the curtain and found out about the fucking stadium!" Harry said triumphantly. Sand looked momentarily shocked. His eyes opened wide behind his glasses before narrowing even further as he glowered at Harry.

Harry loved this part, where he extended his will, his power, and made people do what he wanted. He called it "The Squeeze," and it always took him back to France in the fall of 1944. As part of the 2nd Armored Division, the hard charging "Hell on Wheels" division, Harry and his unit, the 17th Armored Engineer Battalion, had been on the go since the breakout at Normandy. They rebuilt bridges almost as fast as the retreating Germans destroyed them. That day in October 1944 found Harry's unit out of position, too far south, and they were ambushed by a German column. Most of his guys were engineers, but they all knew how to use a rifle when pressed. The fighting was brutal and desperate on both sides.

Harry saw his lieutenant killed by a huge German sergeant. Roaring, Harry charged the man with a fixed bayonet. The German sidestepped that bull rush, and the two men fell into the mud. Punches were thrown, eyes gouged, teeth found flesh. At last, Harry got a grip around the man's thick neck. He squeezed with all the desperate power in his massive arms and shoulders. Harry felt the man frantically try to twist out of his grip, but he pressed on, and moments later a sickening, but strangely satisfying "crack" ended their contest. Harry fell back, exhausted, but moments later, survival instincts kicked in, and he twisted around looking for the next threat. Some groans reached his ears, and he saw that a couple of GIs were helping an injured comrade, but the fighting was over. They'd won. Harry lay back and laughed. He was alive, and it was the greatest feeling in the world.

Squeezing Sand wasn't the same, but it was satisfying in its own way. The smart son of a bitch always seemed like he was looking down at Harry, and now he relished seeing the man clearly uncomfortable.

"That stadium deal..." Sand said, only to be cut off by Harry.

"The stadium deal is gonna happen, just not where everybody thought it was gonna happen," sneered Harry. Everyone in San Francisco had been buzzing about Major League Baseball and the relocation of the New York Giants next year. The team had decided to leave the confines of New York and move to the burgeoning west. The city of San Francisco had bent over backward to make it happen. The team was to play in the old Seals Stadium in the Mission District on the condition that the city build a new stadium for them. Everyone assumed that the new stadium would be built in that same neighborhood, but Harry's source in city hall had confirmed that the city had acquired land in the Bayview Heights neighborhood on the cheap, and that was where the new stadium would be built.

"You had me buy up that land for you cause if it got out that the city and the new stadium were in play, prices would skyrocket. I know 'Emerald City Investments' is a proxy for the city. So now, you got some of that land, but I got some of it too," Harry said with great satisfaction.

Sand paused and then seemed to regain his composure. "What do you want?" he asked icily.

Harry sat down in his overstuffed chair, leaned back, and smiled. "I want the contract to build the stadium. And I'll even sell you my land in the neighborhood. At a nice profit, of course."

"The city has to put projects this big out to bid. We can't just hand it to you."

"Sure you can. You need my land. You need my company. Make it happen."

Sand cast his eyes down, "My partners aren't going to like this," he said.

"Hey, we're all gonna win here," Harry said, rubbing his hands together.

"There's still the matter of the unsecured land. There are the holdouts you were going to deal with," Sand said.

"Well now I have a bigger reason to drop the hammer on them. We'll get the land. You get me the contract." Sand removed his glasses and rubbed his eyes. Got him, thought Harry.

"Very well. We need to move quickly, Harry. I'll let my partners know of the new arrangement, but you must deliver," Sand said while rising.

"Looking forward to doing business with you," Harry said, trying unsuccessfully not to gloat.

Sand gathered his hat and coat and quickly exited Harry's office. Heading out into the empty hallway, he marched toward the stairs. As he did, a small but perceptible smile appeared on his face.

Things are going just as planned, he thought.

CHAPTER 3

Monday brought Kats to the Bayview Heights community on the southeastern side of the San Francisco Peninsula. Parking his Harley Davidson Sportster motorcycle on the Vello & Sons lot, he stood and surveyed the South Basin neighborhood. Armstrong Avenue, which he arrived upon, was little more than a dirt road. Trucks lined both sides of the street, and low Quonset hut buildings made up the majority of the building stock. Warehouses with painted corrugated steel walls were emblazoned with business names such as ACE Steel and Bayview Waste. Industrial remnants—doors, turbines, barrels, flatbed trailers, and empty trash bins that would have been trash anywhere else—were necessary elements, casually cast aside yet waiting for the day that they would be used again. The lack of trees made the peninsula very windy, even on this mild morning. This was the industrial wasteland of San Francisco, the dirty underbelly of the growing, cosmopolitan city that most San Franciscans didn't know or care about.

Across the water perhaps half a mile away, Kats could see the massive Hunters Point Shipyard with its distinctive crane soaring some ten stories above the far eastern edge. Moored at one of the closer docks was what looked like a World War II destroyer. Cranes moved about, and even at this distance, the shipyard looked busy. Vello & Sons looked busy as well. The front of the building and the visible yard were tidy compared to most of the neighbors. Ship masts were visible from behind the building as Kats entered the main door.

Inside the main building, open to the back and onto the waterway, was a busy, strangely ordered environment. Materials, such as long pieces of lumber, were neatly stacked along with brass and metal fixtures. Ropes and canvas were stored together. There were workstations that seemed to have distinct functions. As Kats looked around, Anton approached, smiling.

"Thanks for coming," he said as the two men shook hands.

"Quite the operation you have going here," Kats said as he took in the space with a practiced eye.

"Best hand-built boats in the city. Probably in all of California," Anton said with pride. "Our family has been doing this kind of work for generations, but my father took it to another level."

Kats had to agree. As Anton showed him around the operation, he thought that despite its size, this was less of a factory and more like the personal workspace of a craftsman. Like something you might find in a small studio but expanded to a grand scale.

Kats counted four boats, each over forty feet in length, in various stages of completion. Stepping outside onto the working dock, Kats noted two more boats in the water with workers moving about them. And there on the dock, seated on a folding chair, directing traffic like Michelangelo in his Florence studio, sat the man who had to be Anton's father.

Carlo Vello looked up at his son and Kats as they approached. Dark green eyes were set in a deeply lined, sun-darkened face. Wisps of white hair poked beyond his hat, and he wore dark jeans, heavy work boots, and a large, wool sweater. Even seated, Kats could tell that the sweater hung on him, and once-powerful hands were bony and spotted.

"Father, this is the man I told you about. This is Mr. Takemoto."

"Please call me Kats, Mr. Vello," Kats said with a slight bow.

Vello eyed him, seeming to take the measure of Kats.

"Do you know anything about boats, Kats?" Vello asked.

"No, sir. Can't really say that I do."

"Walk with me," said the older man, who stiffly rose from the chair but straightened himself to his full height. Kats followed with Anton a couple steps behind.

"You see this boat here?" gestured Vello. "It looks like it's done, doesn't it?"

To Kats's eyes, the boat was beautiful, painted, brass polished and gleaming, sails furled. It looked like it was ready to sail out into the bay.

"Most would say that it's ready. But for me, I know that there are a hundred things that need to be done before it's close to being ready. Mostly little things that you might not notice and probably not even care about. But I can't help but see them. For example, do you see those two shutters on the foremost window?"

Kats nodded, "Sure. The green ones."

"Yes," Vello said. "They're not quite even."

Kats looked again, and even trying to discern a flaw, he couldn't see it.

"Trust me. If we went over and measured it, you would see that it's half an inch off," Vello said with a smile.

"Over there at the shipyard," Vello said, pointing across the basin, "they build ships. Big, impressive, powerful ships that are more machine than human. They're even using nuclear reactors to power ships now!"

"That is what sets my boats, our boats, apart from others.

We craft them with our hands, with our hearts. Our boats move with the wind. They're made from wood that was once alive. If we do our job, we bring that wood back to life in the form of the boat. We resurrect that wood and that spirit into something unique."

"This is more than just my family's business," he continued. "This has been a way of life for us for generations and, God willing, it will be for many more."

"It will, Papa," came the voice over Kats's shoulder. Approaching them was the man who had to be Anton's older brother Gianni. Taller, broader of shoulder, and darker haired, the resemblance was obvious.

"Gianni, this is the man I told you about, Katsuhiro Takemoto. My brother Gianni."

Gianni approached and stood squarely in front of Kats, hands on his hips and a couple of inches taller. "The sheet metal shop had their presses sabotaged last night," he said in his father's direction. "Last week, two of our trucks were stolen, and our neighbors, the fish processors, had barrels of oil dumped on their floor. It's only a matter of time before someone gets hurt. We don't need a private investigator," he said to Kats. "We need soldiers to fight."

Kats raised his eyebrows and looked at Anton.

"We need help, Gianni. We don't know who or what we're up against, and Kats can help."

"Papa, we need to fight back," Gianni said as he turned to his father, "I was a soldier. I know how to fight."

"Yes, I know, Gianni. You served honorably in Korea. But who says he's not a soldier?" Carlo said, gesturing toward Kats. The elder Vello looked to Kats. "You're a soldier, are you not?"

"I was," Kats replied.

"Once a man is something, he remains that thing. He can become more, but he adds to his story. I'm a son of Malta. I'm a boat builder. I'm a father. I'm all those things. If you were once a soldier, you're still a soldier."

Kats thought about Vello's words. They reminded him of his own father, who taught him about family and the layers of obligation, both *On* and *Giri,* the obligations we voluntarily take on and those we inherit. We carry many things, and those things make up our story.

"I was a Ranger with the 100th Battalion and the 442nd Regimental Combat Team in Italy, France, and Germany," Kats said.

"The famous Nisei unit" Carlo replied, nodding appreciatively. "Were you involved in the rescue of the Lost Battalion?"

Vello's two sons looked inquisitively at their father, who smiled and said, "You should read more!" Kats was impressed with the man's knowledge of history. "Tell them," he said to Kats.

"I was the scout for K company. We located this Texas battalion that had been cut off by the Germans in the Vosges mountains. They'd been surrounded for six days and were running out of food and ammo. We attacked uphill into the German entrenchments for five days, finally breaking through on the fifth day and rescuing the 1st Battalion. Apparently, Hitler was furious."

"How many men did you lose?" Carlo asked.

"K company had 187 men. Of those, 169 were killed or wounded."

"Were you wounded?" Anton asked.

"Yes, I took a couple but was still able to fight."

"How many did you save?" Carlo asked.

"211 men survived."

The words hung there for a moment. No one said anything. Finally, Carlo broke the silence and said, "If we need a soldier, he'll do, eh Gianni? But let's see if we can be smart about this and not need to fight."

The rest of the morning, Kats huddled with the Vello family reviewing the events of the past several months along with the initial letters and business cards they'd been given by the mysterious agents. Anton took Kats around the neighborhood. They talked to the other business owners who told similar tales of offers, followed by threats, followed most recently by vandalism.

Gianni Vello and several of the other headstrong business owners had created a patrol unit, intending to watch over the neighborhood at night. Of course, they would be armed despite Kats's recommendation that they start with flashlights and whistles. This could get out of hand very quickly, Kats thought, recognizing that he needed to quickly begin his investigation into who was behind the intimidation campaign. The sooner they had that information, the sooner they would be able to form an actual plan to resist and not just rely on an unfocused show of force.

Returning to the city, Kats began his search at the main branch of the San Francisco public library near City Hall. Approaching the public information desk, he smiled at the silver haired, middle-aged woman working behind the desk. "Hello, Gladys," he said.

The woman looked like a proper schoolteacher, the one you didn't want to get for English or history. Looking over her bifocal glasses, she replied, "Good afternoon, Katsuhiro. What can I help you with today?"

"I need to access the gray pages," he said. The reverse telephone directory or "gray pages" was a listing of the names and addresses associated with local phone numbers. The directories were used by law enforcement, but as Kats had learned years ago, the public libraries had them, too. You just needed to know whom to ask.

Handing her a slip of paper with the number that the Vellos and the others had been given, she eyed it and nodded her head. "Give me a few minutes."

"Sure. I'll be over in the maps room."

Forty-five minutes later, Gladys approached Kats, who sat amidst an array of maps showing Bayview Heights and the whole southern peninsula of San Francisco. She sat down next to him.

"This is an odd number," she began. "The current listing in the directory says this number is for K. L. Roy Construction. And it gives an address that doesn't exist unless their office is in the Bay."

"Kilroy?" Kats laughed. 'Kilroy was here' being the famous graffiti American soldiers drew on everything from bombs, planes, buildings, destroyed enemy tanks, and even reportedly in Joseph Stalin's private bathroom.

"Yes, clearly a joke."

"Or someone trying to cover up a number and their identity," said Kats.

"That's what I thought, too. Well, it turns out we still have an older set of reverse directories from 1954. Librarians hate to throw away anything," she smiled.

"The 1954 listing of that number is to an H. W. Charles Construction office. Address is here," she said, handing Kats a piece of paper.

Kats was reminded of something he had told Jimmy Stewart early on about detective work—that he spent more time in libraries than in seedy bars. And knowing a good librarian like Gladys was like having another investigator on staff.

"You're the best, Gladys," he said, meaning it.

She nodded graciously and, lowering her voice, said, "I know you're too polite to ask, but I want you to know that my nephew Jackson is doing very well. He decided that he'd had enough big city adventure and moved back to Pennsylvania a couple months ago."

Kats smiled, recalling the mess that the young man had gotten into: loan sharks, the dirty priest, Chinese triads, and that ridiculous statue. Gladys had been terrified for her nephew, as she'd promised her sister she'd look after him. In fact, she did, but only after the adventurous boy got so twisted up in things, it took a professional, specifically Kats, to unravel that knot.

"That was an interesting one, and hey, I'd never been to Fresno," he laughed.

The next day, Kats found himself at the edge of the Castro District at the corner of Market and Church streets. The intersection was bustling, and Kats sat across the street staring out of a coffee shop window at the three-story building that held the offices of H. W. Charles Construction. Kats noted several people entering the building this morning. Everything looked normal. Then a large truck pulled up in front of the building. A man stepped out of the passenger side of the truck as it sat double parked. Several men exited the building and climbed into the back of the covered truck. Nothing unusual about that, but then Kats observed several large axes and some duffle bags being handed up into the truck. Not your usual construction tools, he thought.

The truck pulled away, and Kats stepped out and crossed the street. Entering Charles Construction, he was surprised to see that the office was more of an open floor plan, with big, drawing desks in the middle of the room, and smaller desks ringing them. The office was busy, perhaps twenty people moving about. To his right a woman's voice asked, "May I help you?"

Turning right, Kats saw a trio of women in a small bull-pen setup. Two young women sat at their respective desks, one typing, the other on the telephone. Standing between them, holding a stack of papers, was a tall, red-headed woman who looked quizzically at Kats.

"Oh hello," began Kats, now noticing that the standing woman was quite lovely. Not as young as he'd initially thought. She was perhaps thirty, and immaculately dressed and coifed. The woman cocked her head, waiting for him to speak. She was used to this kind of reaction and expected the obligatory comment on her looks. Let's get this over with, she thought.

Kats quickly regrouped and smiled. "I think I may be in the wrong location," he began. "I'm looking for a construction company."

"We're a construction company," she said like he was stating the obvious. Hazel eyes and just a few freckles, he noted.

"Yes, but I'm looking for a K. L. Roy Construction company."

At that, the other two seated women looked at Kats, seeing him for the first time. The redhead's eyes narrowed momentarily, but then she shook her head. "Sorry. Can't help you on that one."

"Must be my mistake," Kats said jovially. "Sorry to disturb

you all."

The redhead nodded, "No problem," she said.

Kats started to turn, stopped himself, and asked, "May I possibly use one of your phones to call my office?"

Gesturing to the phone in front of the seated secretary, the redhead said, "Sally, please help Mister…?"

She was trying to get his name. Smart, he thought. "Takemoto. Kats Takemoto. Thank you Miss…?"

"Molly," she offered. He continued to smile at her. "Just Molly," she said.

Turning the phone toward him, Kats opened his small notebook and dialed the number Anton had given him for K. L. Roy Construction. The line clicked and connected, and the phone on the redhead's desk began to ring.

The two seated girls looked at the phone like it was a hissing snake. Kats and the redhead held each other's gaze. She broke character first, raising her eyebrows and flashing what Kats thought was a great smile. He returned the smile, reached into his pocket, and handed her his card.

"Please give this to Kilroy. I want to talk about Bayview Heights."

CHAPTER 4

After the stranger left, Molly Hayes, the office manager for H. W. Charles Construction, closed the door to her office. She'd closed the door because she knew she was going to have an uncomfortable conversation. She sat a moment collecting her thoughts. The sudden appearance of the strange man, Mr. Takemoto, had rattled her a bit. She recalled the meeting with Harry Charles in his private office at the Russ Building several months ago. He'd sat her down and offered her a drink.

"No thank you, Mr. Charles."

"Molly, I've told you a million times. Call me Harry," the big man said as he poured two fingers of scotch for himself.

"Molly, we have something important going on here, and I need your help and your discretion." He winked at her, no doubt trying to be disarming, but Molly felt her stomach tighten instead.

"We're going to be acquiring some land for a real game-changing project," he began. "But we need to do it on the sly. If word gets out that someone is buying up land in this neighborhood, prices are going to skyrocket. And, of course, some may hold out."

Molly nodded. That made sense. She'd been with the company just over a year, rising quickly from the secretarial pool after Harry and others stopped ogling her and realized she knew how to do bookkeeping, billing, scheduling, and most importantly, getting people, mostly men, to work. Part flirt, part schoolteacher, with a healthy dose of salty language when necessary. People quickly fell in line when she told them what was what. In short, Molly Hayes didn't take any shit.

She'd arrived in San Francisco in early 1956 from Ohio, following a short residence in Reno, Nevada. Molly came west to get a divorce from her high school sweetheart, whose star rapidly faded following graduation and who tried one too many times to take his anger out on her. She left Ohio with a black eye, a broken right hand that had delivered the satisfying blow to Bill's nose, and a suitcase containing her life. Once she was free, San Francisco seemed a lot more interesting than a return to Ohio.

She bounced around some odd jobs and received some odd propositions, including being a photo model for some niche magazines—"You OK with being tied up, honey?" At one point she was a hostess at a very high-end club that she was pretty sure was also a bordello, and she also had bartended at an exclusive night club that served mostly women. All had been part of her education in the big city, and she took it in with an adventurer's spirit. For the bartending job at the ladies' club—Ann's 440, though many of the locals still called it Mona's 440 after the original owner—discretion was key. In truth, she liked all the attention she got there, and the tips were exceptional. She still worked a couple shifts each week to supplement her income at Harry's place, but she'd never let him or her other daytime colleagues know about it. So, Molly Hayes understood the need for discretion, but she had an uneasy feeling about the story her boss was selling.

Harry told her they were creating a front company to acquire some land and that any calls to her dedicated line were to be answered as K. L. Roy Construction. "K. L. Roy Construction, get it?" he leered.

"Yes, sir, I get it. What do you want me to say?"

"Just take their information and set up a meeting for us. Tell them Mr. Roy is very interested in moving quickly."

She nodded her head as Harry smiled and acted like this was a sufficient explanation for any woman. That was another advantage to being an attractive woman—men constantly underestimated how smart and observant she was.

So when someone had walked into the office today, looking for the front company, Molly knew that something had gone sideways. Harry Charles wasn't going to be happy. She already had to take the weekly reports and checks over to his private office today, so rather than making that call, Molly decided she wanted to ask Harry some questions herself. Especially since lately crews were being scheduled for nighttime work on no specific project.

Gathering her coat, she stuffed the papers into a leather portfolio and headed toward the door. "Sally, I'm going to the private office. I'll be back after lunch."

As she exited onto Market Street, she walked toward

the streetcar landing and boarded the next streetcar headed toward the Financial District. She didn't notice Kats detach himself from shadows in the alleyway across the street, hop on his motorbike, and merge into traffic a discrete distance from the cable car.

Molly entered the elegant building and took the elevator to the fourth floor. She entered office number 455. Two large men sat on sofas, reading the daily paper. Amos and Andy, thought Molly. At the desk sat Liza, Harry Charles's personal secretary. Bottle blond and breathlessly busty, Liza barely knew how to answer the phones or mix a drink. Molly suspected that she had other talents that kept her on the payroll. She buzzed Charles on the intercom. "Molly is here with the papers," she said.

"Molly," he boomed as he opened his office door. "Come in, honey."

Ignore it, Molly thought as she sat down. "Sir, we had a situation at the office this morning," she began as she recounted the encounter with Kats.

"Who was this guy? Ever seen him before?"

Molly handed him the card Kats had given her. "Japanese American from the name. In his thirties. No accent, so probably born here. Seemed… clever," she said, choosing the last word carefully.

"Tak… Tako," attempted Harry, looking at the card. "Who is this fucking Jap?"

At that moment, voices could be heard in the outer office, their volume rising.

"I'm tellin' you pal, get out!" was heard, followed by what Molly thought was a grunt and then a crash like something heavy hitting the floor. At that moment, Harry's intercom buzzed, and Liza's crackling voice came through, "There's some guy here looking for a Mr. Roy."

"Were you followed?" barked Harry at a confused Molly.

"Why would I be followed?" she retorted. Harry stood up and moved to the door, throwing it open. The scene was almost comic. Liza stood behind her desk, clutching the phone to her chest, trying her best to become part of the wall. The two big men now occupied the same overturned sofa and were scrambling to find their footing. Standing in the middle of the room, hands comfortably crossed in front of him, was a slender Asian man. The Jap, Harry thought.

Kats smiled at Harry and politely asked, "Are you Mr. Roy?"

Harry stepped forward, motioning his two embarrassed bodyguards to stand down. Molly peered from the doorway. "My name is Charles. Harold Charles. Harry to my friends, but..." he said motioning to his men, "it don't look like you're my friend."

"Well, Mr. Charles, the problem is that this Mr. Roy and his company have been trying to acquire some land out in the South Basin."

"Nothing wrong with that," said Harry. "Sounds like good business to me."

"Yes, but good business doesn't include threats, beatings, vandalism, and arson," Kats said. He noted that Molly's eyes darted back and forth between him and Charles as he said this. She knows something, he thought.

Harry sneered at the accusation. "Like I said, I don't know no Kilroy. I got a legit construction company here, and I oughta call the cops for you comin' in here, bustin' up the joint, injuring my men."

"I never said 'Kilroy,' Mr. Charles," Kats said. Harry's eyes narrowed dangerously. Caught in the lie, he was both angry and embarrassed at being so easily outsmarted by this little prick.

"Get the fuck out," Harry growled and motioned for his men to come forward. Amos and Andy started cautiously forward, not wanting a reprise of their earlier encounter with this stranger.

Kats maintained eye contact with Harry but raised a hand toward the two bodyguards, who stopped like dogs, unsure of what to do next. "Mr. Charles, the people down in the basin don't want any trouble. If they want to sell to you, fine. That's their right. But remember, no means no. And we know who you are now."

Kats started to withdraw, keeping his eyes on the men. As he reached the door, he caught Molly's gaze over Harry's shoulder. She stared at him as he turned and closed the door behind him.

For a moment no one in the room spoke. Then Harry let forth a bellow "Fuck!" Turning toward his men angrily, "What do I pay you two for? You let a guy roll in here, toss you around, and insult me?"

"Sorry, boss," said the bigger man. "Yeah, sorry," said the other. "He did that judo shit on us. It won't happen again."

Harry literally growled at that, the low sound coming from deep in his throat. Liza started to pick up the room, and the two big men reset the sofa. Harry stormed past Molly into his sanctum. Turning, she followed him into the office.

"Is that stuff true?" she asked him as he stood pouring himself a drink.

"Close the door, Molly," he said between gulps of scotch.

"Harry..." she continued.

"Close the goddammed door, Molly!" he snarled.

Molly closed the door and stood there with it to her back.

Taking a deep breath, she continued, "Is that what those crews of men have been doing in Bayview Heights these past few weeks?"

"We have to get that land, and some of those assholes need a little convincing," Harry said. "That's business, sweetheart."

"That's extortion, Harry."

"Don't get all righteous with me. This is big boy stuff. We may have done a little pushing, but this is too big to be screwed up by some immigrants who don't know a good deal when they see it."

Good deal for whom, Molly wondered, but clamped her mouth shut.

"C'mon sweetheart," he said, changing tactics, "There's a big score in this, and I'm gonna make sure everybody who plays their part gets a taste."

Molly took a deep breath, prepared to tell him to go to hell right there and quit, but something held her back. She was thinking about the documents, surveys, and photos back at the construction office that had seemed unusual before and now seemed outright suspicious. She wanted to know what was really going on before she made her exit.

"OK, Mr. Charles. So long as no one gets hurt," she said innocently.

"Of course not. We don't want any bloodshed. We just need to make 'em understand. I've got an even better deal to offer, so it's all gonna be fine," he lied with what he thought was charming conviction.

Molly stood, leaving the official papers on Harry's desk, nodded to him, and quickly left the office.

Harry stood for a moment, going over the recent developments. Part of his success as a soldier had been the ability to think on his feet, and Harry felt that old muscle memory kick in. Walking into the outer office, he said to Liza, "Get Franco on the phone."

Turning to the two humbled bodyguards, he gestured toward the door. "Keep an eye on her."

CHAPTER 5

U pon hitting the street outside Harry's office, Molly stood for a moment unsure of where she wanted to go. "Shit," she said loud enough to turn a few heads as she walked down the street. She didn't want to return to the office, and she didn't want to go home. She hopped onto the Market streetcar and exited at 5th Street. Entering the Emporium Department Store, she wandered the first floor, turning over the events of the morning in her head. She made her way to the store's lunch counter, sat, and ordered a coffee and a BLT.

"May I join you?" asked the voice over her left shoulder. Turning, she saw Kats standing there with an innocent expression on his face.

"You've been following me all goddamn morning," she said angrily.

"Yes, and I'm sorry to put you in an awkward position." He gestured toward the seat next to her, and she gave a curt nod.

"What do you want, Mr. Takemoto?" she asked, folding her napkin properly in front of her.

"Call me Kats, please," he said. "What I want is to stop the threats and violence in the South Basin before someone really gets hurt. I told my friends that I'd find out who was behind this, and it's abundantly clear that it's your boss."

"Do you have any proof it was Harry?" Molly retorted.

"I'm not a cop. And I'm not trying to get anybody sent to jail. I'm trying to help those landowners in the South Basin who don't want to be forced to sell. They're not going to go without a fight. They've organized and are armed, but they're not soldiers. If this continues, there will be blood."

Molly looked at Kats's earnest face and shifted uncomfortably, "I was told that no one would get hurt."

"So far that's basically true. Some property has been damaged and a warehouse set on fire, but no casualties. Yet."

Molly looked dejectedly at her coffee and sandwich as they arrived. "I don't want anyone to get hurt either."

"Good. Then maybe you can talk to me about your boss," implored Kats.

"Soon to be ex-boss, I think. I can't work for that asshole," she said. "OK, what do you want to know?"

Over the next fifteen minutes, Molly shared what she could about the secretive K. L. Roy project. Kats would ask about small details, forcing her to try to remember specifics. "Clearly, they have a bigger plan in mind for all that land," Kats mused. "Any thoughts on what he could possibly have in mind?"

"I thought it might be a new housing development. The city is growing fast, and people are moving here in record numbers."

"Maybe," Kats said. "But Bayview Heights has always been the industrial part of town. Cold, windy, giant navy ships going in and out. People who have a choice won't want to live there."

Molly nodded. "You know the weirdest thing about all this is how much money Harry has been throwing around these projects. The construction company is successful, but Harry has been flush with cash, and I don't know where it came from. That's how he's been able to buy those parcels and how he's hired that extra muscle."

"You think there may be another investor? Another player?" Kats asked.

"Early on there were a couple meetings with some investment group named..." she paused, trying to recall. "Emerald something. Guy's name was Sand, I think. Probably in the date book. But after that Harry got really interested in the South Basin and Bayview Heights."

"So you'll help me?" Kats asked as he looked at her. Nice face, he thought.

Molly looked back at him, noting his dark brown eyes and jet-black hair. I just met this guy, she thought. Harry was a jerk and all, but she did feel a bit of loyalty to him and the company. She was about to say sorry but no when Kats spoke again.

"I'm sorry to put you in this position. But ask yourself how you'll feel if someone gets hurt. Even someone from your office. This is headed toward violence. Please, help me."

"Dammit," she said under her breath but nodded her head.

"OK then maybe you can put off quitting for a few days and gather some info for me. Like that date book and anything else that ties Harry to the South Basin?"

"Alright. Let me look into it. Give me a few days. If I find something, I'll contact you. Don't contact me" she said pointedly. Kats nodded, accepting her conditions.

"May I ask you a question?" he said, knowing he was pushing his luck, but wanting to know, nonetheless. She nodded, gathering her things to leave. "Why are you willing to help me?"

She looked at him squarely, her hazel eyes clear and purposeful. "I don't like bullies. I can put up with their juvenile come-ons, their leering, the stupid jokes. I even put up with some of Harry's shady tactics. I'm no angel. But I hate bullies. People think they can pull one over on someone else who's weaker than they are. It pisses me off."

Kats nodded. "Best not to get on your bad side," he said.

"Don't you forget it," she said and then smiled earnestly at him. Great smile.

The rest of the week was a cold, wet, and gray San Francisco December. Molly had hoped to be able to go through the books and documents in Harry's official office, but he'd been there all week, meeting with various foremen and vendors. To all appearances, H. W. Charles Construction was a busy, thriving business. In many ways it was, but to Molly's eyes now, she only saw the shady elements.

Work orders and invoices to new vendors, new "foremen" in closed-door meetings, and Harry's increasingly short temper as he barked orders made for a stressful week. Molly also noticed that Harry's two bodyguards were around the office. She'd rarely seen them in the office before, and their presence now was odd.

Friday afternoon turned even chillier when Salvatore Francona, "Franco," walked through the front door. Well over six feet tall, Franco was broad in the shoulders, narrow at the hips, and looked like a football player, which in his youth, he had been. The story was that he and Harry had served together during the war, and Franco had saved Harry's life somewhere along the way. Harry had found a special place for Franco in the company, who came and went, seemingly as he pleased, and only reported to Harry.

Franco was well dressed, dark haired, and empirically handsome, and the other girls in the office smiled and flirted with him whenever his infrequent visits brought him to the office. Molly found him reptilian. His smile seemed fake, and his eyes were cold and lifeless. Seeing him approach her door now felt threatening.

"Hello, red," he said leaning against her doorway, eyeing her like a meal he wanted to eat.

"Good afternoon, Mr. Francona. Harry was expecting you yesterday."

"Yeah, couldn't be helped. Out of town commitments," he said nondescriptly.

"Anna can buzz you in," Molly said.

"Don't bother. I like to surprise him," he said, winking at her. She forced a smile as he turned and pushed through Harry's door.

"Where the fuck have you been?" Molly heard before the door shut. Inside, Harry slammed his hand on his desk.

"I had to take care of that thing in Sacramento. Remember?" Franco said as he casually sat down across from Harry.

Harry made a face, happy that the loose end in Sacramento was no longer a loose end, so he let go of his frustration with Franco. It had been like that since the war. The man was a magician at getting things done but a complete disaster at following standard protocols and chain of command. Harry had learned how to best use him and, at the same time, keep him out of trouble with the commanding officer.

"We got a situation down at Bayview Heights," Harry said. "I need you to accelerate things there. We're running out of time, and those Emerald City pricks are getting anxious."

"So the last round of negotiations didn't work," Franco said.

"No, they didn't. In fact, I got reports that those local assholes have created a patrol and are marching around the neighborhood at night with guns and flashlights."

"Don't sweat them," Franco said. "Give me a dozen of

our best guys, let me take the kid gloves off, and we're in business."

Harry nodded and went to the door. "Molly," he called across the office, "come in here."

Molly approached and stood in the open doorway facing the two seated men. "Yes, sir?" she asked.

"Where's Tommy and his crew right now?" Harry asked.

"I'd have to double-check, but I think they're working on that demolition in Daly City."

"Get Tommy on the horn and tell 'em to be here tomorrow evening at 6 pm. They're workin' overtime," Harry laughed.

CHAPTER 6

K ats sat on the rooftop of the tallest building in the basin—a four-story remnant of the nineteenth century that had been a machine shop on the first two levels with two empty floors above. The cold night seemed colder as the fog draped the basin in an eerie silver gray. He'd been atop that roof for nearly three hours, and midnight was fast approaching. It was a quick phone call from a nervous Molly the previous day that had led him here.

"There's something going on tomorrow night" she breathed into the phone. "Harry has called in his muscle and their best men."

Kats pressed for more information, but Molly exclaimed, "I can't talk. I think they're watching me." With that she quickly hung up, and Kats was left to decide what to do. He contacted Anton Vello and decided that he'd spend the following night in the basin. Anton had also given a heads-up to his brother and the neighborhood patrol to be on alert.

That evening, a dozen men had gathered in the local church, St. Paul of the Shipwreck, to organize. Gianni Vello spoke first.

"We're ready to defend our homes, our businesses. We'll show them our resolve," he told the nervous men. Several brandished clubs, and two held old rifles. Gianni carried a Colt .45 pistol, his sidearm from Korea. They split into two teams and headed out into the night.

Kats couldn't fault the men for wanting to protect their community but feared they were likely to shoot each other in the dark. He pulled Anton aside. "Come with me," he said as he led Anton out into the neighborhood. Kats had already surveyed the landscape and knew that the best vantage point in the area was the decrepit four-story building they now sat atop.

The two men took up positions on opposite sides of the building, where they could get a 360-degree view of the neighborhood and still maintain eye contact with each other. Kats had a pair of binoculars and, appropriately, Anton carried a nautical spyglass. At his feet was a black canvas bag and a full canteen of water. They settled into what Kats knew was the biggest part of any job—waiting.

They'd seen the patrols walking along the darkened streets for the first couple of hours, but such activity was draining, and these men were neither trained nor fit for such extended work. Kats suspected they were now in someone's kitchen drinking coffee and trying to find their second wind.

Kats looked across the basin toward Hunters Point Naval Yard less than half a mile away. Even at night, it was well lit and bustling with activity. Small ships moved in and out of their docks, and vehicles could be seen driving about the massive grounds.

Anton had risen and crossed the roof. Sitting down, he looked at Kats. "Maybe this was a bust," he said hopefully.

"Too early to tell. Six more hours till dawn."

"Uggh," grunted Anton. Kats smiled in the darkness. Many times his patience and willingness to wait when others wanted to move or act had saved his life and many others. Stillness was a strength, one that only a few really understood.

Just then a low rumble of an engine, or maybe more than one engine, could be heard in the distance. Sound was funny near the water; it traveled, and what seemed close could be far away. The fog, too, seemed to muffle and diffuse the noise, so they only got a general sense of the direction from which it came. Then, to the northwest, they saw three sets of headlights turning off the main street and disappearing behind a row of buildings. Moments later the sound of the engines stopped, and the night became still and quiet again.

Franco sat in the lead truck. He was dressed in dark work clothes and a wool stocking cap. Around his neck was a bandana ready to conceal his face. Ten more men, similarly clad and awaiting his order, squatted in the trucks. This brought Franco back to the villages of France during the war. He knew that half of his men had seen similar action, and those newer recruits had cut their teeth on the Korean peninsula more recently. Harry trusted former military guys. He could relate to them, and he could manipulate them. He created this special unit of trusted men to do the most important jobs. He gave them a nickname "The Commandos," and he used the idea of unit cohesion to get the reluctant ones to fall in line with the program, even when that program crossed some criminal lines. He used financial rewards to keep them happy and incentivized. Tonight, the Commandos would earn their rewards.

Harry had finally given the go-ahead to escalate the conflict, and Franco was prepared to deliver a clear and decisive message to the holdouts in the basin. He could smell the kerosene in the homemade firebombs as he looked at his watch. Go time, he thought.

Extending his left arm out the window, Franco made a circular gesture, and the Commandos quietly assembled outside of the trucks. Two large satchels contained the makeshift bombs. The Commandos split into two groups: one headed toward the warehouses, and the other toward the waterfront. Franco followed the waterfront team.

From the rooftop vantage point, Kats strained to see in the gloom. The binoculars scanned the streets searching for signs of movement. If they're out there, thought Kats, they're well trained. Quiet and stealthy. "Anton," he said quietly. "Go find your brother and the men. Tell them to head toward the warehouse road. But tell them to go quietly." Anton nodded and was gone.

Kats scanned the streets again, sensing that an attack was about to come. Part of him wanted to rush out with Vello and the men to make the conflict open and obvious, but training and experience held him in place. There! A glimpse of movement against a whitewashed wall. And again, and again. There were several men moving down that street three blocks to his west. Kats opened the black bag at his feet, grabbed the powerful flashlight and what looked like a wooden crankshaft, a *tonfa*, which tucked neatly against his right forearm. Reflexively, he surveyed the perimeter once more, checking for other possible activity, and finding none, he headed quickly down the stairs.

Hitting the street, he circled to his left and advanced toward the warehouse row. As he approached the darkened street, he heard shouts coming from the next block. So much for quietly, thought Kats. Then gunshots, several in rapid succession, pierced the night. Running now, Kats rounded the corner to see several dark clad men standing in front of the Ajax Shipping sign in the middle of the block. One held a gun pointed toward the end of the street. At the end of the block, Gianni Vello was shouting from behind a low wall, the patrol having fallen back from the gunfire. The dark clad men were hefting two satchels, and as one kicked in the office's front door, they tossed the satchels inside. A low *whoosh* could be heard, and suddenly orange-red light was pouring out of the open door.

"Fire!" shouted someone at the other end of the street, and Vello's men tentatively came forward despite the guns pointed at them from the fire team. There were four masked men visible, and they began an orderly withdrawal away from the fire toward Kats. Their attention was focused on the other end of the street as Gianni's men surged forward.

Across the peninsula, Franco and his team waited in the shadows. As the shouts rose from the warehouses and the first flames became visible in the night sky, they gathered their packs and headed toward the line of businesses on the water.

As casually as if he were on an evening stroll, Franco lit a cigarette and watched as his men placed satchel after satchel against wooden door frames and crates. Satisfied that all was in place, he walked over to the first incendiary device, blew on his cigarette, and then held the red tip to the det cord fuse, which sparked immediately. He rose and continued his evening stroll to the next waiting fuse.

The fire was already surging as the masked men crossed the street and headed toward Kats's position. Crouching behind a parked car, he waited a beat and then moved toward them in a low run. The squad had turned toward him, and in that instant Kats flicked the flashlight in his left hand to on, momentarily blinding the advancing men. Then he was among them, the wooden *tonfa* in his right hand, braced against his forearm, smashed into one face with a crunch that dropped the man to the street. The solid steel flashlight connected with a knee, and a man howled. Spinning low, Kats rose and led with the extended end of the *tonfa*, which found the solar plexus of another, causing an explosive grunt. Suddenly a handgun was swinging toward his position, causing Kats to dive sideways and roll. Two bullets followed him across the pavement as he took cover behind a car.

At that moment, something exploded in the warehouse, creating a giant fireball that illuminated the entire street. The men of the basin were falling back as the fire rose. Kats heard Gianni Vello shouting orders and organizing the firefighting effort. The four masked men had taken the opportunity to gather themselves and scuttle down the street. Kats started to rise to follow them when a bullet ricocheted off the car in front of him. Another gunman, Kats realized. Two more shots struck the car, pinning him down and giving the men time to disappear down the street.

"Help!" came a voice from behind him. Turning, Kats saw Anton rushing up the street. "Kats, help! The docks are on fire!"

Damn! Kats thought, knowing they'd been tricked. Straight up commando tactics. Use one attack to divert your attention from another target. More men were pouring out into the street. Fire extinguishers appeared, and the men were trying to contain the fire. "Get your brother!" Kats shouted and pointed toward Gianni.

Kats raced toward the docks, seeing the flames a block away. This attack had been precise. Vello's docks were on fire, as were his neighbors'. There were men and women in the streets, trying hopelessly to contain the blaze with garden hoses. As Kats approached, he saw one man standing in the midst of the chaos, unmoving as he appeared to stare at the fire. Carlo Vello. The old man stood with his fists clenched at his sides. Kats approached the man and noticed the tears streaming from his lined face. A moment later, Anton and Gianni arrived with more men, who rushed forward to fight the conflagration. In the distance, Kats could hear fire alarms, but he knew they wouldn't get here in time.

"Look!" someone shouted over the din. All eyes turned toward a massive spray of water that arced over the flames. There in the basin, spraying thousands of gallons of water onto the blaze, was a fireboat. *US Navy* was stenciled on the bow. The tugboat-sized ship aimed its water cannons back and forth. The fire hissed and crackled, but the fireboat was unrelenting. The docks along the basin were the immediate worry, and the boat managed to hit them with both cannons, slowing, then extinguishing the blaze. The land-based fire trucks arrived, and within minutes they, too, were hitting the landside buildings with multiple hoses. Soon the fire that seemed out of control and destined to destroy the neighborhood was extinguished.

CHAPTER 7

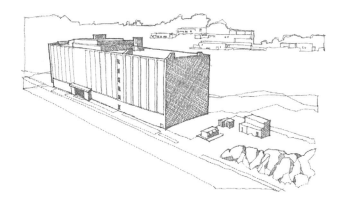

Monday's copy of the *San Francisco Chronicle* was on the passenger seat of Mr. Sand's car as he approached the guard house at the Hunter's Point Naval Yard. His car glided to a halt, and the sentry approached the driver side window. Sand pulled his ID from his breast pocket and held it for the man to read. The sentry reviewed his log sheet, glanced nervously at Sand, and gave a crisp salute. "Do you need directions, sir?"

"No," Sand said as he rolled up his window and entered the busy base. His destination, the largest single building on the base, was easy to spot. Seven stories tall, concrete and steel, yet the most disconcerting thing about Building #815 was the complete absence of windows. It was a giant, concrete box that squatted in the center of the naval yard. The building also had its own secondary security, as the facility itself was classified. Even though it was in the midst of the bustling shipyard, 815 seemed to repel both visitors and attention. Busy men and women moved across the yard but studiously avoided getting too close to it, and trucks, jeeps, and cars all gave it a wide berth. The building defied any sense of outward activity. There was only one visible entrance: a two-story high portal in the middle of the building with oversize double doors and a small sentry office. Sand parked his car near the post and approached the entrance.

Two guards, armed with machine guns, flanked the sentry post, but Sand approached casually, walked past them, and entered the small outside office. Inside sat another guard, a lieutenant, who rose and saluted.

"Good morning, sir."

"Good morning, lieutenant," Sand said as he signed the logbook.

The young officer handed Sand two badges that he clipped to his jacket as he turned for the entrance. The second badge, a square plastic enclosed holder, contained a piece of photographic film. Sand had gotten used to the device, but the dosimeter made many people nervous. Designed to detect exposure to radiation, it had been first used by workers on the Manhattan Project. After being worn, the film was removed and developed. If you'd been exposed to a significant amount of radiation, the film would show that exposure. Of course, there was nothing that could be done at that point other than to get your affairs in order.

Sand passed through the large doorways and entered a broad corridor. Two more heavily armed guards came to attention and passed him into the heart of the Naval Radiological Defense Laboratory.

The NRDL had quietly established itself at Hunters Point

in 1955. To Sand, the innocuous name belied a truly fright-ening purpose. The lab was tasked with detecting and study-ing the effects of radiation on military and civilian targets. Though the American public was well aware of nuclear en-ergy and nuclear weapons, their perception was still rooted in the 1945 display of atomic fire seen at Hiroshima and Nagasaki. That had been devastating and truly frightening, but those early weapons were firecrackers compared to the hydrogen bombs and warheads that now made up the US's and unfortunately the USSR's arsenal. Sand knew that the world should not, and literally could not, understand the destructive capability that each nation had at its increasingly nervous fingertips. No one would sleep at night, he thought grimly.

Hunters Point had been a center of nuclear research since 1948, when several of the target ships from the atomic tests in the South Pacific had been towed to the yard for investiga-tion. The highly classified results were shocking. The nuclear fallout from the blasts had penetrated every surface of the exposed ships. The clean-up crews at Bikini Atoll had been woefully unprepared for their work, and hundreds of those men had received high levels of radiation exposure. The *USS Independence*, an old light aircraft carrier used as a target ship, was towed into Hunters Point and had resided there for nearly three years, leaking radioactive waste into the bay. In 1951 it was finally towed out to sea and scuttled. Men like Sand knew that ship also contained several thousand barrels of radioactive waste, all of which sat thirty-some miles west of the Golden Gate Bridge, near the Farallon Islands, like a ticking time bomb.

Sand walked at a leisurely pace through the huge build-ing, taking it all in. He passed officers, lab technicians, and scientists all intent on their various work destinations. He made mental notes for his debrief in Washington that would certainly follow this meeting. Sand walked to the end of the first floor, where a large conference room was situated next to the main offices of the NRDL director. No sense being on the upper floor in a building with no windows, thought Sand. A guard snapped to attention as Sand approached and opened the door for him to glide through.

Inside the well-appointed conference room was an elongated table that could easily seat twenty people. Today it held just three others. At the head of the table sat Vice Admiral Hyman Rickover, though today he was in civilian clothes. To his left sat NRDL Director, Dr. William Sinclair, a stuffy, self-important man who annoyed Sand. To the admiral's right sat Nelson Winslow, the west coast bureau chief of the National Security Agency and technically, Sand's boss.

"Good morning, Sand," Winslow said with a hint of irony. Sand was the codename that everyone involved in the current operation knew him by, but only Winslow knew his real name. Like Winslow, Sand had been an initial Truman appointee in 1952 when the NSA had been formed. Since then, the two men had risen in the ranks, Winslow on the administrative side, Sand on the operational side. Winslow had become a political animal and didn't like getting his hands dirty anymore, yet Sand knew that Winslow was very effective at his job and ruthless when it came to making the hard decision.

Sand sat, nodding to the admiral who returned the gesture. Director Sinclair spoke first. "What the hell has been happening over in Bayview Heights? Explosions, fires, bad press? The shipyard sent a fire tug the other night..."

"Why did you send that tug?" asked Sand. "If that fire had

destroyed the docks and those buildings, we'd be ready to take control of that land."

"I didn't order it," snapped Sinclair. "The watch commander of the shipyard ordered it, and I couldn't very well tell him not to."

"Of course not. That would make you look bad," jabbed Sand. Sinclair's face reddened, and Sand suppressed a smile.

"Your operatives are a bit messy," Winslow said. "Can they get this job done, or do we need to find alternatives?"

"There are few alternatives," Sand said. "From the beginning we knew that we couldn't be direct and needed to use third parties to keep our distance. It's the same reason that eminent domain couldn't be used. It was all too public, and too many questions would have arisen if the government was seen as taking over the land."

Winslow sat back and made a pinched face. "We've had these pieces moving for years now. We got the New York Giants to move to San Francisco and are going to build them a fucking stadium to provide cover for this operation. Having it thwarted by some locals is unacceptable."

We? thought Sand. The Giants move had been his idea, his operation, and he recalled how crazy it was when he first proposed it to the leadership back in DC. But the very audacity of the idea was what made it work. The government needed to take control of a large parcel of land around Hunters Point without anyone knowing about it. They had to create a buffer zone around the shipyard and the NRDL that would limit ongoing human contact and discourage local action. A new baseball stadium surrounded by parking and a road system for moving thousands of people and cars was just the trick. Oddly enough, Giants majority owner Horace Stoneham practically leapt at the opportunity to leave the

Polo Grounds in Upper Manhattan for the west coast and a new stadium.

"Gentlemen," Admiral Rickover said, finally chiming in, "I don't care to know the particulars of the local operation. I just need you to finish up before Operation Sunshine next year."

Operation Sunshine was the plan to sail the *USS Nautilus*, the world's first nuclear-powered submarine, under the polar ice cap. The *Nautilus* had been launched in 1954, and its ability to travel underwater for extreme distances made it a strategic asset for the US and a tactical nightmare for the Soviets. The long-range test was also part of the proof of concept for the SLBM, or submarine-launched ballistic missile program, that the navy had in the works. The Soviets may weaponize space, but the US could weaponize the oceans.

Sand knew how important Operation Sunshine was to the navy and to the president. After the Soviets launched the Sputnik satellite two months ago, all hell broke loose in the corridors of power. The NSA knew that Sputnik was basically a bowling ball thrown into space, but that didn't change the perception of the event around the world. The Russians had beat the United States into space, and that made Eisenhower furious. Operation Sunshine was meant to be a visible celebration of US naval technology and power.

But Sand also knew the dirty secret of the *Nautilus* and of all the planned nuclear warships: they produced significant radioactive waste. And they leaked radioactive material. A lot of it. That was why the NRDL had been founded: to study and eventually correct those rather significant problems. Nuclear energy had to be seen as safe and controllable by the American public, or the military would lose support for its continued use and expansion. Because the lab and the shipyard were bleeding radioactive waste, they needed to create a buffer zone to prevent too much contact with the locals. Intermittent exposure, such as coming to an occasional ball game, wouldn't likely cause radiation poisoning, but anyone living in the wash zone would be at risk. God help those locals living in the basin these past ten years, he thought.

"Of course, Admiral. We know what we're up against time wise," Winslow said.

"Our proxy has been given the greenlight to increase the local pressure, which unfortunately made headlines in the *Chronicle*," continued Sand. "I expect that last weekend's events will move many of the holdouts. I'm also working on the local utility companies to begin major system maintenance in the area that will ensure power outages, lack of water, and maybe a sewer main backup or two."

"What will that do to the lab?" asked Sinclair nervously. "Our work here is critical, and we can't have it being impacted by your operation."

"The base has its own backup power generators, a separate water supply. And if a little shit backs up in your toilets, well, we all have to make sacrifices, Dr. Sinclair," Sand deadpanned.

"Are you sure that our proxy is still in the dark?" asked Winslow.

"I have him under control and in the appropriate amount of darkness," Sand replied.

"Gentlemen," Rickover said, standing, "In the new year it will be announced that I'm heading up the new Naval Reactors Branch of the Bureau of Ships[2]. The long-term future of the nuclear navy is tied to this project and to Operation Sunshine. We have to assure the American public that nuclear energy is safe and poses no risk to them or their communities. I'm committed to making it safe, but I'm also a military man, and right now a nuclear deterrent is the only thing keeping the Russians and the Chinese at bay." The admiral collected his briefcase, coat, and hat. "Get this done," he said to the room as he exited.

CHAPTER 8

Monday morning's newspaper was open in front of Molly Hayes as she read the page 3 story about the near-tragic fire in the South Basin early Saturday morning. Several people injured, no fatalities, and hundreds of thousands of dollars in damages to the local businesses and buildings. The story noted that arson was suspected. There was also a quote from one of the local business owners, a Gianni Vello, who declared, "We aren't afraid and won't be forced to sell." Molly's lips thinned as she finished the story. Someone is going to get killed; it's only a matter of time. She dreaded going into work today and acting like everything was normal. But she still needed to find out what exactly Harry was trying to do and get that information to Kats. She finished her coffee, dressed, and headed out the door.

Arriving at the Castro office, Molly was surprised at how busy it was. In addition to the regular staff, at least a dozen "contractors" were present. She noted that a couple of them had black eyes, and one had an arm in a sling. Harry was holding court in his office with several men. Franco was parked on the couch inside.

As Molly approached her adjacent office, she could hear Harry berating the assembled men. Molly pretended to shuffle papers across her desk as she turned an ear toward the open door. "And still these assholes are talking about fighting back," he bellowed as he held the morning paper open to the story Molly had just read. "Gianni Vello," he sneered, looking at the paper, "His old man is the one who refused to budge and that gave balls to the rest of 'em."

"Well, maybe we should take the old man out of the game," offered an unfamiliar voice.

"Nah, wouldn't matter. I hear the old man has cancer. The bad kind. But his kids might not be smart once he's gone."

"Then we should put some heat on the Vello kids," said Franco. "I know where one of 'em will be Saturday night."

"How ya know that?" grunted one of the men.

"Cause unlike you palookas, I can read!" laughed Franco. He tossed the folded paper to Harry. "One of the kids is a poet. Says right there he's reading at the Six Gallery on Fillmore."

"One of those fucking Beat poets," sneered Harry. "Their shit don't even rhyme." Harry glanced up and caught Molly staring before she quickly looked away. Harry walked to the door, poked his head out, and gave her an oily smile.

"Hey, sweetheart. Can you bring us some coffee?"

"Sure thing, Harry."

Harry stared at her for a moment, seeming to think about something. Then he turned and closed the door.

Molly's heart was racing. She knew that Harry suspected something, but she also knew that someone named Vello was in trouble. Trying to keep her cool, she headed to the kitchen and prepared a small cart with a coffee service. She returned to Harry's office a few minutes later and was about to knock on the door when she heard her boss's booming voice say, "Ants stadium contract." Ants Stadium, she thought. What stadium?

She knocked and entered. "There she is," said Harry with an overly sweet tone that set Molly on further edge. The other men descended on the coffee like vultures, but Harry and Franco merely sat and watched.

"Do you need anything else, Harry?" she asked in her most casual voice.

"Nah, all good," he quipped with a smile that didn't quite reach his eyes.

Molly quickly turned, closed Harry's door, and retreated to her own office.

The rest of the day was a blur of normal office routine and a growing sense of dread that she needed to tell someone about. The only person she thought she could tell was the clever Japanese PI, Kats, who would know what to do. She knew she couldn't just have a conversation with him from her office. Too many ears and eyes. Gathering her thoughts, she eyed Harry's door and dialed Kats's number.

Kats was sweating despite the morning coolness in the air. He stood in the small dojo built in the back of his home, having just completed the Gendai Jiujitsu *kata* or form for the second time, improving on what he thought was a sloppy first run through. He could hear his father's voice saying "Again." He'd begun his martial arts training as a child after having watched his father practice as long as he could remember. The fluid motions, the sharp smack of fist meeting padded target, the blur of short sticks... all had fascinated him as a small boy. One day when he was eight, his father had turned to him as he watched from his usual place on the step and beckoned him to the tatami mats. His training started that day and had never truly stopped.

As he stretched and contemplated a third run-through of the challenging *kata*, the phone in his front office began to ring. Kats grabbed a towel and headed into the front of the building. "Takemoto," he said as he answered the phone.

"Mr. Takemoto... Kats. It's Molly Hayes."

"Oh hi," he said, a bit surprised to hear from her. "Good

morning, Molly."

"I don't have much time. Can you meet me at lunch? I have some information you need to hear."

"Pick a public place with a lot of people, and I'll meet you there."

Molly thought for a moment, "City of Paris," a favorite of hers on Union Square.

"I'll find you there around lunchtime. And Molly, act casual and watch out for someone following you."

During her lunch hour, Molly gathered her things and casually told the office girls she was going shopping. She walked briskly toward Union Square, occasionally looking back to see if she was being followed. No one there, she thought, but she knew that many of Harry's men had been soldiers and wondered if their training included surveillance. She walked into the beautiful City of Paris department store. Passing under the ornate rotunda with its skylight, she turned upon entering the store and headed to a row of phone booths by the coat check. She thought this a clever way to search for a tail. Closing the door to the booth behind her, Molly once again scanned the halls for any of Harry's men. Not seeing any, she took a deep breath and tried to relax.

A soft knock on the door made her jump, and she saw Kats standing outside the booth. Opening the door, she smiled and started to speak, but Kats took her by the arm, and they moved deeper into the store.

As they walked through the store, acting like a couple doing their Christmas shopping, Kats spoke in a low voice. "Are you in danger?"

"I don't think so. I didn't see any of Harry's guys following me. Maybe I'm just being paranoid. Listen, I overheard some things that have me very worried. Harry and his guys were talking about a man named Vello and his sons. I think they're going to hurt the sons."

"I know Carlo Vello and his sons. They're a family of shipbuilders in the South Basin."

"Is one of them a poet?"

Surprised, Kats said, "Yes. In fact, the younger son, Anton, is a poet."

"He's in danger. They know he's performing somewhere this weekend, and I think they're going to go after him."

"Thank you, Molly," said Kats as he turned a looked at her concerned face. "That's very helpful. Is there anything else?"

"I heard them talking about something, but it doesn't make sense to me."

They approached the coffee counter, and Kats bade her sit down. He ordered coffee for her and tea for himself before imploring her to continue.

"Go on."

"Harry and the crew were talking about an ant stadium."

"Ant stadium?" repeated Kats, also confused.

"I know. What kind of ants need a stadium?"

Kats smiled, "Maybe Gi-Ants Stadium? As in the New York Giants baseball team that's moving to San Francisco next year."

"Giants Stadium," she mused. "I read about that. Makes sense, but what does Harry have to do with Giants Stadium?"

"I don't know. The team is going to play in Seals Stadium in the Mission District temporarily. The city is building a new stadium, but everyone figures it's going to be in the same location as the old stadium..."

"What if Harry knows something?" said Molly. "What if the new stadium is being built down in Bayview Heights?"

"Seems kind of crazy to build out there," Kats said. "That's the windiest part of the city and, frankly, no one goes out there. It's been the city's dumping grounds. It doesn't even feel connected to the city."

"And there's a lot of cheap land out there," Kats continued. "Just having several parcels, even big ones, isn't necessarily going to be a huge payday. Harry's willing to break the law, maybe even kill someone, to get that land. There must be something else."

"Harry's not dumb," she said, thinking out loud. "Why else would he do that unless he had an end game in mind?"

Molly's mind was racing, trying to make the pieces fit together. It was all there, she thought, but somehow she still couldn't see it. She was replaying what she'd heard in her head, *ant stadium...* Then it clicked. Harry had said "ant stadium contract."

"What would the contract to build a stadium be worth?" she asked, recounting the memory to Kats.

"To a legit contractor, it would be worth millions. To a contractor who might skim, cut some corners, take bribes from subcontractors..." Kats let the thought hang in the air. "Somebody might kill for that kind of money."

"That son of a bitch!" she exclaimed, which caused Kats to laugh. She sure doesn't hold back, he thought.

"I have some friends over at city hall who might be able to shed some light on the stadium situation if I ask quietly. Let me follow up with them. You should keep your head down and make sure your boss isn't suspicious."

"I can do that," she replied.

"And give me your phone number," he said, "in case I need to reach you."

Molly looked at him for a moment, smiled, and wrote it down, along with her home address.

"Will you make sure that the Vello boy doesn't get hurt? Harry's guys are tough, and they seem to be getting desperate."

"I'll make sure Anton is safe. Thank you again, Molly."

She rose, nodded, and headed toward the store exit. Glancing back over her shoulder, she saw Kats watching her, and she smiled. Great smile.

CHAPTER 9

A s the weekend approached, Mrs. Harada reminded Kats of his promise to "investigate" her daughter Emiko. Reluctantly, Kats agreed to follow her on Friday, knowing he needed to shadow Anton Vello on Saturday night. He'd also reached out to his contact at city hall, Tak, an old army buddy whom he hoped could provide at least a hint of information.

Takiyuki Ozawa had been a classmate in the Minidoka camp high school. Like Kats, he'd immediately volunteered for the military when the US government allowed the Nisei, the second-generation Japanese Americans, all of whom were US citizens, to enlist, provided they sign a loyalty oath. The idea of the oath was offensive to some, yet for young men like Kats and Tak, eager to prove themselves to the world, they signed the oath and found themselves in the army. In the summer of 1943, they began training at Camp Shelby in Mississippi as the 100th Battalion. The following year they were deployed in the invasion of Italy. Later the 100th merged with the newly formed 442nd Infantry Regiment. There were 4,000 Nisei soldiers, with all White officers. Over the next twelve months in Italy, France, and Germany, they'd amass more than 4,000 purple hearts, 4,000 Bronze Stars, 500 Silver Stars, 8 Presidential unit citations, and 21 Congressional Medals of Honor. These young Americans, who had everything to prove, became the most decorated unit of its size in US military history.

When Kats arrived at Tak's desk in the planning department at city hall, he received a huge smile, and Tak pushed himself up from the desk, hopped over on his one leg, and the two old friends exchanged a fierce bear hug.

"Sit, sit," said Tak as he slid back into his chair. "What can I do for an old '*katonk*' today?"

Kats laughed at that. *Katonk*. He hadn't been called that in a long time. *Katonk* was the Hawaiian slang term for Japanese from the mainland, like Kats. It was meant to refer to the sound of a coconut hitting the ground and the emptiness of the mainlanders' heads. The mainlanders had called the Hawaiians "Buddha heads" for their pidgin English and island dialect. There had been huge cultural differences between the Hawaiian Nisei and the mainlanders, and it had taken a long time for them to build trust and respect. But once forged in training and then in combat, the bond was unbreakable.

Tak was a junior member of the city's planning department. After returning from the war, he'd used the GI Bill to go to college in Berkeley, getting his degree in urban planning. He'd been with the city for six years and was shaping the future course of this rapidly growing city.

"I'm investigating a land deal down in Bayview Heights, and I was hoping you might be able to shed some light on some shady business."

Tak tilted his head and made a pinched face. "Man, I think I know what you're going to ask, but I really can't talk about it."

"Look, I don't want to get you in any trouble, but there are some people there who are going to get hurt in all of this. Maybe even killed."

Looking around the office, Tak lowered his voice. "This is top-secret stuff. The mayor has insisted on keeping this info under wraps."

"OK. How about if I propose a hypothetical, and you tell

me if I'm completely insane or not."

Tak thought for a moment and then nodded.

Kats began to muse out loud. "So, everyone knows that the New York Giants baseball team is moving to San Francisco. They're going to play in the old Seals stadium next spring. And the city is going to build them a new stadium as part of the deal to bring them to the west coast."

Kats paused, and Tak nodded. All this was common knowledge. The Seals had been a minor league baseball team in the Pacific Coast League and their stadium, which seated over 20,000, was serviceable as a temporary option, but not a long-term solution. When the Giants announced their plan to move earlier in the year, the Seals had been forced to look for another home.

"Now, everyone assumes that the new stadium is going to be built in the area around the current stadium in the Mission District. But what if that's not the case?"

Tak kept up his poker face. Kats continued.

"A stadium takes up a lot of space, especially these new stadiums that baseball and football teams are building. There aren't many options in San Francisco with so much development happening since the war. But there's one area that's still cheap, with available land, and a population that's not politically connected. Bayview Heights. If I were going to build a new stadium, I might look there as an option because I think I can get the land. Hypothetically, of course."

Taking a deep breath, Tak said, "The city hasn't officially committed to a location for a new stadium." He stopped there, letting what wasn't said hang in the air as he looked at Kats. That unspoken communication had served them both well in Europe, and Kats was sure he was right about Bayview Heights.

"So hypothetically, would a contract have been awarded before any official announcement?" Kats asked.

"No. Any contract that big would need to go to bid and eventually be approved by city council."

"No exceptions?"

"The only exception for circumventing the public bid is if there's some extraordinary circumstance, like national security or public safety or environmental issues."

"Hmmmm," mused Kats. On a bit of a flyer he asked, "Have you heard of a guy named Charles? Harry Charles? Owns a construction company?"

Tak's face went blank, and he sat back in his chair, almost ramrod straight. He looked around the open floor office at the busy workers as if they might be spies.

"How do you know about Charles Construction?" he asked quietly.

"He seems to be a central figure in my investigation into some trouble down in Bayview Heights. Seems that someone has been buying up land and putting heat on the locals to sell. It's bad, and it's going to get worse."

"Shit," whispered Tak. He paused, trying to decide his next move. Suddenly he burst into a big smile and switched to Japanese.

"Remember how we used to talk over the radio or in the field when we thought the Germans were listening?" he asked, smiling the whole time and nodding his head, just two old friends chatting.

Kat's returned the smile, nodded, and replied in somewhat rusty Japanese "Of course. What do you know?"

"That guy you mentioned," he said, not wanting to use Charles's name, "he was talked about in a meeting last week with my boss, the mayor, and few others on the team. We were told he's working on a special project and we're to co-operate with him and keep the details quiet. We all thought it was some economic development project, like maybe a big company moving into the area. Now I'm wondering if it's related to the stadium."

"Could this guy get the contract for the new stadium that way?"

"I don't see how," Tak paused. "There was another meeting that my boss and the mayor had right before ours. Some Fed came out of the mayor's office. Now that I think about it, those guys looked spooked."

"How do you know he was a Fed?"

"Because the mayor mentioned the Office of something or other from Washington and even said the guy's name. Sand. John Sand."

"So why would the federal government be interested in a baseball stadium in Bayview Heights?"

"That I don't know, but the government has been interested in the Heights for a while now. Obviously, the naval yard is a huge deal. But a few years ago, there was some classified environmental study, and the feds got some major infrastructure modifications from the city. Rumor had it, they added something big to Hunters Point."

"*Kuso*" said Kats.

"Shit is right," replied Tak in English.

"Can you get me access to that environmental report?"

Tak shook his head. "No way, man. That could cost me my job." Kats slumped a bit in his chair, wondering how to proceed. "But I might be able to review the file as part of my work for that construction company we talked about and give you a synopsis. Over dinner. You're buying."

Kats had to keep himself from hugging the man right

there. Instead, he politely nodded, rose to leave, and switched back to English, "So nice to catch up with you, Ozawa-san. I hope to see you again soon. Please tell your parents that I send my very best. "

"Of course. Happy Holidays, Takemoto-san."

CHAPTER 10

I t was the last Friday before Christmas, and Kats wasn't happy. His conflict about following a friend who was nearly family and his sense of obligation to another near-family member, Mrs. Harada, had weighed on him all week. He could hear his father's voice telling him that he needed to do as Mrs. Harada asked. It was *Giri*, the idea of necessary obligation that was characteristic of Japanese culture. He had to do it, even though his American side felt it was wrong. I'm thirty-three years old and still listening to my father, he thought.

The Haradas lived just down the street, and Kats knew where to wait for Emiko to depart and not be seen. Shortly before 8 pm on a cold, damp night, she emerged from the

96 | HUNTERS POINT

home she shared with her mother and walked up to Sutter to catch a cab. Kats walked his motorcycle down the alley across the street. Once Emiko entered her cab, he followed at a discrete distance. They went up Franklin and turned east on Broadway. Headed toward North Beach, Kats thought. A few minutes later, Emiko exited her cab at the corner of Broadway and Kearney in the heart of the North Beach neighborhood. Maybe she's secretly a Beat poet.

He watched as Emiko entered Tommaso's Italian restaurant. Parking his bike, he waited a few minutes before strolling by the front of the restaurant to peer in. Near the back, he saw Emiko with a small group of women. Dinner with friends. Probably some of the girls from the bank where she worked.

Figuring he had a bit of time, Kats walked down the street and ordered a hamburger and a Coke at a local diner. He sat in the window of the diner where he had line of sight on the front of Tommaso's. He ate leisurely and scanned the newspaper, with one eye trained across the street. Finally around 9:30 pm, Emiko and her friends emerged from the restaurant. Kats rose, left his money on the counter, and started to walk toward his bike around the corner. To his surprise, the ladies didn't hail a cab. Instead, they turned the corner, crossed the street, and headed up Broadway. Midway down the block, they turned and entered some establishment. Kats thought he might know where they went.

He strolled down the block and, reaching the point where they'd disappeared, saw the entrance to a club most locals knew about. Ann's Club 440. A sign next to the entrance proclaimed "A Continuous Show from 7 pm" and featured a picture of a large Black woman in a white tuxedo with tails, top hat, and cane—"Gladys Bentley, The Brown Bomber of

Sophisticated Songs." Kats knew the club and knew the performer. He'd seen Bentley several times over the years. She was a great singer and consummate entertainer. She'd been a star in the Harlem Renaissance in the 1930s before coming west. An avowed lesbian who dressed in men's clothing, she was a long-time regular at Mona's Club 440, then Ann's 440, which was famous for its live entertainment and its diverse crowd that included a significant lesbian clientele.

Kats knew that all were welcome at Ann's, so after waiting a few minutes, he walked up the stairs and entered the bustling club. Bentley and the band were in full swing, and the place was full of people, smoke, and music, which provided enough cover for Kats to slide along the wall as he tried to locate Emiko. It took a minute, but he saw her on the dance floor doing the Cha-Cha with an elegant looking woman who wore a suit jacket, pleated trousers, and a tailored shirt. This doesn't mean anything, Kats thought. Lots of people came to Ann's for the entertainment and to dance. Then as the music stopped, Emiko and her dance partner embraced and kissed. This may be hard to explain to Mrs. Harada.

Keeping an eye on the dance floor, Kats angled toward the bar, trying to decide what he should do. Kats was aware of San Francisco's growing reputation as a gay and lesbian mecca. He had friends who were gay and was happy when people could be themselves. But he knew that many did not share his low-key approach, and these changes frightened them. Sadly, he suspected that the older Japanese community might fall into the latter category. As his mind raced with this new information, he managed to find the bar and waived to one of the bartenders.

"What the hell are you doing here?" came the voice behind the bar as Kats finally looked at the bartender.

"Molly?" he said stupidly. Eyeing her up and down, she wore a white tuxedo shirt, a black vest, a bowtie, and a frown. Her long, red hair was pulled back into a ponytail.

"Yeah, and again, what the hell?" she asked in a low voice.

"Umm, I'm kind of on a case. Something for a friend. What are you doing here?"

"I work here obviously. I've been tending bar here on weekends for a while."

"Right, sure," he said, still trying to find his balance, like a fighter who'd been caught with a good one-two punch.

"Look, this isn't something I want folks to know about, especially at my day job, you know? They already give me enough shit."

"Right, sure. I get it. You being a lesbian is none of their business."

Molly leaned in closer to him, "I'm not a lesbian. I get great tips here and a lot of nice attention from the patrons. There are a lot of great people here. They accept the straight divorcee from Ohio, and I accept them. Get it?"

Kats nodded, respecting the idea of simply being accepted for who you were. He was about to order a drink when another familiar voice came from behind him.

"What the hell are you doing here?" said Emiko as she approached the bar. "Did you follow me?"

"Emiko," Kats said, surprised and suddenly back footed. "Hey there."

She looked at him, a combination of anger and embarrassment painting her face. She repeated, "What are you doing here?

"Umm," he began.

"He's working on a case for me," Molly said, coming to his rescue. "He needed to update me on his progress."

Looking back and forth, Kats managed, "Yep, a case. Big case. Surprised to see you here."

Emiko blushed. It was her turn to stammer. "Yeah, well…"

"Hey, your private life is your business," he offered. "Can I get you a drink?"

She nodded and said, "Vodka tonic." Kats ordered two that Molly delivered with a smile and a nod of encouragement to him.

"Kats, I'm trying to figure out who I am," Emiko began. "My life has been really good since I stopped trying to be something I wasn't. But you know how much pressure my mother has put on me to find a man and get married."

Kats nodded. "Japanese parents," he said, and they both knew all the good, bad, and considerable expectations that carried with it.

"Mom wants me to get married and have kids more than anything."

"Actually, I think your mom wants you to be happy," offered Kats. "I bet if you told her you were happy and safe, she'd be really supportive."

"I've been trying to find a way to tell her, but there never seems to be a good time. She will be very…" she searched for the right word, "disappointed."

"Look, when I told my parents I was enlisting back in '43, my mom was terrified, and my dad was angry. They mostly got beyond that and were ultimately supportive. You just have to let them feel what they feel for a while. I know she'll come around."

"You think?"

"Japanese parents stand by their kids, no matter what. Think about what our parents endured during the war for us. Your mom is a fierce little samurai when it comes to you and your brother. She always will be."

Tears streamed down Emiko's cheeks as she smiled, thinking about her mother. "Well, my brother and his wife gave mom the grandson she wanted, so some of the pressure is off me," she laughed.

Over Emiko's shoulder, Kats could see the woman who had been her dance partner earlier. Kats gestured toward her, "I think your friend is worried about you."

Turning, Emiko looked at the elegant woman, nodded, and held up a finger to indicate she needed a minute.

"Her name is Sydney, and she teaches at San Francisco State. We've only been going out a few months, but we have a lot of fun together. She's been really supportive of me."

"She sounds like a good person to have in your corner," Kats said.

"You are too, Katsuhiro." She kissed him on the cheek. "I'll talk to mom. She's going to be so disappointed that I won't be marrying you!"

Kats watched her leave. Molly leaned on the bar. "That was very sweet of you," she said to him. "I only caught a bit of it, but you did a good thing there."

"I hope so. Being different is hard. But at least this city is becoming more open and accepting of different people," he mused, looking around at the variety of people in the bar. Molly smiled in agreement.

"Thanks," he said looking at her. "I appreciate the help there."

"You're welcome," she said, looking at his earnest face. "You're different than I thought."

"How so?"

"I guess I expected a private detective to be more..."

"Sam Spade?" he interrupted.

"I was going to say more of an asshole," she laughed.

"Kind of the same thing," Kats replied with a smile. "But I will take it as a compliment."

Their eyes held each other for a long moment. Molly blushed, and Kats took a sip of his drink. "Well, now you can focus on our case," she said, breaking the tension.

"Yes, of course. Tomorrow I'll be over on Fillmore with Anton. He's doing a reading at the Six Gallery along with some other Beat poets."

"Sounds interesting."

"Not really my scene."

"Please be careful."

"Always."

Kats took a final sip of his drink, put some cash on the bar, and gave Molly a small wave. She nodded and turned to patrons at the other end of the bar.

"Good evening, Katsuhiro," said yet another familiar voice over his shoulder. Turning, he found himself face to face with a striking, silver-haired woman in a well-cut, blue suit jacket. He tried to place the face and then realized she wasn't wearing her glasses.

"Gladys!" he said to his favorite librarian. "You look fabulous. Enjoying the show this evening?"

"Always, my boy," she said with a wink. "So, you know Molly?"

"Yes, a bit."

"Lucky boy."

Maybe, thought Kats. Maybe.

CHAPTER 11

The next morning, as Kats sat drinking a cup of coffee in his kitchen, there was a gentle knock at his door. Without waiting for a response, his door clicked open, and Mrs. Harada stepped inside. She was carrying something in a *furoshiki*, a cloth wrapping typically used for gifts.

"*Ohayo gozaimasu,*" she said.

"Good morning," returned Kats. He was surprised she'd waited until 9:05 am to come calling. He'd been carefully formulating his plan since departing Ann's 440 the previous night.

She placed the *furoshiki* on his counter. "Is that what I think it is?" asked Kats.

"I made you some musubi," she said simply. The Hawaiian comfort food of fried Spam, rice, and seaweed was one of his favorites.

Inwardly, Kats did a backflip; outwardly, he demurely stated, "Most kind. *Arigato gozaimasu.*"

Turning, she asked obliquely, "Did you have a good evening?"

"Well, yes and no. I was able to follow Emiko to a restaurant in North Beach."

Mrs. Harada made a face at the mention of the artist and bohemian enclave.

"She met some friends there. Looked like some of her girlfriends, probably from work."

"She didn't get home until very late," quipped Mrs. Harada. "Dinner couldn't last that long."

"Well, after they left the restaurant, they got into a cab. I was about to follow them on my motorcycle, but I noticed I'd picked up a nail in my tire. No way to follow them. Very sorry." He hated to lie to her, but he was giving Emiko time to speak with her mother.

"Katsuhiro-kun, I thought you were a good investigating person."

"Well, you kind of get what you pay for," he joked.

"That is what the musubi is for."

Not the first time I've been paid with food, he thought. Part of the job.

"Look," he said in his most placating voice, "Christmas is coming up, and Emiko will have some time off. I bet if you asked her to help make Christmas *sukiyaki*, she might be more open to talking with you." Hopefully.

Mrs. Harada seemed to ponder that, and she gave a firm nod. "If that doesn't work, you will have to investigate again. And you can come over for *sukiyaki* on Christmas."

"Of course," he said, hoping Emiko was true to her word. And he congratulated himself on scoring *sukiyaki* for Christmas.

That afternoon Kats called Anton Vello to let him know he had some information he needed to share with him. As expected, Anton mentioned that he'd be in the city that evening, performing at the Six Gallery. Kats said he'd come out and they could chat after the show. He didn't want the young man to be worrying when he should be focused on his art.

Kats arrived at 3119 Fillmore, the Six Gallery, shortly before 9 pm. Kats realized he'd been to the gallery several years before when it originally opened as the King Ubu Gallery. Small world, he thought. The place was already spilling out onto the street. Men and women stood about, smoking, talking, and laughing in the chill night air. At the entrance a hand-painted sign announced "Six Gallery Poets" featuring the names Ginsberg, Kerouac, McClure, Ferlinghetti, and Vello. The MC was Kenneth Rexroth. Even Kats had heard of several of them.

He entered and quickly surveyed the nearly full room. The minimal, low stage at the back had a dark curtain behind it, and small tables circled the room. The walls were adorned with paintings that ranged from beautiful to primitive. The bar was busy making espressos and pouring glasses of wine. Looking for a place to stand, Kats saw a familiar face waving him over to his table in the back.

"Hey, Shig," said Kats as he approached his friend who'd gotten him mixed up in this whole scene just a couple of weeks ago.

"Hey, man. Good to see you. You here because of Anton?"

"Yeah, I need to see him after the show. You?"

"Big night tonight. Jack Kerouac is back in town supporting his new book, *On the Road*. Ginsberg has a new holiday poem. Up-and-comer like Anton. This is a great lineup. And the boss is reading," he said, winking, referring to City Lights owner Lawrence Ferlinghetti.

Kats noticed Anton sitting at the side of the stage talking to a middle-aged man, with wide-set, smart eyes. Shig, following Kats's eyes, leaned over and said, "That's Ken Rexroth he's talking to. The MC and the godfather of the poetry scene here. If Ken likes you, you're golden, and Ken has a great eye for talent."

Kats nodded and settled in for what he was sure would be a unique night.

Rexroth was an excellent master of ceremonies. He

kept the room engaged and the poetry moving. As the evening progressed, Shig, as well as most of the audience, got progressively more lubricated and animated. Despite his comfortable state of inebriation, Shig managed to provide Kats with useful commentary and context on the various performers.

Allen Ginsberg opened the evening. Fresh off the legal vindication of his book *Howl*, he was a local celebrity. He joked with the familiar audience before launching into a hilarious parody of his own work called "Prowl" about a red suited burglar who only worked one night of the year—December 24.

Michael McClure was next and certainly more serious. Shig explained that McClure was a staunch environmentalist who talked about nature and spirituality. He read a poem called *A Fist Full* from his most recent book of the same name.

The next and certainly most energetic performance was a reading by the man who'd become a Beat icon with the success of the just-published *On the Road*. Jack Kerouac took the stage wearing workman's clothes and slicked back hair. He looks like a dock worker, thought Kats. A tough dock worker.

As Kerouac read excerpts from his book, he prowled around the small stage, an intense energy about him. When he talked about his characters wanting to "Burn, burn, burn" you could almost feel the heat. Sitting next to the stage was another tough-looking man, about the same age as Kerouac, who between sips of wine from a large bottle, would interject "Yeah, man!" or "Burn, baby!" as Kerouac preached like a Baptist minister.

"Who's that guy next to the stage?" Kats asked Shig.

"That's Cassady. Neal Cassady. Fixture in the scene for a while. Everybody wants to either fight him or fuck him. Supposedly he's the model for Kerouac's character Dean Moriarty in the new book."

Kerouac finished to rousing applause and a fierce hug from a laughing Cassady. Rexroth called for a short intermission, and Shig headed to the men's room.

Kats had to admit he was enjoying himself even though he was working. Poetry had never really done anything for him. But now he realized that poetry on the written page was a shadow of what it could be when spoken, or more accurately, performed well. He was about to order his third espresso when Anton Vello came over and sat down.

"Hey, Kats. Enjoying the show?"

"Yes, I am. Very much, in fact," Kats replied truthfully. "Looking forward to your piece later."

"Yeah, Kerouac is a tough act to follow," he mused. "What did you want to tell me, by the way?"

"I've made some progress on who and what is behind the trouble in Bayview Heights, but let's connect after the show, and I'll go over everything then. You should focus on your poetry."

"Yeah, it's been hard to focus. Dad is getting worse. We know he doesn't have much time left. My poem tonight is inspired by him."

"I'm sure he's very proud of you," Kats said.

"Thanks. Catch you later."

Kats surveyed the room. He watched Kerouac and Ginsberg holding court at opposite sides of the gallery. Shig was talking with his boss Larry. Men, women, Black, White, Latin, Asian, young, and old—quite a collection of different people here, thought Kats with a smile.

"Is this seat taken?" came a voice over his shoulder. Turning, Kats found himself staring at Molly Hayes, who gave him a bemused smile. Before he could answer, she seated herself to both his pleasure and concern.

"What are you doing here?"

"Thought I'd check out the show. And I thought you could use some help."

"Molly, this could get dangerous. You could get hurt."

"I can help. I can identify Harry's men and be your lookout. Believe it or not, I can take care of myself."

"Of that I have no doubt but..."

At that moment, Shig returned to the table, "Well, hello," he said with an enormous grin as he sat down.

"Hi, I'm Molly."

"Good evening, Molly. Shigeyoshi Murao. Shig to my friends," he said as he shook her hand.

"Good evening, Shig," she replied, and he laughed.

"How do you know my dear old friend Kats here?" he asked as he slapped Kats on the back.

"Oh, he's been following me for weeks. Can't get enough of me," she joked. Kats felt his face redden, and Shig pounded the table with laughter.

"She's part of this case you dropped on me *baka*," Kats retorted.

"Is that Anton?" she asked as she spotted the young man approaching the stage.

"Yes, he's up next," interjected Shig.

As the show resumed, Rexroth introduced Anton, who took the stage with a humble bow and small notebook in hand. "Thank you, Ken, and thank you to the Six Gallery for hosting us."

"I want to dedicate this poem to two men who have shaped me. First is to our friend Michael McClure," he gestured to the poet seated in the audience now. "Michael's work touching on nature and the environment has inspired me. He's been a friend and wonderful mentor into this world of words." Anton took a breath to steady himself.

"And this poem is for my father, Carlo Vello, and his lifelong love affair with the sea. This is called *Poison Fish*."

Over the next five minutes, Kats watched Anton cast a spell over the audience. At first, he didn't get the reference to a "steel black fish consuming itself and the world" or the "poison wake of its passing" until Anton said "Nautilus," and it clicked. He was talking about the American nuclear-powered submarine that had been navigating the Pacific for months now. The *Nautilus* was the first of what would certainly be many more nuclear-powered ships, or "poison fish," to pollute the seas. To an environmentalist like McClure, these ships would contaminate the world. To Carlo Vello, a man all about the wind and the water, such vessels were epochal to that world. Anton's poem captured the fear and the threat, but more importantly it captured what was to be lost in this atomized world.

As he finished, the room was silent for a moment, then erupted in thunderous applause. Kats found himself joining in enthusiastically. He saw Neal Cassady and Jack Kerouac shouting thunderously from the bar. Ken Rexroth came on stage, whispered something in Anton's ear, and gave him a hug. Shig appeared at Kats's side and said, "Told you the kid was good."

The show continued for another hour. As he sat with Molly, Shig regaled them with insight, gossip, and intrigue about the scene that seemed Shakespearean in its scope.

"Are you a poet?" Molly asked Shig.

"My talents sadly don't include the written word, as much as I love it. By day I manage City Lights Bookstore. By night I try to swim in this sea of art, music, and literature." Clearly, Shig was drunk, thought Kats. He's laying it on thick!

"Shig is a free speech champion," Kats said in a serious voice that made Shig blush in turn. "Remember the obscenity trial over that book of poetry this past summer?"

"Of course," Molly said.

"Well, that guy," Kats pointed to Allen Ginsberg at a nearby table "is the poet who wrote the book. And this guy," pointing to Shig, "is the unlucky son of a bitch who sold the book to an undercover cop."

"And was charged along with my boss with distributing obscenity," said Shig as he pointed to Larry Ferlinghetti across the room. "Quite the day at City Lights."

"But you all were acquitted, right?" asked Molly.

"Oh, yes, but it was still great press for the store. Better press for Ginsberg," Shig said with a hint of resignation. "But really it was a win for art and free speech. That's what was at stake."

Kats raised his espresso cup to Shig, "To free speech," and they clinked glasses.

Rexroth called Larry Ferlinghetti to the stage, and he closed the show. Shig leaned in and said, "Larry doesn't get enough credit as a poet. Everyone thinks of him as a successful business owner and publisher, but mark my words, he'll be one of the greats." Kats nodded, but he had one eye on Anton as he watched person after person come up and shake his hand or buy him a drink. He was happy for the young man and glad he hadn't told him yet of the possible danger he was in. Let him enjoy this.

"Kats," Molly said into his ear, "I just saw one of Harry's men at the door."

He reached around her waist and pulled her close to him. She didn't resist. He spoke into her ear, like young lovers on a date as he turned to look at the door.

"Dark hair with a brown jacket?"

"Yes."

Kats watched the man and noticed that he exchanged a look with another man at the bar. He's not alone, thought Kats. And she smells great.

"Shig, is there a back door?"

"Yeah, just past the office down the hall from the bathroom."

"Where did you park?"

"Anton picked me up. We're in the alley over off Steiner by Greenwich."

"OK, I need you to sober up and get over to Anton. You need to tell him there may be trouble here, and he needs to slip out the back. Act casual, like you're going to take a leak. But get him out the back and meet me over on Steiner. And you need to take Molly with you."

"Got it," Shig said as he wiped his face with his hands and stiffened his resolve. "Casual."

"What about you?" asked Molly as Shig rose and casually walked across the room.

"I'll run a little interference on these guys and meet you over on Steiner. Just go out the back. Don't make eye contact with Anton, and don't look at the guy by the door. Just act like you're out on a date."

"Right. OK." She rose and looked toward the back, but before she left, she leaned over Kats and kissed him. He found himself kissing her back, and all too soon, she pulled back enough to make eye contact. "Just like I'm on a date," she said with a smile and turned for the back.

Kats watched her walk away, using the time to both appreciate the view and to collect his thoughts. You're working, man! He saw Shig and Anton talking. Shig was pumping his hand like a fan, trying to keep things casual. First Anton, then a moment later Shig, headed toward the hallway in the back. Kats watched the two-man team. They exchanged glances, trying to decide if they should follow or if this was nothing. The one at the bar jerked his head toward the back, and the man at the door started to make his way through the crowd.

Kats stood up and appeared to lurch a bit as he did so. He took a couple of shaky steps on an intercept course with brown jacket man. As the man approached, Kats stumbled into a young woman carrying a glass of wine. As she was about to fall backward, Kats caught her and plowed the two of them into brown jacket. Spilled wine, apologies, and swear words ensued. As they righted themselves, brown jacket angrily pushed Kats, who allowed himself to fall backward again to great dramatic effect. He was caught by two strong hands.

"Not cool!" shouted an angry voice over his head. Kats was hoisted to his feet by Neal Cassady, the scene-making tough guy, who confronted brown jacket. Cassady was clearly also drunk, but he wore it like a familiar friend. Brown jacket fired a right cross to Cassady's head, which to Kats's surprise, merely seemed to awaken the man. Cassady responded with a growl and a tackle that took both men to the floor. The second man was crossing the bar, and Kats thought he might need to step in to prevent his unexpected benefactor from being outnumbered, when suddenly America's most famous

Beat writer, Jack Kerouac, bellowed like a barbarian and punched the second man in the jaw. Kats felt a pang of guilt at having instigated this fight, but clearly Cassady and Kerouac were familiar combatants. Plus, they genuinely seemed to be enjoying themselves. Just another Saturday night on the road.

Kats knew he had to get Anton to safety, so he made his way out the front door during the confusion. He looked around, knowing that there may be others, but no one seemed to notice his departure. As he headed around the corner, he checked his back once again and, satisfied, broke into a run around the block.

Shig, Molly, and Anton rounded the corner from the alley behind the Six Gallery and headed toward Steiner, the next street. "The car is over there," Shig said as he pointed toward the corner.

"What's going on?" Anton asked as they trotted down the block.

"Some guys were here to hurt you," said Molly as she scanned the quiet streets. "And there may be more of them."

"OK, got it. And who are you?" Anton asked.

Franco smiled as he watched the three emerge from the alley and scurry down the street. Not only did they get the Vello kid, but also that Jap who fucked with their plans and that uppity bitch Molly! He emerged from the shadows across the street onto the sidewalk and stepped into a pool of light cast by a lonely streetlamp. He made a circular motion over his head, and multiple shadows detached themselves from buildings down the block and began to converge on the retreating trio.

As they arrived at the alley entrance off Steiner, Shig looked around for Kats. Shit, he thought, where is he? Anton was scrambling for his car keys and waved for them to follow into the car. As he approached his old Ford Mainline, Anton noticed that it was leaning oddly to the left.

"Shit! The tires are flat!" he exclaimed.

"That's not a good sign, is it?" Molly said.

"Probably not," Shig said as they turned and looked back up the alley entrance. Several dark-clothed men were gathering there. Shig pushed Molly behind him and looked for a way out of the alley.

There were six men blocking their exit. Molly recognized several of them. Then they parted and she saw Franco approach, smoking a cigarette.

"Good evening, Molly," he said smugly. "Didn't know you were a poetry fan."

"Go to hell, you knuckle-dragging Neanderthal," she spat.

"Such a mouth on you," he smiled his reptilian smile. "And you," he said, pointing at Shig, "My guys got a score to settle with you."

"Um, I don't think that's the guy boss," said one of the men behind Franco.

"All them Japs look alike to me," said another.

"They think I'm Kats," Shig whispered to Molly. He decided to run with it.

"Do you know karate, too?" whispered Molly.

"God, no."

Stepping forward, Shig waved his hands in circles and made his best samurai face. He'd seen enough karate over the years to make a show of it. He hoped these idiots wouldn't know the difference.

"Get 'em," said Franco, and his squad advanced.

Shig let out a fierce, "Kiai," that stopped their advance, but only for a moment.

The first man stepped into range, and Shig made a passable punch to his chest, but he lacked the power that real training provided. In a moment, Shig was held around the neck in a very large arm. The next guy grabbed Molly by the arm but couldn't fully secure her. She delivered a well-aimed kick to his groin that dropped him like a stone. Before she could find her next target, someone grabbed a handful of her hair and yanked her off balance. She hit the ground.

"Run!" Kats shouted as he appeared behind the thugs. Everyone, even Franco, who was normally attentive to battlefield situations, was caught off guard. Kats was among them. A straight right hand into a stomach crumpled the first man who held Molly with a whoosh of expelled air. Kats dropped and spun, sweeping the legs out from the next man. Two down, but he'd lost the element of surprise.

As hands moved to grab him, he dove deeper into the alley, rolling and coming upright next to Anton. He hoped to draw the men into the cul de sac and give his friends space to run. Anton appeared frozen as Kats stood next to him. "You need to run. Follow me."

Kats launched himself into the massed men, leading with his feet. Hands and fists hit him as they struggled to pin him down. The only advantage Kats had was that these guys were getting in each other's way. He took the blows and stayed close to the throng to keep them occupied.

Anton moved forward, pulling Molly to her feet. Shig shouted, "C'mon!" as he cleared the alley.

Molly and Anton were blocked by Franco, who pulled a black .45 pistol from his jacket. "Give it up, kid," he deadpanned.

Anton pushed Molly behind him as Franco approached, the gun in his right hand. "You're lucky, kid," he said, gesturing slightly with the gun, drawing Anton's eyes toward it. "We gotta bring you in," echoed as his left fist buried itself in Anton's belly. He went to his knee with a groan, and Franco followed him down, bringing the butt of the pistol down across his head.

"Bastard!" Molly yelled as she leaped forward onto Franco. Her hands sought his face as she ripped and clawed at him. Momentarily blinded, Franco swung wildly with his empty hand, connecting with Molly's face in its backhand arc. She hit the ground with Anton. Blood covered Franco's face as he savagely glared down at Molly.

"Fucking bitch," he said as he kicked her several times. She lay motionless.

Turning toward the scrum behind him, Franco saw that his six guys still were struggling to keep the slippery Jap from getting free. As Kats twisted and rolled, he stood up, but one of the prostrate men grabbed his leg, momentarily locking Kats in place. Franco stepped forward and clubbed Kats across the head with his gun. Kats fell forward in a daze.

"Jesus Christ," he said to his battered men, "he's one fucking guy. Get him up and get the kid in the car," gesturing toward Anton.

Two men pulled Anton up, and the larger one threw the slight man over his shoulder like a sack of grain. They quick-timed it down the street.

"What about the girl?"

"Leave her. She's mine," Franco said malevolently. "But first, you boys want some payback?" he nodded toward Kats being dragged to his feet by two men who held his arms.

"Hell, yeah," said one, who stepped forward and buried

his fist in Kats's midsection. Another punched him across the side of the head, and Kats buckled, his legs turned to water.

Franco knelt next to Molly and pulled her head up by the hair. "You should see this, red." Molly blinked through tears, trying to rise, but her body wouldn't listen.

"Boss! Trouble!" came a cry at the mouth of the alley. Franco dropped Molly and turned to look down the street. There, running up the dimly lit street, were several men, led by the other Jap that had gotten away.

"Banzai!" Shig yelled as he led his Beat army into battle. Cassady and Kerouac bellowed behind him, eager for more action.

"Go!" ordered Franco, but his men were already in retreat. They dropped Kats, and all ran, disappearing into the night like cockroaches.

Shig arrived, running first to Molly, who said, "I'm OK. Help Kats." Shig rolled Kats over onto his back, his face bloodied but his eyes open.

"Banzai? Really?" Kats said through bloodied lips.

"It was all I could think of," returned Shig.

Behind Shig, Kats saw two concerned faces as he looked up at Cassady and Kerouac.

"You look like hell," Kerouac said. Kats sat up and started to rise. Cassady offered him a calloused hand and pulled him to his feet.

"Thank you," Kats said to the two men.

"Sometimes ya gotta fight to keep the peace," Cassady said, and Kerouac smiled in agreement.

Molly had been helped to her feet as well as Kats reached her, her right eye already swollen and darkening. "I'm OK," she assured him.

"I'm so sorry you got caught up in this."

"It's OK. But they got Anton."

"We'll get him back," Kats said. "We'll get him back."

"Helluva first date," Molly said. "What do you do for an encore?"

"Plane crashes and shark attacks," he replied.

"Sign me up."

CHAPTER 12

"**A**re you fucking kidding me?!?!" Harry Charles shouted into the phone at his private office. Franco and another man, who sported a black eye and a bandage across his evidently broken nose, looked at each other and then at their shoes. It was Sunday morning, and they were already tired.

The voice on the other end of the phone was nervous. "We did just like you told us. We called that Vello guy, but we got his kid, named Gianni. We told him he needed to sell or the other kid would end up floating in the bay. That's when he told us the old man was in the hospital."

Harry held the phone away from his ear, his head shaking. "And because he's in the hospital, he can't sign a god damned thing," Harry said bitterly.

"Yeah, boss. Sorry," came the voice over the phone.

"Sit on him. I'll send you back up later today," he said as he slammed the phone onto the cradle.

"Fuck me!" he shouted to no one in particular. "The old man is in the hospital, and he's the only one who can sign over the property. And the guy is terminal. If he fucking dies now, we gotta wait for the courts and lawyers to settle things."

"Nobody said kidnapping was easy," quipped Franco. Harry's head snapped around, and broken-nose guy visibly flinched. Franco just smiled. He'd known Harry for too long to be worried. Plus, it was true. They'd been operating outside the law for years now, but kidnapping and blackmail were different from the strong-arm stuff that Franco and Harry were so aptly suited for. Mistakes were bound to happen.

"We need to get that land locked up to secure this deal with the city," Harry lamented. "If we gotta wait weeks for the transfer, we're fucked."

"Yeah, eventually we need to own the land," offered Franco, "but right now we can *control* the land."

Harry squinted at Franco, "What?"

"Remember back in '44 as we were advancing with Patton and the 3rd army?"

Harry nodded. Of course, he could never forget it. Some of the scariest, most intense, and most amazing moments of his life.

"Remember how we'd move into an area, clear, and secure it? We controlled that area long before HQ designated it as liberated or 'owned' by us. We need to control the land for now, and eventually we'll own it. Having the one kid is a good start, but we probably need to work on the other son. Make sure we control him, too."

"Yeah," nodded Harry, suddenly seeing a pathway. "When the old man dies, the kids will inherit the land. Control the kids, control the land."

He needed some intel on the older Vello kid, and he had an idea of who to call.

Kats awoke with a start; for a moment he was still fighting. He looked around through a swollen left eye and realized he was on Shig's couch. He knew that because Shig was next to him on his overstuffed chair, snoring away.

He groaned as he sat up, his head throbbing. Maybe a couple of cracked ribs, too, he thought. Cuts and bruises covered him. Still, it could have been much worse.

"Shig," he said, shaking the man's foot. "Wake up."

"Oh, man," groaned Shig as he rubbed his face and sat up. "I'm sore," he complained as he rotated his shoulders.

"Yes, your life is hard," Kats replied. The irony was lost on Shig, who wandered into his kitchen to make coffee.

Looking at the clock, it was nearly 9 am. He recalled the conversation with Gianni Vello late the prior night.

"You were supposed to watch him!" Gianni had yelled into the phone. Kats had no reply and let the elder brother vent his anger. "My father is in the hospital," he continued. "I can't tell him my brother is missing. They say he doesn't have much time."

"Perhaps it's time to call the police," Kats offered in a neutral voice. He wasn't sure the police would be able to help. They knew who took Anton but had no proof of it. Charles would just act shocked, deny any involvement, and maybe dispose of Anton if the heat got too high.

"They took him for a reason," Gianni said. "They want the land and will use Anton to get it. The police don't help folks like us, and if we get them involved, Anton gets hurt."

Kats had to agree. "They'll probably contact you with their demands. Be ready for that. Keep them occupied, and stall while you're cooperating. I'll find your brother."

An angry response started up Gianni's throat, but instead he said, "Find him for my father," and hung up the phone.

Kats now mulled over his promise to find young Anton and knew he was on a literal deadline.

"Where's Molly?" he asked Shig, trying to piece together the fuzzy details of the aftermath of their battle.

"I gave her my room, remember?" Shig replied, pouring hot water over the coffee grounds in the glass carafe.

Kats poured a cup of coffee for himself and one for Molly

and opened the door to Shig's bedroom. She lay on her side, seemingly sleeping peacefully. Her hair mostly covered her battered face. As he sat down on the bed she stirred, muttered a salty expletive, and sat up. Kats handed her the coffee.

"You look terrible," she said to him.

"Good morning to you, too."

She sipped the coffee, touched her faced, winced, and eyed him. "So, this is your job?"

"No, mostly I follow people, occasionally take some pictures, and find folks when they don't want to be found."

"Well, now we have to find Anton," she replied.

"Yes, *I* do," he said with emphasis.

"I think you need my help," she replied.

"Mine, too," Shig said as he entered the room. Molly smiled and raised her cup to him. He gently bowed.

"Guys, this is dangerous stuff. You can get hurt. You did get hurt," he said to Molly.

"I took worse beatings from my ex-husband," she said, breaking his heart a little bit. He looked at her a moment. She tried to look tough, but he knew she was putting on a good front.

"And I was in the army too," Shig said.

"You were an interpreter." [3]

"Still, army!"

"All this is meaningless unless we can figure out where they stashed Anton," Molly said.

"You know Harry's operation better than anyone. Where would you hide a Maltese Beat poet?" Kats asked.

"The main office and the warehouse for Charles Construction are too obvious. We could send the cops there. Harry doesn't want to end up at San Quentin for kidnapping."

"Maybe they could use a construction site? The holidays

would have most of them empty until after the New Year," Kats said.

"Too many other folks have access to those kinds of sites," replied Molly. "Harry would want control."

"Does he own any other properties?" Shig asked.

"No, even his private office is in a public building, so…" she trailed off.

"Wait, wait, wait," she said, searching her memory. "There was another older warehouse that is owned by one of Harry's shell companies in Mission Bay. I saw it several times in the books. But I don't remember the address."

"Mission Bay is a pretty big neighborhood, but we could stake it out," Shig said enthusiastically.

"Too big, and too much time," lamented Kats.

"Well, let's get the address," Molly said.

"What do you mean, get the address?"

"I know where the books are. We could get the address if we get the books."

"Are you suggesting…" Kats began.

"Yeah," interrupted Molly, "let's break into Harry's office."

Shig clapped his hands, smiled, and said, "This is gonna be fun!"

CHAPTER 13

Sunday crawled by. Molly and Kats set a rendezvous point several blocks from Charles Construction's office and agreed to meet there at midnight. Shig initially protested being left out but admitted stealth wasn't his strong suit. Kats returned home, applied some liniments to his varied injuries, and fell back asleep. When he awoke, it was already early evening and dark. He packed a satchel with a few tools he thought might be required for their planned breaking and entering. What have we gotten ourselves into, he mused as he dressed in a dark turtleneck and black chinos. Grabbing a black stocking cap, he headed toward the door. He stopped at the mirror by the front and took in his reflection. He pulled the hat on low over his forehead and then turned the turtleneck up over his mouth and nose. I look like a damn ninja, he thought as he took off the hat and pulled the collar down.

Kats parked his motorcycle behind the all-night diner that was their meeting point. He checked his watch. 11:47 pm. Three minutes later, Molly walked up the street wearing a long trench coat.

"The trench coat is a nice touch," he joked. "I left mine back at the office."

"Ha," she replied. "I know you said to dress in dark, comfortable clothing, but it's cold!" she said, removing the coat and placing it behind Kats's bike. Underneath she wore tight pegged black pants, black Chuck Taylors and, like Kats, a black turtleneck. But hers clung to her like an inky, wet blanket. She looked amazing, and Kats drew a deep breath.

Noticing he was staring, she asked, "What? Is this not OK?"

"No, you look great…" he stammered. "I mean you look… ah yeah, that's fine."

In the darkness, Molly felt herself blush. Then she remembered that they were on a mission and not a date.

They walked casually down the street, a couple of late-night Beats. They stopped across the street from Harry's office and stepped back into the shadows of an alley. The lights were out on both floors, and the street seemed quiet. As Molly started to move forward, Kats put a hand on her shoulder. "We wait and watch first," he said quietly. "Stillness is a strength," he repeated the mantra his father had told him many times in his training.

"Is that an army thing?" she asked as she leaned against the dark wall.

"It's certainly a Ranger thing, but I learned that first training with my father."

"Was he a soldier?"

"No, he was a salesman at an import company."

"How does a salesman learn about strategy and combat?"

Kats settled into a comfortable position where he could see the street, Harry's building, and Molly without shifting his head.

"As a young man in Japan, my father learned the martial arts in school. He was very talented in these activities, and he got to study with a man named Jigoro Kano. Kano was the founder of a martial art that many around the world now know: judo."

"Wow. So your father taught you judo?"

"Actually, my father taught me jiujitsu, which is the traditional Japanese martial art that Judo is based upon. Where judo has now become a sport, jiujitsu is purely about combat."

"So that's how you could fight all those guys the other night," she mused.

"Yes, but credit the US Army and the Ranger training with a lot of that, too."

"Still, your father must be a great fighter."

"He is, but he's actually more of a pacifist than anything else."

"Seems like an odd combination," she replied.

"He taught me that *budo*, the martial arts, are only to defend and that aggression was antithetical to 'the way,' as he called it. He was adamantly opposed to my joining the army."

"But you were fighting for a just cause. And don't some folks deserve to get punched in the nose?"

"Well, I believed so, but my father was pretty staunch in his beliefs. There's a special kind of stubborn that Asian parents have, especially with their kids."

"That must have been difficult for you."

"It caused some issues between us," he said.

"So where's your family now?"

"I have two older sisters: one in Chicago, and one in Washington, DC. Both are married."

"And your parents?"

Kats paused for a moment, not used to talking so much about himself and his family.

"They returned to Japan a few years ago."

"Oh," said Molly, not expecting that particular answer. "Sorry. I didn't mean to pry. Just a Midwestern thing. We're as open as a book about stuff and just assume others are as well."

"It's OK," continued Kats. "My parents, well my father actually, felt more comfortable returning to Japan."

"Was that because of the camps? Because of internment?" she asked somewhat hesitantly but still wanting to know his story.

"Certainly, that was part of it," Kats said in a very matter of fact voice. "My father never talked about it, but I know he was angry about how he, and all the Japanese Americans, were treated. He came to this country as a land of freedom and opportunity. He had children here who were American citizens. He was successful at work and built a life here, and when it was all taken away arbitrarily, yes, it made him very angry. He felt betrayed."

"I barely remember that happening during the war."

"Most folks... most White folks don't. And most Japanese folks don't talk about it now. It's like we're collectively ashamed of what happened, and we ignore it. Even after the war, most people didn't want to hire folks who looked like my dad. There was too much baggage. He could only get a job working in a candy factory. He never said anything, but I know that offended his dignity. Eventually my father couldn't continue to ignore it, and ultimately it led to him leaving his adopted country for his mother country."

"That must have been hard on you and your sisters."

"It was. But the hardest part was when I volunteered to join the army during the war. My father was furious. He couldn't understand how or why I'd volunteer for a country that had essentially imprisoned all of us. Many of the older generation felt like that, but guys my age, born here, felt like we had something to prove. He and my mother were both scared for me, but my father covered that fear with anger."

Kats realized he'd been talking for what felt like a long time. It was something he rarely ever did. Somehow Molly coaxed it out of him, and he was grateful for the chance to share. She smiled and put a hand on his.

"What about you?" he asked, changing the focus. "You said you were from Ohio. How did you end up out here?"

"Ahh, well, that's a sadly common tale. I spent a little time in Reno to get a divorce from Bill, my high school sweetheart. San Francisco seemed like a more interesting choice than returning to Ohio."

"Yeah, you said something about your ex-husband yesterday..." he let the rest of the sentence hang in the air.

"Yeah, he had a drinking problem and a temper." Pointing to her still swollen eye, she said, "Not my first black eye."

"Sorry," he said, squeezing her hand. For a while they sat in companionable silence, reflecting on the truths they'd shared, wondering what it meant.

Finally, Kats brought things back to the point at hand. "Tell me again about the building," he said, nodding toward Charles Construction.

"As I told you, I still have keys to the door, but Franco must have told Harry about me, and I'm pretty sure they would have changed the locks. There's a door on the roof. The girls go out there on their break to smoke and gossip. We're supposed to lock the door, but I found it open lots of times. That may be the best option."

"And inside?"

"The billing records are in my office, and that's where I remember the Mission Bay warehouse being referenced multiple times. The address is there."

"OK then..." Kats stopped. A light had come on somewhere inside of Charles Construction on the lower floor. "Look," he said to Molly.

She stared at the light coming from deep inside the office. "I think that's the light from the kitchen on the first floor."

"Someone's there. We need to be quiet."

They waited several more minutes and watched the light go off and the building go dark again. While they were waiting, Kats formulated a plan that he shared with Molly.

"What if there are a bunch of them?" she asked.

"If there's more than a couple or if anything goes sideways, we abort and meet back at the diner. I'll lead them away, and you get out. Got it?" She nodded.

"First thing, I get up onto the roof and make sure I can get in through the door. If that's locked, we go to plan B."

"What's plan B?" she asked.

From the satchel, Kats pulled out a small pry bar, "Plan B."

Heading to the back of the building, Kats and Molly found themselves at the base of a rusted fire escape. Kats took a tentative step onto the metal. It held but groaned in protest. He took a second step and slowly transferred his weight, which seemed to quiet the old metal. He signed to Molly, and she nodded her head in understanding. Then he slowly made his way up the four small flights of steps and over the low parapet wall onto the rooftop. Crouching there for a minute, he listened and let the night settle about him again.

Kats produced a small flashlight and noted the many cigarette butts on the roof. Crossing to the door, he crouched next to it and raised a hand to the doorknob, giving it a slow turn. It easily slid open. He was reminded yet again that the best designed security was always subject to human error and general laziness.

Now the hard part, he thought.

Kats moved into the upper vestibule. According to the plan, he'd estimated fifteen minutes to get into position downstairs. Molly had provided a good description, and he remembered enough of the general layout from his first visit a couple weeks ago. Seems like a long time ago, he thought.

Putting his back to the wall, he glided down the rooftop stairs and into the upper hallway. Closed office doors lined the corridor, and a large open staircase led down into the main bullpen area of the office. The only light came from the streetlights outside the windows. Whisper silent, he moved to the top of the stairs and listened. He slowed his breathing and closed his eyes. *Where are you? I know you're here somewhere... There!*

From the office space underneath the stairs, he heard the distinctive sound of movement on a leather couch. *The guard is lounging on the couch in Harry's office!* Certainly, that was the most comfortable place in the office. His finely tuned internal clock told him eight minutes had gone by.

Moving slowly down the stairs, Kats put one eye toward where he knew Molly's office was near the front of the building. She'd be waiting outside, and his job was to get to her office window, open it, and get her up and through to the office. Passing by Harry's office, he peered into the open door and could vaguely discern a shape on the couch. Kats paused to listen and noted a soft snoring. *He's fallen back asleep.*

Moving to Molly's closed office door, he recalled her saying, "My door squeaks." He turned the knob and ever so slowly cracked the door. *Sqeeeaakk.* Kats froze, listening for motion in the other room. Nothing. Having once voiced its displeasure at being awoken in the middle of the night, the door barely made any further sound. Kats moved inside, pulling the door closed behind him.

The office was covered in the silvery light cast from the window, which he quickly unlatched and peered outside. Molly rose from the shadows behind a shrub. *She's a natural,* he thought. Leaning out the window, he grasped her upstretched hands and hauled her up the wall and into the office. In the semi-darkness, Kats could see that Molly's eyes were wide with excitement. He looked at her and made a small gesture in front of his own face. *Breathe*, he silently told her. Instinctively, she followed, and in a few breaths, she felt calm enough to begin.

She went to her desk, opened the top drawer, and grabbed a small keychain. Moving to the filing cabinet, she inserted the tiny key and opened the top drawer. Kats handed her the small flashlight, and just as he'd shown her, she placed her body between the light and door and moved the light as close to the paper as possible. Kats listened at the door.

Several minutes passed. At the cabinet, Molly closed the top drawer and moved to the second. He could tell she was getting frustrated. Kats was about to step over to her when the phone rang in Harry's office.

BBBRRRIIINNGGG... BBBRRRIIINNGG... The guard answered on the second ring.

"Yeah," said the man holding the phone to his ear and trying to disguise any sleep in his voice.

"Heckman, you'd better not be asleep," said the sharp voice on the other end of the line. "The boss told me to call and make sure you two assholes weren't asleep at the switch."

"Course not. Me and Baker are here playing cards." Baker rose from the overstuffed chair where he'd been sleeping, gave Heckman a thumbs up, and walked over to listen. "The place is quiet as a tomb."

"Just keep your eyes open. Franco said that redhead Molly was helping the Jap. If she shows her face, put her in a bag and bring her over to Mission Bay."

"Bag in the bay, got it," he said, wiping his eyes.

"Not put her in the bay, you idiot. Bring her to the warehouse in Mission Bay."

"Yeah, yeah, bring her to Mission Bay," Heckman said. The phone clicked off.

"He sounded pissed," Baker offered, trying to be helpful.

"No way anyone is coming back to the office. What's she gonna do? Clean out her desk?" Heckman said.

Baker snorted a laugh. "Still, we should probably walk through the office again. Maybe make some more coffee in the kitchen."

In the other office, Kats and Molly looked at each other. They'd clearly heard the two voices in the other room. Kats knew he could take two out without much problem. He had darkness and the element of surprise. But if they were attacked, Harry would know the office had been compromised and might move Anton again or, worse, panic and look to cut his losses by simply disposing of the young man. No, we need him to think all is going according to his plan.

Molly leaned in and whispered in his ear "You heard what he said about Mission Bay?" He nodded. "So let's let them take me to Mission Bay."

Kats paused for a moment, processing the audacious move. Shaking his head, he leaned in and whispered back, "Too dangerous."

"You follow us to Mission Bay, and we find Anton," she said like it was the most obvious thing in the world. He shook his head firmly again. He'd already lost Anton, and he didn't want to lose her.

Standing back, Molly walked over to her desk. She seemed to be eyeing the phone on her desk. She looked at Kats, then at the phone, and nudged it toward the edge of the desk. *No!* Kats shook his head. *Yes,* she nodded back, nudging the phone closer to a very loud fall.

She pointed toward Kats, then toward the window, before making a motion with her fingers like legs running. *Please,* he gestured. She tilted her head, smiled mischievously, and pushed the phone.

Kats was moving even before the phone clattered loudly to the floor. He grabbed his satchel and was out the window in one fluid motion. Behind him he heard Molly swear into the darkness. "Shit!"

Heckman and Baker were in the kitchen preparing to make another pot of coffee when something crashed across the office. "Shit!" they said simultaneously and ran toward the sound.

"Someone's in the office," Baker hissed.

"No shit," Heckman replied and produced a .38 revolver from his shoulder holster. He signed to Baker, and the other man moved adjacent to the door. Despite their slovenly appearance, the two men had been valued members of Harry's unit during the war. Their training kicked in, and they prepared for a possible intruder. Baker pushed open the door, and Heckman strode forward yelling, "Freeze, asshole!"

Molly raised her hands, "Don't shoot!" she exclaimed and acted a bit more scared than she was, as she recognized these two men.

Heckman turned on the office light. The open filing cabinet, the overturned phone, and Molly's cat burglar outfit made a convincing tableau.

"Holy shit, it's Molly!" Baker said behind Heckman. "The boss was right."

"And we got her," Heckman said with a smile.

Thirty minutes and two phone calls later, Heckman returned to the office, where Molly sat on a chair and Baker held the .38 across from her.

"The boss wants us to bring her to Mission Bay," he said entering the room. Molly had largely remained silent, pretending to glower at her two captors. "What's in Mission Bay?" she asked.

"Never you mind," Heckman said. "We can do this easy or do this hard." He held forth a length of rope.

"You was always nice to us, Molly, and we don't want to hurt you, but we got our orders," Baker said, hopefully.

"Fine," she said, extending her hands in front of her. They tied her wrists together, put a work shirt over them to cover the bindings, and walked her out the front door and into a waiting car.

The eastern sky was just starting to lighten as the car pulled away. A moment after it turned the corner, a motorcycle exited the alley across the street and followed.

CHAPTER 14

Anton sat in an uncomfortable wooden chair in a small, windowless office. His back hurt, he was hungry, and he had to pee. Still, he hadn't really been hurt, and after spending that first night tied to the same wooden chair, he was at least free to move around the office and stretch his legs. After being pushed into a car late Saturday night, the next hour or so got jumbled. There was talk, there was squealing tires, there was a coat thrown over his head. Once the car stopped, several men walked him a fair distance, and when they removed the coat from his head, he was in the office.

Over the past day and a half, he realized he was in a warehouse of some kind. Whenever the door opened and when they took him to the bathroom around the corner, he could see rows of crates and shelving. And the place smelled musty like an old storehouse. He also realized to his dismay that he was being held as leverage against his father.

A series of men had come and gone, and he could tell he was being well guarded. They said little to him and didn't make eye contact. The only one who spoke to him was the same man who seemed to lead the group from Saturday night. He was tall, dark haired, and had what seemed to be a perpetual smirk on his face. He had cold eyes, and Anton suspected he'd hurt him without a second thought.

It must have been Monday morning when there was a commotion outside the door. He heard some angry voices and a woman's voice. Molly? he thought. A moment later the door opened, and Molly was pushed through. Anton moved to catch her.

"Molly! Are you OK?" he asked her.

"Good as could be expected," she quipped, "but are you OK? Did they hurt you?" she asked, looking him up and down.

"He's fine. For now," Franco said as he entered the office carrying a cup of coffee. He was flanked by two more men who stood by the door.

"But red," Franco said, turning to Molly, "you're starting to really chap my ass."

A sharp retort formed in Molly's throat, but she thought better of vocalizing it at that moment.

"Kid, it looks like you're going to be with us for a while," he said. "Your old man has complicated things," he said cryptically.

"Why are you doing this? What can possibly be so important that you burn down businesses, hurt people, and kidnap me?"

Franco sat on the desk, sipped his coffee, and looked at Anton. "Land, kid. It's all about the land."

"Our dock? My father's house? Hardly seems worth it."

Franco laughed out loud and slapped his leg. "You don't know, do you?"

"Know what?" Anton said, looking back and forth at Molly and Franco.

Franco smiled, a big shit-eating grin that was more frightening that his usual smirk. "Your old man owns half the basin. Most of those businesses pay rent to him!"

"No way," Anton said. But in his head, he was turning over the idea. His father was famously frugal and secretive about his finances. They never had fancy things, yet they always had money for new equipment when necessary, and they never missed a payroll. Even when the ship building business slowed down and Anton got accepted to the University of San Francisco, his father had insisted on paying for everything.

"Your old man is loaded, kid. But you see, some folks really need to get that land he's sitting on. We offered more than a fair price, but that stubborn bastard wouldn't budge." That's my father, thought Anton.

"So you use Anton to get something over on his father," Molly said.

"Yeah, we need him. But you, red. I'm not sure what to do about you," he said malevolently. "Harry's call, but I know what I'd do with a traitor."

Kats sat outside the dilapidated three-story warehouse on 3rd Street near the Mission Creek Channel. This area of town had been an industrial dumping ground since the 1906 earthquake. Now it was dominated by the Southern Pacific rail yard. Dozens of warehouses, transportation companies, and light industrial buildings surrounded the otherwise unremarkable building that now held Molly and most likely Anton as well.

Monday morning was clear and sunny, and Kats was trying to decide if the fire escape to the rooftop or the alley side of the building might prove to be the best manner of access. A car approached the front of the warehouse and parked on the street. Out stepped three men, one of whom Kats immediately recognized. Harry Charles.

As the men entered the warehouse, Kats sprinted toward the fire escape and quickly found himself on the rooftop. Seagulls moved across the roof, but it was otherwise unguarded. The access door was locked, but Kats used his small pry bar to force it open. In a moment he was inside.

The warehouse was three stories tall with an open central corridor that ran the length of the building. Gantry machinery for moving materials covered the visible ceiling. Kats looked down to the lower floor and saw several men moving. He found a metal staircase and moved to the second floor, seeking a vantage point where he could see the activity on the first floor. He could see men milling around the one end of the warehouse where the administration offices were located. There were at least six men as well as Harry. Too many for a frontal assault, he thought darkly.

Kats moved into a position behind some crates that allowed him to look down and across to the office end of the warehouse. One of the guards entered the office. As the door opened, Kats caught a glimpse of several people inside—Molly and Anton included! His heart pounded in his chest, and he took several deep breathes to center himself. Now what?

Harry Charles was angry and scared, but he was trying hard not to show it. Kidnapping was serious shit, and though he desperately wanted the South Basin land, he also didn't want to end up in prison. He found himself walking an unfamiliar tightrope. But like his days in combat, at some point you realize that the only way through is forward. Harry now realized he was at that point as he approached the office.

Several of his men were waiting outside the office, including Heckman and Baker. "I hear you two caught Molly at the office," he said.

"Yes, sir," Heckman said as Baker nodded.

"Good work. Maybe Santa Claus will bring you something nice." The men laughed to break the tension.

"What exactly was she doing?" Harry asked.

"We caught her in her office, boss," Heckman said.

"Yeah, she was going through her file cabinets. Looked like billing," Baker added.

Billing, thought Harry. That could be a problem. Molly did much of the official billing for Charles Construction, but the real accounting was a separate matter. His ledgers were locked in his safe at the private office, but he wondered if Molly might have some dirt on his cooked books. His eyes narrowed at the thought.

Turning to the other men, "And you guys said she was there in the gallery watching the kid on Saturday night?"

"Yeah, she and the kid snuck out the back together."

Molly and the Vello kid together? he thought. Had she been feeding him information all this time?

"Boss, there's a guy here to see you," said one of Harry's crew who approached the office.

Harry looked startled by that. Who knew he was even here? "What guy?" he fired back.

"Says his name is Sand."

How the hell did he know I was here, thought Harry. "Send him over."

John Sand, in his customary gray suit and tie, overcoat draped over his arm, walked calmly over to the group of men. He was by far the smallest man there, yet he exuded a confidence that irked Harry. Little shit, he thought.

"Happy Holidays, Harry," Sand said.

"What the fuck are you doing here? I thought you didn't want to know the details," Harry said.

"Unfortunately, the details are finding me," Sand replied.

Harry nodded his head at his men, and they dispersed. Turning away from the office, he led Sand to the center of the building, where the glass rooftop let in the bright morning sunlight.

"We're close to sealing the deal," Harry said, "We just..."

"You're not close," interrupted Sand. "I know that Vello is in the hospital. Probably not leaving it alive. Once he dies, the land will pass to the sons. You're trying to force the father to do something when you should be focused on putting leverage on the sons."

Harry stared at Sand, thinking through what he said. "What are you really doing here?"

"This is getting sloppy," Sand said flatly. "Too many people saw your fight outside the gallery Saturday night. Kidnapping only works if the father is alive and conscious. He's barely that. And a body in the Bay attracts way too much attention for my investors."

"So what are you offering?" Harry asked.

"I'm offering you leverage on the son," Sand said with a smile that didn't reach his eyes.

Kats had been observing the conversation between Harry and this small newcomer but was unable to hear from his vantage point. They moved toward the open center of the warehouse, which allowed Kats to slip closer to them on the second floor. Fortunately, there was no real work going on in the warehouse that day, so he easily shifted over to a point that was almost directly above the two men.

"Alright, Sand. What have you got on the sons?" Harry asked.

"Nothing yet on the younger son, but the older brother, Gianni, is in deep to Jimmy Lanza."

"Jimmy the Hat?" Harry replied, recognizing the West Coast mafia family name.

"Yes, Jimmy 'the Hat' Lanza. Gianni has a gambling problem. He owes them big. He's been dipping into company funds to stay afloat, but now that money is coming due."

"OK, but how does that help us?"

"You need to bring Lanza into the deal."

"No fucking way," began Harry.

"You wanted the stadium contract. Did you really think you could keep the mob out of a deal that big? Bring Lanza in on the deal. Promise him contracts for his boys and a piece of the union money. In return, he leans on Gianni to sell. They're much more practiced at that kind of leverage, and I hear they've even recently reminded Gianni of the position he's in."

Harry was turning this over in his head. Jimmy the Hat? This was serious gangster territory. In Harry's mind, he was still the good-guy American soldier he'd been back in the war. Sure, he bent some rules, busted a few heads, but that was just business stuff. He'd worked hard, and he deserved what he got. He still had this image of himself as the All-American war hero, but this... this was apparently who he was becoming.

"OK, OK," he said to both Sand and himself. "We use Lanza. And we hold onto the younger brother, too, for now. Insurance."

Sand nodded in agreement. "And no bodies in the bay. Way too much heat and attention."

Right, thought Harry, but he also had at least one loose end that needed to be addressed. Molly. What did she know, and what was she looking for back at the office? And why was she helping Vello in the first place? What's the connection?

Time to ask.

Kats's mind was racing with new information—a stadium contract, the Lanza crime family, and this mysterious Sand, the one that Molly had mentioned. He heard them say 'no bodies in the bay,' but he also knew that if Harry and his men got desperate, all bets were off. He watched as Sand turned and headed toward the exit and Harry headed toward the office.

Molly heard Harry's voice outside the office door and was steeling herself for the coming confrontation. She knew that Kats was out there somewhere, but she'd be in here with Harry. Harry might have some qualms about hurting her, but Franco wouldn't. Franco would kill her in an instant and not bat an eye.

Harry pushed open the door and stared at her and Anton. None of his usual quips, thought Molly. Not a good sign. Harry took off his coat and leaned against the wall. "Molly," he began quietly, "did I not give you a chance? You were just a divorcé from Ohio, but we gave you a chance, and you betray me for your boyfriend here?" he pointed at Anton.

Boyfriend? thought Molly, surprised by this unexpected line of questioning. Before she could answer, Anton was at her side, putting his arm around her. "Leave her be, Charles. Your issue is with me and my family."

"Never would have thought about you two together," he said. "We all wondered where you disappeared to on weekends, Molly."

Molly looked at Anton, who squeezed her shoulder. Go with it.

"She was just trying to help me," explained Anton.

"Yeah, after you grabbed him, I was looking for information that could help us," she said, looking first at Anton and then at Harry. She was totally improvising.

"That why you thought you could steal accounting records? Dumb, Molly. I thought you were smarter than that. You'll never see those records."

"I was desperate, Harry. I couldn't let you hurt, Anton."

"And here we are now. So here's what's gonna happen. You two are gonna stay as our guests while we sort out some issues with your brother and old man," he pointed to Anton.

"And then what?" Anton asked.

"Then if everybody's smart, we all get paid."

CHAPTER 15

It was 7 pm the next day, Christmas Eve. Businesses had shut down. People were headed home or out to the bars and restaurants to celebrate. Kats had spent the past thirty hours preparing for his return to the warehouse. He'd gone to the Army Surplus store, then on to Chinatown for fireworks, and the markets where he bought some odd ingredients for the dish he was planning on serving up later.

Shig had called during his preparations and insisted on being part of the operation. "I feel responsible for the kid," he exclaimed. "If something happens to him..."

"I won't let that happen."

"You have to let me help. I did good the other night, right?"

"Yes, you did," Kats had to admit. He also realized that having Shig as a backup might be a good idea. "OK, come on over."

Shig arrived that afternoon, still driving Anton's car, which Kats thought would be useful. Sitting in his kitchen, he explained his plan to Shig, showing him the various devices and props he'd prepared. Shig listened wide eyed, asking a few questions, and ultimately slapping his knee in delight, "That's fantastic!"

"Hopefully, yes, but if something goes wrong and I don't come back, you need to go to the police. I know the Vellos don't want to do that, but Molly is in danger now, too."

The two of them loaded two dark green duffel bags into the trunk. Shig got in the driver's side and Kats rode shotgun as they drove over to Mission Bay. Kats had him circle the block in different directions, learning the streets and traffic pattern. They parked on a dark street and sat silently in the car, letting their eyes adjust and listening. Stillness.

They checked watches. It was 8:45 pm. "If I'm not back by 11 pm, something went wrong, and you need to go to the police. You don't try to rescue us. Am I clear?"

Shig nodded. "Am I clear, Shigeyoshi? You go to the police. Your word?"

"Yeah, man, my word."

Kats opened the door and stood outside the car, taking in the street. He could smell the contents of the trunk even now, through multiple layers of wrapping. Clenching his teeth, he opened the trunk and hefted the two bags across his black clad shoulders, gave Shig a thumbs up, and headed toward the warehouse.

For the past two days, a rotating cadre of unhappy men had stood watch over Anton and Molly. Now on their second boring tour of duty, Heckman and Baker were playing cards with Johnson and Johnson, the two brothers from Washington who were the demolition experts on Harry's crew. Tonight they were pissed off at having to spend Christmas Eve in a dank warehouse. The two prisoners weren't even treated like prisoners. More like valuable cargo. Harry had left explicit instructions that the kid wasn't to be touched, "We need him," he said.

"What about Molly?" asked Baker, who was clearly troubled by the thought of hurting her.

Harry made a face, "We need her for the moment. We'll move 'em on Christmas Day to a better location. Meanwhile, don't fuck this up!"

They brought in cots for Anton and Molly and set up a couple extra outside for them to take breaks. Take-out from Chinese restaurants, Mexican restaurants, and back to Chinese restaurants had been the highlights of their days. Molly and Anton were strangely quiet, whispering to each other and asking for bathroom breaks and something to read.

The guys had been playing poker for over three hours, and Heckman was down $10. Could be worse, he thought. Baker's down $20. They had a radio playing in the background. It was Christmas music that seemed sadly out of place.

"Want a snort?" the elder Johnson asked, offering a splash from his ever-present flask.

Baker looked at Heckman. Something a bit troubling about a perpetually drunk demolition man, said the look. They waved off the hooch and rose to stretch and get yet another cup of coffee.

"Christmas fucking Eve," Heckman said. "I should be with my family."

"You hate your family," Baker said.

"Not as much as I hate you assholes," he said with laugh. "Can we change the game? Maybe gin rummy instead?" They all nodded. "And for god's sake change the damn radio station. I can't listen to any more Christmas music."

Baker changed the station, and Elvis Presley's *Jailhouse Rock* filled the room.

They returned to the makeshift card table, and as Johnson began to shuffle, something hit their noses. Heckman made a face, looked around, and said to Baker, "Did you fart?"

Even through the petroleum jelly lining his nose, Kats could smell the durian. It was awful. The spiky Southeast Asian fruit was a delicacy to some but widely reviled for its smell that some likened to raw sewage and death. Shig had aptly described the smell as "worse than a dead skunk's rotting asshole," and he said he wasn't a poet. Upon returning to the warehouse, Kats had begun the careful process of placing a dozen of the ripe fruit around the office end of the warehouse. Even outside, the smell would waft through open windows and vents. He managed to place several of the fruit inside as well, each well hidden from a casual search. The other items were ready and in place. Now all he had to do was wait.

"Oh my god! What the fuck is that smell?" Johnson cried. Baker looked like he was about to gag, and Heckman took off his glasses, wiping his eyes, which had begun to water.

"Must be something backed up from the sewer," Heckman said. He walked to the nearby window that was already partially open. He lifted the window completely and stuck his head outside. "Christ, it's even worse outside!"

Inside the office, Molly and Anton were banging on the door. "Let us out!"

"Shut up!" yelled Johnson as the other Johnson headed toward the main door.

Pulling his gun from the shoulder holster, Heckman said

to Baker, "Watch them," and he headed outside. He found Johnson on the street, and they both sniffed the air. "It's worse back in there," Heckman said. He was on alert. Guns drawn, they headed back inside.

"What's goin' on?" asked a visibly green Baker as they ran up.

"Either a sewer line broke in here somewhere, or something is wrong," Heckman said.

"I checked the toilet, and it's working fine," said the other Johnson, also looking a bit green.

At that moment, Baker turned, trying to make it to the garbage but instead emptying his stomach onto the wooden floor. Johnson took a deep breath, tried to fight it too, but followed Baker's lead and spewed onto the card table.

Heckman hovered for moment. He felt his stomach roil, but he closed his eyes and slowly swallowed. Fight it, he said to himself. The urgent need to vomit seemed to pass, and he opened his eyes. As he did, he saw two quick flashes of light, followed by the actual sounds of detonation.

When Kats saw the vomiting begin, he knew it was time for phase two of his plan. From his second-floor hiding place, he dropped two of the smoke bombs he'd purchased at the surplus store. With a flash and a muffled pop, they quickly filled the area with white smoke. Kats heard shouts from below, then a couple of gun shots, before a voice yelled, "Hold your fire, dammit!" A moment later he heard someone say, "Circle up," and he was ready.

Kats lit the fuses on the two improvised flash pots he'd mixed that day. Equal parts fireworks and ground red Tien Tsin peppers, they looked like brown bags of flour. He hefted the two over the railing, followed by more smoke bombs, which went off immediately. Three seconds later, the flash pots exploded.

Heckman had his guys circled up, weapons ready and extended. Smoke filled the room, but they all knew it was the same white smoke they used in the war to hide movement. The real attack would be coming, and they were ready. More smoke bombs went off with a flash and pop, so it took a second for Heckman to realize that a small sack had appeared on the floor near them. It took another second for him to realize it had a lit fuse. We're dead, he thought.

The flash pots exploded, but instead of shrapnel ripping through them as he'd expected, dark red powder filled the room, carried on the wings of the smoke. For a second, Heckman, Baker, and the Johnson brothers thought it was a dud. Then their eyes, noses, throats, and lungs began to burn. They began to cough and stumble blindly about, trying to get out of the cloud.

Kats dropped to the first floor, his mouth and nose covered in a mask, his eyes protected by a pair of goggles. He raised the *tonfa* to club the four guards, but there was no need. They had no fight in them, and were crawling about blindly, wheezing and retching.

Moving to the office door, he stepped through to find Anton and Molly holding their hands over their faces. "Kats!" they yelled in unison. Molly hugged him and allowed a moment to hug her back. "What was that?" she asked.

"Chinese Pepper bomb," he laughed. "Here, cover your faces with these," he handed them handkerchiefs, "and hold onto me. We're going out the front door."

Pushing open the door, they held onto Kats as he led them through the slowly dissipating cloud and into the cool night air. Down the street, they found Shig anxiously waiting by the car. "Well, Merry Christmas!" he shouted and jumped up and down as they climbed into the car. A moment later, they were gone.

CHAPTER 16

Shig drove them through the night toward Bayview Heights. Anton insisted on getting to his father's bedside. They arrived at the southside hospital just minutes before midnight. They all started to come in with him, but he insisted they go home. "I'll be safe with Gianni and the boys. And take my car," he said to Shig. Molly hugged Anton and kissed him on the cheek. Anton embraced Shig as well. He then turned to Kats and with great solemnity extended his hand. "Thank you," he said as they shook hands. "Thank you for getting me back to my father."

Kats nodded. "*Gambatte.*" Good luck. They watched Anton enter the hospital and then turned to look at each other. She smiled at them both for a moment. Then the stress of the past several days and the façade of being strong came crashing down, and she found herself crying in Kats's arms. He held her there, stroking her hair until she composed herself.

"I need a drink," she declared. Then she wrinkled her nose. "And a bath. Definitely a bath."

"I know a place," Kats said, opening the car door.

Molly closed her eyes and lay back in the wooden *ofuro*. The soaking tub was in the back bathroom of Kats's Japantown home where Shig had dropped them off. She felt the tension of the past several days, along with the aches and pains of her various escapades, slowly leave her body.

Next to her was a small pot of hot green tea and some kind of rice cake that Kats had brought in while she was showering off in the adjacent room. He'd explained to her that you had to wash before you got into the bath, which seemed like a ridiculous step to her at the time, but now as she luxuriated in the hot water, she wondered how she would ever go back to a western bath.

Knock knock.

She opened her eyes to see Kats at the door. He was wearing a robe and looked freshly showered. He held some towels in his arms. She waved him in, too comfortable to care that she was naked. He made a little bow with his head, set the towels on the chair next to the tub, and turned to leave.

"Stay. Please."

He sat down on the floor next to the high-walled tub. A less distracting view, he thought to himself. He poured a cup of green tea and handed it to her. She sipped it and said "Bitter."

"This is *sencha*, which is traditional Japanese green tea. Only westerners put sugar in tea," he smiled.

She lay back and closed her eyes. "This is amazing," she said. She brought her hand over the tub edge. Instinctively, he reached out and clasped her hand.

"I knew you would come for us," she said. "Anton did, too. He said you were like a twentieth century samurai. He explained what that was to me, too."

"Really? What did he say?" Kats asked, now curious.

"He said the samurai were like medieval knights, in service to their lord and to honor."

"That's a nice image," he said, knowing that the reality of the samurai, the ancient Japanese warrior class, was more complicated and bloodier than most westerners would understand. Kats decided that the history lesson could wait for another day.

Molly turned onto her side and rested her chin on the

edge of the tub. Their faces were close. "I liked the idea of being a lady rescued by a brave knight."

"A brave knight with stinky fruit and pepper bombs," he deflected.

"A clever knight who rescued us without resorting to his sword. That's most honorable."

Kats felt his face blush red, and he looked away from her clear eyes.

"You know, the first time I met you, I thought you were clever. I even used that word to describe you." She paused and raised her hand to the side of his face. "But a truly clever man would be in this tub with me."

Kats smiled, and their lips came together in a warm, wet kiss. He slid out of the robe, and Molly saw for the first time his corded muscles that were crisscrossed by many, many scars. Still, she thought he was beautiful. Kats slid into the hot water with her. By the time they left for the bed, the water was barely warm, and the room was awash from their movements.

Molly was awake and knew it was Christmas morning from the sunlight poking in at the edges of the window shades. Kats lay asleep at her side, and she languidly looked him over. She'd never been with an Asian man, and that sense of difference was exciting. Even his skin was different from other men she'd been with. People said Asians were yellow, but to Molly, he was a warm golden color. He was smooth, almost hairless, which made touching him a different sensation. And the scars. So many of them. Some that looked like the slice of a knife, others that looked like darkened splotches, and two that she knew were gunshots. A twentieth century samurai, she mused. He had the scars to prove it.

He rolled over toward her, and she allowed herself to be wrapped in him. Smiling, she fell back asleep.

Knock knock.

Molly jerked awake from a deep slumber, but Kats was already up and pulling on pants and a t-shirt. He smiled. "Hey."

"Hey."

"You can stay in bed. I'll send whoever it is on their way."

She lay back down hoping Kats would return to bed. A few moments later, she heard a door open and then close. Then Shig's voice could be heard. Smiling, she rose and got dressed.

"Merry Christmas! I brought bagels," smiled Shig as he entered without waiting for an invitation. "The Jewish place was the only thing open this morning.⁴" He busied himself in the kitchen, and Kats knew there was nothing to do but go with it. In a matter of minutes, coffee was brewing, and bagels were toasting. Molly entered the kitchen, wrapped in one of Kats's shirts.

"Merry Christmas, Molly-chan!" Shig said as he gave her a hug and winked at Kats.

"Merry Christmas, Shig," she kissed him on the cheek. "And you brought bagels!"

"God's gift to gentiles," he said.

"I didn't even know what a bagel was back in Ohio," she said, grabbing one and a dollop of cream cheese. "I'm sure we had them somewhere, but they weren't part of my family's menu."

"I never had crawdads until I was in Mississippi," offered Kats. "Or frog legs until I was in France."

Shig raised his cup of coffee in a toast, "Here's to trying a whole world of experiences." Molly and Kats looked at each other as they toasted, "New experiences."

Later that morning, after dishes were put away and Molly's clothes came out of the wash, the phone rang.

Kats answered. "Hey... Merry Christmas... Yeah, all good... Uh huh... Yeah, sure... What time?... OK... Can I bring friends?... Great... See you soon."

"What's up?" asked Shig.

"That was Emiko Harada."

"Amy!" said Shig.

"Yes, Amy. We're all invited over for *sukiyaki* if you're interested."

"*Mochiron!*" Of course, shouted Shig.

"Of course," smiled Kats, taking Molly's hand.

"Of course," she said.

That afternoon, they walked down the street to the Harada's home. Molly wore one of Kats's sweaters and one of his white shirts over her black chinos. *It smells like him,* she thought. *She looks amazing,* he thought. *I'm hungry,* Shig thought. Kats carried a bottle of sake in a gift cloth and a small potted plant that looked like a miniature pine tree to Molly. "Bonsai" he said.

"Amazing."

Upon arrival, they knocked, and a moment later the woman Molly had seen at 440 answered the door.

"Merry Christmas, Emiko," Kats said.

"Hey, Amy! Merry Christmas," Shig added.

"This is Molly," Kats said, and the two women shook hands. "Hi!"

"Come in, come in" she replied. As the boys entered, they took off their shoes. Molly followed suit.

"*Irasshaimase!*" came Mrs. Harada's voice from the kitchen.

Welcome.

"*Ojama shimasu*" said the boys in unison. It meant sorry to disturb you, the traditional reply.

As they entered the cozy house, Mrs. Harada toddled out of the kitchen. "Murao-san" she smiled at Shig. "*Shibaraku deshita ne.*" It's been a long time. Shig clasped her hands in his, bowing slightly "Yes, it's been too long," he replied in English.

"Katsuhiro-kun," she smiled at him.

"Merry Christmas, *O-bachan*," he said and kissed her cheek. "Molly, this is Mrs. Harada, a very dear friend to my family. *O-bachan*, this is Molly Hayes."

Mrs. Harada looked at Molly for a moment. Her white skin, her red hair. For a second Kats worried he'd made a mistake bringing her, but Mrs. Harada smiled broadly and took Molly's hands. "Welcome to our home," she offered warmly.

Over the next several hours Molly got a crash course in Japanese culture. She learned about *omiyage*—gifts and their importance. She learned about *mochi*—the sweet and savory rice cakes that were part of the holiday tradition. She learned about *sake* and decided that warm was the best way to drink it. And to her delight she learned about *sukiyaki*, the Japanese hot pot stew that was cooked with thin sliced beef, tofu, mushrooms, noodles, and the most wonderful broth. They taught her how to properly use chop sticks and to hold her rice bowl as she ate.

Molly asked Kats, "Why do you call Mrs. Harada *O-basan?*"

"*O-bachan.* It literally means 'Grandmother' but refers to the special relationship we have. She's close, like family, so it's OK."

She nodded toward Emiko across the room, "And why

do you call her Emiko and Shig calls her Amy?"

Shig interjected, "Lots of Nisei, second-generation Japanese Americans, have English names. Some take on English names like Emiko did by using 'Amy.'"

"Do you guys have English names, too?"

"Actually, I don't," Shig said. "But this one," he pointed toward Kats, "is Paul."

Kats nodded "My middle name. My sisters Aiko and Michiko are also Katherine and Francis."

"My middle name is 'Maire,' the Irish version of Mary," Molly told them.

After dinner, Kats, Molly, and Emiko finally had a chance to speak as Mrs. Harada was in the kitchen. "I recognized you from the bar last week," Emiko said. "You really are working on a case with her, Kats."

"I really am," Kats said earnestly. "Did you have a chance to talk to your mother about, you know..."

"I did. It made for an interesting Christmas Eve, but you were right. She was worried, but she just wants me to be happy. And she explained some things that I didn't know. Did you know that until Christianity was introduced to Japan, the Japanese were very laid back about same-sex relationships? And there's a term in Japanese: *dōseiai*. Do you know it?"

Kats shook his head.

"In the Taisho period of Japan, the early twentieth century, it meant 'same sex love.' Mom told me all this and said she had friends back in Japan who were *dōseiai*. She told me not to be scared." Emiko gave a little cry, and her eyes filled with tears.

"That's wonderful," Kats said, and he squeezed her hand. They all sat there for a few moments, and smiles returned as

Shig came over to join them.

"We had an interesting Christmas Eve, too," Molly said with a sly smile.

Before Emiko could follow up on that tease, Mrs. Harada brought out a plate of *daifuku,* sweet bean rice cakes and summoned them all to the table. Green tea and *sake* were mutually poured, and Kats felt a warmth of friendship and family that he'd not experienced since his parents had returned to Japan several years ago.

Though it was Christmas, Kats was mulling over the information he'd overheard in the warehouse regarding the Vellos and the basin. He needed to broach it all with Anton. He also wanted to check in on the young man and see how he was doing. Kats used the Haradas' phone to call Anton. *No answer.* Kats dialed Carlo Vello's number. "Hello?" answered a male voice.

"Yes, hello. This is Kats Takemoto. I'm trying to reach Anton Vello."

"Just a moment."

Kats could hear someone approach the receiver and it change hands. "Hey, Kats," Anton said in a tired voice.

"Hey, Anton. Sorry to disturb you, but we wanted to check in and see how you're doing." Shig and Molly had approached him at the mention of Anton's name. Concern showed on their faces.

"Actually, Dad passed away a couple of hours ago. We just got back to the house."

"Anton, I am... we all are so sorry. I'm here with Molly and Shig."

There was a heavy breath on the end of the line, "Thank you," he managed.

"Can we help in any way?"

"No, not right now. Can I call you later? I need to be with my family."

"Go," Kats said, and the line clicked closed.

CHAPTER 17

Christmas night had ended on a more reflective mood than it had started. Still, they'd parted with warm smiles for Mrs. Harada, who promised to make them *shabu-shabu* sometime. Molly had no idea what that was, but she enthusiastically agreed.

Despite the good feelings of the season, Kats brought them back to the situation at hand as they stood in the street. He reminded Molly that Harry's men still were out there and it may not be safe to return home.

"What do you suggest?" she asked, arching an eyebrow.

"If you had a friend to stay with for a few days, that could work." He paused. "Or you're welcome to stay with me," he said as neutrally as he could manage.

Molly looked at him for a moment, then over to Shig, who was grinning from ear to ear. Molly winked at him and said to Kats in her best impersonation of his neutral voice, "That would be acceptable."

Kats exhaled, realizing he'd been holding his breath, and Shig laughed and clapped him on the back.

"I need to get some things from my place, though. Can we swing by there?"

A quick side trip to Molly's apartment in Hayes Valley was uneventful. Still, Kats had insisted on reconnoitering the place first. Once satisfied there were no watchers, they entered her place while Shig waited outside with the car running. Ten minutes later, she had a full suitcase, and they were out the door.

Shig dropped them off at Kats's place and said good night. They entered the house and realized they were alone again.

"Can I make you some tea?" Kats asked.

"Mmmm, do you have any *sake?*"

"I think so," he said and turned toward the kitchen. Molly carried her bag up to his room on the second floor, thought about unpacking, but decided a drink was more urgently needed.

She found Kats in the kitchen, holding a small ceramic bottle under the tap. "You seemed to like it hot," he said, and she sat down at the table. Kats brought over the *tokkuri* and set down two small cups—*choko*. He poured her drink and then passed the *tokkuri* to her. "Traditionally, one doesn't pour their own drink." She took the bottle and gently poured for him.

He held up the small cup, "To Carlo Vello." She nodded, and they both drank.

"I never met Anton's father. What was he like?"

"He was a son of Malta, a shipbuilder, and a father," Kats repeated what Carlo had told him. She looked at him quizzically. "Something he said to me the first time I met him. I would say he was also an artist."

"An artist? Like Anton's poetry?"

"A different type of artistry. The art was in the work. The way he made boats, they were floating works of art. In anything we do, first there's ignorance. Then there's skill. Then there's craft. Then for a small percentage, there's mastery. And beyond that, for an even smaller few, there's art. That place where technique, skills, and craft disappear, and the art of whatever it is you do comes through."

"Wow. I wish I'd met him." They poured another drink.

"He actually reminded me of my father," Kats said. "I think that's why I took this case. I liked Anton right away and, like you, I don't like bullies. But it was meeting Carlo that convinced me to help."

"How so?" She liked hearing him talk.

Kats paused a moment, and his head cocked to the side. "I saw how Carlo cared for his family and wanted so much to provide for them, just like my father. He was this fiercely protective and principled man in the face of a much bigger opponent, just like my father. Part of me wanted to help Carlo because I hadn't been able to help my own father."

"But you were just a kid back then." She poured for them.

"Seventeen when the war started. I thought enlisting would be a way to help my family. Instead, it tore us apart."

"You said that the other night. I can't understand how he could be angry with you for serving your country. And serving it well."

"My father believes in peace. That *budo*, the martial arts are only for defense and protection. And he'd never condone killing, even for king and country."

"Sounds extreme," Molly said, taking a drink.

"Not really. He taught me control above all else. Control your body, control your mind, control your emotions. The discipline he taught me saved my life more than once."

She stood and came around the table. Pushing his chair back, she straddled him and wrapped her arms around his neck. "Don't you sometimes want to just let go? Be free, be wild?" She whispered the last words into his ear.

Kats breathed in the smell of her hair, her skin. He kissed her neck, and his hands ran up her back. "Letting go has always been hard for me," he said. "It hasn't always ended well."

"Try," she moaned into his mouth.

He did. Three times.

The next day was a Thursday, and Kats had errands to run. Molly, finally feeling the exhaustion of the previous days catch up with her, opted for staying in and revisiting the *ofuro* tub. Kats happily prepared the bathroom and the tub. He kissed her and said, "Lock the door behind me."

Many offices and businesses remained closed, and the city took on a slightly less hectic persona, which locals always appreciated. City Lights Bookstore was of course open, and Kats found Shig behind the counter in his usual perch late that afternoon.

"Got time for a coffee? Or a Coke for you?[5]"

"Always," smiled Shig, who left a young man named Michael in charge as they walked across the alley to Vesuvio. As they were entering, two familiar faces were exiting.

"Hey, Jack. Hey, Neal," Shig said to Kerouac and his buddy Cassady. "Guys, you remember my friend from last weekend. This is Kats Takemoto."

"I recognize this guy," Kerouac said. "Yeah, from the fight!" added Cassady.

"Yes, that's me," Kats said as he shook hands with both men. "Thanks again for stepping in the other night."

"That was actually fun," Kerouac said. "Kind of thing I may have to write about," he added.

"Who were those bastards?" Cassady asked.

"Some guys messing with Anton," Shig answered.

"The Vello kid? He was good," Kerouac said, and Cassady nodded.

"Yeah, you let us know if you need an assist again," smiled Cassady.

"Will do," Kats said, and they all shook hands again.

Kats watched the two men as they departed. Then he looked over at Shig with a smile, saying, "You and your Beat army."

"Power of poetry, baby," he laughed.

As Kats sipped his double espresso and Shig had his umpteenth Coca-Cola, Kats recounted what he'd heard about the Vello family in the warehouse. Shig was particularly troubled by the mention of Jimmy Lanza and the connection to Anton's brother. "A very heavy dude with lots of muscle behind him," Shig opined.

"Yeah, and that could be coming down on Anton. I need to talk to him, but he has so much to deal with right now."

Shig looked reflective. "You know if you'd asked me a couple months ago, I'd have said that Anton would vote to sell cause he wanted to get as far away from ship building as possible. He really wants to be a writer."

"And now?" Kats asked.

"Now it seems like all this shit they're going through has made him more engaged with the family business. I'm not sure he'd sell."

"Nobody wants to be forced to do anything. Maybe if

there was a legit offer that would allow the family business to relocate."

Shig nodded, looking sage and wise. Kats suspected Shig practiced that look, as he'd seen him use it oftentimes in the bookstore.

"OK, I have another question for you," Shig said seriously.

"Fire away."

"What's going on with you and Molly?" he laughed.

Kats made a quizzical face and raised his hands, "I don't really know. We haven't had a chance to talk about it. We just keep having sex."

Shig made a pouty face, "Aww, that's terrible" he said mockingly.

Kats tried to regain the initiative, "We haven't even had a proper date."

"So fix that! *Baka yo!*" Stupid.

"Yeah, yeah, it's not just that. She's... she's White."

"Yeah, I noticed. You've had *hakujin*[6] girlfriends in the past."

"Yes, but they never last. There's pressure and scrutiny and sometimes outright hostility coming from every direction."

"Man, you handle pressure and hostility better than anybody I know."

"I think it's harder on them. My father might not approve of my dating a *hakujin*, but it seems like the whole world doesn't approve of a White girl and an Asian man."

"This city is changing, man. All kinds of people, colors, and combinations happening here. I see lots of mixed-race couples around here. It might be different back in Ohio where she's from, but here in San Francisco..."

"Yeah, there are mixed-race couples, but most of them are

White men and Asian women. Lots of soldiers stationed in Japan or Korea or the Philippines come back with an Asian wife."

"Do you like this woman, Kats?"

"I think I do. I'd very much like to get to know her better."

"Then just be brave, like I know you are, and do it."

"Be brave... Funny, that's what Mrs. Harada told Emiko the other day."

"Good advice. My advice is to take that beautiful red-headed *haukujin* out on a proper date and see what happens."

"You're both sage and wise, Murao-san."

"Don't fucking forget it. C'mon, I gotta get back, and you can use the phone in the shop to make a dinner reservation."

Kats returned home. Dinner reservations were secured for 8 pm. A proper date, he thought. He found Molly in the bedroom, unpacking as he'd suggested. Her suitcase contents were strewn about in what might have been loosely termed "organization." The closet door was open, and his dresser drawers were ajar. Molly sat on the bed as he entered, and she smiled nervously at him. "Sorry. I started to put things away, and it got a little out of control."

"No problem," he said as he took off his jacket and hung it in the closet. He noticed her staring downward at something on the bed, and then he realized it was the small gray watch case that didn't contain a watch. Usually it hid in the back of his sock drawer, but now there it was like evidence from a crime scene.

"I was putting some things in the drawer, and I noticed this case. I'm sorry. I didn't mean to snoop," she looked embarrassed. Kats just nodded. "Is this what I think it is?" she asked him.

"What do you think it is?" he asked cautiously.

"Is it the Medal of Honor?"

Kats made a small grunt, "No, it's not a Medal of Honor."

"But it's a commendation of some kind, right?"

"Yes. It's a Silver Star."

She opened the case again and the medal lay there. A small, bright silver star in the center of a larger bronze star wrapped in a laurel. The red, white, and blue ribbon looked brand new.

"Wow. How did you... what happened?"

He took a breath and began carefully.

"We were in the Vosges Mountains in eastern France, October 1944, and we had to take the city called Bruyères. The Germans were getting desperate, and the fighting was..." he paused looking for a word. "It was intense."

Molly wanted to ask many more questions, but she didn't want to press too hard. "Is that when you were shot?" Her hand instinctively went to her own left shoulder to mirror one of his gunshot scars.

"Yeah. Twice actually." She thought about the other scar on his right side. It was smaller but more precise than the shoulder wound.

"You must have done something extraordinary," she said, trying to put him at ease.

"I did my job," he replied harder than he'd intended.

"Kats, you're a hero."

"Please don't say that. I know a lot of guys who were far braver than I was, and a lot of them didn't make it back. And honestly, when I look at that," he pointed to the star, "all I can see are those faces."

She looked at him and felt a wave of empathy and compassion well up in her. He's so strong for everyone else. Who's strong for him? she wondered. She moved over and hugged him. They stayed that way for a long time.

They walked through the cold, foggy night toward dinner. Kats had offered to drive, but Molly wanted to walk. "I'm still enough of an Ohio girl to not mind the cold so much," she smiled. He was happy to oblige, though he'd always found cold and damp weather to be particularly chilling. Wrapping themselves up, they headed out toward Tommaso's, the same Italian restaurant he'd followed Emiko to days before. It looked good, he thought, and he did have a love for pizza—one of the better things he brought home from his time in Italy. Molly put her arm through his, and they casually walked up Kearny toward the restaurant.

Traffic was light, though the sidewalks were busy enough. As they walked and chatted about nothing in particular, Kats noticed a couple of looks that came their way as people walked past them. From a distance, they were just another couple out for a stroll on a chilly San Francisco evening. Up close, Molly's red hair jumped out, as did Kats's black hair and Asian features. Theirs wasn't a combination that people saw every day, and they gawked a bit. Molly didn't seem to notice, but the observer in Kats certainly did. Perhaps too much. By the time they arrived at the restaurant, it felt to Kats that every eye on the street had been looking, judging them.

The hostess welcomed them and walked them toward a booth in the back near the wood fire pizza oven. Kats imagined every head turned as they walked through the restaurant. They did get a fair number of looks, mostly because Molly was strikingly beautiful. Half the guys in the restaurant noticed that, and most, but not all, didn't even see the guy she walked in with.

"How'd you find this place?" asked Molly as they looked over the menu.

"Through a case," he answered truthfully. "I hope you like pizza."

"I love it. You know I was really surprised how much better pizza is here in San Francisco than back in Ohio."

"Any favorites?" he asked.

"Anything except those little fishes."

"Right, no anchovies," he laughed, trying to find his ease and simply allow himself to enjoy being out with her.

They ordered a large pie with sausage, pepperoni, mushrooms, and onions. Kats surprised Molly by not eating his slice with his hands, but rather with a knife and fork.

"It's how I learned to eat pizza in Italy. Besides, pizza tastes better with a knife and fork," he opined.

She put her slice on the plate and followed his lead. "Delicious!"

Between their second and third slices, a well-dressed couple in their thirties was seated at a nearby table. They seemed to be in some conversation with the hostess about something. All Kats heard was, "We're full tonight." The couple appeared to reluctantly sit. This time Molly did notice the incident. "What's their problem?" she asked.

"Maybe they don't like the view," Kats said.

"Well, I like this view," she said to him and grabbed both his hands in hers, squeezing. They ordered dessert, and while they were waiting, Molly said, "That woman keeps looking over here at me. At us, but mostly at me."

"Just ignore it. We can take dessert with us, maybe walk to Washington Square Park."

"What's her problem?"

"She probably hasn't seen too many red-headed Irish women out with a Japanese man."

"Then she probably hasn't seen this either," Molly said as she slid closer to him and planted a very big, very public, kiss on him.

Molly had one eye on the woman, and she saw her roll her eyes and make a disgusted face. Even Kats heard her pained grunt. Uh oh.

Molly rose from her seat and walked over to the couple. Kats threw some cash on their table and followed Molly.

Molly stood next to the seated woman, who was making a show of applying her lipstick in a small compact mirror.

"I couldn't help but notice you were staring at us and making comments. Do you have something you want to say to me?" Molly asked her pointedly.

"Since you asked, dear... I was thinking that a pretty girl like you really should keep better company."

"You don't know me or my friend," Molly replied.

"I have no interest in your friend." She sneered at the word "friend."

The woman's husband grunted a laugh and watched the drama like he was watching a sporting match.

Molly struggled to find words. She'd never been on the receiving end of such bigotry and racism, and she struggled with a response. "How can you be so small minded? This man," she gestured toward Kats, "is a war hero."

"On whose side?" laughed the woman, and her partner roared and slapped the table.

Molly felt her face turn hot. Even her ears were burning. "You fucking bitch," she said.

There's that salty mouth, thought Kats. She does have a

way with words.

The seated woman looked momentarily taken aback. "I guess I should expect gutter talk from someone like you," she said.

"Like me?"

Kats stepped behind Molly, "C'mon, let's just go," he said, but she continued to stare at the woman.

The woman rose from her chair and faced Molly. The restaurant was now watching.

"Yes, someone like you, who would run around in public with a Chinaman like a common whore. What's the coolie paying you, sweetheart?"

Molly's hand was moving even before Kats could react. It arced up and made near perfect contact with the woman's left cheek. The smack was audible across the busy restaurant, and the woman fell back, stumbling into a passing waiter, and they both landed on the floor with a thud and the clatter of dishes and silverware.

"Hey!" said the woman's companion, no longer amused by the show. He pushed his chair aside and moved toward Molly as if to strike her. This time Kats did move, and anger blazed within him. With his left hand he moved Molly aside and fired the edge of his right hand into the man's open neck. The man's eyes went wide, and he grabbed at his throat, but Kats's fury wasn't done. He kicked the man's knee, which crumpled him to the floor. Kats instinctively followed him down and realized he was about to drop his knee onto the prone man when he caught himself. This could kill him, he thought with horror, and as quickly as it had flared, his anger was gone.

He stood and took Molly by the arm, "We need to go," he ordered. She nodded and grabbed her coat, and they were out the door and onto the street. Kats led them quickly around the corner, down an alley, and then across another street. Molly's adrenaline was still pounding, and she followed instinctively. Finally, he slowed, and the realization of what he'd done hit him, almost as hard as he'd wanted to hit that man.

"Are you OK?" he asked Molly.

She nodded. "Yeah, sorry about that. I guess I lost my cool."

"Yeah, so did I," he said disgustedly. He turned and started walking down the street. She followed.

"I can't believe those people. I've never... " she tried to find the words, finally summing up with, "Racist assholes."

"It's not against the law to be a racist asshole," Kats replied. "Assault and battery, on the other hand, is."

She caught his arm, "Are you mad at me?"

"No. I'm mad at myself. I lost control back there and almost really hurt that guy."

She looked at him, not sure what to say at that moment.

He took a deep breath, realizing that his own heart was racing. It had been a long time since he'd reacted angrily like that, and he felt ashamed.

"I can't lose my temper, Molly. If I lost my temper every time somebody said something stupid or racist, I'd be in jail. Or dead."

"You shouldn't have to deal with shit like that," she said, defending him and herself at the same time.

"You're right. I shouldn't, but I do. So do people who look like me or are Black or Latin. We get this all the time. And by being with me, you're probably going to get a lot of that, too. Have you thought about that?"

She paused, "Honestly, no. I've never really dealt with

anything like this. But she just made me so angry. How can they be so small minded?"

He had a lifetime's worth of thoughts on that subject but said nothing. He took her by the shoulders, "I just don't want you to get hurt."

"I know. Thank you. But I'm not afraid of a fight."

"I've noticed."

"More importantly, I'm not afraid of a fight if it's something worth fighting for," she said, looking him in the eyes. They nodded to each other, kissed, and Kats took her hand.

They walked circuitously around the neighborhood, finding themselves in Washington Square Park. They found a bench, sat, and watched the night in the city like a moving picture. Molly finally spoke. "Was that the kind of control you were talking about last night? The control your father preached?"

Kats nodded. "Tonight was like a lesson that my father taught me twenty years ago."

"Tell me," she said.

"I was fourteen years old, a few years before the war. I'd been training with my father since I was eight or so, and I was getting pretty good. I think my father saw something in me then. Something that worried him. I had a temper. No, actually I *have* a temper," he said with emphasis.

"You're one of the most levelheaded people I've ever met," Molly said, not believing him.

"Perhaps now I am, tonight notwithstanding. But when I was younger, yeah, I had a bit of a chip on my shoulder and a temper. That worried my father."

"Kids get in fights," she said. "I got in fights!"

"Yes, but most kids don't have years of training in *budo*." He was quiet for a few moments.

"Back in our neighborhood before the war, there were a lot of different people living there. Asians, of course, but also White families, Hispanics, and some Black families, too. I was coming home from school one afternoon and saw this kid, Anthony, being pushed around by some other boys. Anthony was probably eleven or twelve and Black. Quiet kid. I didn't really know him, but I saw him around the neighborhood and at school. There were three older White boys, high school age, surrounding him, being young and dumb like so many young men are at that age."

A young couple walked past them, arm in arm. "Good evening" the young man said. Kats and Molly both nodded and watched the two stroll across the park.

"So these guys are picking on Anthony, and they push him down as I'm walking toward them. The kid's school bag spilled out, and these boys are laughing and calling him names. Names that still make me mad."

Molly nodded.

"I yelled for them to stop and then helped Anthony get up and gather his books. As I was turning to face these guys, one of them, the bigger one, punched me in the face."

"I don't remember thinking about hitting him back. I just did. What I do remember was the red-hot anger I felt. I beat the hell out of the one kid and got in some shots on the other two before they ran away. That was my first real fight."

"You protected a smaller boy. That's a good thing."

"I kind of thought so too, at the time. I helped Anthony home, he thanked me, and because of him, the whole school knew about me the next day. I instantly got a reputation as being a fighter. I never had to fight again in school because of that reputation."

Kats looked at Molly, "If it was just some kids fighting,

no big deal, right? But it was a big deal. That kid I beat up—his name was John—ended up in the hospital with a concussion and a broken jaw. His family called the police, and the only reason I wasn't arrested was because Anthony and one other witness from across the street said that John and the others started the fight. But my father was furious and so disappointed in me. 'Anger is the enemy' he had told me so many times, and yet, anger led me to really hurt that kid. I could have killed him, and the scary thing was I didn't think about it. I just did it."

Molly squeezed his hand, "I'm sorry I put us in that situation tonight," she said.

"You reminded me of the importance of that lesson. We all need reminders," he said and gave her a kiss.

They rose and started their walk back to Kats's home. Molly stopped him. "Will you teach me?" she asked.

"Teach you to fight?"

"Yes, no... not fight. But to defend myself and maybe help others."

He looked at her and kissed her hand. "Yes, I can do that. Lesson one: no more slapping people in restaurants, even if they kind of deserve it."

"Deal."

CHAPTER 18

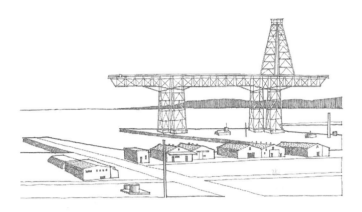

The next day Shig called to tell them that there was to be a memorial service for Carlo Vello on Sunday at St. Paul of the Shipwreck Church, followed by a wake at Carlo's home. He agreed to pick them up so they could go over together. Molly looked through the employment notices in the *Chronicle*. She circled a few options but noted that she'd pick up some more shifts at Ann's until something panned out. She'd be working there tonight.

Kats put in a call to Tak over at the city's planning department. His friend answered on the second ring.

"Kats, hey man. Sorry. You were on my list of calls to make today."

"So, you have something for me?" Kats asked.

"Yeah, I do, but I can't talk about it here. Can you meet me after work today, 6ish? The bar at Jun Fan?"

"Sure," Kats replied, noting the Chinatown location. Jun Fan was a restaurant deep in the heart of Chinatown, favored by the local Chinese population. It was as close to a secret meeting place as he could imagine. "See you later."

That evening Molly insisted on coming with Kats before starting her shift at Ann's 440. Despite the chilly evening, they bundled up and hopped onto Kats's motorcycle for the short trip. They headed into Chinatown and made it to Jun Fan just before 6 pm. Tak was already at the bar and halfway through a beer.

As they approached the bar, Tak looked up and was momentarily surprised that Kats wasn't alone. "Unfortunately, she's part of this and may have some information that might help us piece things together," Kats said after making their introductions.

"OK, sure, but let's get a booth," and Tak grabbed his cane and began to slowly walk toward the restaurant.

"Oh," Molly said involuntarily and half raised her hand to her mouth as she noted Tak's gait. He looked back at her. "I'm so sorry, I didn't mean to..."

Tak smiled graciously. "No problem, Molly." He tapped his lower left leg with his cane and landed a metallic "clank."

"That's new," Kats said, noting the prosthesis.

"Yeah, trying out some new wheels," Tak said as he raised his left trouser leg to reveal a steel rod that ran into his shoe.

Molly stared, and Tak said, "I'm still a better dancer than this one," he pointed to Kats.

Probably true, thought Kats, and he smiled at his friend. Tak was more than an army buddy. They shared both terrible and wonderful experiences together, and each had saved the other more than once. Tak was even there that fateful day in France 1944.

It was Tak who'd found Kats inside the German bunker, covered in blood, sitting cross-legged with the bloody bayonet in his hand, dead German soldiers everywhere.

"Kats! Kats, are you hurt?" Tak felt for wounds, and finding none that were life threatening, he looked into Kats's unfocused eyes. "Katsuhiro? Come back. It's over."

Kats blinked several times, his eyes coming slowly into focus. Seeing Tak's concerned face brought him back to blood-soaked reality. He dropped the knife and hugged Tak, sobbing into his friend's embrace for a long time.

Sitting down at a booth, they ordered another beer for Tak, tea, and dim sum for the table. Kats noted that Tak looked stressed, so he let him sip his beer and gather himself. Tak looked across the table at his friend and said in Japanese, "You've stepped in some shit."

"I thought as much," Kats replied in Japanese. "Lay it on us," he continued in English.

"I was able to review the environmental report on that whole area. It was done by the Department of the Navy about five years ago. It's bad, but I've seen a lot worse. It talks about wastewater contamination, some chemical spillage from the base, some industrial runoff—kind of what you'd expect from that area."

"So, that doesn't sound so bad," Kats mused.

"That's what I thought, too. But I was able to access some of the special permitting and projects the city did for Hunters Point over the past four years. They paved over a ton of land. Pavement prevents offgassing of any hazardous materials. The city partitioned off their water and sewage systems. They created new catchment areas for wastewater even though there were already systems in place. They built... no, they overbuilt those systems. They added backup power generation on the site. They essentially isolated the base from the city."

Kats and Molly looked at each other and leaned closer. "Why?" they said together.

"If that environmental report was really bad and there was some kind of contamination happening, then all the stuff they did would make sense. But the report was mild at best," Tak said.

"But they still made all those changes," Molly said.

"Exactly. I think that report that is in the file and officially 'classified' is bullshit. I think it's in there just in case someone was ever to look."

"So, there's contamination of some kind at Hunters Point," Kats said, "and they're covering it up."

"There's more," Tak continued. "I found a reference to some sort of accident in 1953. The files had been heavily redacted or outright missing. But from what I can piece together it was bad, and it spurred a ton of activity by the navy, the city, and the Feds. There were blanket permits handed out, variances, and other easements of code around the base. They started building like crazy out there. They also started talking about containment and remediation."

"Remediation? Like how to clean something up?" Kats asked.

"Except with remediation you try to let Mother Nature do the heavy cleaning. You plant things, you drain things, you till the soil. Something to get nature moving in the direction you want it to."

Tak took a drink and made an unconscious scan of the room. He was sweating. "But here's the scary part."

"There's more?" Molly asked. "Jesus."

"In the file there are still some technical notations. Like lab results and numbers, but most people would never really look at them or even understand them. I knew a little bit about some of them because of my stint over in the Public Works Department when I first got started. Public Works monitors water."

Kats felt his stomach tighten and his jaw clench. "Go on."

"There was one notation that didn't make sense. And I only found it on one document, scribbled in the margin. It said, '30 ppb' and was underlined."

"PPB?"

"Parts per billion. Imagine one drop of something in 500 barrels of water. That's about 1 ppb. But most everything we track in the water supply—lead, bleach, oil, bacteria, even shit—we measure that in ppm, parts per million. The only thing we measure in ppb that would be enough to scare these guys? Radiation."

Kats and Molly looked at each other and back at Tak. No one seemed to breathe for a moment.

Kats began quietly, "So you're saying that evidence points to a radiation leak into San Francisco Bay, and the government, the navy, and maybe the city are covering it up."

Tak could only nod. Molly's fists were clenched on the table as she looked at him. "So our friend Anton and his family and all those other businesses in the basin have been exposed to this radiation?"

"That seems to be the implication."

"And that radiation could cause people to get sick, right? Like cancer?"

"Yes."

She and Kats both thought of Anton's father who lived and worked just a few hundred yards away from the naval yard. The man who loved the sea and spent so much time there at the water. "Fucking bastards," she declared.

"Fucking bastards is right," added Kats. Turning to Tak, "So what the hell did they build out there?"

"That's the $10,000 question. Seems like it would be related to the radiation contamination. But that information is a classified military secret. You'd have to be a general or a senator to get that info."

"A general, huh? I happen to know a general," Kats said.

Across town, another meeting was taking place, and Harry Charles didn't like the way it was going. He felt uncomfortable and out of his element sitting in the plush office of Jimmy "the Hat" Lanza, the unofficial head of the Lanza crime family. Unofficial because his boss, Michael Abati, had recently been having some problems with the Feds over, of all things, his immigration status. Jimmy was the underboss, but with the scrutiny on Abati, the family had turned to him, the son of the original founder of the San Francisco syndicate.

Harry knew exactly who he was dealing with, and that made him anxious. He'd had run-ins with the mob as part of the dark side of the construction business over the years. But he'd paid off the right people, looked the other way when supplies went missing from job sites, and generally viewed the mob connection as part of the cost of doing business. Now he was escalating to a whole other level, and though Sand had made the need for it obvious, Harry still didn't like it. He felt out of control, and that feeling had started with his very first call to Lanza to set up a meeting.

Lanza's lieutenant had taken the call and informed Harry that "Mr. Lanza is engaged at the moment." When Harry requested a meeting at his office, he was told bluntly that Mr.

Lanza doesn't come to you; you come to Mr. Lanza. "It's a sign of respect," said the lieutenant. Respect my ass, thought Harry. It's a power thing, and he's showing me he has power. But he needed to make this arrangement, so they set the meeting at Lanza's office on Pier 23 near Fisherman's Wharf.

Harry knew that arriving with a platoon of his men would make him look weak, so he tapped Franco to accompany him. And because there would be operational details that needed to be worked out, Franco was the natural choice. They arrived at Pier 23, a true working pier that housed over a dozen fishing operations within its two-hundred-yard length. They entered the huge front doorways and could see the building stretch before them over the bay. Several large men were waiting for them inside, and they gestured for Harry to follow. To the right of the main entrance, like a stubby appendage, was an area called the "shed" that extended to the side of the main pier. Only about forty yards in length, it was the private domain of the Lanza family.

The family had long-standing connections to the waterfront. Fisherman's Wharf had been co-owned by Jimmy's father, Francesco Lanza, since 1935. The shed was their dock, their warehouse, their offices from which the legitimate and the not-so-legitimate businesses all operated. They passed under the high archway, noting the heavy wooden doors that could seal their portion of the building. Like a fortress, Harry thought. They walked halfway inside, and Harry saw the wide doorways at sea level for boats to come and go. During Prohibition, one of the main sources of the Lanzas' revenue was bootleg liquor. Having your own dock and access to the bay certainly made smuggling easier. They approached a wide stairway that led to the second level suite of offices. Two of the men followed them inside as they entered the office suite and were standing in a large outer waiting room. Large glass windows overlooked the pier and warehouse below.

When they were finally ushered into Lanza's office after waiting several minutes—more power plays, Harry thought—they were greeted by a handsome, smiling man in his fifties. He might have been a banker or a politician the way he dressed and carried himself. Lanza looked different from the recently published photos of him in *Life Magazine*, where J. Edgar Hoover himself had declared Lanza a "Top Hoodlum" and one of America's most notorious gangsters.

Lanza invited them to sit. "Thank you for meeting with us, Mr. Lanza," Harry said.

"Please call me Jimmy. And I'll call you Harry. And this gentleman is?" he asked of Franco.

"This is Franco," Harry said with a tilt of his head.

"Salvatore Francona. Honor to meet you," Franco said in an unusually deferential tone.

Lanza said something to Franco in Italian. Franco nodded and replied in surprisingly fluent Italian. Harry stared at his man, wondering what was said, but not wanting to ask.

Harry had hoped to make this deal short and simple, but Lanza knew far more than he had thought or hoped. He knew that Charles Construction was getting a major contract for Bayview Heights, and he succinctly laid out the deal—10% off the top, money from the local union dues, use of their "preferred" material suppliers, and "jobs" for their people. By "jobs," Harry knew that meant paying for people whose only work was a monthly visit to the jobsite to pick up their check. In return, Lanza would make sure that the Vello kid sold his property to the appropriate shell company. They'd take a small commission on that sale as well. Harry listened with increasing anger but knew his hands were tied at this point. There's a ton of money to be made in this deal, he reminded himself. Cost of doing business.

"So how are you going to get the Vello kid on board?" Harry asked. "We need to get things moving again."

"Soon enough, Harry," Lanza replied. "The boy just lost his father. One has to pay respects to the father. We'll give him that time."

"And can my men help?"

"My men will handle things. Have your boys stand down," smiled Lanza.

Harry caught the insult of "men" and "boys" but said nothing.

Lanza stood, indicating the meeting was over. "Pleasure meeting you both, and I look forward to working with you," he said like they'd just closed a business deal. In a way they had, Harry thought.

"Thank you, Jimmy," Harry said as they shook hands.

"*Grazie, Padrino,*" Franco said. Thank you, Godfather. Lanza smiled.

Harry kept his cool until they were outside the building and then erupted like a volcano. "Fuck!"

"It could have been worse, Harry," offered Franco with unusual circumspection. All Harry could do was scowl at the world. It could have been worse, but still...

Turning to Franco, he said, "What the fuck was goin' on with you and Lanza back there? Acting like a couple of goombahs. I've seen you kiss less ass on a four-star general."

Franco shrugged, "Respect. It's an Italian thing."

"What did he say to you?" Harry asked, now curious.

"He asked where my family was from back in Italy. He was just checking to make sure we didn't have a blood feud. Again, an Italian thing."

"Fucking wops. I need a drink," and he turned toward the waiting car. Franco watched him for a moment and then followed.

St. Paul of the Shipwreck Catholic Church had served the Maltese community in Bayview Heights since 1915, and that Sunday it was packed. The service for Carlo Vello had brought out the entire community. Kats, Molly, and Shig sat near the back and mostly just observed as dozens of people came up to Anton and Gianni to pay their respects after Mass. The boys now knew that Carlo owned many of the properties these folks lived and worked in, but there clearly was a great deal of respect and love for the hardworking boat builder. Anton seemed to be holding up OK, but Gianni was brooding and less engaged with the congregation. They also noticed that Gianni's lower left arm was in a cast. Before the Mass had begun, they briefly paid their respects to the two brothers. Kats asked him about his arm. "Shop injury," Gianni replied without further comment.

After the service, there was an open house wake at Carlo's house. Over the next several hours, a long retinue of well-wishers and respect-payers came through the house. Anton dutifully met them all, while Gianni retreated to his father's study with his wife and young son. The guests brought with them a dizzying array of Maltese dishes, and despite the solemn occasion, Kats, Molly, and Shig found themselves enjoying this new cuisine. They particularly loved the *stuffat tal-fenek*, which was Maltese rabbit stew, and the small cheeselets called *gbejna*.

As the afternoon drew to a close, the last of the guests bade farewell, leaving only the family lawyer, an older man named Grech who had business to discuss with the Vello boys, and Kats and his friends, who were finally ready to share their findings to the brothers.

As they all sat down in Carlo's study, Anton poured them each a glass of grappa from their father's liquor cabinet. Anton raised his glass, saying, "Thank you all for being here for us," he nodded toward Gianni, "and thank you for honoring our father. *Sa-ha*. To Carlo."

"To Carlo," they all repeated. The grappa burned on the way down, and there was a moment of silence. Then Mr. Grech spoke up.

"Boys, I was instructed by your father to read his last will and testament to you after his wake. As you know, it was his wish to be buried at sea, and tomorrow I understand you'll be taking him out for his last voyage."

The brothers nodded, and Grech continued. "His declaration is actually rather short. I'll read it."

To my sons, Gianni and Anton, I leave the entirety of my estate to you as joint tenants. Family is the most important thing, and it's my wish that you two act together as a family. To do this, you must work together. Please take care of our employees. They've been loyal to us and are, in their way, like an extended family to ours. The world is changing, but it is my hope that in you both, I have built something that will last and carry our family name forward. I love you both. Your father—Carlo.

"What does it mean, 'joint tenants?'" Gianni asked.

"It means that you and your brother each own the whole of the estate, but it also means that because you're equal, you have to agree on all decisions," Grech explained.

Gianni looked disgusted, "So I need my brother's permission to do anything?"

"Essentially yes. But also he needs yours," the lawyer said, attempting to placate the elder son.

"Relax, Gianni," Anton said. "Let's just talk this out."

"I don't want to relax, brother. I want to settle this and get on with my life." He pointed to Kats, "And I don't understand what they're doing here at a family meeting."

"I explained to you what had happened at the warehouse. Kats saved me. And because of that, we learned why those men are trying to force us to sell."

Gianni was silent. He, too, had been shocked by the revelation of the extent of their father's holdings. That revelation now fed his current agitation.

"Kats tells me that there's more to the story, and he wanted to share that with us all here. And Mr. Grech, as our family attorney, I'd like you to stay."

Grech nodded, and Kats stood.

"As was mentioned, during the course of my..." he paused and turned toward Shig and Molly, "during *our* investigation, we learned some significant information."

"We learned that because of the extent of your father's holdings, this outside group, led by one Harry Charles, has been trying to put pressure on your family to sell to them. We believe that they've been secretly given a huge contract to build a new stadium down here in Bayview Heights."

"A stadium? What kind of stadium?" Gianni asked.

"A baseball stadium for the New York Giants. They're relocating here starting next season."

"So our land is going to be worth even more," brightened Gianni. "Anton, we absolutely should sell for top dollar. You never wanted to be a ship builder. This way you can go off and be a writer."

Anton nodded, "I do want to be a writer, but I also want to respect our father's wishes. I used to think selling was the right move, but now I'm not so sure. What surprises me is your change of heart. You wanted to stay and fight."

"And look what that got our father. Nothing. Our shop burned. Our work destroyed."

The two brothers locked eyes.

"Gianni, what happened to your arm?" Kats asked, breaking the tableau.

"I told you. Shop accident."

"And do you know a man named Jimmy Lanza?" Kats followed.

Gianni's eyes blazed. He looked back and forth at his wife and son seated on the couch but said nothing.

"Brother, we can help you, but you have to tell us," Anton implored. "Please."

Gianni's wife, Lilly, concern etched on her face, repeated, "Please, Gianni."

Face red and breathing heavily, Gianni suddenly collapsed into his chair, "Alright!" he sobbed. "Yes, I know Lanza. And yes, I owe him money."

"How?" Anton asked.

"Gambling. Cards, horses." Turning toward his wife, "I'm so sorry, Lilly."

"Did Lanza do that to your arm?" Kats asked, already knowing the answer.

Gianni nodded. "They said the next time it would be worse. They threatened my family. I'm sorry, Anton. I dipped into the business accounts to stay even, but that wasn't enough."

Anton nodded, and Grech chimed in, "Perhaps selling is a good idea then. If you can get a fair price, it could clear your brother's debt and set you up to start over somewhere else."

"But our men would be out of work."

"Yes, but that really isn't your responsibility," Grech said.

"My father felt differently, Mr. Grech."

"We have to protect my family, Anton," Gianni said as he held his wife and son close to him.

"We have to protect you, too, brother," Anton replied.

"I think you and your family need to get out of town for a while, Gianni," Kats said. "Lanza has too many men and too much influence around here for us to ensure your safety."

"I can't leave you all here to face this alone."

"Brother, you need to take care of your family. Think of it as a vacation. Go, and you take Lanza out of the equation. That way we can focus on this Harry Charles."

Lilly looked at her husband "You've always promised us a vacation," she said plaintively.

"Yeah, Daddy. You said we would go to Disneyland!" Carlo Junior said.

"You want to go to Disneyland?" Gianni smiled at his son, who clapped his hands and nodded emphatically.

"I want to go to Disneyland," Shig whispered, which elicited an elbow from Kats.

"OK. How would this work?" Gianni asked.

"Go home, pack, and hit the road. Stay away for a couple weeks, and hopefully we can settle all this so you can come home," Kats said. "Check in with us every day or so, and make sure we know how to contact you."

"We could leave tomorrow after you take care of your father," Lilly said. Gianni nodded and hugged them both.

He turned and hugged his brother, "I'm so sorry, Anton."

"I know, G," he said, using the childhood nickname his brother always smiled at. "We will get this right and get you home soon."

Kats watched, not wanting to disturb this emotional moment, but he cleared his throat and said, "There's another outside element to all of this that you need to know."

The room looked perplexed.

"There's something very troubling going on at Hunters Point that may be related to all of this."

He continued, explaining what Tak had shared with him, painting an ominous picture of the current state of the basin and Bayview Heights. In the end, the group sat silent, shocked at the possibilities.

"Poison fish," Anton said quietly. Kats looked at Molly, who looked at Shig, and they all remembered Anton's powerful poem at the Six Gallery. Now it held a new and terrible meaning. "This radiation... It can make people sick, right?" Kats nodded. "It causes cancer?"

"Yes," Kats said.

At that, Gianni let out a howl of pain, and with his good arm he swept Carlo's desk of its contents, which crashed to the floor. He stood, chest heaving and eyes unfocused as his wife and son came to him. Anton held a hand over his heart, and tears silently streamed down his face.

Molly moved to Anton, hugging him, and he buried his face in her neck. Kats could see his shoulders shake. Shig was wiping tears from his own eyes as he approached Kats. "This isn't right," he said throatily to Kats, who nodded and put a hand on his friend's shoulder.

"What are you going to do?" asked the attorney Grech. "You need evidence. And I don't understand this connection between the naval base, a radiation leak, a stadium, and these people wanting to buy your land. It makes no sense that they'd want to buy up contaminated land."

Shig asked, "Is it possible that they wanted to buy up the land because it was contaminated? Like they knew it but wanted it anyway?"

Molly spoke up, "I used to work for Charles Construction, and they were using a series of shell companies to buy up pieces of the basin for the past year or so. But I never thought that Harry Charles was the mastermind behind it all. It always felt like someone else was pulling his strings. Someone else was supplying him the funds to buy these properties. There was a man named Sand," she looked at Kats, who was nodding, "who seemed to represent some group that was pushing Harry."

"Then there's all that development that's been happening on the naval base," Anton said. "That must be related to this."

Gianni cut in, "You're all talking about this like some mystery. There's no mystery. Those people killed our father with their poison. We have to tell the authorities."

"We have no proof, Gianni," Kats said. "But we can get some."

"How?" Shig asked.

"We need to figure out what's going on at Hunters Point. That seems to be driving all of this: the development, the accident they reference, the flurry of buying property. This whole thing seems like an elaborate cover-up."

"Again," Shig said to Kats, "How?"

"First, I know someone who has the clearance to get us some answers. Hopefully he can help."

"Sounds a bit..." began Shig.

"Thin?" Kats said.

"Yeah, pretty damn thin."

"That's why I'm going to break into the base."

"Are you nuts?" Molly demanded. Anton shook his head, and the whole room looked like Kats had just proposed going to the moon.

"That is a US military base with some kind of top-secret

shit going on. You get caught, and you go to federal prison for espionage," Molly said.

"If they don't shoot you first," offered Shig. Kats looked at his friend. That wasn't helpful.

"First of all, I have no intention of storming the gates of Hunters Point. But we do need to do some serious recon to prove what we think is happening. And let me remind you that every day over 10,000 people go on and off that base without any special clearance. Most recon is blending in and keeping your eyes open."

"So you're going to..." Shig began.

"Walk in the front door," finished Kats.

CHAPTER 19

The next day, New Year's Eve, the Vello brothers took their father's ashes out on the last boat he'd worked on and returned Carlo to his beloved sea. As they sailed past Hunters Point, they both eyed it like a malignant growth squatting on the bay. Neither said a word, but both had tears in their eyes.

Returning to the dock, Gianni was met by Lilly and young Carlo. They'd brought the family car over, loaded with suitcases. He and Anton looked at each other one last time. "Go. Call us when you get there." Gianni nodded and got into the drivers' seat of the red-and-white Chevy Bel Air. As they drove off, Carlo waved out the back window to his uncle, who smiled and waved back. OK, they're safe, thought Anton.

As the Bel Air reached the top of the road and turned toward the hills and the highway, a dark blue Buick started its engine and slowly creeped down the road following the Bel Air at a distance.

Over the next three days, Kats laid out a surprisingly simple plan to gain access to the base. Anton was reminded that one of their craftsmen, Stefano, had worked over at Hunters Point years ago. They sat down in the shop office with Stefano, and he explained that in 1947, he'd worked for the American Bridge Company. They were charged with building the enormous battleship crane. Standing some ten stories tall, the steel superstructure still dominated the horizon of the base.[7]

"How did you access the base when you went to work?" Kats asked the man.

"We were issued a pass with our name on it along with our company. The men who worked for Bethlehem Steel and Dupont and the other companies had the same kind of identification," Stefano said.

"So every day you had to show the pass to enter?"

"Technically, yes, but most of the time when the shifts changed, you had hundreds of men entering and exiting, so you just flashed the pass and the guards waved you through. It really didn't matter unless there were inspectors or visitors on base. Then they paid more attention."

Kats and Anton looked at each other. *Not so crazy after all.*

Stefano continued, "There's security there. It's in layers. It was easy to get onto base and then just go to your worksite like we did. But getting access to the buildings was much more difficult. There were guards at all the important buildings."

"And you think it's the same today?" Kats asked.

"I know it's the same. My son Marco works out there for the steel company. Same procedures." He laughed, "They even have the same ID."

"Do you think we could get a look at your son's ID?" Anton asked.

"No need. I still have mine," Stefano said as he reached into his jacket pocket and pulled out his wallet. He opened it up and dug into it, producing a worn, slightly yellowing card. Kats reached out, examined the card, and nodded to Anton.

"Stefano, we need to borrow this," he said.

Stefano looked momentarily concerned, "No trouble for my boy, right?"

"No trouble. We promise," Anton replied.

Kats went over to the entrance of the base and observed the inflow and outflow pattern over the course of the day. Morning and late-afternoon shift changes were the busiest, though workers and military personnel were perpetually moving on and off the base. The main gate was always open, always guarded, and always busy.

There did seem to be a pattern upon entering the base. Workers entered through the southern side of the gate and exited on the north side of gate. There was a gatehouse at the southside where it appeared the incoming workers showed their ID cards to the guards. It appeared that they almost never broke stride and were barely glanced at as they entered. He also noted a number of Asian faces in the blue-collar mix, so he wouldn't stand out. Promising, Kats thought.

By Friday morning they were ready. Kats had arrived at the Vellos' lot early wearing his workman's coveralls, boots, and hat. He carried a toolbox like many of the other men. "Nice touch," Anton said, pointing at the tools. Kats smiled and opened the toolbox. On the top layer was a standard assortment of tools, like one would expect to find. Raising the top off, he revealed a brown paper bag and what looked to be a small thermos.

Anton scowled at that layer as he asked, "What's that?"

"Lunch," Kats said. Then he lifted the bag to reveal a camera and a long, telephoto lens. Anton nodded.

The plan was for Kats to enter with the morning shift, spend the day milling around like a worker, and then leave with the afternoon shift. Anton would collect him where they dropped him off. Anton drove Kats to within a quarter mile of the base entrance and turned down a side street. Waiting until the road was clear, Kats exited the car, tugged his hat lower on his head, and started walking toward the front gate.

It was cold and overcast, so Kats turned up his collar. As he approached the gate, dozens of other men, and a smattering of women, were filing toward the entrance. He heard bits and pieces of conversations, but the group was mostly muted. Kats fingered the ID card in his pants pocket. He watched the queue in front of him for cues on how to present it and act while passing through the gate. He glanced to his left and right and noticed that the men around him held a card that reassuringly looked similar to the one he palmed. If he was stopped at the gate, the fallback was to say that he'd found the card and was trying to get a picture of the new ships to sell to the newspapers. Thin, but they'd agreed to not letting Stefano or his son take any heat. If he was stopped or confronted on the base, Kats agreed to dispose of the borrowed ID card so that it couldn't be traced back to Stefano. Kats realized that in a pinch he might have to eat the card. Hopefully it wouldn't come to that.

The crowd of workers, coming in and exiting, moved with practiced familiarity. Kats followed like a bird in a large flock. Approaching the gate, he mimicked the casual wave of the card that everyone else affected, and in a moment he was in. Only in the perimeter, but in. Kats allowed himself a deep breath. Now the hard part. Everyone else had a set destination, a particular building, a dock, an area. He had to look like he had a job and a destination while poking around the base. Keeping his eyes open, he looked for something that might provide him with a bit of cover.

On his left Kats noted a taller building with open, garage-style doors on the lower floor. On the side of the building, it said 351. A machine shop! The reinforced concrete building was three stories tall with an extended tower that climbed to five stories in its northwest corner. The machine shop was busy, but not too busy.

The trick to making this work was to look like he belonged. To do that, he needed to look busy. Kats entered the machine shop through the open side door. Lathes, drill presses, and pipe fitting tables were arrayed about the floor. The walls were covered in tools, so Kats walked over to the table, opened his toolbox, and made a show of grabbing tools off the walls. He noted that there were clipboards and forms on some of the tables, and sitting on one, like a cherry on a sundae, was a battered hard hat. Kats scanned the room as he closed his toolbox. He grabbed a clipboard, marched across the room, and confidently took the hard hat, placing it under his arm as he walked out of the building. Act like you belong.

Rounding the corner, Kats placed the hard hat on his head, hefted the clipboard in his left hand, and appeared to read it. He looked up and down and then marched down the street, occasionally stopping to check the clipboard and looking around.

The base was an odd mix of civilian and military buildings, but even the military buildings didn't bristle with overt security. As he moved deeper onto the base, toward a large congregation of buildings, that changed. In the heart of the grouping was a large, white painted building of six, seven, maybe even eight stories. What made it difficult to tell was the complete absence of windows. There were also a number of armed naval guards, and it was clear that building 815, its only marking, was something classified. The silent but clear message the building was sending said "stay away."

Kats turned from the main access point of 815 and walked up the street, away from the building. He was looking for a place to observe the building, and he found a three-story, glass walled structure that must have been built during the war. Dirt and dust were everywhere, and as he entered the open doors, it was evident the building was being transitioned into some kind of storage. The bottom floor was covered with crates, old office furniture, machine parts, and even an old Jeep. There were two mezzanine levels with more storage, but the building was open to the glass-paneled roof. Kats noted the metal stairs to his right, and he quickly found himself on the third floor. He found a discrete position with a sight line to the windowless building, opened the toolbox, and pulled out the Exacta camera and the 400mm telephoto lens. Quickly assembling the pieces, Kats checked his film again and raised the view finder to his eye. Turning the lens to bring it into focus, Kats could see the faces of the guards nearly 300 feet away. He could also see their machine guns.

Slowly panning the camera up and down the building, he noted very little that gave any clue as to the nature of the building. The only markings were the numbers 815 and the stenciled "Restricted" signs on the walls. Kats snapped a few photos and then turned the lens to the small guardhouse outside the entrance to 815. Big enough for a couple of guys, he thought. He watched as an officer came out of the guardhouse and spoke to the guards. The officer then entered 815. A couple of minutes later he exited, and Kats took a photo out of habit. He decided he wanted to get a better perspective on this building, so he needed to get higher. Looking across the mezzanine level, he saw a ladder leading up to the roof. Hefting the camera, he crossed the building and climbed up the rusty ladder. Kats pushed open the skylight and found himself on the open rooftop. There were narrow steel walkways between the glass panes of the roof, and he carefully made his way to the edge. Careful not to expose too much of his silhouette above the low rooftop wall, Kats looked around.

815 squatted in the midst of several other buildings, and Kats could see the bay beyond the base. Other than the lack of windows, there was nothing remarkable about this building. Kats paused and let the open air clear his head. Stillness. This time when he looked, he looked with "slow eyes," as they'd taught him in Ranger training. Take your time. Take in the details, and look at things that don't seem important. Look at the edges and not just at the obvious target. Kats allowed the whole picture to wash over him. Then at the far end of the building, perhaps fifty feet away from 815, he saw a small puff of what looked like smoke. It came from a low, pillbox-like structure approximately the size of a car but maybe three feet tall. Kats waited a few moments and there it was again. Another puff of smoke or maybe steam?

Kats scanned the perimeter of the building. Now he noticed that there were more of these little pillboxes, equally spaced around 815, and his heart began to beat faster. There was a familiarity to this design. Could it be?

Snapping several more photos, Kats paused and then decided to head back into the building. For two reasons, he took up his vantage point of being able to see the entrance to 815 again. One, his training had taught him the value of patience and waiting to see if something might develop at this mysterious building. He had the time. Two, it was late morning, and he was ready for lunch. His training and experience taught him the importance of meals and hydration.

At 12:33 pm, a car rolled slowly down the road, approaching 815. Kats raised the camera and peered through the lens at the approaching vehicle. Black and official looking.

It parked by the entrance to 815, and a driver jumped out and opened the rear door. An older man, in a long peacoat, stepped out, and Kats snapped a photo of him. He doffed a naval cap. Officer, thought Kats. High ranking to have a driver. From the other side of the car, a civilian emerged on his own. Medium height, maybe forties, glasses. Ordinarily, his would have been a nondescript face, but Kats had seen him just days ago in the Mission Bay warehouse. This was the same man who had met with Harry and was now in the company of a naval officer! Kats zoomed the lens in and shot several photos.

The two men walked toward the guardhouse, and the officer inside came out and gave a crisp salute, which the older officer casually returned. Definitely high ranking. The junior officer handed them both badges, which they took and, removing their outer coats, clipped them to their jackets. Kats got a good look at the senior officer's chest, which was filled with hardware. Must be an admiral. Then the junior officer handed them each something unusual. It was a small, grayish badge that each man clipped to their lapel. Kats zoomed in on the badge as far as he could. Click.

The men turned and entered 815, leaving Kats to wonder why an admiral, escorted by this same man, would be visiting this decidedly unfriendly building.

Vice Admiral Hyman Rickover wasn't happy to be back at Hunters Point, but the newly appointed director of naval reactors branch of the Bureau of Ships had a situation to deal with. Sand had been ordered to the meeting by his immediate boss, the West Coast NSI Chief Winslow. He didn't know why, and that made him anxious, though his deadpan nature would never reveal that truth.

Their last meeting had been in the main conference room on the first floor. This time they headed into the office of NRDL Director Sinclair, who sat at his desk looking nervous. Winslow stood and nodded a greeting to the admiral. Sand and Winslow's eyes met for a moment. Sand hadn't expected pleasantries from the man because they were professionals and well beyond such conventions, but he did see that Winslow was angry. This could be interesting.

Rickover sat looking at the NSI chief and commented, "Why am I back here, Winslow? I thought we were on track and that your men," he glanced at Sand, "had things in hand."

Winslow had years of experience walking the fine line between deference to power and candor. So he began patiently. "After the incident here in '53 and steps that followed, we all realized the need to construct a curtain to contain that information."

Rickover sat stone-faced, and Winslow continued.

"Part of that curtain included the recruitment of an asset inside the city's public works department. Since that department is charged with environmental management, any breach of security would likely flow through that department. We wanted to make sure we had eyes and ears there before anything could get out."

"Asset?" Rickover grunted. "You put a spy inside the government of an American city," he said bluntly.

Careful, Sand thought as he watched Rickover scowl.

"The asset has seen evidence that someone is digging into the Bayview Heights information. There were files that, by themselves, might be happenstance, but when requisitioned with certain other files, led our asset to believe they were looking at Hunters Point."

Sand spoke up, "We sanitized the environmental reports.

They showed a bit of contamination that one would expect from an active naval base like Hunters Point, but nothing more."

"Yes, but our man noted access to the building permits we were issued after the incident. There were dozens of them issued, along with other documents. It's possible that some notes were included that shouldn't have been there. There could be enough circumstantial evidence to make someone suspicious. Or at least curious."

"Do you know who accessed this information?" Rickover asked.

"Yes, it was a member of the city's planning department. A man named Tak Ozawa. And," he turned to look at Sand, "he's working on the city's stadium project."

Sand made a slightly pained face, which Winslow knew was the equivalent of someone else screaming in rage.

"What do we know about this Ozawa?" Rickover asked, now leaning forward a bit in his chair.

Winslow produced an 8×10 black-and-white photo that looked like it came from a city file. "Exemplary worker. Been with planning for six years after graduating from Berkeley. Started working for the city after college. Military service, too. Lost a leg in Europe."

"The 442nd?" Rickover asked, and Winslow nodded and continued.

"Once our asset reported this, we began surveillance on Mr. Ozawa. A few days ago, he met with two others—a man and a woman—at a Chinatown restaurant. It might have been a friendly meeting after work. The tail noted that the other man was also Asian, most likely Japanese American. We were later able to identify that man as Katsuhiro Takemoto, a local private investigator." Winslow produced a photo of Kats, most likely his photo on file with the local police department as a registered private investigator.

Not good, Sand thought, and Rickover barked, "A damn PI?"

"The two of them served together in the 442nd. In fact, Takemoto saved his unit and earned a Silver Star."

Sinclair, the NRDL director, finally spoke, "What does this mean to the lab?"

Winslow looked to Sand, who stepped forward, "Nothing. We carry on and make sure that *Nautilus* is ready for Operation Sunshine. We'll secure the adjacent lands and create the buffer zone we've planned."

"But this PI," fretted Sinclair.

"I'll handle the PI. He may suspect something, but so long as he can't prove it, we're fine."

Rickover let out an exasperated breath. "My confidence in this operation of yours grows less and less. After the debacle in '53, you were this close," he held two fingers very close together "to being completely shut down."

Debacle, thought Sand. Yes, I suppose a prototype nuclear reactor dumped into the bay rightfully qualifies as a debacle.

"Now we have intelligence leaks to go with the radiation leaks," Rickover said sardonically. "The navy must have this base operational, and Operation Sunshine needs to go off without any problems. The future of our nuclear deterrent is on the line here."

"Admiral," Sand began, "we have one more landowner to secure, and that's in process. Once we have that property, we can begin the cover operation that will move people out of the contamination zone and create space for Sunshine and all future operations."

"Your fish is here, and they're on schedule to make the additions to her before Operation Sunshine," added Winslow.

Rickover looked unconvinced, but nodded, "Let's go take a look at her."

Kats remained in place for another hour on the chance that some others might be joining whatever meeting was occurring inside 815. He decided he needed to examine the pillboxes that lined the grounds around the building. Repacking the camera, he emerged again as the hard hat guy with a clipboard. He strode purposefully out and away from 815. He walked farther and farther east, toward the water. He passed down streets and around buildings, and he kept seeing the pillboxes at regular and increasingly predictable spaces.

The last one he found some fifty yards from the water's edge, near the fingerlike extension of land that jutted outward into the bay. He stopped, examining the pillbox. It was a roughly eight-foot-by-eight-foot structure, but only three feet tall. It had a flat metal "roof"' that covered an open vent that extended downward. Kneeling next to the structure, Kats could feel the warm air coming from below through the large gaps in the sides. Listening, he could hear a low-level industrial hum. He found a small rock and dropped it into the shaft. He waited a moment but heard nothing. Deep, he thought. Just like Italy.

The elevator stopped, and the four men exited into the true heart of Hunters Point: a massive underground complex. They stood in what had started out as a huge sea cave. When Hunters Point was established as a commercial shipyard in 1870, the engineers had discovered the cave and seen it mostly as a geological nuisance. They built around its presence and largely ignored it. By the turn of the century, the US Navy had taken an interest in Hunters Point, though it officially remained a commercial establishment. In 1907, President Theodore Roosevelt wanted a demonstration of America's naval power. Roosevelt ordered a fleet of sixteen battleships and many more smaller support vessels to circumnavigate the globe on a "goodwill mission" that would last over fourteen months. All the ships were painted a peacetime white, and hence became known as the Great White Fleet.

Hunters Point, declared Roosevelt, was the "World's Greatest Shipyard," and he made it the major launch and staging point for the Pacific leg of the mission. From that time on, the navy began to use Hunters Point as an unofficial west coast base. By World War I, this included the excavation and buildout of the sea cave into an underground storage facility. By the 1920s, further tensions with Japan expanded the above-ground naval yard and resulted in the underground work being designated a military secret. Over the past three decades, the navy quietly expanded the underground operation to include submarine pens, dry docks, and maintenance bays.

The navy officially purchased Hunters Point in 1940, as most in Washington saw the coming conflict with Japan as inevitable. By the time Hunters Point officially became a US military base, it had been secretly operational for years, and now Rickover, Winslow, Sinclair, and Sand stood in the massive, manmade cavern as dozens of men moved busily about under the fluorescent lights.

They were some 100 feet below the 815 building, and the massive underground complex was easily 100 yards across and twice as long with smaller tunnels leading to offices, laboratories, machine shops, storage, and even kitchens and personnel quarters. The ceiling, a web of metallic scaffolding in the main area, was sixty feet above the cold black water. The channel to the bay lay at the eastern end of the complex. There in the main mooring, stretching out over 300 feet in length, was the black metallic fish with the number 571 on its conning tower. The *USS Nautilus*, the world's first—and still only—nuclear-powered vessel.

The admiral strode confidently toward the sub. This is very much his progeny, Sand thought. He knew that as a trained engineer, Rickover had his hands deep in the development and testing of the nuclear power plant that now drove the *Nautilus*. He'd been pushing the teams at Westinghouse who developed the Submarine Thermal Reactor, or STR. When the first fully operational prototype was delivered from the National Reactor Testing Station in Idaho, the next step was to install it in a working submarine. Westinghouse had delivered the STR to Hunters Point in early 1953. The navy had brought in the *USS Walrus*, a World War II-era sub that was scheduled to be decommissioned and scrapped. The STR was installed to test the ventilation and cooling system components before it would be fully integrated into the final build of the *Nautilus* across the country at the Groton, Connecticut Naval Yard.

The first tests had been a success. Run in the confines of the submarine dock, they'd provided proper cooling and ventilation. The second level of testing would have the *Walrus* dive out into the bay and running the same systems while underwater. Should have been easy, reflected Sand.

On a cold March night in 1953, the navy and the US government learned how dangerous it was to try to harness nuclear energy. When the hydraulic system in the aging submarine couldn't handle the unexpected power levels being generated by the STR, it started a cascade of system failures that left the frantic crew and engineers on board with only one choice. They had to vent sea water into the overheating chamber and jettison the STR to prevent it from potentially going critical. For the next twenty-seven months, that refrigerator-sized component sat in the shallow waters off Hunters Point, bleeding its deadly energy into the bay.

The president was terrified that the American public would find out. The navy was embarrassed, and Rickover was furious at the engineering failure. They all frantically began trying to develop a solution that would remove the STR from the bay. The energy it was giving off prevented divers from getting within fifty feet of the wreckage. They'd need to design a special vehicle, and that would take time.

The incident was classified so that only those with the highest-level clearance knew what was happening. Sand, Winslow, and the NSA were brought in to protect the secret. They came up with the idea of creating the NRDL, or the Naval Radiological Defense Laboratory at Hunters Point. It was classified a top-secret project whose official mission was to study the effects of the radiation and develop better ways to detect contamination. Building it provided the necessary cover and funding for its true, ultra-top-secret mission to develop a submersible capable of removing the STR and containing it.

In June 1955, the specially designed submersible, piloted by two volunteers, was able to attach flotation devices to the wreckage, which rose to the surface one moonless night and was collected by a shielded navy tug that transported it to shore and eventually into the NRDL storage facilities. Sand was reminded of something he'd heard many times by the higher-ups: "Nuclear power must be seen as safe and controllable by the American public." It was around that time that Sand had been tasked with covering up the incident and, at the same time, try to minimize civilian exposure to the contamination. Not an easily reconcilable task, but he'd come up with a surprisingly bold and innovative solution while at a baseball game. By the time of the seventh inning stretch, he was already trying to figure out which team might be lured away from its current home and into the new stadium Sand had dreamed up.

As Rickover led the way toward the Nautilus, several officers emerged from the boat and met the Admiral with a round of official salutes followed by good-natured handshakes. Rickover was beloved by these men who were at the forefront of the next generation of the navy—the nuclear navy.

Winslow turned to Sand and Sinclair, "Rickover will be hours with these guys," he said.

"Perhaps I should get back to work then," Sinclair said as he turned to go.

Winslow watched him retreat and turned to Sand, "Walk with me."

They moved away from *Nautilus* and across the metal gantry that took them to the far side of the submarine bays. As they cleared the moored boat, they could see the collection of cylindrical bays and tubes that splayed across the floor.

Sand walked in silence, waiting for Winslow to begin. He had all day.

"The latest reports show promise that this," he inclined his head toward the machine parts, "portion of Operation Sunshine will be ready on time."

"Good news for the admiral," Sand said.

"And the navy. They're pushing hard inside the Pentagon

to be the primary nuclear deterrent. If the submarine launch system performs well during Sunshine, they'll have the inside track over the air force."

"What are you hearing about their missile program?"

"That is what I wanted to tell you. I've been informed that the president is going to create an independent space authority, separate from the air force. They're calling it NASA, for National Aeronautics and Space Agency. The air force is furious."

"I'm sure they thought space exploration was going to be theirs."

"Which is why this turf war with the navy over the country's nuclear arsenal is so critical. Each side believes that their future funding, and therefore their relevance, is tied to whoever controls the keys to the nuclear kingdom."

"And the other sub?" Sand asked. The navy was hedging its bets on the SLBM system, so they had developed a simpler system that required the submarine to surface before launching its missile. The *USS Grayback* had been doing test runs in the Pacific for the past two months.

"Due in shortly. Their new test missiles are here already," he pointed across the way to a sleek, jet-like device. "They'll run some secret trials here before the official ones later this year."

Staring at the tubes and containers designed to house and launch nuclear ballistic missiles from an underwater submarine, Sand felt tired. Old and tired. Going from hot to cold war was hard enough, but having the territorial pissings of generals, admirals, defense contractors, congressmen, and senators interfere with the main point of defense—to protect the country, made all the work men like him had done for their entire careers seem like a carnival sideshow.

Winslow changed the subject back to his real concern, "What about the leak? Are you confident in getting this land deal closed?"

"Yes. There was a bump in the road, but we have the inside track on the family now. I was able to provide some necessary leverage to our proxy."

"What about this investigator? He may already know too much."

"I'll see to him personally."

Chapter 20

A s Kats scanned the expanse of the base, his mind was taken back almost fifteen years to the coast of Italy, north of Salerno. It was September 1943, and the 100th Battalion had joined in the advance up the Italian peninsula. Kats had been assigned to a recon mission outside the town of Gaeta. It was some 150 kilometers southeast of Rome on an outcropping of coast that jutted into the Mediterranean. A German artillery battery on the hillside above the coast had resisted multiple Allied airstrikes and would need to be dislodged by a bloody assault up the hill by American infantry—the 100th Battalion. In advance of that attack, detailed reconnaissance was needed, so Kats and a dozen others had been dropped 5 kilometers south of the hillside by a PT boat on a nearly moonless night. Using two inflatable boats, the men quietly paddled to the rocky shore.

Over the next twenty-four hours, they moved cautiously toward Gaeta and the artillery battery. They moved inland when necessary and tried to avoid notice by the Italian civilians, though the Italian population was increasingly sick of the war and had begun rumblings to oust Mussolini and sue for peace with the allies. Still, it only took one loyalist to bring a squad of German infantry down on them, so they moved cautiously. By the following night they were in position outside the German battery. Kats had been assigned a sea-level approach as he hugged the rugged coastline, creeping forward. Their mission was to spread out and determine the best approaches to assault the battery—from the coast and up the hill, or from behind the hilltop, which necessitated checking multiple locations for German positions. They were there to reconnoiter, not engage, and ordered to meet at dawn at the rally point. They're dug in there like a tick, Kats thought.

As he moved forward, he was almost directly below the battery several hundred feet above. He stopped to take a sighting and, sitting there, he quieted his breathing, his eyes, and his mind to allow the nighttime scene to fill his consciousness. In a moment he became aware of a low, mechanical hum coming from above him in the darkness. Looking up, he saw nothing out of the ordinary until... there! A whisp of smoke, no steam, from a dark patch up the hill. It was only because he was looking up that he could see the steam in contrast to the starry sky.

He quietly moved up the hill and discovered a knee-high structure that appeared to be a covered vent. He could feel the warm, moist air flowing upward into the cold night and realized there was a facility of some kind underground. This changed everything, he realized. There could be a whole battalion underground waiting for an Allied assault. Moreover, there could be a series of tunnels and passageways that would allow the Germans to move behind his unit as they struggled up or down the surrounding hills.

The vent was approximately three by three feet, with a cover of corrugated steel and a wire mesh grate that he easily pulled back. Looking down, he could see nothing. He dropped a stone, expecting to hear a solid clack, but none came back. It can't be that deep, he thought. Taking a chance, he pulled his flashlight from inside his jacket. He placed his body between the light and the German position above. He leaned over and into the vent, pointing the flashlight downward. He took a deep breath and readied himself to run in case this crazy move drew a sentry. He thumbed the switch on, and the beam of light pierced down the metal shaft. Kats blinked furiously, his eyes having to adjust to the sudden light. A moment later he could see down the shaft and some forty feet or so came back a black, rippling light. Water! That wasn't what he was expecting.

Clicking off the flashlight, Kats rolled onto his back and let his ears scan the area for any sign he'd been noticed. Nothing. He let his eyes readjust to the darkness and began to think why there would be water underneath the hilltop. He also realized that this might be a way into the German base and decided he needed to know.

Opening his field pack, he pulled the black, nylon rope each man had been issued. Eighty feet, he thought, as he examined the black weave, approximately as thick as his finger. Good for going down, less so for going up. He unspooled the rope using his outstretched arms as the measure. Then he added a series of knots to the rope at six-foot intervals. Next, he looked for a way to anchor the rope on top of the vent. He gathered two pieces of wood, each over six feet long and thicker than his arm. He hefted them and checked for signs of rot. Satisfied that they were solid enough, he made an "X" and used the rope to secure them together. He placed the makeshift cross over the vent and let the rope drop down the shaft. He tentatively stepped onto the wood, which bowed slightly but held his weight.

Kats stripped off his coat and shed his helmet. He secured his .45 pistol in his holster and sheathed his knife on the opposite hip. The flashlight was the last of his equipment in his belt as he crawled over the edge, grabbed the rope, and slowly began his descent into the shaft. He had to go slowly enough so that he didn't sway and crash into the metal walls.

It reminded him of basic training, where day after day they made the recruits do pull-ups. He'd always been strong, and on day one of basic he impressed his drill sergeant by doing fifteen straight pull-ups. By the end of Ranger training, he could do thirty-eight.

Kats counted the number of knots he passed and realized he was nearly forty feet down. He could feel more moist air coming from below. One more knot, and his feet swung clear of the shaft. Then his head followed. He stood on the knot, swaying some twenty-five feet above the dark water in a giant manmade cave that stretched a couple hundred feet across and cut much further back into the hillside.

Toward the hillside end of the cave, electric light bathed that end of the cavern with a cold luminescence that reflected off the dark shapes of three docked submarines. A German submarine pen, hiding under their artillery battery! No wonder they were defending this so doggedly.

Kats looked back the other way, realizing he was in the sea channel that led outside into the Mediterranean. He couldn't see the exit from here, and it would be concealed outside so that passing ships or aircraft would never notice it.

There were at least a couple dozen men moving about the submarines, on the concrete docks and back into the facility cut into the hillside. There must be supplies, ammunition, and space for the crews, he thought. HQ needs to know about this.

Kats also took a second look at the channel as he swayed above. The ceiling was crisscrossed with steel scaffolding. Probably good against bombs from above. But what about a bomb from below? He knew that the sappers would love to have a go at this one. Smiling, he adjusted his grip and began the ascent back toward the surface.

Now as Kats recalled that mission many years ago, he wondered what to do. Gaeta had ended very well. Several days later, he led a sapper team back to the vent along with a platoon of commandos. They entered the base from the water as the 100th began its assault from the hills behind the base. Once the commandos moved in, the sappers blew the roof of the channel, trapping the subs in their pen and their surprised crews off guard. That was a good day.

Back then Kats had tools and the might of the US Army behind him. Now he was alone and ill prepared for that kind of recon mission. But getting back on base for another chance at this would be highly unlikely. "'Go for Broke" was his unit's motto and one that they were extremely proud of. He sometimes felt that it had made them do foolish things to live up to their own growing reputation and to prove to the naysayers and the skeptics that the Nisei troops were as good, or even better, than their White counterparts. They all felt like they had more to prove, and that had cost a lot of lives.

First things first, he thought, I need the right tools. Without those, this was a scrub. He stood and began to casually walk back toward the street of buildings at the center of the base. He checked his watch. 3:15 pm. He had less than two hours before the shift change. Anton would be looking for him. He gave himself until 5 pm to find what he needed; otherwise, he'd stick to the plan and leave with the main shift.

He strode purposefully toward nothing as he carried the clip board in his left hand and his toolbox in the right. Walking back through the streets, his eyes scanned left and right looking, looking for... there! Seahorse Towing & Maritime Supply. A civilian company working with the navy, located on the base to better service their biggest client. There was a closed office door and an open double garage door that led onto the floor of their one-story building. Kats could see crates and walls of material that ought to have what he was looking for. But how to get it? It was one thing to walk out with a hard hat and clipboard. Finding and taking a coil of rope was another matter. As he contemplated the situation, a loaded flatbed truck pulled up in front of the supply company, and its driver jumped out and walked over to the office doorway and entered. As Kats looked over the truck, he noticed that the flat bed was covered in a large canvas tarp that was held down by a crisscrossing of rope. A bold plan formed in his head as he removed the hard hat and set the tool kit and clipboard aside. He walked over to the truck.

Lifting the tarp, Kats could see that the flat bed contained a hodgepodge of boxes and machine parts. Delivery or pickup, he wondered? Taking a chance, he started to untie one end of rope that was attached to the truck bed. Working quickly, he undid one side and tossed the rope end over the truck and began working on the other end when he heard, "Hey, what are ya doin'?"

Turning, Kats saw the driver approaching him. "John told me to help you unload," and he nodded his head toward the building. The driver looked momentarily confused as he looked back toward the office and then at Kats. "Alright, thanks," he said and began untying the other ends of rope. Kats grabbed the first rope and quickly wound it around his arm the way sailors organized their ropes. He tossed it next to the rear wheel of the truck and started on the next piece. In moments, they'd removed four lengths of rope, and now Kats was helping the man pull the tarp off.

"What do you want to move first?" Kats asked. "I'll hand

it down to you." He lithely jumped up on the truck bed. The man, overweight, tired, and near the end of his shift, looked grateful to not have to heft the boxes off the truck. "Let's start with those," he said, pointing to the boxes marked *Industrial Strength*. Kats slid two of the suitcase-sized crates to the edge. He hopped down and then pulled the first box down, turned, and handed it to the driver, who took it in both arms with a small grunt. The driver turned and began walking toward the open garage doors. As he entered the building, Kats moved behind the truck and grabbed the coils of rope by the rear wheel. He didn't run but quickly moved across the road and was gone by the time the driver returned thirty seconds later.

Kats returned to the storage facility down the road from Building 815. He found a quiet corner on the second floor and began his preparations for the night's activities. At 5 pm he heard several whistles indicating the end of a shift. Anton would be waiting for him, and when he failed to show up, no doubt the young man would be worried. Molly and Shig, too. Can't think about that right now, he chastised himself as he tied the four pieces of rope into a single, usable piece for the night. It was about ninety feet long and not terribly thick. As he'd done in Italy, he meticulously added knots at six-foot intervals that would provide necessary hand and footholds. He had also found an old tire iron in the back of the Jeep stored on the ground floor. As he cautiously picked through the storage facility, he found a waxed canvas bag that he could wear around his shoulder. He added a wrench and screwdriver to the bag, along with the camera and flashlight, and settled in atop a stack of crates to wait for darkness.

Anton fidgeted behind the wheel of his car. The shift change had started more than forty-five minutes ago, and still no sign of Kats. Molly sat next to him, peering intently toward the gate. They'd not spoken for several minutes. Anton drew a deep breath and said, "We probably shouldn't stay here too long. It'll start to look suspicious."

"Give him more time," Molly implored. "He's too smart to get caught," she said, trying to sound confident. Anton nodded, understanding that she needed his reassurance.

"You really care about him," he said matter of factly. She blushed a little. The color was easy to see on her pale, white complexion.

"I do, and I know it's crazy 'cause we hardly know each other. But he makes me feel... I was going to say 'safe' but that's not it exactly. I feel..."

"Protected," finished Anton.

"Yeah, protected. Like nothing can get to me."

"I've only known him as long as you, and I agree. He was amazing at the warehouse. So composed, and very observant. You can see him taking things in."

"The first time I met him, the one word that popped into my head was 'clever,' and he certainly proved that." Molly recounted the first encounter with Kats that led to Harry and how Harry had been tricked into giving away his silly secret identity. They both laughed at that.

"He'll come back," Anton assured, "but we probably need to move. I've seen a couple people looking at us as they walked by." Anton started the engine.

"OK, but we come back at the end of the next shift," Molly said.

"And the next, and the next if we need to. He'll come back."

CHAPTER 21

K ats awoke without moving a muscle. Time in the field had taught him to reach out with his ears, nose, and eyes before movement might give him away. He smelled the cold night air and felt the moisture. He heard the now quieter sounds of the base, a distant motor, a foghorn in the distance. As he opened his eyes and looked out a window, he saw the thick fog had rolled in. Excellent, he thought. Checking his watch, it was 10:09 pm.

He moved to the ground floor and took stock of the situation. Most of the civilian operations were now closed, though he could tell that the ship works, the steel foundry, and some of the other large ones were on their second shifts. At the eastern edge of the base, the massive battleship crane was lit by a revolving navigation light. The base and the crane jetty were prominent enough that they needed to create a lighthouse on top of it to alert passing boat traffic. It also helped illuminate the eastern end of the base.

Naval personnel moved about the base, and the guards were still visible at their posts, bathed in pools of light from fog-shrouded lamp posts. His civilian work clothes weren't out of place, but they were definitely less common. Look like you belong.

Kats had assembled several ten-foot-long aluminum pipes from the storehouse. They were about three inches in diameter and lightweight. What they were used for, he had no idea. Tonight, they would be a disguise. Placing his hard hat on his head, his pack slung under his arm, he hefted the pipes onto his left shoulder and marched out of the building.

Walking east, he moved past several closed buildings. A few other workers were headed west, presumably toward the exit on that side. On the next street over he saw headlights followed by a jeep carrying two men driving west. Guards? That meant they might be coming down his road next. Not wanting to chance that, he turned a corner and walked up to their road and looked around the corner. Taillights were distantly visible. He glanced back to the east and his destination. The crane cast shadows across the broad expanse of the approach to the water. As the light passed through the night, it created an eerie effect on the fog. It looked like the air was moving, which would help conceal him if necessary. Let's hope it doesn't come to that, he thought.

As he stood in the shadows of the last large building, he set the pipes down and stared out across the ghostly expanse of the eastern side of the base. It was very exposed. A couple of small buildings and, of course, the series of metal pill boxes that had started this whole operation. On a clear night, the lighting would have made crossing unnoticed very difficult. Tonight, it was at least possible. Kats noted the rotational time of the light atop the massive crane. Just under eight seconds according to his watch. He knew he'd have to work on the west side of the selected pill box to avoid the light. But the west side faced the more populous end of the base and made observation possible.

Timing his moves to avoid the light, he selected a pill box that was far enough from the center of the base but not too close to the water's edge. Crouching on the western side of the low structure, he surveyed the opening. He removed some screws to open an access panel. It was tight, but he could slip into the vent. That wasn't the problem, he realized. As he opened the panel, he became aware of the low whine of an engine. He stuck his head into the vent and could feel the warmer air coming upward almost like it was being pushed up. Then he realized what the sound was—a turbine spinning in the shaft to circulate the air from below. That could hurt. Retrieving the flashlight from his pack and pointing as deep down the shaft as he could to prevent light escaping and giving him away, he clicked on the light. Turbine. He couldn't see beyond the spinning blades.

Kats grabbed two small stones from the ground and, positioning his upper body inside the shaft, he dropped the first stone. *One Mississippi, Two ...* CLANK. He repeated the drop and got the same result. Forty-some feet, he estimated. But how far beyond that was the exit? Ninety feet of rope gave him a little wiggle room, but not much.

Kats was able to tie off his rope to a group of pipes at the corner of the vent. Then he took his pack and positioned the elements he might need. He put the wrench and the tire iron near the top of the zippered pouch. The camera was below that. Kats took his pocketknife and clipped it to his belt, and a pack of matches went into his front pants pocket.

He took another look down the shaft with the flashlight. At the center of the spinning turbine was a hub, which he knew was his target. He measured off about forty feet of rope and circled that up over his shoulder. He couldn't let the excess rope fall into the turbine; it might foul the mechanism and create a hopeless knot of rope. Worse, it might cut the rope and end this adventure right there. He moved the pack into an accessible position across his chest and prepared to enter the shaft. Slow and steady, he thought.

As he entered the shaft feet first, he found the knots

in predictable places and began his descent. In the aluminum-covered shaft, his breathing was amplified, and every brush against the wall or creak of the rope seemed like an alarm. He knew he was getting close to the turbine, as he could feel the increase in wind past his face, and the whine of the electric motor was more audible. Pausing, he anchored his feet on the small knot. With one hand he removed the flashlight and checked his distance to the fan. Just under ten feet. He sighted the center hub, clicked off the light, and continued. He reached out in the darkness with his feet, looking for that solid metal landing. *CLACK!* He felt the reverberation up his leg as he touched the spinning blade. He tried again, and this time he found solid footing. He slowly allowed more weight to transfer from the rope to his foot until he was sure it could hold his weight. Satisfied, he stepped onto the hub, which was about eighteen inches across.

Turning on the flashlight, he examined his position. The blades were spinning fast, but not propellor fast. Maybe 120 rpm, he estimated. Don't want to stick my hand in there, but maybe the tire iron, he thought. Bloody noisy, though. He spotted a junction box about a foot above the spinning blades. A black cable entered there and connected to the hub he was standing on via a crossbeam under the blades. The junction box didn't appear to have a lock on it, but its front panel door was closed. Too far to reach over by hand. Kats stood on one foot and, using the rope above to balance himself, reached out with his booted right foot and was able to flip the panel door open after three tries. Pointing the flashlight at the interior, he saw several dials and connectors. A prominent red color switch was toggled upward. Flip the switch! He reached out with his foot again, but the box was too small and the switch recessed enough that his boot wouldn't fit. He pulled back and, using one hand, untied his right boot and carefully removed it. Setting it on the hub, he decided to take off his sock, too, to give him more feel. He stood and again reached out with his bare foot toward the junction box.

The switch was recessed several inches deep, and he stretched even farther trying to find the mechanism with his toes. The stretch also put significant weight on his arm that had to hold him steady on the swaying rope. Sweat was running down his face, and he had to blink to clear his eyes. Several times his toes seemed to brush the mechanism but couldn't find it. *Kuso! Shit,* he thought. He pulled back to the center to rest his arms and gather himself. Kats stood on the small island, took several deep breaths, and shook out his arms. He then stretched forward till his head was level with his knees in a move that would have impressed a ballet dancer. He remembered what his father had taught him about too much effort. "You must learn to fall into sharpness, Katsuhiro. Trying too hard robs you of technique and makes you sloppy. Breathe and allow yourself to fall into proper form."

Reaching out this time with his foot, Kats allowed his mind and his muscles to relax and lengthen. His foot found the interior of the box, and he was able to stretch even further. His toes found the switch this time! Applying downward pressure now... Stuck! *The damn thing is stuck.* He closed his eyes, took a breath, and on the exhale found just a bit more length in his muscles to stretch even further and *CLICK!* The switch flicked to the off position. Just as it did, the pressure from his foot caused him to slip a few more inches. He caught himself with the rope, but the sudden shift caused his plant foot to shift, and it knocked his boot off of the hub. It bounced on the blades momentarily and then fell into the darkness below.

Kats hauled himself back onto the hub as the blades slowed and eventually came to a halt. He stared down at his naked foot. To most people losing a shoe or a boot was embarrassing. To a soldier, losing a boot was almost as bad as losing your rifle. Boots affected your mobility, which directly impacted your ability to fight. Armies since Napoleon's had worried about soldier's feet. Trench foot, the debilitating condition made infamous during World War I, had sidelined thousands of soldiers.

Kats recalled one night during his Ranger training when they'd assembled for a midnight run. Nothing unusual about that until the training officer had ordered them to remove their boots. The men looked at each other and slowly complied. The officer chided them, "What are you gonna do if you lose your boots? You gonna quit? You gonna lay down and die?" *No, sergeant!* they replied. As the run began, he heard many yelps and cries to start, and he certainly felt every rock and branch despite having reasonably tough feet from training with his father. But by the time the five-mile run ended, no man was complaining, and they even laughed at how much they'd cried at the outset. Lesson learned.

Kats was now able to see below the fan, and it looked like another twenty feet of vent before it opened into something larger. Kats unspooled the remaining rope, stepped between the blades, and lowered himself to the end of the shaft. There was some light below, and clearly it opened into a structure of some kind, but he couldn't tell what until he braved entry. He let his legs clear and followed the rope down until his head emerged just below the vent edge. What he saw astounded him.

He hung some forty feet above the water. To what he knew was the west, the tunnel extended for another seventy yards and then opened into a massive, well-lit cavern. From his vantage point, it looked like there was at least one submarine docked in the pen. He'd thought his experience in Italy would be comparable, but the scale of this dwarfed that operation several times over. He looked back up the channel and could see the dark corridor of water extending back toward the bay. He could see a metal catwalk running down the center of the channel above the water, just tall enough for a man to stand. It extended in both directions and was about thirty feet from the ventilation shaft. *Too far to swing.* He noted that the ceiling of the channel was crisscrossed with metal lattice work and pipes.

Wrapping the hanging rope around his lower leg, Kats eased onto a steel pipe and smoothly swung, hand over hand, toward the catwalk and quietly dropped onto it. Then he secured the rope so he could get back out. A casual look wouldn't notice the line stretching from the shaft to the catwalk, and he hoped not to be here long enough for a closer inspection.

Kats opened his pack and removed the camera with its long telephoto lens. He focused the lens down the channel and shot a couple of images. He started to move forward but stopped and looked at his feet. One bare foot and one booted foot stared up at him. He felt out of balance, like a car with one flat tire. He quickly removed the boot and sock and left them on the scaffolding. The cold, damp metal was actually less slick in his bare feet, and he padded slowly forward.

As he moved toward the center of the cavern, light began to creep into the tunnel. He got to within thirty feet of the chamber, mostly still in shadows, and lay down on the metal surface like a sniper. The submarine was ahead of him, slightly to his right. From this vantage point he could make out the identification number on its conning tower. 571. That's the *Nautilus!* America's first, and so far only, nuclear vessel. It had been all over newspapers, magazines, and television since its launch in 1955. He aimed the camera and shot several images of the submarine. The chamber wasn't very active. He saw a couple of technicians working on something at the far end of the docks, and there were a few men moving across the concrete expanses that must lead to storage and repair stations.

To the far right of his vantage point, spread out in array like a set of tools, were three black metal tubes that he initially thought were torpedoes. *Too big.* Then he saw the metal stabilization fins. Missiles. He snapped image after image. Kats realized that his heart was racing, and he forced himself to relax and once again looked through the chamber like he was trained to do. This time he saw fuel tanks, crates, and a forklift.

In the far corner, behind that forklift, was another piece of machinery that almost looked like a sleek jet airplane. Easily fifty feet long, Kats stared at it intently. He raised the camera and, using the telephoto lens, was able to get a clearer image. It wasn't a jet airplane, but another type of missile. This one looked like a German V-1 rocket. He'd encountered those in the final weeks of the war after the 442nd had secured a German airfield and discovered several of the so-called "Buzz Bombs" in the hanger. They were winged rockets that carried a high explosive payload and had been part of Hitler's terror weapons in the final stage of the war. This one was much larger and looked far more sophisticated.

Kats's mind was reeling from this discovery. The investigator in him wanted to move forward and discover more of Hunters Point's secrets. But the trained soldier in him remembered one of the key lessons learned about reconnaissance: you had to deliver the information to make it worth a damn. Slowly, he got into a crouch and crept back down the channel toward the covering darkness.

He was more than halfway back to the ventilation shaft when a klaxon sounded behind him from the docks. Like the electric braying of a sheep, it echoed down the channel. Could they have seen me? Then to his horror, he heard an electric buzz, and overhead, fluorescent lights embedded in the ceiling down the length of the channel began to flicker on. Below him, he could see running lights along the water's edge lining the channel come to life as well. His once-dark tunnel was now brightly illuminated from above and below. He broke into a run and saw the water in the channel below swell as another black submarine surfaced, moving into the base.

Ensign Keith Elder looked up from his work on the dock. The entrance signal alerted the base to the arrival of the *USS Grayback*. The sub was expected. The ensign had been assigned to Hunters Point for almost a year now, but the arrival of a sub through the sea channel was always an impressive sight. He stood, wiped his brow, and watched the lights come on down the tunnel. Then he saw something that seemed out of place. It was an outline of something on the service walk. "What the fuck?" he said out loud. The outline started to move, and then it ran down the walkway. Elder ran to the nearby phone that connected to the operations center.

As Kats ran down the catwalk, the submarine passed underneath him like a half-submerged whale. He reached the rope and untied it as he heard a different kind of klaxon emanate from the docks behind him. Not wasting time, Kats let the rope drop free as he made his way hand over hand back toward the vent entrance. Grabbing the rope, he began to ascend the vent as fast as could manage. This time he wasn't concerned with keeping quiet, so he was able to use his feet against the steel walls as he hauled himself back up the shaft. By the time he pulled himself clear of the surface pillbox structure, he could hear sirens going off across the base.

Across the open spaces he could see headlights come on and begin moving. To the northwest and southwest he could see multiple flashlights. Perhaps 200 yards away. That left the east as the only viable option. He turned, and a quick scan didn't provide many options. The crane. Kats took a moment to cut the rope from the pipes and cover the breach as best he could. Might slow them down a little.

In a half-crouch, Kats quickly scuttled across the open expanse toward the giant battleship crane at the base's edge. Careful not to silhouette himself against lights in front of him and moving to avoid the sweep of the navigation light, he saw that several men had gathered at the southern base of the crane, flashlights and rifles in hand. Kats put the last building on the approach between himself and the men as he circled north. He peered around the corner of the building at the men around the small utility building. He looked to his left and saw that the edge of the pier was only about forty feet away, and he could keep the building between himself and the guards. He checked them again. They appeared to be using a radio, and a moment later four of them peeled off and headed west into the base, leaving two armed with machine guns. The sirens continued to wail into the night, and he knew his time was running out.

Kats slipped to his left and made it to the dock's edge and looked down. It was about eight feet to the water, and the concrete edge of the dock extended down halfway to the water, creating an overhanging ledge. The support structure must be underneath, he thought.

Looking back, Kats could see a truck approaching the guards. He adjusted his pack, secured the closure as best he could, and slid over the edge of the dock. He found that there were grooves in the concrete, and he was able to brace his feet underneath on the support structure. He clung there like a barnacle and listened.

The three-quarter ton Dodge M37 truck skidded to a stop at the foot of the battleship crane. The ensign jumped out along with four more armed men from the back. "Have you men seen anything or anyone come this way?" The two local guards looked at each other and shook their heads. "No, sir. What are we looking for?"

"Not sure. Possible breach of a secure building." Turning to his men, he said, "Give me a sweep of the perimeter of the dock." Splitting into two teams, they approached the edge of the dock and peered over it.

From his position, Kats could see beams of light flashing over the wall to the east of him. They're checking the wall. Below him, Kats could see the frigid waters of the bay and realized he had to get out of sight. He slid down the wall and pulled himself underneath the overhanging wall, the lower half of his body in the icy water. Moments later he heard footsteps above and saw the beam of light cross over his hiding place and then move quickly down the wall, back toward the base. Kats realized that he couldn't feel his feet, and he had to clench his jaw to keep his teeth from chattering. He knew that hypothermia could set in quickly in water this cold. He needed to get out and get moving to warm himself up again, but he had to give the patrol time to clear. He mentally counted out two more minutes and began pulling himself up again toward the edge.

As he did, his legs didn't seem to want to cooperate. They felt like dead fish flopping from his waist. Using his upper body, he brought his head above the edge to sight the guards. Their truck was still there, and he could see two men. The others were gone, hopefully moving west. He began slowly sliding laterally down the side of the dock toward the giant crane. If one of the guards looked over, all they might see would be fingers curled over the stone edge. He moved deliberately, not wanting to make noise or, worse, slip into the bay.

He reached the base of the crane, and as he hauled himself upward, he again sighted the guards. Satisfied, he began to climb the giant metal leg. There were stairs running up the structure like a fire escape, but they were too open and obvious. Instead, he climbed the outside rigging. Halfway up the leg, he could see across the base and out into the bay. Approaching from the south bay were two patrol boats, their search lights cutting across the black water and moving toward the crane. Moving quickly now, speed his ally, he climbed up to the lower side of the crane's horizontal superstructure. He nestled into a corner joint just as the first boat approached and began to sweep the end of the dock and surrounding waters with its search light.

He felt momentarily safe. It was human nature not to look up as often as we did on our horizontal plane. If they did look at the superstructure, he was in a dark crevice and would look like a dark blotch on the dark metal crane. He would be invisible until dawn. He checked his watch. 2:32 am. He had about four hours of solid darkness, and then things could get ugly.

He realized that the sirens had stopped, but the base was still highly active with vehicles and men moving about. He took out the camera and sighted the long lens back toward the pillbox he'd used. He could see two jeeps parked there and several men standing around the vent. Well, they figured that out, he thought.

He turned the lens downward to look at the two guards left by the opposite foot of the crane. One held a walkie talkie that he occasionally kept to his ear. He also noted that the small truck was still parked there next to them. That could be useful.

Kats looked across the level of the crane where he sat. There was a walkway that crossed over to the other side, and he thought he'd be able to come down behind the two guards. He knew he couldn't hurt them because they were just a couple of cold swabbies doing their duty. But there were ways to incapacitate them without hurting them too much. But before he was going to try anything, he realized he had to get some feeling back in his freezing feet and legs. He began rubbing the still wet pants to encourage more blood flow. He grasped his bare feet in his hands to transfer some much-needed body heat into those extremities. While he did so, he continued to watch the movements across the base and noticed an interesting pattern. Most of the activity was centered in the middle of the base, but there was also some to the west and to the north. The south end of the base was largely quiet and dark. As he surveyed the area with the long lens, he could see little other than a patrol boat that went into and out of the channel on its search pattern. That part of the base was just a few hundred yards from the civilian side of the basin and the Vellos' dock.

After about thirty minutes, enough feeling had come back to his feet and legs to attempt a quiet crossing of the crane. His two guards below, a tall guy and a short guy, had succumbed to the late hour and a sense of disconnect from the action. They leaned against the superstructure and eventually sat on the lower stairs, blowing into their cold hands to keep them warm. There was enough noise still coming from the base and water lapping at the walls to provide enough cover for his crossing some sixty feet above the guards. He moved deliberately even though he was well covered on the walkway. Unless they hit him directly with a flashlight, there was almost no chance of him being seen.

Once on the south side of the crane, Kats looked down the structure and could see the men sitting on the lowest level of the crane foot, each smoking a cigarette. He began slowly creeping down the vertical ladders, now being cautious and silent. He made his way down two sets of ladders onto a metal landing some twenty-five feet above the guards. He stopped like a panther in a tree, listened, and considered his options. He knew he could take them out, but how quickly and how quietly was the issue. The truck was parked next to the small crane office building. Knowing standard military protocol, Kats figured the keys were left in the ignition in case someone else had to move it. He was counting on that fact. Below he heard the men shift.

"I gotta hit the head," said a voice. "Just take a leak over the edge," said the second voice. "Yeah, that ain't gonna cut it. Can't hang my ass over the edge." The other voice laughed. "Use the head in the office."

The tall guard stood and headed into the small office via the door on the far side of the building. He also left the walkie talkie with the other guard. This was Kats's opportunity. He quickly slid down one more level and took a sighting of the smaller guard. He was standing, smoking, and looking back toward the base. The ladder was behind him. On silent feet, Kats moved down the ladder and paused. The man puffed on. In two long steps, Kats was on him, throwing his right arm across the man's neck, securing it with his left arm. The shocked man spit out his cigarette and with it his oxygen supply. When he tried to draw another breath, he found a vicelike grip around his neck. He clutched at the arms holding him, feeling a terrible pressure coming down on the left side of his neck. His arms frantically waved, and his feet kicked, though they now felt unattached from his body. His eyes became unfocused and, in another moment, unconsciousness took him.

Kats held the man in the so-called sleeper hold for another two seconds, making sure he was unconscious. The man would awaken within an hour with a massive headache, probably embarrassed, but fine. Kats hefted him in a fireman's carry and deposited him in the shadows of the crane. He looked at the man for a moment and then stripped off his navy peacoat and his hat. Turning, he grabbed the walkie talkie and moved toward the truck. He listened for signs that the tall guard was returning but heard nothing. He quietly entered the truck and, there in the ignition, just as he'd predicted, were the keys.

The engine started on the first try, and Kats threw it into

gear and accelerated. As he looked back in the mirror, he saw the other guard run out of the door, "Hey!" he heard. Kats waved the swabby's hat out of the window, which drew a reply, "Very funny, asshole!"

As Kats drove toward the center of the base, he slipped on the peacoat and the hat. It wasn't a great disguise, but it might get him past a quick look. As he approached the center of the base, a squad of men was walking up the street. He pulled the hat a bit lower on his head and kept his eyes forward as he passed them. Looking into the side mirror, he searched for any reaction. Finding none, he continued past the next building and made a hard left.

Once off the larger road, he turned off the truck's lights and continued southward. At the southernmost building, he pulled into the shadows and parked the truck. The relative quiet of the night returned, and he checked his mirrors and the southern perimeter. Clear for the moment. Opening his pack, he took out the tools and the Exacta camera. He wound the 35mm film back into its container and removed it from the camera. The plastic cartridge went into his pocket, and he looked for a moment at the camera. It's heavy and can slow me down, he thought. But it's from *Rear Window*! Making a command decision, he stowed the camera and long lens back into the waxed canvas bag and cinched it closed. He removed the peacoat and, using the sleeve, wiped down the steering wheel and the tools he left on the seat. Remembering his promise to Stefano, he took the work ID and shoved it in his pocket. A last check of the perimeter, and he slid out of the truck into the cold fog.

From the corner of the building he could see the line of the chain link fence at the perimeter of the camp, some forty yards across the expanse. Beyond that was a service road for the utility companies, and beyond that, the basin. He knew that the fence would likely have barbed wire at the top, so he prepped the peacoat. Moving in a low crouch, he zigzagged across the field, finding the small bits of cover—a barrel and a group of shrubs where he paused again to assess. The fence was some ten yards away and as predicted; barbed wire ran across the top of it.

He crossed the last of the camp and leaped onto the fence. Scrambling up it, he threw the thick cotton peacoat over the barbed wire. Then he slid over it to drop on the far side. A quick look back showed no activity, but looking up at the peacoat stuck to the barbed wire, he knew that when the sun rose in about an hour, the sentries would see his escape route. He moved across the service road toward the water. There he found a cluster of low, green brush, and he waded into the middle of it.

In the cover of the brush, he took a sighting across the basin. He knew roughly where he needed to go, but he couldn't tell for sure. His eyes scanned the horizon looking for something familiar, and then he realized there was a black hole in the watery black of the bay. *Double Rock!* He remembered seeing it from the Vellos' dock; they'd even pointed it out to him. Using that as his point of reference, Kats made a mental sighting of his target. He picked out a group of city lights on the hills behind it and began to strip off his clothes. He knew that he had only a few minutes before his body would seize up with hypothermia once he entered the frigid water, and clothes would only slow him down. Modesty kept him in his skivvies, and he slung the pack across his back and tightened the strap. He tore Stefano's ID into tiny pieces and set them adrift in the waters. Last, he took the film cartridge from his pants pocket and put it in his mouth. Taking a deep breath, he slid into the dark water.

Kats had swum in the bay before. More accurately, he'd been pushed into the bay during summer beach excursions. That had been cold, but this was the bay in January, at night. The cold hit him like an electric charge. Taking a quick look at his target lights, he began swimming. As a kid he was a good swimmer, but it had never been much of a priority until preparations for the Italian invasion had begun in full. Men were taught to swim with a full pack and a rifle. Most of the guys would initially panic as the water soaked their clothes and weighed them down. The trick was to remain calm and let your body's natural buoyancy help you float. Now Kats found himself taking about ten strokes, raising his head, and searching for the lights. He estimated that it was about half a mile to the Vellos' dock.

Rising again to take a sighting, he found Double Rock to his left and knew that the commercial channel was just ahead to his right. As he was about to dip his head and continue, the far-off whine of a motor carried across the water. Then over his head he saw a search light swing across the basin. He turned to see a patrol boat approaching around the tip of the base. He had no chance of making it to the channel before the boat arrived, and they'd surely spot him if he didn't move. With a sudden surge of adrenaline, he turned and sprinted toward the darkness of Double Rock some fifty yards away.

The patrol boat arrived in the basin just as Kats pulled himself out of the water and behind some rocky cover. He was panting and shivering at the same time. He hugged his arms around his legs, trying to find some warmth. The boat moved to the opening of the channel ahead, slowed its motor, and idled there for a few moments as its search light scanned the waters. Kats heard the motor gun, and the light swung toward him. He slid down into the tidal ditch behind the rocks, clutched the pack to his chest, and forced his twitching muscles to quiet themselves. He saw the light move overhead, linger on the larger of the two rocks above, and then move off. The motor churned, and the boat turned back toward the base. Kats lay there for few more moments before he allowed himself to unclench and look up at the retreating boat. As he did so, his body began to tremble uncontrollably. If my muscles stop trembling, I'm in trouble, he thought. His survival training had taught him that trembling was the body's way of trying to warm itself. When the muscles stopped trembling, you were likely too far gone and would succumb to the elements. He'd stories of men who had frozen to death but were found completely naked because their body's temperature regulators had ceased to function before they died. They couldn't tell they were freezing, and in their last moments of life thought they were hot.

He knew he had a few hundred more yards to swim, but before he would re-enter the water, he began to jump in place. Then he shadow boxed and shook out his arms. In a few moments, his heart rate was raised, and he felt better. Taking a sighting of the channel, he entered again into the frigid water.

Molly sat in the kitchen inside the office of the Vellos' boatyard. She and Anton had returned for the night shift change to no sign of Kats and were now truly worried. They'd return for the morning shift, and if Kats didn't show up, they'd have to have a serious discussion about next steps.

Around 1 am, she and Anton had walked out onto the dock and looked across the waters of the bay at the naval base in the distance. It looked both tantalizingly close yet far away at the same time. Be safe, Kats, she thought as she realized that her fists were tightly clenched at her sides. "Come inside. I'll make us some tea," Anton said as reassuringly as he could manage. That was several hours ago. Anton had slept for a bit on the office sofa, but Molly merely paced around the workshop and looked anxiously from the clock to the telephone.

Dawn is coming soon, she thought as she stepped onto the dock. She lit a cigarette and hugged herself against the cold and the rising feeling of dread. What if they captured him? What if they thought he was a spy? That thought made her wryly recognize that, technically speaking, he was a spy. And she and Anton, maybe even Shig, were part of a spy ring. I'm so far from Ohio, she thought.

She was about to go back inside when she heard something from the water. A fish maybe? She moved to the edge of the dock and looked down into the channel. There, on the ladder leading down into the water, was a shape. A man! "Kats!" she yelled and swung down onto the ladder. He looked up at her as she reached down and took his arm. He was ice cold to her touch. She tried to pull him upward, but neither of them had the strength to climb the ladder. Kats looked at her with half-closed eyes, and she knew he was fading. "Anton! Help!" she yelled into the night. Moments later, she heard Anton at the top of the ladder, and together they pulled Kats up and onto the dock.

"We've got to get him warm," Anton said as he rushed over to grab a canvas tarp that he threw over Kats. Molly slid under it and wrapped herself around him. His eyes were closed, and his lips were blue. She put her hands to his cold face to try to warm him. In his cheek, she felt something hard, and opening his mouth she pulled the film cannister out and handed it to Anton. "You did it, Kats. You made it back," she said. His eyes fluttered. "Mission accomplished, soldier." At that, his eyes opened, and a moment later they were able to focus. He smiled.

"Welcome back, Kats," Anton said over Molly's shoulder. Kats nodded. "What the hell were you doing there? That was crazy," he said.

Kats lay his head against Molly's chest and closed his eyes again. "Just training for my escape from Alcatraz."

CHAPTER 22

Kats awoke in an unfamiliar bed in an unfamiliar bedroom. He did recognize the red-haired woman cradled in his arm. As he shifted, she stretched and opened her eyes. "Hey," he said.

"Hey, yourself," she replied and kissed him. "We were so worried about you."

"Yeah, sorry about that, but something came up and I had to look into it. I didn't think I'd get another chance."

"What did you find?"

Kats made a long exhale, "Let's get Anton. You guys aren't going to believe this."

Sitting around the Vellos' breakfast table, Anton, Molly, and Shig, who'd arrived after Anton had called to update him, listened to Kats's recounting of the last twenty-four hours on Hunters Point. Their expressions moved from shock to anger and back to shock. "Fucking missiles?" Shig cried. All Kats could do was nod. Anton was quiet. Molly looked angry, and she spoke first.

"Who the hell is this guy Sand?"

"At first, I thought he was the representative of the investment group that has been backing Charles Construction. That explained why he was there in the warehouse when they had you two," Kats said. "But seeing him on the base with the admiral makes me believe he's government. Maybe military."

"And you're certain it was the same guy?" Anton asked.

"Positive."

"So the US government is funding Harry Charles?" Molly said. "Why would they do that?"

"Perhaps they're using Charles as their agent," Anton replied. "Seems likely that they'd use a shady character like him to do some shady business." Kats nodded in agreement.

"I can't believe the government and the navy would do something like this," Molly said.

"The government does all kinds of questionable things," Shig said knowingly. "They just don't get caught most of the time."

"But now we have this," Anton said as he placed the small film cartridge on the table.

"We've gotta get that developed," Shig said.

Kats stared at the cartridge. "Yes, but we can't just take that to the local photo lab. And anyone who helps us with developing that could also get in trouble."

"What about the newspaper?" Molly asked. "Surely, they'd want to break this kind of story."

"Maybe," Anton replied, "but we could still be in trouble for stealing and leaking military secrets."

"No, going to the press is the only real threat we have against the government. If we take it to the papers, we lose that leverage," Kats said, and they all nodded in agreement. "I think I know where we can get the film processed discretely."

"One of those private photo clubs over by Barbary Coast?" Shig said with a grin.

Molly made a loud snort and then covered her mouth with her hand, looking embarrassed. Kats and Shig looked at her, and her eyes went back and forth between them. "What?" she said.

"Something you want to share?" followed Shig, now truly interested.

"No. Not really."

"So, yes, kinda," Shig pressed.

"I, uh... Yeah, I know about those places."

Shig looked intently at her and merely tilted his head to the side, like a dog listening to a whistle. Even Anton was smiling.

"I did some modelling at one of them when I first got to town."

"What does this have to do with our problem?" interjected Kats.

"Absolutely nothing. Go on, Molly," Shig replied.

"It was just some cheesecake stuff. It was good money. The guys would come in with their own cameras, the girls would dress up in various costumes or swimsuits, and they'd photograph us. The studio had a darkroom in the basement that these guys could use to develop the prints."

Shig smiled approvingly.

"We're taking it to The California School of Fine Arts," Kats said loudly.

"CSFA? Why there?" Shig asked.

"Because Dorothea teaches there."

"Wow, that's right. I haven't seen her since..." Shig trailed off.

"Yeah, Minidoka. And then we saw her a few years ago at a show at that gallery. I think she can help."

"Who are you guys talking about?" Molly asked.

"An older woman from Kats's past," Shig said with a wink.

Molly's eyebrow cocked, and she looked at Kats.

"Don't listen to him," Kats said. "Dorothea is a photographer I met years ago. She was working for the War

Relocation Authority documenting internment. She took some photos of my family here in San Francisco and again in camp."

"She's actually kind of famous," Shig said with a smile.

"Yeah? Like how?"

"Dorothea Lange. You know that photo from the dust bowl of that Okie mother and her kids? The one where she's staring off into the distance with this grim look on her face?"

"Sure, that was on magazine covers and stuff," said Molly.

"It was called 'Migrant Mother,' and Dorothea took it. She also won a Guggenheim Fellowship," Shig said.

"And now she teaches at CSFA," finished Kats. From the office next door, the phone began to ring. Anton left, and they heard him answer the call.

"But you said she used to work for the WRA, right?" Molly asked. Shig nodded. "That's the government, Kats. She worked for the government. Can you trust her to help?"

"Dorothea always was a bit of a rebel and a progressive voice. All I can do is ask."

Anton appeared at the kitchen entrance, "We have a problem. Gianni is missing."

The drive headed down SR1 along the coast was one of the most beautiful in the country, but Gianni couldn't enjoy it. Lilly and little Carlo amused themselves that first day, singing songs and playing a never-ending game of Eye Spy, but his mind was elsewhere. And his arm hurt. They made it over 200 miles down the coast and then pulled into the lot of a motel on Morrow Bay, just outside of San Luis Obispo. There was a small pool, which was all Carlo cared about. As the boy swam, Lilly looked at her husband, concern written across her pretty face.

"Gianni, it's going to be OK," she said reassuringly. He looked at her, managed a thin smile, and squeezed her hand. He knew he had to get her and Carlo out of harm's way, but he was also ashamed of himself for not being there to stand with his brother. He was also ashamed of himself for noting that the hotel Lilly had booked for them in Pasadena was just a short drive from the Santa Anita Racetrack.

The next afternoon they arrived at the beautiful Huntington-Sheraton Hotel in Pasadena. The hotel had been the showcase of rail baron Henry E. Huntington and sported the first Olympic-sized swimming pool in California. Now owned by the Sheraton Corporation, the opulent resort had been Lilly's first choice for this important family trip. Gianni had to admit, it was beautiful, and Lilly and Carlo were thrilled. The next day, they lounged by the enormous pool, Gianni thinking Carlo would never be satisfied with a motel pool again. The day after, they made the trip to Disneyland. Carlo was mesmerized, and he and Lilly spent the day holding hands and chasing their son. It had been a wonderful day.

By the next morning, which they again spent poolside, Gianni was getting anxious. That nagging tickle at the back of his mind was again forcing its way into his consciousness. After lunch, he kissed Lilly and told her he wanted to get out and go for a drive. "Just to clear my head," he smiled. "I'll be back by dinner."

Thirty minutes later he found himself at Santa Anita Racetrack. The park was the home of the Santa Anita Derby, an annual springtime tune-up race for the Kentucky Derby. Today it was local action, and he grabbed a program, checked his watch, and settled in for the races. By 4 pm, he was down $100, more than half of what he'd allowed himself to bring.

The next race was the last of the day and his last chance to get even.

He scanned the race sheet again, feeling that added pressure but at the same time loving it. Favorites had been missing all day, so he decided to bet the exacta on two secondary horses. He thought for a moment to box the bet but said to himself that fortune favors the bold! Throwing down the last of his money at the window, he collected the ticket and made his way back to the track as the race began.

A mile and a quarter later, Gianni threw up his hands and shouted with the crowd, "Yes!" He felt his heart pounding in his chest, and he was smiling. That sweet, sweet feeling of winning was a rush. Better than booze, maybe even better than sex, and he breathed it in because it had been a while since it had visited him. He gathered himself and headed to the window to collect his winnings. In his head he was doing the math and thought he'd just about paid for this little family vacation from that one race. Maybe he could get back here one more time before things cleared up back home and they had to leave.

He handed over his ticket, and the cashier counted out $1,800. He smiled and winked at her, thinking this was a good day. That thought lasted nearly five whole minutes. As he headed back toward his car, he saw a man standing near it, smoking a cigarette. As he approached, the man, black hair slicked back, turned and looked directly at him, "Hey, Gianni." Gianni stopped some fifteen feet short of him. He turned quickly to run back but was surprised by two more men coming up behind him.

"Where ya, goin?" the black-haired man said sarcastically. The two trailing men grabbed Gianni by the arms and brought him forward to face the apparent leader. The black-haired man reached into Gianni's breast pocket and pulled out the wad of cash. "Looks like it was your lucky day," he said.

Gianni scowled back at him, "Doesn't feel so lucky now," he said.

Black hair smiled and nodded. "Well, we have some other business to take care of, too.

Get him in the car."

Gianni instinctively stiffened and resisted, which made black hair step forward and put a finger in his face. "We can do this easy or hard. You wanna ride in the trunk or the back seat? Or maybe you want us to go pay a visit to the Huntington Hotel and say hi to your family?" Gianni's eyes widened in fear, and he shook his head no.

"Good. Then get your ass in the car." Black hair took Gianni's car keys and tossed them to one of his men. "You follow us" he ordered.

The two cars moved through the late-afternoon traffic, heading west toward Burbank. Franco wondered how people managed in this sprawling city, and he missed the tight confines of San Francisco. They pulled into the Pacific Breeze Hotel and brought Gianni into their two adjoining rooms. "Sit," Franco said with enough menace that Gianni sullenly complied.

"Watch him. I'm gonna go call the boss," he said to his men. He left just as they turned on the TV. Franco headed to the hotel lobby and the small bank of phone booths to make his call. Closing the door, he reached into his pocket and dumped a handful of change onto the small metal ledge. Inserting the coins, he dialed, and moments later a woman's voice answered.

"Yeah, sweetheart, it's Franco. Put him on." Moments later Harry's voiced blasted through the receiver.

"You got him?"

"Good afternoon to you, too. Yeah, I got him."

"Don't start that shit with me. This should have been handled weeks ago. Now you just gotta get him back here so we can renegotiate that shitty deal with Lanza."

"We'll hit the road in the morning."

"Yeah, fine. Just get him here tomorrow." Harry hung up.

Franco listened to the dial tone for a moment and then hung up. He walked across the lobby to the bar and ordered a double scotch. Not the expensive stuff Harry had acquired a taste for, just good, old-fashioned, feel-it-in-your-balls scotch. He sat there drinking the amber liquid. Feeling the burn down his throat, he was a man wrestling with a decision. He threw some cash on the bar and walked back to the phones. Slamming the door behind him, he pulled a piece of paper from his jacket pocket and dialed the phone number written there.

"Yeah, tell him it's Franco."

A few moments later, a friendly male voice came on, "*Buona sera*, Salvatore."

CHAPTER 23

"Hold for the general," said the female voice on the other end of the phone. Kats sat in his office, happy that two days of calls and callbacks had finally brought him to this point. A moment later, the line clicked. "Hello, Kats. Happy New Year!" came the unmistakable voice that most Americans, at least those who had been to a movie in the past twenty years, could identify.

"Happy New Year, Jim, or should I say 'general,'" Kats replied. Jimmy Stewart, actor and brigadier general in the US Air Force,[8] laughed and then said, "No need to salute. How's the PI business?"

"Well, that's actually why I'm calling," Kats began. Then over the next twenty minutes, he relayed the events of the past several weeks to his friend. When he came to the part about his excursion onto the naval base, he was particularly delicate, knowing that Stewart, despite their friendship, was an officer in the air force and a lifelong Republican. He didn't mention the underground complex or the mysterious Sand and the admiral. But he laid out the information about the environmental contamination and the likelihood that his client had died of cancer caused by that exposure. Stewart took it all in and quietly said, "That's quite a story. One that frankly makes me angry."

"I'm sorry, Jim. I didn't want to put you in a tough situation..." Kats began.

"No, I'm not angry with you or anything like that. It makes me angry when we as a service or as a country don't live up to our ideals. We should be better than that."

"Well, I'm glad to hear you say that because now I'm definitely going to put you in a tough situation." Kats explained that he needed to find out what had happened at Hunters Point a few years ago and why they were trying to acquire land around the area to cover that activity up.

Stewart was quiet for a moment. "Kats, this could be classified information we're talking about here."

"I know."

"And you know I'm a commissioned officer. A general for God's sake."

"I know, and I'm sorry to make this ask, but we have very few options, and I truly believe peoples' lives are at risk."

"Hmmmm... you know if you weren't a former solider, I don't think I could help you. But I know your service, so let me look into it."

"Thank you, Jim."

"Don't thank me yet. I'll look into it and we can go from there."

"We'll stand by."

Across the street, two men sat in a dark sedan watching Kats's office. One of them exited the passenger side of the car and walked to the corner where a phone booth was nestled next to a flower shop. He dialed the number from memory and waited. The line clicked on. "Yes?"

"He's here. What do you want us to do?"

"Stay there. I'm on my way."

Kats heard the front door of the office open as he was in the back. Must be Mrs. Harada here to clean, he thought. He stepped out into the office to say hello only to find the mysterious Mr. Sand standing there, looking about the simple room. Kats fought to keep the surprise off his face and out of his voice as he said, "Can I help you?"

Sand smiled and looked at him with cool eyes. There was nothing imposing about the man except his eyes when they focused on you. Like a bird of prey, thought Kats.

"Mr. Takemoto. Nice to finally meet you. My name is Sand."

Kats said nothing but gestured to the chair in front of his desk for Sand to sit. He took his own seat, "Have you been looking for me?"

"Well, it feels that way. Certainly, it seems like we're circling each other lately."

"How's that?"

"You have a client in Bayview Heights."

"I'm really not at liberty to say."

"Oh, don't play coy with me, Mr. Takemoto. I know all about you. And your client. And your friends." That was a threat, thought Kats.

"You're a decorated soldier. Silver Star for Bravery in France. Youngest son. Two older sisters: one in Chicago, and one in Washington, DC. Parents returned to Japan four years ago."

"Five actually."

"They never applied for citizenship after the McCarron-Walter Act of 1952. They could have become citizens but never did. But they might want to visit their children here in the States. It would be a shame if they ended up on the wrong list."

Not sure my father wants to visit, but my mother is another case, Kats thought.

"Your PI license is subject to renewal in a year. I'm sure you'd like to get that renewed. You're friends with Shig Murao. His federal obscenity charges were dropped last summer, but they could be reinstated. We may lose, but how much will it cost him in time, money, and even reputation? Molly Hayes. Did you know there's a warrant out for Miss Hayes back in Ohio? She may not even know it. Her ex-husband filed assault charges. And don't even get me started on the things the IRS can do to people."

Kats waited patiently for the real conversation to begin. All this was preamble to whatever Sand really wanted to say, so he waited for the posturing to pass.

For Sand, a bit surprised that the usual stuff wasn't seeming to have an effect, pressed further.

"What about espionage, Mr. Takemoto? There was an incident out on the point a few nights ago. I'd hate to see a decorated veteran brought up on charges of spying."

"An incident?" he replied neutrally.

Now Sand realized he was talking too much and giving away his position. He caught himself and sat back in the chair. Time to counterattack, thought Kats.

"What about kidnapping, Mr. Sand?" he began.

"I don't know anything about kidnapping," Sand replied nonchalantly.

"Gianni Vello is missing. The people you're working with kidnapped him. They may hurt him. They may kill him." No response.

"How about extortion?"

"Please, Mr. Takemoto. When we want to do something, we don't extort. We just do it."

"Except when you don't want people to know it's you doing it."

Silence. *Touché.*

"Someone has been moving pieces around like a chess

board. Harry Charles. The Lanza crime family. The city itself.
Sure, it looks like Harry Charles is behind it, but Charles isn't
smart enough to pull all this off. He's a hammer. A tool being
wielded by another hand. Perhaps your hand, Mr. Sand."

"Here's what I know," Kats said, sitting forward. "Hunters
Point has been leaking radioactive contamination for years."

"Yes," Sand said casually. "We told the public about the
contamination following the clean-up from Operation
Crossroads. The *USS Independence* was brought in for study,
and it did leak some radioactive contaminants. We moved
the ship offshore and scuttled it.[9] Any residual contamination
is just that. Part of a small accident that occurred years ago."

"Yes, that's what your official report said. What about
the real report?"

"The real report is the one we say is the real report, Mr.
Takemoto. Don't you realize that? We give people the truth
that they want. They want to believe that nuclear power is
safe and will make them safe. They want to believe that we're
strong and will keep them safe from the Russians. They want
to believe that we're winning the Cold War. They want to
go to work, raise their kids, and watch *Lucy* on TV."

Sand sat back, crossing his legs, "And do you know how
many jobs Hunters Point provides? Not just military jobs
but civilian jobs. If you were to cause the base to close, even
for a short time, the economic repercussions to the city, the
region, would be huge. Believe it or not, Mr. Takemoto,
we're trying to protect people in Bayview Heights."

"How does a stadium in Bayview Heights protect people?"
Keep him talking, thought Kats.

"What's the matter? Aren't you a baseball fan, Mr.
Takemoto?"

"I love baseball, but I'm more of a Yankees fan than a

Giants fan."

"Well, think about the jobs. Thousands of jobs created by the building of the stadium. Then ongoing operations, concessions, transportation."

"Who do you work for, the chamber of commerce?"

"Hardly," Sand replied with a twitch of annoyance.

"Alright, Mr. Takemoto. I'll share a thought with you. Now this is purely hypothetical, you understand."

"Of course," Kats replied sardonically.

"If, and I do say again, *if* there was some kind of contamination around Hunters Point, it would behoove us to get residents and businesses away from that, would it not?"

"Unless you were completely evil, heartless bastards, yes it would."

"We're not complete bastards, Mr. Takemoto."

That remains to be seen, thought Kats, but he nodded for Sand to continue.

"So if one were able to move people and businesses out and set up an operation that takes up a large plot of land, is surrounded by a sea of asphalt and unused green space, that might be a nice buffer zone, eh? And what if people didn't live in the area but only visited there, say, at most 77 times per year?"

Kats immediately did the math; a baseball season was 154 games, half of which would be at home. Genius.

"How did you get the Giants to move?"

"Surprisingly easy. Professional sports have always been a business, but ever since the war, they've become big business. Teams aren't beholden to their longtime fans. They're whores. They follow the money. They followed it right where we led them." Sand caught himself, "Hypothetically, of course."

The two men stared at each other, saying nothing. But a grudging appreciation for the other's wit passed between them.

"What do you want from me?" Kats asked.

"I want you to go away. You and your friends. I want you to find something else to do. Go write poetry with Mr. Vello. I don't care. Just get out of our way and keep your silence. Or don't and, well… There are others who are less patient than I am. Others who only see this in pecuniary terms."

"And you don't?"

"I actually want to protect people, Mr. Takemoto, but to do that, I need them to move out of the way."

"That may be your objective, Sand, but your partners aren't concerned about hurting people. If they hurt Gianni or any others, I'll take you down."

"You don't even know who I am, Mr. Takemoto," Sand said as he rose and put on his hat. "Best you never find out either."

Kats watched the door close behind Sand, and he sat there for a moment, sitting back in his chair. He reached out with his right hand and opened the top drawer of the desk. He removed the film cannister and held it in front of his face, eyeing it with a new purpose.

CHAPTER 24

The California School of Fine Art had been established in the city nearly 100 years before, and the small, private art school had developed a reputation for excellence in many disciplines. One of those was fine art photography. The program had begun in 1945 with the hiring of Ansel Adams to head the department. He brought in a series of all-star lecturers and faculty, including the woman in whose office foyer Kats now sat.

Dorothea Lange was an award-winning photographer and photojournalist. She was a Guggenheim Fellow, co-founder of *Aperture* magazine, and an old friend. Kats would always remember the day he met her because that day was, in many ways, the worst day of his life.

It was April 16, 1942, on Van Ness Avenue, not far from where he sat now. Kats, several months shy of eighteen, along with his mother, father, two older sisters, and 110,000 others of Japanese ancestry, had been ordered to assemble for "relocation" out of the newly created West Coast Exclusionary Zone. They'd been given two weeks to reduce their lives down to two suitcases each. Houses had to be sold or boarded up, businesses liquidated, family pets given away or put down. In some ways, the Takemotos were lucky. Their home in Japantown was paid for, and Kats's father had transferred the deed to his American-born son. They made arrangements with the local bank to provide a caretaker to check in regularly. There was money for the taxes, and Kats's father, Shuzo, had optimistically said, "This will only be for a short time. They'll see that we're good Americans." The rest of the family wasn't so sure.

Standing on Van Ness in front of a tire store, Kats dumbly looked around, not fully registering what was happening. The older folks, most dressed in their best clothes, looked like they were going to church. The children played and were excited to not be in school. It was like everyone was in denial about what was really going on, and it made Kats want to scream. From behind, he heard the click of a camera shutter. He turned and was surprised to see a middle-aged White woman behind the camera. A hot flush of anger rose in him. *My family is herded off like criminals, and this hakujin is taking pictures.*[10] Their eyes locked for a moment, and just as he was turning away he heard her say, "I'm sorry."

He turned back and looked at her again. "Sorry about what?" he asked sharply. "Sorry about taking the picture, or sorry about all of this?" he said, waving his arms. "Sorry the whole world has gone to fucking hell?"

She lowered the camera. She was an experienced photo-journalist by this time. She'd documented the Great Depression and had seen poverty, desperation, and sadness. But this feels different, she thought. This was Americans turning on other Americans. They may look different and come from other places, but seeing these families, especially these kids, she could only see the injustice of it all. This is us acting out of fear. So she did something that photojournalists weren't supposed to do. She talked to her subject. One angry, young Nisei boy.

"I'm sorry about all of it. I'm sorry that America isn't living up to its own ideals." She looked around. "This isn't right."

Kats felt his anger recede. "Why are you here?"

"I'm working for the War Relocation Authority to document this... process."

"Trophy photos for politicians?"

"Not the way I'm shooting it. I see the commonality between all of us. I see the humanity and the patriotism on display. That is what I'm seeing in my lens. And hopefully when the powers that be see my images, they'll see what I see."

Kats nodded.

"What's your name?" she asked.

"Katsuhiro Takemoto," he said. "But everybody calls me Kats."

"I'm Dorothea. Dorothea Lange." She extended a hand and stepped forward. Kats noticed that she dragged her right leg and limped when she walked. He stepped forward too and shook her hand. She noticed him staring at her leg. "Polio." He nodded. They both knew too many people who'd been impacted by that disease.

"Can you help me, Kats? Can you tell me a bit about some of these people so I can better understand them and better tell their stories?"

"I can try."

"Good. Because I use this…" she held up the camera, "to teach people how to see without a camera.[11] And they need to see this."

For the next two hours, Kats walked with her among the crowd. He knew many of the people and shared their names with Dorothea and what he knew about them. There was the Matsumoto family. The father was a dentist, Kats's dentist in fact. Their son Peter[12] was a good baseball player. The Ashizawa family owned the hardware store in Japantown.[13] The Morozumis had a bakery. Dorothea took it all in, though Kats wasn't sure how all this helped her tell the story.

As the buses were finally loaded and the convoy prepped to leave, Dorothea had turned to Kats and thanked him. She offered him some cash, but he said no. She shook his hand and said, "Be strong. You, your family, all of you will get through this. I've seen the resilience and strength of people. You'll get through this."

Kats nodded, and a wave of emotions that he'd been fighting back all day washed over him. He felt his face flush. "I'm scared," he said quietly. Dorothea stepped forward and hugged him, and he embraced her back, feeling tears on his cheeks.

"It's OK to be scared. We're all scared right now. Don't let fear define you. Fear makes people do the wrong thing, like all this," she gestured. "Real strength is being scared and still doing the right thing."

Wiping his face, Kats nodded and walked toward his bus.

He waved to her and stepped on board, thinking he'd never see her again. He was wrong.

He heard the office door open, and out stepped a young woman. "Hi, I'm Linda. I'm Professor Lange's assistant." Kats stood and shook her hand, and she gestured for him to sit. "When was the last time you saw her?"

"Maybe five years ago at a gallery opening," he thought out loud, "The King Ono?"

"The King Ubu," she smiled. "Yes, that was opened by several of our faculty. Well, since then she's been dealing with some health issues. The doctors say it's related to the polio she had as a child."

"What's wrong with her?"

"She gets tired easily and she has lost a lot of strength. She gets around pretty well. She still teaches, and she's the professor that freshmen don't want to get, but seniors love her."

"Sounds about right," he smiled.

"Just thought you should know that before going in. But please... she's excited to see you."

Kats knocked and entered the sunny office that was lit by a large bay window behind the desk at which she sat. Dramatic backlight, he thought. As he entered, Dorothea slowly rose and came around the desk.

"Katsuhiro," she said and extended her arms.

He quickly stepped forward so that she didn't have far to walk. "Professor," he smiled as he hugged her. He could tell she was thinner than she'd been a few years before. Though she was in her early sixties, she seemed older. She gestured for him to sit, and they eyed each other across her cluttered desk.

"You look good," she said. "Are you happy?"

He smiled at the unconventional question. It was so un-Japanese to ask. "I have friends. I have good work. I have..." he thought of Molly.

"Someone?" she explored. "It's good to have someone, Kats."

"Yes, it is. How's your husband, the professor?" he asked.

"Paul is very well and getting closer to retirement," she said. Kats knew he was a prominent economist over at UC Berkeley. "He keeps trying to get me to teach at Berkeley. He knows the commute here twice a week is hard, but I love it here. San Francisco is my adopted home."

For the next ten minutes they chatted about life, politics, work, and family. His eyes scanned the comfortable, cluttered space. He noted on one shelf, in a simple black frame, was a print of Dorothea's most famous image *Migrant Mother*. Her eyes followed his, and she nodded. "Yes, my baby," she said. "I have a complex relationship with her. I never even knew her name, you know. In my notes, it just said something like migrant mother, thirty-two years old.[14] That's true of so many of the images I took. A moment in time, a moment in the life of that person. One of millions. But if you capture the right moment, that moment and, in a way, that life, goes on forever."

"That's a beautiful thought," he said.

"She's also the first line in my obituary."

He frowned, "What are you talking about?"

"She's my most famous image. I've shot thousands, proba-bly millions, of images, but that's the one that will be printed next to my obituary. After that image came out and it got all the attention... at first it was great. But after a while, I really resented that image because it became how people defined me. I've done other things I wanted to tell them, but they always came back to that image. As I've gotten older, I see that how others define you is less important than how you define yourself. I'm proud of her," she nodded toward the photo, "but she doesn't define me."

Kats smiled and marveled at the amazing artist, the amazing person she was. He thought back upon their strange journey to this place. It had been one day in early 1943 when a group of visitors had come to Minidoka. The camp was quietly buzzing because there were government officials visiting there. Some thought it meant something important. Others simply thought they were inspecting the prison they'd created, but everyone was curious. Kats and a group of other young men had watched intently at a distance when his sharp eyes fell upon a photographer with the group. A woman.

He moved closer but the armed guards escorting the visitors kept him from getting too close. There she was—the same woman photographer he'd met almost a year ago. What was her name? Dorothy? Something like that, and he doubted she'd even remember him. It had been an awful day for him and his family, and she was just there doing a job. He watched as she sighted through her camera, taking shot after shot. Then she stood and scanned the base, and as her eyes passed over his location, she stopped and stared at him. She moved forward, pushing past the guards, and approached him.

"Your name is Kats, right?" she asked with a smile.

"And you're Dorothy," he said a bit hesitantly.

"Dorothea. Yeah. Wow, you remember."

"I remember."

"So this is where you and your family ended up," she said, looking around. Kats followed her gaze, realizing that this cold camp in the middle of Idaho was his home.

"Want to help me again? I'm here following up for the WRA, and I'd love to get your insight again."

"Sure," he replied, and though the guard eyed him, Dorothea put an arm around his shoulder, and they walked through the camp. She captured image after image, and he did his best to explain what life was like for them in camp. He introduced her to his family and friends, including a young Shig Murao, in the camp library. At the end of the day, what had been intended by the officials as a perfunctory visit had become a deep dive into the reality of internment. Years later, Kats would see those images and be shocked that so many of the children were smiling and adults looked dignified even in the midst of ramshackle barracks. It truly was an example of strength and resilience.

"Write down your name here," she said, handing him a small leather-bound notebook from her bag. He did so, and she handed him her WRA-issued card. "I suspect we might see each other again someday."

They'd seen each other again, though it would be nearly ten years later. Kats had seen a story in the *San Francisco Chronicle* about the emerging "Beat" art scene in North Beach. The story highlighted several established artists who were helping that movement, and there was Dorothea's name as a teacher at CSFA and one of the elder statesmen to these young artists. They mentioned the upcoming opening of a new gallery, the King Ubu, and Kats thought it would be interesting to go. Because he knew very little about modern art or poetry, he recruited Shig to go with him.

The space was packed, and they mostly kept to the perimeter, observing the patrons who were obviously familiar with each other. Dorothea arrived a bit late, making an entrance with her husband. The gallery founders greeted her like a

VIP, which Kats supposed she was. As the crowd slowly parted, she looked around and saw Kats standing there with a smile. She immediately came over, pushed aside Kats's extended hand, and gave him a hug. It had been a wonderful night. They'd spent the next hour or so catching up, and she introduced him to the gallery founders who were also faculty at CSFA. Kats reintroduced her to Shig. They exchanged contact information and promised that it would not be years before their next meeting.

Three days later, Kats was surprised by a courier delivery to his office. He opened the roughly 12-inch-by-12-inch package and found himself staring at his own image. The framed photograph was of him, from that fateful day in April 1942, when he and his family had reported for relocation. He stood, holding his two suitcases, looking over his right shoulder. His young face was anxious as he looked toward an uncertain future. Kats recalled that was the moment when he had heard the camera shutter and turned to see Dorothea standing there. He stared at the photograph for a long time.[15]

Now, sitting in her office, Kats was sorry he hadn't come to see her just because she was his friend, and he made a promise to himself that he'd do so. But today he very much needed her help and hoped that he wasn't pushing that friendship with his ask.

"I need your help, Dorothea. I'm working on a case that's gotten very big and very scary."

"Well, I love a good detective story."

He pulled the film cannister from his pocket. "I need your help with this."

She smiled and said, "You know the drug store will develop that for you?"

"What's on here can't be seen by a drug store employee. Or a newspaper. It probably shouldn't be seen even by you, but I don't know who else to turn to."

"What's on that, Katsuhiro?"

"Secrets. Secrets that some powerful people don't want disclosed. Secrets that could get you, me, and my friends in trouble."

"And what will you do with these photos?"

"Try to make things right for some people who have been victims of government secrets and didn't even know it."

She looked at the cannister and at him. "You know I've worked for the government many times during my career. Proudly worked for them." He nodded. "But I've also seen the government do terrible things. What they did, no, what *we* did to you and your family and all the other Japanese Americans is just one example. So maybe helping you can square that ledger a bit." She smiled at him, "Let's go find a darkroom."

Kats helped Dorothea to the outer office, and her assistant Linda told her that the main darkroom was currently open. They walked slowly to the basement where it was located. Entering the room, Dorothea turned off the main lights and flicked on the red light that bathed the room in an eerie glow. Dorothea seemed to come alive in this familiar environment, and her movements became stronger and more purposeful. She was clearly in her element as she checked the chemicals and the equipment before beginning.

She began the familiar process of exposure followed by chemical bath steps that she'd done thousands of times. "You know it's been a while since I developed any film. But I've always loved the process. People think that the art of photography happens the moment you snap the image. That's only half of it. It's in here that you truly find the image and bring it out of darkness and into light. And to life."

Kats knew he was watching a master at work and was smart enough to just get out of her way. As they were looking over the prints in the washing process, it became evident what Kats had shot. There were military men, including a couple of good close-ups of them. But it was the images of the submarine, the base, and the missiles that made Dorothea whistle. "What have you gotten into, Kats?"

"That's what I'm trying to piece together."

In the glowing red light, he could tell she was thinking about something. "You have an idea?" he asked.

"There's someone here at CSFA that might be able to explain this stuff to you."

"What kind of artist knows about atomic submarines and missiles?"

"The kind of artist who used to be a nuclear scientist."

She walked to the phone hanging on the wall and dialed a number.

"Linda, yes. Can you see if Jess Collins is around today? Yeah, call me back in Dark One. Thanks."

"Is this someone we can trust?" he asked skeptically.

"Well, I trust him. He's no fan of this arms race madness we seem to be in. You actually met him several years ago. Jess was one of the founders of the King Ubu gallery. He worked on the Manhattan Project before becoming disillusioned with these weapons and focusing on art."[16]

The phone rang, and Dorothea answered it. "Yes? Excellent. Can you ask him to come down here and keep it quiet? Thanks."

Kats and Dorothea stepped outside the darkroom, and several minutes later a slender young man in his thirties, short brown hair matched by thick brown eyebrows, came walking down the corridor. He waved gently at Dorothea.

"Good afternoon, Jess," she said. "I'm glad you were on campus today."

"Robert and I are working on a new project together, so I'm over here a lot lately."

"Jess this is an old, special friend of mine, Katsuhiro."

"Everyone calls me Kats," he said, extending his hand.

"And everyone just calls me Jess. Nice to meet you. Was there something you wanted to show me?" Jess asked as he pointed toward the darkroom door.

"Well, yes," began Dorothea, "but first we need to talk about it." She gestured toward the benches in the hallway. Sitting, she continued.

"As I said, Kats is a very dear friend. He's also a private detective." Jess's bushy eyebrows raised at that, but he said nothing.

"I've been investigating some events in Bayview Heights and Hunters Point."

"The naval base," Jess said.

"Yes, and I found out some things that I don't fully understand but I think are troubling."

"But?"

"But the means by which I found them out are..."

"Illegal?"

"In a word, yes."

Jess looked at Dorothea. "Are you involved in this, too?"

"Mostly after the fact, but I believe there are some very concerning things going on out there. Knowing what I know about your background and your stance against the military, I was hoping you might look at some photos."

Jess was quiet, and Kats could tell he was wrestling with some internal struggle. He waited patiently, knowing those internal battles couldn't be rushed.

"I was in the army," Jess finally began. "The Corps of Engineers. They drafted me out of CalTech. I'm not against the military," he said emphatically. "I worked on the Manhattan Project, making plutonium for atomic bombs. But seeing what those bombs did, and knowing I had a hand in that, made me start to question the direction of all that research. I had dreams—nightmares, really—about the end of the world. So I quit. Decided I'd rather paint and make art, maybe use that to make the world a little better. But I'm not against the military."

"Sorry, I didn't mean to paint you in that light," Dorothea said.

"Well, I'm also not a fan of unchecked authority. Show me what you've got."

As they moved around the photographs, still hanging and drying in the lab, Jess would stop, furrow his eyebrows, and twist his mouth in an expression of concern. Finally, Kats could take no more and asked, "Well, what do you see there?"

"That's the *Nautilus*. Doesn't take a nuclear scientist to tell you that because that sub has been all over the news for the past couple of years. But that facility it's in…"

"An underground submarine pen at Hunters Point," Kats said.

"I'd never heard anything about that. Most likely no one has. But the real concerns are these," he said while pointing to a photo in front of them. "These are ballistic missiles."

"Like long-range missiles?" Kats asked. "Like the German V2 rockets?"

"The V2 was a bottle rocket compared to where the technology has gone today. What's interesting is that these appear to be designed for installation in a submarine. I still have friends in the industry and have heard talk about this new program. They call it submarine-launched ballistic missiles. They built an atomic sub to carry the next generation of atomic warheads right to the doorstep of the Russians."

"Is that illegal?" Dorothea asked.

"No. But the thought of more and more of these types of weapons is terrifying. And it certainly is troubling to have a secret base with nuclear weapons so close to the city."

"Do these weapons and ships leak radioactivity?" Kats asked.

"Well, no containment system is 100% effective, but for the most part, labs and manufacturing facilities like we had for Manhattan are very secure. I can't say about this nuclear submarine. I certainly hope it's safe." He pointed to the photo of the officer and civilian outside the windowless building.

"See here," he pointed to the men's chests. "That little badge they're wearing... that's a dosimeter. It measures exposure to radiation. We all wore them when I was working on the Manhattan Project. This means the entire building is part of whatever work they're doing."

Jess paused. "See, that's the thing about nuclear energy and this whole atomic age we live in. It's been painted as this amazing technology and power source that will light our homes and keep democracy safe. People love it. But they don't understand it. They don't understand how powerful the weapons have become. The hydrogen bombs in our arsenal and the Russian arsenal are thousands of times more powerful than the bombs dropped on Japan. People can't even begin to comprehend the destructive power each side has. They don't understand the radioactive waste that's produced in the making of these bombs. That waste remains deadly for thousands of years. Thousands! Where are we going to put all that? The government wants to paint a pretty picture about all of this, but the reality should terrify people."

They sat in silence for a few moments, letting that thought sink in.

"Dorothea, it's always a pleasure to see you. I imagine we won't speak of this again?"

"Probably not. Thank you, Jess."

"Yes, thank you, Jess," Kats said, shaking the man's hand. Jess nodded, "Good luck." and he left them.

"What are you going to do now, Kats?"

"Jess confirmed what I'd feared. But at least now I have the images to make the powers that be do the right thing."

"What's the right thing, Kats? I worked for the government for years at the WPA documenting programs to help the farmers in the Dust Bowl. That was a good thing. I also worked for the government to document what they did to you and your family. That was wrong, but most Americans went along with it because they were scared. Frightened people are more likely to compromise what they believe in, in exchange for security. People are scared of that Russian satellite. They're scared of communists in the government, in the universities, even in Hollywood of all places. So showing them something they believe is there to protect them isn't likely to bother them."

Kats thought about her words. Would the public care that there was a secret military base at Hunters Point? Would they care if it was contaminating the area so long as it provided a nuclear umbrella they thought would protect them? Especially since it was Bayview Heights, a part of town that was largely neglected and ignored because its residents were the least powerful in the city. His whole plan now seemed a pointless exercise, some Quixotic notion of justice that almost no one would care about.

"You once told me not to let fear define me and that real strength is being scared and still doing the right thing."

"Sounds like something I'd say," she laughed.

"Well, maybe we can use the threat of taking it public to make them do the right thing, at least for Anton and his family and those folks in Bayview Heights."

CHAPTER 25

Kats arrived at his office to find a telegram slipped through the mail slot of his front door.

> *K. Found your story. Need to see you. Ticket waiting SFO on American for Friday. 918 N. Roxbury, Beverly Hills. — J.*

Day after tomorrow. He picked up the phone and dialed Anton. A moment later, the man picked up. "Yes?" came his anxious voice.

"Sorry, Anton. It's Kats." He knew the young man was on edge, waiting to hear something about his brother. So far there had been nothing, which was almost worse for the family.

"It's OK. I thought it might be Lilly with some news."

"I wanted to ask about Lilly. You'd said she didn't want to leave in case Gianni came back."

"Yeah, but she's been worn out by all this. She really needs to get back here to family."

"Well, how about I collect her and bring her home?"

"Really?"

"Yeah, I have to go to LA on Friday. My contact has some information that might help us, and I could go and get her afterward and bring her home."

"That would be fantastic. Thank you."

"OK. Just call her and let her know I'll be there sometime later Friday afternoon. And can you get her and Carlo plane tickets on American back from LAX?"

"Will do. Is Molly going with you?"

"I know she'll want to come, but my contact might be a little sensitive about a new face in the room. Can you keep an eye on her for a few more days?"

"Of course. You really think Charles might try to grab her again?"

"Not likely, but he's probably getting desperate, and desperate people make unpredictable decisions. I'll bring her down to you on Friday morning on my way to the airport."

Friday morning was gray and cold as they headed south from Japantown. Molly was quiet, and he could tell she was disappointed about not being able to go with him. She at least said she understood. Kats had packed light, not planning on being there overnight, but a change of clothes went into his shoulder bag along with a manila envelope that contained a dozen black-and-white photos that he knew he might need to show his friend. Then I have to explain how I got them, he frowned.

The docks behind the Vellos' workshop were being cleaned and repaired from the fire, but progress was still being made on the boats in their slips. Anton may want to be a poet, but he's showing surprising skill and leadership in the boatbuilding arena, Kats thought. The young man stood on the dock holding a cup of steaming coffee as he spoke to one of the craftsmen in what Kats thought must be Maltese.

"Good morning, Anton," he said.

Molly gave Anton a hug, "How are you holding up?" she asked.

"Better than Lilly, but I'm worried. Thank you again for collecting her, Kats."

"I should be back late tonight. Tomorrow at the latest."

He turned to Molly, "Stay out of trouble," he said with a smile, but meaning it.

"You, too," she replied, also meaning it. She kissed him.

Sixty minutes later Kats sat aboard the American Airlines DC7 as it taxied out of the gate toward the runway. Minutes after takeoff, the four turbo prop engines carried the airliner above the signature San Francisco cloud cover and into a bright sunny sky. Not usually one to wax poetically, Kats thought of the myriad shades of gray that made up San Francisco. Seems like so many of its people were shades of gray as well. Not wholly light, not wholly dark, but complex mixtures of both. Closing his eyes, he thought it best to leave the poetry to Anton.

Two hours later, just after noon, he was walking through sun-filled LAX airport in search of a cab. He grabbed a big yellow Checker cab and slid into the back seat.

"Beverly Hills, please. 918 North Roxbury," he said.

"Fancy neighborhood, pal," said the cab driver. "That's where the movie stars live."

"That's what I hear."

Driving down the tree-lined road, Kats looked back and forth at the beautiful houses along the way. Some were veritable mansions, and others were smaller and more modest. All were immaculately tended. The cab slowed to a stop in front of an English Tudor style home. Two floors with trees in front and a stone entranceway. You wouldn't know that a huge movie star lived here. That's probably the way Jim wants it.

Walking up the stone pathway, he approached the heavy

door and rang the bell. Moments later he heard footsteps and the door swung open. "Hello, Kats!" Stewart said with a genuine smile.

"Hi, Jim. Thanks so much for seeing me." They shook hands, and Stewart waved him inside. Kats wasn't sure what he had expected of Stewart's home, but what struck him the most was how normal it seemed. Of course, the home was beautiful, but it looked well lived in, as one would expect of a family with four children. Comfortable and laid back, just like Jim, he thought.

"Gloria is shopping, and the kids are at school," Stewart said as he led them into the kitchen. "How about some lunch?"

"Sure," Kats replied and watched as Stewart puttered about the kitchen making ham sandwiches. They ate and talked of small things, including the latest on Hitchcock's movie and Jim's next film. Kats knew that they were dancing around the real conversation to come. Surprisingly Japanese, he thought.

During a pause in the small talk, Stewart looked pointedly at Kats and shook his head. "You..." he searched for the words. "You have stirred up a hornet's nest." Kats nodded but said nothing. "Let's go out to the garden," Stewart said.

The backyard was much bigger than the front yard would suggest. Stewart had purchased the extra lot in part for privacy but more so that he could indulge his passion for gardening. And the garden was beautiful. Flowers, trees, and shrubbery that looked well tended but not overly so the way many European gardens looked. To Kats's eye, the backyard was an idyllic retreat from the hectic life of a public figure.

"This is beautiful, Jim. You have a talent for gardening."

"Well, I can afford some very talented help," said the always modest star. "I do love it out here, though." As they walked, Stewart turned serious. "I did some digging into what we talked about," he said gravely. "I don't like what I found, but what I found is also classified material."

"I wouldn't ask if it wasn't important."

"And I wouldn't share this and compromise national security for just anyone. You see, I did some research on you, too."

Kats simply nodded.

"I knew you'd served. I knew about the 442nd and their exploits. That was one of the reasons we hired you last year. But you never mentioned you'd been awarded the Silver Star."

"You were awarded military commendations also," Kats said. "You don't talk about them either."

"It's different for me. I'm an actor, and people would think that all that puffery was just more hogwash from Hollywood. I get enough attention. Too much sometimes. But you..."

"Would you want to brag and pound your chest about killing people?" Kats asked in a quiet voice.

"Some would."

"But would you?"

"No, and I know you're not that kind of man either."

"Thank you," Kats said.

"Your file says the award was for combat in the Vosges Mountains in October 1944. It says you saved your platoon but little else. Would you tell me what happened?"

They sat down on a comfortable bench that looked at the small pond near the rear of the garden. Kats recognized that this was the price for Stewart to share his secrets. He wanted to be sure of who he was giving them to. Kats drew a deep breath, feeling the need to center himself before sharing the story. "Yes, it was the Vosges, just after the battle, in a town called Biffontaine. We'd fought house to house against some tough German resistance but had taken the city. Our guys were exhausted, but two days later we were ordered back into action to relieve a battalion of Texans that had been cut off by the Germans."

"The Lost Battalion," said Stewart. Kats nodded.

"Those guys had been surrounded for days by the Germans, and no one could get them out. We'd tried air dropping food and munitions to them, but those mostly ended up in the hands of the Germans. Hitler had apparently made the destruction of this battalion a priority among his generals, so the stakes were high. They sent us in, and I was part of the advance scouts looking for ways to flank the Germans, but they were deeply entrenched into the mountainside."

He looked across the placid scene in front of him, so at odds with the death and chaos of his memories, but he continued. "Eventually we were pinned down in foxholes and behind trees even though the Germans were just yards above us. Command ordered a charge, and like a bunch of crazy samurai, we attacked up that hill screaming, 'Banzai!' at the top of our lungs." He paused. "We lost so many men."[17]

Stewart watched his friend, not wanting to press. He gently put a hand on Kats's shoulder and waited for him to continue.

"I found myself up the hill, a bit ahead of the rest of the squad. I could see the concealed bunker that was spitting out machine gun fire. I was out of grenades, so I had no choice but to dive into one of the openings and take the fight to the men inside."

Stewart shook his head. "How many men were in there?"

Kats looked at his hands. "They said there was a dozen."

"Were you injured?"

"Shot. Twice."

Stewart nodded and knew better than to congratulate or compliment his friend. Those who'd not been to war might marvel at the bravery, the so-called heroics, but soldiers knew better. He squeezed his friend's shoulder, and they sat quietly for a time. Stewart began.

"So, some of what I'm going to share with you is classified. Some of it is military. Some of it is classified because of politics. It would embarrass certain powerful people and agencies." He paused, knowing he was about to cross a line.

"Right now, we're facing the greatest threat to America and the free world that we've ever faced. I don't say that to be dramatic either. The Russians are catching up to us in the arms race, and the fact that they got that damned satellite into orbit last year sent shock waves through the government and every branch of the military. People are actually scared in Washington."

"We're not just in an arms race. We're now in the 'Space Race,' and everyone believes we're losing. Remember that stupid televised launch of our Vanguard missile[18] last month?" Kats nodded. "When that blew up on the launch pad, Eisenhower was furious. People started talking about a 'missile gap' between our rockets and the Soviets' rockets."

"That was a spectacular failure," Kats said, remembering how he'd watched it on television with so many others across the country. "So they rushed that launch because Sputnik had gone up in October?"

"Exactly. They were supposed to be launching in February this year, but the Soviets caught everyone by surprise. We began scrambling. In fact, there will be a new agency of some kind coming soon that will oversee and coordinate all civilian space-related activities."

"Not the military?"

"No, and that's where things get messy. Right now, my colleagues in the air force are in a turf war with the navy over who will be the lead in our nuclear capability. We have long-range bombers, B-52s, tactical bombers, and some short- to medium-range surface-to-surface missiles. The navy can't touch that right now. They have some carrier-launched bombers, but their plan is to arm submarines with missiles. Missiles that could potentially be launched from a boat underwater. You saw the *Nautilus* launched a few years ago? Imagine nuclear-powered submarines that could stay underwater for weeks—months—at a time and creep right up to the coast of the enemy and launch from there. The politicians believe that if the Soviets have the upper hand in space, we need to have the advantage here on Earth or, more accurately, under the ocean."

Kats's mind was racing, recalling what he'd seen in Hunters Point. "How far along are they on that work?" he asked cautiously.

"Apparently pretty early in the process, but there's a huge amount of money and political capital being spent to make it happen."

"So how might a naval base like Hunters Point play into that scenario?"

Stewart nodded and looked out across his garden, his mouth a tight line. "For over a decade, Hunters Point has been the center of nuclear research for the navy. In 1955 they officially opened the Naval Radiological Defense Laboratory there on the base. Apparently, it's a giant, windowless building in the heart of the base. The official reason it's there is to study the effects of radiation and contamination caused by nuclear weapons. You have to understand that it's critical to our leadership that the American public believes in atomic energy. That it's the future, it's safe, and it's controllable. But it's all bullshit."

Kats had rarely heard Stewart curse, so he knew this information had somehow angered, maybe even offended, his friend.

"About five years ago, things at Hunters Point escalated significantly and rapidly. Over the past five years, they've quadrupled in size and easily as much in funding. So I asked around a bit, and this is where it applies to your folks there in Bayview Heights."

"In 1953 they were doing some field tests on a prototype of the nuclear reactor that now powers the *Nautilus*, but something went wrong. That reactor had to be dumped into San Francisco Bay, and for a couple years at least, it sat out there, poisoning the area while the navy and the government tried to figure out how to contain it. They built out the base including all those new buildings as part of the effort to contain the secret."

"My god," Kats said. This is so much worse than they'd thought.

"The government had to tell the city of San Francisco and the governor. Everyone was furious. But there was nothing they could do. They invoked some national security provisions and kept it all confidential. But the city did get a promise from the navy that once they contained the accident, there would be no more nuclear research or nuclear weapons on the base. And the government had to agree to clean up the area. As far as anyone I spoke with knows, the navy has followed through on that promise."

Kats listened intently, his stomach twisted in knots. Taking a deep breath, he pulled the manila folder out of his coat pocket. "Jim, the navy and the government broke that promise all to hell." He opened the envelope and pulled out the stack of black-and-white photos and handed them to Stewart. He began to flip through them.

"That's Admiral Rickover," he exclaimed. "And that's the *Nautilus*. But where is she? Those look like missiles."

"There's an underground submarine base at Hunters Point, and it looks like they're preparing those submarine-launched missiles you talked about."

"When were these taken?"

"A few days ago."

"By you?"

Kats nodded and looked intently at Stewart, wondering if he was looking at his friend or at a US Airforce general.

"Goddammit, Kats. This is serious." He continued to look through the photos. "These," he held them up, "could get you sent to prison."

"I really am sorry I involved you, Jim. Truly. But there's more." Kats pulled out the photo of Rickover with Sand and pointed to the gray man. "This guy works for some government agency. Some intelligence agency. He showed up in my office this week."

"What did he want?"

"He mostly used scare tactics with threats to me, my family, my friends. But what he really wants is for me and my clients to go away quietly. He wants that land sold and the people out of the area. They're trying to create a buffer zone out there because he knows how badly the area is contaminated. They used a proxy to buy up the land and promised this guy, Harry Charles, the contract for the redevelopment of the area for his efforts. Charles has been using strong-arm tactics to force reluctant sellers, and he's graduated to kidnapping and extortion."

"Kidnapping?"

Kats told him the highlights version of the incident with Anton and Molly. Stewart actually laughed at the pepper bomb. "But now it looks like they grabbed the other Vello brother, Gianni," and he told him about the plan to get the elder brother out of town and how he'd now been missing for several days.

"In fact, I'm going to collect his wife and son from their hotel over in Pasadena. They've been hoping Gianni would come back and didn't want to leave, but we need to get them home. Then we have to sort out Mr. Charles."

"What are you going to do?"

"Well, this new information might provide a bit more leverage with Mr. Sand and the government. It ultimately must be Anton and, hopefully, Gianni's decision about what they want for their homes, their business, their lives. Now they can make an informed decision," he paused. "But I don't like bullies."

"Neither do I, and it offends me when we don't live up to our ideals as a government."

"So what are you going to do?" Kats asked the general and movie star.

Stewart sighed and sat back on the bench. "Well, tonight I'm going to take Gloria and the kids out to dinner. Maybe the Brown Derby. They all love that place. I'm going to have a glass of wine and do my best to forget about Hunters Point." He clapped Kats on the shoulder. "But first, I'm going to drive you to Pasadena to get your friends."

"Jim, thank you, but I can get a cab."

"I know you can, but I'm going to drive, and you're going to tell me exactly how you got onto a top-secret military base so I can make sure you can't do it again!"

An hour later, they pulled up in front of the Huntington Hotel. Kats jumped out of Stewart's Cadillac, "I'll get them and be right back."

"I'll be right here." Kats ran inside, and an astonished car valet approached the blue Cadillac. Stewart smiled, "We'll just be a minute; my friends are checking out."

Ten minutes later, Kats emerged from the hotel lobby carrying three suitcases and leading Lilly and her son to the waiting car. Stewart got out of the car and approached them, taking Lilly's small bag and opening the car door for her. She looked at him with wide eyes, momentarily forgetting her troubles.

"Aren't you …" she began.

He smiled, "Jim. Nice to meet you."

Lilly looked at Kats, who shrugged his shoulders. "I needed a ride, and apparently movie stars do that here in LA."

CHAPTER 26

The late flight got them into SFO after 9 pm and back to the Vello residence at 10:30 pm. Anton greeted his sister-in-law and nephew with a fierce hug. They wanted to go home, but Anton insisted they stay at the main house instead, sending one of his men to collect fresh clothes for them.

"Where's Molly?" Kats asked.

"She was pacing around like a caged animal. Eventually she insisted on going to work at Ann's. I drove her there a few hours ago and told her I'd pick her up at 1 am. Sorry Kats, but that girl is fierce when she gets her back up."

"I know. It's OK. She should be safe there in public. I'll

get her later. Meanwhile, I have a story for you."

Over coffee in the kitchen, Kats recounted meeting with his "unnamed" source in LA. He didn't want to compromise either of his friends with too much knowledge in case things got complicated later. The revelation of the atomic reactor being dumped into the bay hit Anton hard. "Right out there!" he pointed. "Every day it was poisoning people, literally killing my father. Bastards!"

"I understand your anger. I do. But you also need to be thinking about your family's health and safety. The people who work for you, too. Staying here may not be an option. As you said, this land is now poison."

"So I should sell to these fuckers? Let them win?"

"I think there may be a way to sell but not let them win. At least not the way they'd hoped."

Anton looked skeptical "OK. How?"

"It seems pretty clear that you weren't the only ones lied to in all of this. I think that Harry Charles and his guys have been played in this, too. I bet he was promised some things that just aren't going to happen. I bet he has no idea about the environmental damage out here."

"Kats, he's a thug. A criminal. If he gets burned in all this, don't expect me to feel any sympathy for him."

"He's an opportunist. A survivor. We can use that and maybe get him to work with us. Or at least not work against us."

"And get back Gianni," Anton said. "He has Gianni."

"Maybe. Probably. But if we show him there's no upside to keeping Gianni, we get him back without storming the castle."

"If you're going to confront him, I'm going with you."

"Absolutely not. If he does have Gianni, bringing you

284 | HUNTERS POINT

over gives him complete control of your father's estate."

Anton scowled but couldn't argue the point. He changed the subject. "So if we could sell for a good price, I actually have an idea where we might go."

"Really?"

"Yeah, there's a growing boat-building community across the bay in Sausalito. There are even some folks starting to live on houseboats there."

"Sounds like you're thinking like a shipbuilder, not a poet."

"Yeah, crazy isn't it? If you'd asked me a year ago, I'd have said I wanted out of the family business. But now, with the way my father died and knowing what he wanted for me and Gianni, it changes things."

"I get it. Fathers and sons. My father has been back in Japan for years now, but I can still hear his voice in my head telling me to do things. And you know what? I usually do," Kats laughed.

The phone in the office of City Lights Bookstore rang. It was after 11:30 pm, but Shig Murao, the ever-present manager, picked up. "Yeah?" he said gruffly.

"Shig, hey. It's Kats."

"Hey, man," replied the other man, all the gruff leaving his tone.

"Can you meet me for a drink? I've got a story to share."

"Sure. Where do you want to meet?"

"I have to pick up Molly at Ann's later, so how about there?"

"See you soon."

It was Friday night, and Ann's 440 was hopping. The

singer Johnny Mathis was performing. Mathis, a longtime San Francisco resident, got his start singing at Ann's in 1955. Tonight he was the returning hero, with two popular albums to his name and a recent hit song from the movie *Wild Is the Wind*. He'd finished two sets by the time Kats and Shig arrived but had one more set in him before the end of the night. They found their way to the end of the bar. Molly was wearing the standard uniform for the wait staff—white shirt, black vest, and bow tie. A good look on her. She and another woman were busy making drinks, but when he caught her eye, she smiled and gave him a wink.

"What will it be, gentlemen?" asked the other bartender. Kats looked at her for a moment, noting the slightly deep voice and strong jaw line. Her long blond hair framed a very pretty, if well made-up, face, and Kats remembered where he was. This was the 440, and it was where all kinds of people could come and be themselves. That meant transvestite bartenders, lesbian waitresses, gay clients, and straight tourists alike. Gotta love San Francisco, he smiled.

"I'm feeling saucy," Shig said, clapping his hands. "How about a Brandy Alexander?"

"I'll have a beer, please," Kats said.

The bartender smiled and gave Shig a quizzical look that he didn't notice as he looked around the club.

"Hey, aren't you that guy from the trial last year?" she asked Shig who, at the mention of the trial, immediately focused on the questioner.

"Yes, Shigeyoshi Murao, defender of civil liberties and freedom of speech at your service."

"Pleasure to meet you, Shigeyoshi. I'm Lola."

"Please call me Shig, my dear."

"I just wanted to say, Shig, that you're a hero. Standing up to the government over those ridiculous obscenity charges. Well done. This round is on the house." She squeezed his hand before turning to make the drinks.

Shig couldn't have smiled wider, thought Kats, but he, too, knew the adulation was well deserved.

"Hear that, Katsuhiro? I'm a hero!"

"I heard" Kats smiled.

"And I think I'm in love," he said, eyeing Lola.

"She's lovely, Shig," he said, and left it at that.

Their drinks arrived, giving Shig another opportunity to flirt with Lola. Molly came to the end of the bar and said, "Glad you're back. Success?"

"Yes, on multiple levels. Lilly and Carlo are home, and I found out some important information."

"Can't wait to hear it, but I've got thirsty customers."

"Go. We're here until you close."

Johnny Mathis returned to the stage to a huge roar from the patrons. He wore a dark suit and tie, his black hair slicked back in a pompadour. Clearly, he was happy to be back in the familiar confines of San Francisco. "Thank you, all! It's so good to be here with you. In fact, it's Wonderful Wonderful!" and the band began his hit song.

Sometimes we walk hand in hand by
the sea and we breathe in the cool salty air
You turn to me with a kiss in your eyes
And my heart feels a thrill beyond compare
Then your lips cling to mine
It's wonderful, wonderful
Oh, so wonderful, my love

Mathis swung through his last set, and the crowd, well lubricated and grooving, was enthralled. Kats had hoped to have a conversation with Shig but ended up enjoying himself too much to worry about nuclear weapons, environmental devastation, kidnapped clients, and an exciting, but potentially complicated, new relationship.

Shig was well into his third Brandy Alexander and showing the tell-tale blush that many Japanese got when they drank. Kats had never really suffered from the so-called "Asian Flush," but his sisters did, as well as many of his friends and colleagues. Most simply powered through the red cheeks in the name of a good time. Kats knew Shig could easily walk home from here, so he clapped his friend on the back, and they stood applauding the young star singer.

Once the show was over, many cleared out of the club, and Kats saw the manager whisper something to Molly, who nodded and then looked over to Kats, giving him a thumbs up. A few minutes later, she came from behind the bar, tie loosened, and joined them. "Can we grab a table? I've got one hell of a story to tell you guys."

They found a table near the bar and sat down. Shig smiled broadly at the two of them. "I'm so happy to see you guys!"

Kats laughed. "You're a bit drunk."

"Still happy to see you."

Kats began to recount findings of the past few days, including the revelation that there had been a serious nuclear accident out in the bay. This seemed to sober Shig up a bit, and Molly clenched her fist on top of the table. "They really did kill Anton's father, didn't they?" she asked.

Kats nodded, "They may not have pulled a trigger, but yeah, it seems clear that Carlo died from exposure to radiation."

"Like all those who died years after Hiroshima and Nagasaki," said a surprisingly bitter Shig.

"There's something else I need to tell you." He looked back and forth at them, both of whom he was now worried about. One of his oldest and closest friends, and this new woman, whom he was growing ever fonder of. "A man came to my office a couple days ago. He was one of the men who was at the warehouse. He seems to be working with Harry. His name is Sand."

Molly's eyes went wide. "Sand? Glasses, mouse brown hair, kind of short?"

"That's him."

"He came in and met with Harry at least once that I remember. He was a developer or represented a group of developers. Money guy."

Kats shook his head. "That's a cover. He works for the government. Most likely one of the intelligence agencies." Kats took a sip of his now warm beer. "He knew about all of us. Me, Anton, and you guys. He threatened you guys if we didn't back off this case."

"How can he threaten us?" Shig said incredulously.

"Yeah," Molly added, "they can't touch us."

"It's the government. They could make lots of bad things happen. He said they could reinstate the obscenity charges against you, Shig. And Molly, I hate to tell you this, but apparently there's an arrest warrant out for you back in Ohio."

"What?!?!" she exclaimed. "For what?"

"Assault. Apparently, your ex-husband filed charges."

"That son of a bitch."

"You assaulted your ex-husband?" Shig asked.

"He deserved it," she said tersely.

Shig looked at Molly with a newfound respect. "Look at us! Couple of law breakers," he laughed, and she laughed with him, clinking glasses.

Kats realized this wasn't the reaction he was trying to elicit from his friends. "This is serious. I don't want you guys getting into trouble. I know Anton wouldn't want that either."

"Buddy, we're not afraid, and we're not bailing on you!"

"No way, Kats," added Molly.

Part of him was mad, but truth be told, Kats was really moved that his friends would risk so much to help. *Really good people*, he thought. "OK, if you're going to help, you need to do as I tell you." He looked back and forth at the two wry grins on their faces. "You have to at least try to do as I tell you," he amended.

"Oh, we can definitely try. Right, Molly," said Shig, nodding effusively. "What's the next move, boss?"

"I know it sounds crazy, but I think we need to talk to Harry Charles."

"What?" Molly said with a wrinkled brow. "That bastard has extorted, burned, bullied, and even kidnapped us and now Gianni, and you want to talk to him? We should call the police or better yet go and burn down his office and his home!" Kats marveled at this red-headed firebrand, and he took her by the hand.

"Let's call that plan B," he said. "I don't think Harry knows exactly who he's dealing with, and I'm completely sure he doesn't know how contaminated that land is."

"Why would that matter to a guy like Charles?" Shig asked.

"Because he's looking to make money. Harry may be a thug and yes, a criminal, but he's a businessman at heart."

Kats looked at Molly, expecting an argument, but she twisted her mouth and nodded. "If he's not going to get the score he was promised, he may be willing to deal with us."

"Or he could just grab you both, and then we're even more screwed," Shig countered.

Kats nodded, "That's also a possibility, which is why you're our backup."

"Me? What can I do? I'm not exactly the soldier you are."

"No, but you talk more than anybody I know, and if Harry does make a move against us, you need to go public with the whole story."

"They won't believe me. It's just a story."

"I have some proof that will make them believe you."

Kats turned to Molly. "I'm thinking it might be better to meet Harry out in public. Not in that private office of his. Maybe we could meet in the construction site office. There would be a lot more people. All of them are not in on the shady side of his business, right?"

"Probably not, but everybody I talked with there knew that Harry was operating on the edge. I wouldn't assume it's safe."

"Where then?"

Molly thought. "Harry used to have a standing card game every Tuesday night. It was at the Olympic Club."

"Harry plays golf?" Kats asked.

"Yes, badly, but it's not at the golf club. They have an in-town clubhouse on Post near Union Square."

"That's fancy," Shig said.

"Yeah, I thought so, too, when I first learned about it. I think it was part of Harry's attempt at respectability. He'd play with lawyers, business owners, stockbrokers, and the like, hoping to be accepted into that world."

"Sounds very Great Gatsby," Kats said, and Shig did a double-take. "Yeah, I read books, too." Shig laughed and clapped him on the back.

"Think he's still doing that with all that's going on?" Kats continued.

"Harry's a creature of habit. I saw him have a cup of coffee every morning at 10:30 am like clockwork. He wore the same suit on Fridays for months. The one time he didn't wear it I asked him what happened, and he said the trousers were wearing out and he had to take them into the tailor."

"OK, so Tuesday evening we pay him a visit at the club."

"You know that's a private club, right?" Shig asked.

"Well, we have a couple days to figure that one out. You ready to go?" he asked Molly, who nodded and grabbed her purse and coat.

"You coming?" Kats asked.

Shig smiled and, eying Lola behind the bar, said, "I think I'll have a night cap."

"Umm, you know she's..."

"Of course, Katsuhiro. I know this city and all of these people are my people," he gestured, expanding his arms. "That's the beautiful thing about San Francisco. I'm always happy to talk to someone who appreciates literature and the importance of the First Amendment."

"And someone who appreciates you."

"That, too."

Harry Charles's car dropped him off at the curb, and he walked through the white doors off Post and into the Olympic City Clubhouse just before 7 pm. He should have been looking forward to his weekly poker game, but the gnawing in his stomach had only gotten worse over the past several days. Several shitty days, he thought bitterly. The attendant at the front desk smiled at him obsequiously, "Good evening, Mr. Charles."

"Evening, John," he nodded and handed his coat to the valet. He'd realized the necessity of learning the names of people since joining the club. He still couldn't fully believe he was a member of a country club, let alone one as posh as The Olympic Club. He'd even taken up golf a couple years ago, taking lessons and dutifully losing money to the much more experienced members in the weekly skins game. Though it was all part of his plan for entrance into high society, Harry still chaffed at the game. "Fucking pussy sport," he lamented every time he strode to the first tee box. But those same smug assholes thought they were good card players, and Harry had found himself invited to the Tuesday night game. He was a wolf among the sheep. He'd played cards with men all over Europe and in the backroom gaming houses of the Barbary Coast and Chinatown once he arrived in San Francisco. These college boys never had a chance, but they liked Harry's gruff, working-class charisma and the stories he told, so accommodations were made.

"Your party is in the 1860 room," John said, and Harry turned toward the double doors at the east end of the lobby, trying to get into a suitable frame of mind to take their money.

Outside and across the street, Molly adjusted Kats's tie. "You look good in a suit," she said to him.

"You sound surprised," he replied.

"Well, khakis and jeans are more your style, but it's nice to see another side of you." She was wearing a pleated skirt, a white blouse, and a demur sweater that covered her distracting figure. She looked like a typical office girl, and that was part of the plan. She held a folder stuffed with odd papers taken from Kats's office, but once inside the manila shell, they looked official. "Ready?" she asked him. Kats nodded and, taking her hand, they crossed the street.

As they entered the posh lobby of the club, they drew the scrutiny of the front desk attendant. Clearly, they weren't members, and the clerk was used to having to shoo away tourists and the occasional process server. "May I help you?" he asked with the tone that only years of experience could produce.

"Yes, please!" Molly said in an exasperated and overly feminine voice. She rushed to the front desk and loudly placed the folder onto the flat surface. Kats waited in the middle of the lobby, with his hands folded in front of him. "I must see Harry Charles immediately," she practically gasped.

"Miss, this is a private club. Emphasis on 'private.' I'm not at liberty to summon people. I'm not at liberty to confirm that a 'Harry Charles' is even a member here. I'm sorry."

"You don't understand. I'm from his office at Charles Construction. We've been trying to get a hold of him this evening. There's been an accident at the Thompson project. A fire. He's needed immediately. Please, you must get him."

The man looked nervously at Molly, trying to process what to do. His eyes moved to Kats standing there. Molly followed his gaze, "Oh, that's Chan, our driver. We need to get Mr. Charles to the site immediately."

"What's your name?" he asked Molly.

"I'm Mrs. Hopkins," she said, giving the name of one of the senior secretaries from Harry's office. Likewise, the Thompson project was an expensive office development near the Presidio. That should get Harry's attention, she thought.

"Wait here," he said and signaled the coat check attendant to watch the desk. He disappeared through the double doors. Molly turned and walked toward Kats.

"Chan?" he whispered.

"I had to improvise."

Harry sat in a blue cloud of cigar smoke, half a tumbler of scotch at his side and holding garbage cards. Fucking garbage all night, he thought. He knew he was off his game, and the smaller than usual stack of chips in front of him attested to that fact.

"Call, Charles?" asked Simon Talbot, a lawyer with one of the big downtown firms. The man was tall, soft around the middle, and part of the old established families that ran San Francisco. Harry hated him.

"Yeah, Simon, I fold," he said, tossing his cards onto the table.

Talbot laughed, "You're off your game tonight, Charles." Harry could only nod as he took a long sip of his drink. Across the room the door opened, and instead of the usual waiter, John entered and headed immediately toward Harry.

As he approached, he leaned over and said quietly in Harry's ear, "Mr. Charles, sorry to disturb you, but could I have a moment?"

Harry nodded and said, "Deal me out, boys. I'll be back for your money later." The table laughed. That good old boy laugh that wasn't real, but it was expected. Harry stood and followed John, who stopped in front of the door and outside of earshot from the group.

"Terribly sorry, Mr. Charles, but there's someone here from your office. A Mrs. Hopkins with some unfortunate news about a project of yours."

"What fucking project?" hissed Harry.

"She mentioned the Thompson project and a fire."

"Fuck!" Harry bellowed as he pushed aside the smaller man and opened the doors. He strode into the lobby expecting to see his long-time secretary and instead saw Molly and that Jap!

Staring intently at the two of them, he strode forward, chin leading, his normally aggressive stance. Kats instinctively stepped around Molly and eased into his Water stance, waiting. Seeing that this could go bad very quickly, Molly pushed past Kats and raised her hands to the advancing man. "Harry, we just want to talk."

Harry started to shout something but realized he was someplace that frowned on such outbursts. He stopped, his chest rising and falling as his fists clenched.

"We need to talk," she repeated.

He looked back and forth at them and let out a long breath. "So, no fucking fire?" he asked.

"No fire," said Molly flatly. He looked across the lobby at the member bar and motioned with his large head. Molly and Kats looked at each other and followed.

Harry slid into a corner table, far away from the other members in the room. Kats and Molly sat down, and a waiter approached the table. "Scotch rocks," Harry said and made a gesture with his hands toward his two "guests" to order.

"No, thank you," said Molly, and the waiter retreated. For a frozen moment, the icy stares met across the table, and Kats wondered if there might be violence. Then, like a balloon losing its air, he sank back in his chair, and he shook his head.

"What the hell are you doin' here, red? Thought I'd seen

the last of you."

"Sorry, Harry, but we needed to tell you some things, and we have to get Gianni back."

"The fucking Vello kid," he shook his head. "I don't got him, red."

"What?" Molly and Kats said together.

"Yeah, welcome to my shit show," lamented Harry just as his drink arrived.

"Where is he then?" Molly asked.

"The Hat has him." Molly and Kats looked quizzically at him. "Lanza. Jimmy 'the Hat' Lanza has him. All because of that fuck Franco."

"Franco? Your man Franco?" Molly said.

"Not my fucking man. Bastard sold me out to Lanza." Harry's face was flush with anger just thinking about it.

"What happened?" Kats asked.

"We was tailin' Gianni. Followed him to LA last week. I sent Franco to bag him and bring him back before Lanza could nab him. But that wop traitor took the Vello kid to Lanza instead. Fucker told me, 'Sorry, it's an Italian thing.'" Harry took a swallow of scotch and grimaced at the memory.

"Now Lanza is just sittin' on the guy. Waiting me out." He took another drink.

"Waiting for what?" asked Molly.

"For the fucking banks, red. I'm running out of time and cash. I leveraged everything to acquire that land in Bayview Heights."

"But you had that outside investment guy," Molly said.

"Yeah, I took his money, but I threw in everything I could as well to buy up that land. The score is supposed to be huge. New houses, office buildings, retail space, and a brand-new baseball stadium. But now everything is stalled because of the Vello lands. We needed to secure those parcels to make this work. And now Lanza has the one kid and will sit on him until the banks foreclose on me and he can pick up the pieces for scratch. I never should've listened to that bastard Sand and gotten into bed with those pricks."

"Sand has been playing you, Harry," Kats said cautiously. He knew the man was on edge, but he needed to know the whole story before they could explain their plan. "I know he promised you the new stadium contract and apparently a whole lot more development." Harry grunted. "But other than a stadium, there won't be any more development in that area. Not for a long time."

"What are you talking about? They're planning a whole huge development out there."

"They won't. They can't. Harry, that land is poison. It's full of radioactive contaminants," Kats said.

Harry shook his head, "They told me about that leakage from that old aircraft carrier they cleaned up after the A-bomb tests. Not a big deal."

"It's much worse than that, Harry." Charles looked at Kats, trying to gauge his veracity. He looked at Molly, who nodded solemnly.

"How bad?" he asked.

"People dying of cancer bad. Carlo Vello was poisoned by the radiation coming from Hunters Point. The navy and the government know about it. Your guy Sand isn't a developer. He works for the government, and his job is to keep all this quiet."

"They won't let people live out there, Harry," Molly said. "They aren't going to let you or anybody else build out there."

"But the stadium?" began Harry.

"That they'll build. It's essentially cover for the land acquisition. A stadium is limited usage. People come in and out a hundred times a year. But they don't live out there."

"So all that land I'm sittin' on..."

"Mostly worthless," Molly said, actually feeling a bit sorry for the man.

"Fuck!" bellowed Harry as he slammed his huge fist down on the table, this time not caring who might see.

They let that sit for a moment. Then Kats offered, "What if you could get even? Would you be willing to help us?"

"Get even?" Harry laughed without mirth. "Get even with Sand, with Lanza, with that shit Franco? Sign me the fuck up."

CHAPTER 27

T wo nights later a strange round table of characters sat on the upper level of Vesuvio in North Beach, nursing their drinks. The place was chosen after numerous attempts to find a neutral location, but eventually the local bar became the obvious choice. On one side of the oval table sat Anton and Molly. On the other side of the table sat Harry and two of his men he simply identified as Heckman and Baker. At the ends sat Shig and Kats. The idea of all working together had been exciting at first, but this first coming together of the team was a bit awkward considering that just days ago, these men across the table were essentially enemies at war. But this is how it's done, thought Kats. Find another enemy, a bigger threat, and suddenly your interests align with a former adversary.

Kats looked back and forth at the table and realized he

needed to break the ice. "I know it's strange to all be sitting together..."

"Very strange," Anton said, eyeing Harry.

"But we now have common enemies, and the only way we can take them down is to work together," Kats finished.

"So how do we do this?" Shig asked.

"We start with what we know. Lanza must have Gianni stashed at their headquarters in Pier 23. Harry described the area to me as a fortress," Kats said.

"Yeah, they got a section of the pier all to themselves. The old docks were where smugglers brought in booze during Prohibition. Now it's guns and drugs," Harry said.

"How many men?" Anton asked.

"At least a couple dozen," Harry replied.

"And Gianni?"

"Probably somewhere on the second level. They had offices and lots of rooms up there. I think Lanza may have an apartment of some kind up there, too."

"We can't just walk in there this time, Kats," Anton said.

"I'm hoping we can come up with some diversion that might allow me to get in there and find Gianni."

"But then you still need to get him out," Anton said. "We don't even know for sure that he's there. All this may be for nothing."

"I can get Lanza to produce your brother," Harry said matter of factly.

"How?"

"By proposing a deal with him. What would interest him? What would make him bring Gianni to a meeting?" Harry asked. "You," he said pointing at Anton. "The one way to get this deal done fast is to get the two of you together to sign over the property." Everyone looked back and forth at Anton and Harry. Kats slowly nodded his head.

"Lanza is a businessman. He'll wait me out if he has to, but I'm sure he'd rather get paid sooner than later. Plus, if the land goes into default, then the fucking banks are involved, and there ain't no guarantee he can get all the property. He'd want to lock this up now."

"So you set up a meeting by telling him you'll bring Anton ..." Kats said.

"That should get his attention."

"That's super risky," Shig said. "We're handing Lanza the one piece he doesn't have. If this goes sideways, we're..."

"Fucked," Anton said. "And pardon me, Mr. Charles, I'm still not convinced you're not playing both sides of this. I walk in there with you, and you turn me over to Lanza and again we're..."

"Fucked," Molly said. "What about me?"

"What about you?" asked Anton.

"Well, Harry and Lanza had thought I was your girl, remember? What if Harry brought me to Lanza saying I'd be leverage to get you to sign. That gets us in the room, gets Gianni in the room, and we don't risk Anton."

"But we do risk you," Kats said, shaking his head.

"I can't let you do this for me," Anton added.

"C'mon, guys," Molly said, "we don't have many options here, and if I'm there with Harry, he's on the line, too. I'd turn him over to Lanza if he has second thoughts," she said, looking at Harry with an evil smile.

"You would, too, wouldn't you, red?" Harry replied smiling.

"In a fucking heartbeat," she finished. "Plus, I know you'd get me out," she said, looking at Kats.

"Getting in is the first problem. We'll need to do some

recon."

"My guys are good at recon," Harry said, nodding toward Heckman and Baker.

Anton looked skeptical. "We was all combat engineers. The 17th Armored Engineer Battalion," and Heckman and Baker said in unison. "Our motto was always, 'We pave the way.'"

"Hell on wheels," Kats said, remembering their unit's reputation.

Harry looked at him, nodding. "That was us," he said. "We built bridges, blew up buildings, and cleared mine fields, all while Nazis were shootin' at us."

"We can use that," Kats said. "We're going to need a big diversion—probably several big diversions—to pull this off." Kats thought for a moment. "Do you have a bulldozer?"

Harry snorted, "Of course."

"What are you thinking?" Shig asked.

"Armored support," Kats smiled.

Over the next two hours, a plan began to form, and tasks were assigned over the next two days with the objective to make the move against Lanza on the third night. "They won't be expecting anything from the water," Kats said. "Anton, we need you to get me close, and from there I can paddle into the dock."

"We can take one of our sailboats, but how are you going to get to the dock? Swim again?"

"I was thinking of a surfboard. Can we blacken one up? I'll need to carry some gear."

"We can do that."

"And speaking of water," Kats remembered the sight of the fireboat at the Vello docks, "do you guys have access to anything like a fireboat?" he asked Harry.

He shook his head. "Not really our thing," he said.

His man Heckman raised a hand and said, "The city has one." Everyone turned to the usually quiet man. "Yeah, I've seen it. I always liked tugboats and stuff. It's docked somewhere around here and has water cannons mounted on it."

"That could be useful," Shig said, "But how..."

"We could borrow it," Baker said with a smile. Kats looked at Harry, who grinned.

"My guys are good at borrowing stuff. We find it, scope it out, and make a move on it."

Kats nodded and said, "OK, see if you can borrow one for us!"

"Here's the other thing. We don't want a firefight with Lanza's men. You and Molly would be on the inside. So is Gianni. We need Lanza's men distracted, not dead."

"Easy to say when they aren't shooting at you," Harry replied.

"If they're shooting at you, then something went wrong. We need something that will change the battlefield, which is something they taught me in Ranger school. Add a new variable—something unexpected that takes away the enemy's numerical or tactical advantage. That throws them off their game. Smoke bombs are a good example."

"Like your pepper bomb at the warehouse," chimed in Shig.

"Shit, that was you?" Baker asked as he looked at Kats. "That was awful, man. I about clawed my eyes out for an hour and was wheezing for days after it."

"Sorry about that," Kats replied.

"Hey," Heckman said, slapping his partner on the arm, "he could have shot our asses. Be thankful."

Baker brightened with an idea. "Hey, could you teach us how to make those pepper bombs? Please?"

Kats looked at Shig, who shrugged. "Talk to me after we beat Lanza."

"Roger that."

"Back to our situation. We need confusion. Chaos."

"How about a few well-placed grenades?" Harry offered.

"You have grenades?" Anton asked incredulously.

"Not really. We got a lot of dynamite, though."

Shig raised his hand and looked thoughtful. "Did you know that the Chinese used monkeys with explosives strapped to them against the British ships in their harbors?"

The table was silent for a moment, as they looked back and forth at each other.

"We don't have any monkeys," Molly said, trying not to laugh.

"Are you saying I'm the monkey, Shig?" Kats asked.

"Hopefully not, man."

"I ain't doin' that either," declared Baker.

"No dynamite," Kats said, but he paused a moment. "Probably no dynamite. But I do like the monkey idea."

"Really?" Shig said, looking both surprised and proud at the same time. "I thought you were going to say it was stupid."

"It is stupid. It's a terrible idea," he said with a half-smile. "But even terrible ideas can be valuable. They lead you to other ideas."

"Like what?" Molly asked.

"The animal idea. There's something to that."

"What are you thinking?" asked Shig, intrigued. "Dogs? Rats? Sea lions?"

"Sharks?" Harry said.

"Let me think on this a bit. I do know we need to make a shopping trip to Chinatown tomorrow. Can your men arrange for transport of what we get?" Kats asked Harry, who nodded at Heckman and Baker.

"You two, go with him and get him whatever he needs."

"I like shopping," Molly said with a smile at Kats.

"Fine. You can come, too."

"I'll get the boat and surfboard ready," Anton added.

"OK, meet me in Chinatown tomorrow at 9 am on Stockton, between Sacramento and Clay. Bring a truck."

By 9 am Chinatown was already bustling with the visible and invisible energy it manifested every day. To many, especially the tourists who increasingly flocked to Chinatown, it was an open and obvious energy, all about restaurants, curio shops, and exotic displays from the mysterious Far East. But there was also a mostly invisible energy of everyday life in a crowded, complex neighborhood that only those who lived there or truly paid attention would ever see. It was into that hidden world that Kats needed to go today.

"I haven't been to this end of Chinatown before," Molly said.

"Not surprising. This is the working end of the neighborhood. Dozens of businesses don't have storefronts or even official names around here. But they've been here since the earliest days of San Francisco."

Just then they saw a large truck round the corner onto Stockton. Kats had to smile at the familiar sight of a WW2-era, two-and-a-half-ton truck, known affectionately as a "Jimmy." They were everywhere during the war, and Kats had ridden in them many times. True workhorses. The truck parked, and Baker and Heckman jumped out.

"You brought a Jimmy," Kats laughed.

"Of course," Heckman said.

"Yeah, Harry picked up a bunch of them as surplus. Got a great deal, plus we all know how to fix 'em," Baker said.

"Well, now we're going to fill her up." He turned and pointed to a nondescript three-story building behind him. "First stop."

With Kats leading, they walked down the alley and came to an unmarked, battered red door. Kats knocked, and a few moments later an eye slot opened, and Kats leaned into a conversation with a hidden gatekeeper. Molly tried to hear the exchange, but the words were obscured, and those she did catch sounded like a mélange of English and Chinese phrases thrown together. The eye slot closed, and Kats turned around. "Should just be a minute," he said confidently.

"Do you speak Chinese?" Molly asked him.

"No. That wasn't really Chinese either. There's a pidgin dialect that traders, smugglers, thieves, and locals use. It's more like the language of commerce."

Behind him they heard levers and bolts moving, and the door opened inward. Kats led the way, followed by Molly, Heckman, and Baker. They entered a gloomy hallway that led to a wooden door at the end. Their gatekeeper, a stoop-shouldered Chinese man who could have been forty or seventy depending on the light, led them into the building.

"Where are we?" Molly asked in a hushed tone.

"This is Si Han's. The largest fireworks factory in San Francisco."

They walked onto the huge factory floor that took up half the block and rose upward three stories. Dozens of men and women were working at various machines. Open crates of rockets, firecrackers, and every kind of novelty explosive you could imagine were strewn about in a puzzling organizational scheme. Copious amounts of gunpowder were evident as well.

Heckman and Baker looked around with more than concerned faces. "There's a fireworks factory in the heart of San Francisco?" Heckman exclaimed.

"There are actually about half a dozen," Kats said calmly. "This is just the biggest one."

Baker looked about, "How has this not burned the neighborhood to the ground?"

"The Chinese invented gunpowder and fireworks. They've been handling this stuff for centuries. They know what they're doing."

An official-looking man in a jade green jacket approached them and threw his arms wide while smiling, "Kats!"

"Hey, Sonny," Kats said, shaking the smiling man's hand. "Guys, this is Sonny. Sun Tsin Han, the owner of this establishment."

"Well, my father technically owns it, but he just wants to play Mahjong at Jun Fan's."

Sonny was thirty-something, wiry, with glasses and a receding hairline. His green jacket was well cut and stylish and made from Chinese silk,. Molly noted that he was wearing Italian loafers. Quite the mix, she thought.

"What brings you to Chinatown?"

"I have a wish list for you," Kats said as he handed a folded piece of paper to Sonny. He read it and then looked at Kats.

"The 4th of July is months away," he quipped.

"I know it's a lot, but we have a special occasion coming up."

"Yeah, I'll bet you do," laughed Sonny. "When do you need it?"

"End of day," Kats said. Sonny blew out his cheeks. "For you... yeah. I won't forget what you did for me and my father." He turned to look at Molly. "This guy," he said pointing at Kats, "saved our asses. I still get goosebumps thinking about the dude with the crossbow!"

"Crossbow?" Molly and the crew looked at Kats, who shook his head.

"Story for another day."

"Hey, gotta ask. Who's paying for all this?" Sonny asked.

"We are. Bill it to Charles Construction," Heckman said, handing Sonny a business card. "We'll call it drywall."

"Right, drywall!" laughed Sonny.

"Thanks, Sonny. We have a few more stops around Chinatown today."

"Anybody I know?"

"You know everybody," Kats replied.

"True," Sonny nodded.

"We've got some special requests." Kats said. "I need to go see Lim Ya-Leng."

"The Tiger Lady," Sonny acknowledged. "Good luck with that."

Kats turned to Heckman and Baker. "The pallets will be ready this afternoon. Leave the truck, and Sonny's men will load it up."

The two men nodded, but when Kats turned for the exit, Baker leaned over to Heckman, "Pallets? How many firecrackers do we need?"

Molly turned to follow Kats. "Next stop?" she asked.

"We go to see the Tiger Lady," he replied with an unreadable expression on his face.

They walked through Chinatown on the cool morning until they stopped in front of a large but unremarkable souvenir curio shop. "Lim's Oriental Store" was emblazoned on a well-worn sign above the double door entrance. They walked into row upon row of "oriental" gifts and souvenirs for tourists. From the overpriced "jade" jewelry, the impractical enameled chopsticks, smiling Buddha statues, incense, and an odd assortment of Chinese martial arts weapons, including a Wushu sword and an iron fan, tourists loved the strange mix of eccentricities.

Lim's Oriental Store had been founded by the original Tiger Lady, Lim Po Chin, a woman who was such a tough and relentless negotiator, she became known as the Tiger Lady. The store was the official business, but it had been a front for the real black-market trade that the Tiger Lady oversaw like a fierce mother cat. She had strict rules as to what she would deal—no drugs, no prostitution, no guns. In part this had been to avoid messy entanglements with the local Tong gangs because that was their territory. The other reason was that she was married to a minister. The two had a unique bond and clearly saw the world in different ways, but they had a successful marriage that resulted in two children. The elder son followed more of his father's path and became a doctor. Their daughter, Lim Ya-Leng, or Gracie to her American friends, had gone to the University of San Francisco to be a journalist. However, her talents seemed to align more with her mother's, and several years ago, she'd taken over the family business, becoming the new Tiger Lady. Some of this was public knowledge, but Kats knew the full story in detail because he used to date Gracie.

The group made their way through the store to the counter, where an elderly woman looked up at their approach. "We need to see Ya-Leng. Please tell her it is Katsuhiro." The clerk's face registered no surprise or emotion. She simply rose and walked to the phone on the back wall. She lifted the receiver and a moment later appeared to speak to someone. She nodded several times, looking back at Kats, and then hung up the phone. She returned to the counter and made a small bow.

"I'm told to tell you," she gestured toward Kats, "Go fuck yourself."

Molly, Heckman, and Baker looked momentarily shocked and then burst into laughter. Kats felt his face redden. "Where did that come from?" Molly asked.

"It's complicated. We have some history." Molly arched an eyebrow. "Yes, that kind of history. Years ago, we were young after the war, in college..." She nodded, and Heckman and Baker grinned like Cheshire cats. Kats turned back to the old woman behind the counter.

"Please ask Lim Ya-Leng if we may have an audience with her. Tell her it's business and we have money." Grandma finally smiled at the word "money," and she turned to make another call. A minute later she smiled at Kats, beckoning him and the rest behind the counter and through the closed door.

"In back. Knock on round door," she waved them through.

The back of the store held a large room filled with dusty inventory. Blocking their path across the room was a round, double door with gold and mother of pearl inlays featuring dragons, tigers, and various Chinese emperors. Two large desks sat outside the door, and two bespeckled men pored over ledgers and paper manifests that were stacked behind them like returned library books. They didn't even look up at the party.

Kats approached the large door and knocked twice before pushing. The heavy door swung easily open, and inside an American office awaited. A couch, a conference table, and a small bar was to their right. To their left was a television console and hi-fi record player on a long credenza. In the center of the room, a beautiful modern desk stretched in front of an equally beautiful young Chinese woman who wore a red cheongsam, a fitted short-sleeved dress with a high collar accentuating her neck. She leaned back in her chair, scowling at Kats as they approached. Then in perfect, American English she said, "Long time, Kats."

He nodded and smiled, "Hi, Gracie. Thank you for seeing us."

"Well, anything for an old friend," she said sarcastically. Molly noted the exchange and realized Gracie was now looking her over, like a predator looking over its dinner. "Who's your friend?"

"This is Molly," he gestured toward her, "and these gentlemen are..." but Gracie cut him off before he could finish.

"Hi, Molly," she said brightly, but no one would confuse the tone with the actual meaning behind it. Molly nodded her head "Hello."

"She's very pretty, Kats. You always liked your *gwaipo* pretty."

Molly started to say something, but Kats put a hand on her arm, and she held her retort. "How's your mother?" Kats asked, changing the subject.

"Retired and terrorizing the other ladies at the Chinese Women's Society. She'll be pleased to hear that you came by.

She always liked you, despite being Japanese."

Kats nodded appreciatively. "She's a fierce and capable woman. And you've grown into the new Tiger Lady. Congratulations."

"Yes, I'm putting my journalism degree to good use here," she waved her hands.

"Gracie, normally I'd be very happy to banter with you; doing that was always fun. But we have some friends in danger, and we need some special supplies. That's why we came to you."

"You have money?"

"We do."

"Good, because whatever it is you need, it's going to be expensive."

"I figured as much."

"So, what do you want?"

"*Shé,*" he said succinctly. "A lot of them."

"*Shé?*" she laughed. "What the hell are you thinking?"

Molly, Baker, and Heckman looked back and forth at each other, hoping someone understood what was going on. No one did.

"I need a distraction," Kats said, "and a barrel full of *shé* would be an ideal distraction."

Gracie slapped her desk, "You crazy son of a bitch!" She smiled at him and looked at the confused faces of the party. She said to them, "Snakes. He wants a barrel of snakes!"

"What?" said the three of them in chorus. Kats simply nodded. Molly looked at him aghast, and Baker and Heckman seemed to be squirming at the thought.

"Why would she have snakes?" Molly asked.

"The Chinese eat snakes," Kats said. "Most every restaurant in Chinatown serves snake. It's not on the Western menus, but they all have it. The locals know how to ask for it."

"And we can't import snakes," continued Gracie, "so there are local snake farms here in Chinatown. Delicious, but they do bite."

"Fireworks factories and snake farms," Baker said, shaking his head. "Good lord, what else is going on down here?" he asked.

"You probably don't want to know," Kats said. "This is another world."

"I can get you snakes," Gracie said. "When?"

"Tomorrow night. Can't sit on them too long. We will need them the night after next."

"I'll arrange to have them ready for pick up. You need to provide transport," Gracie said.

"These two are in charge of logistics," Kats said, pointing to Heckman and Baker, who looked nervously at each other. "I also need something special."

"I'm all ears."

"*Yanjingshé*. Maybe two or three."

"Cobras? You want fucking cobras?" Gracie exclaimed with a laugh. "What kind of party are you throwing?"

"Umm, cobras?" interjected Molly. "This is sounding crazier and crazier."

"Your girl is right, Kats," Gracie said. "Those fuckers are mean."

"I'm counting on it," he said.

"But you know they remove their poison glands?" Gracie said.

"I know that, but my friends won't," he said with a smile.

"I'll see about your specials. And payment?"

"We got that handled," Heckman said. He produced a card

and handed it across the desk. "Send the bill here. Maybe put piping on the invoice."

Gracie eyed the card, gave it a twirl, and put it in her desk. "Does that conclude our business?" she asked.

"I guess it does," Kats said. "Thank you again."

Gracie eyed him and his crew for a moment, stood, and came around the desk. Molly noted she was taller than expected, and the dress clung to her curves like a second skin. An unusual sensation of jealousy mixed with competition washed over her. We all have a past, she thought. Some sexier than others.

Gracie stood in front of Kats, and the two locked eyes for a moment. "I was angry with you, Katsuhiro, but you know I never could stay mad at you. Now I'm very curious who's on the other end of this slithering surprise."

Kats smiled at her. "I can't say now, but if this works, I'll tell you then."

She gave a nod, "Deal. Over dinner. You can bring the *gwaipo*. She looks fun."

Molly wasn't sure how to interpret that, but in moments, she and the rest of the team were walking back through the shop. Catching up to Kats, she asked, "What does *gwaipo* mean?"

"Roughly translated it means 'White devil woman.'" Molly couldn't help but laugh.

Once outside, Kats turned to Baker and said, "Good news. We're going to make some pepper bombs." Baker smiled, clapped his hands, and looked like a kid being told he was going to the circus. Heckman smiled at his longtime partner. The two were accomplished explosive experts from their days as combat engineers and from many legitimate jobsites since the war. Still, the opportunity to learn a new kind of explosive was, he had to admit, professionally interesting. They spent the next two hours in and out of Chinese markets purchasing bundles of red peppers, flour, ground pepper, and several other ordinary ingredients. Like baking a horrible cake, Heckman thought.

After lunch they returned to Sonny's, who had three large pallets of fireworks ready for them. They carefully loaded them into the back of their truck, and Baker and Heckman returned to the Charles Construction offices, which had become the makeshift war room. Molly and Kats drove toward Fisherman's Wharf and parked several blocks from Pier 23.

"Ready for your first recon mission?" he asked.

"Just tell me what to do."

"Look like you belong there. That's the most important part of recon."

"OK, so what should we do?"

"Let's go for a walk," he smiled at her.

They strolled past several of the long piers that contained so much of the local fishing and maritime industry. Fishermen, stevedores, sailors, truck drivers, and buyers from restaurants and groceries moved up and down the street. They walked east along the Embarcadero, happy to be outside and out of Chinatown.

"So, you and Gracie," Molly began.

"Yeah, that was a long time ago. Like I said, we met during college."

"But it didn't end well?"

"It ended like most relationships do when you're young. Believe it or not, the Japanese-Chinese thing is tricky."

"I get it. The Irish and English seem very similar to the

outside world, but that history is more than tricky." She paused for a moment, turning toward him, "We both have a past. That's OK."

He kissed her, took her by the hand, and they walked in a companionable silence for a ways. As they approached Pier 23, he said to her, "OK, don't change your pace, but try to take in little details. People, doors, windows, things like that. We're going to walk in and see if we can walk past the Lanza section and onto the main pier. Ready?"

"Ready."

As they entered the broad doorway to Pier 23, Molly realized that during her time in San Francisco, she'd never been inside one of the iconic piers along the waterfront. The working piers were a tough part of town, and while she wasn't scared, she also recognized that it might not be smart for a single woman to wander the Embarcadero alone. They were also working piers, and despite her love of seafood, she really had no reason to go inside. Now as they walked in, she saw the immense scope of these mammoth buildings that stretched up and down the city's waterfront. Easily three stories tall, the main pier stretched more than two football fields into the bay. It was hard to see the other end from the street entrance. The rooftop was corrugated steel, and the latticework of steel scaffolding held it all together like a gray spiderweb. And despite the lateness in the workday, the pier was busy. Open crates of fish, wooden pallets, melting blocks of ice, several small trucks, and so many bins of crabs! Transactions seemed to be happening everywhere as the last of the day's catch was being sold to Russian Hill restaurants that would have it on a plate by 8 pm tonight. As they walked forward, Molly's eyes were drawn to the small, side pier that extended off like a stub some thirty yards in length. There was another set of large wooden doors, open now, but they looked like they could repel an army. Beyond them looked to be a warehouse, and she could see a set of stairs going up to a second-floor mezzanine.

As they walked, Kats said, "Don't stare," and she quickly realized she'd been staring as they walked. He slowed and pretended to look at a crate of fresh-caught Pacific Halibut. "Look over my shoulder," he said to her. "What do you see?"

"Big, heavy doors. Stairs going up to another level."

"How many guards?""

"Two guys standing around the door. No... three! There's a guy above in some kind of elevated perch."

"Very good. What else?"

She moved closer to him and pretended to be evaluating the fish but now scanned the scene again. "Wooden floor, just like in here. I can see light coming in from the sides. Wait... there are docks and water access in there, too."

"Yes. That's how I'm planning on getting in."

She bent down and pretended to be lacing her shoe. "I can also see a skylight in the center of the roof."

"Really?" he said. She stood and they walked a few steps, this time with him turning and appearing to check a lower bin. There it was: a skylight. And it was open. That's interesting.

Not wanting to spend too much time in front of the Lanza compound, they walked to the end of the main pier, taking in the building structure, the windows, the floor, and the outside docks, which they assumed would be the same as the Lanza section of the building. As they returned toward the street entrance, Kats said, "Follow my lead," and taking her hand, they began walking toward the guards and the wooden door. Kats smiled at Molly, who smiled back. As they approached the doors, one of the men, wearing a dark, navy overcoat, stepped forward, raising a hand.

"Hey, pal. Private property," he said gruffly.

"Oh, so sorry," replied Kats with a smile. "Thought this was all part of the pier."

"Well, not this part," the man replied and gestured with his thumb toward the front. Just then, behind his head, Kats saw a door open on the second-floor mezzanine and a woman step out. Light shown behind her, and for just a second Kats could make out an office space. Lanza's office, just like Harry had described. Kats made a deferential bow, and he and Molly headed for the main door.

As they walked away Molly said, "When you talked to the guard, the guy up at the top pointed something that looked like the barrel of a gun toward you. Maybe a rifle."

"Or a machine gun. Good eye, detective!"

The next day was spent at the offices of Charles Construction. Harry sent the office girls home for the day, along with the other staff who hadn't been with him since the war. The remaining crew, eleven men, were all veterans of the war and experienced combat engineers who'd served with Harry. They knew him, and he trusted them. Kats and Harry explained what they were doing, planning the operation like they would have done in the forests of Europe.

Kats showed Baker and Heckman how to mix the ingredients for the pepper bombs. As they discussed how to use them, the two engineers commented that they should make a directional charge that would send the noxious fumes away from themselves and toward the enemy. By midafternoon they'd built two steel cannisters that looked like huge mortars. They packed the explosives and pepper mix into them and assured Kats that these would send a cloud away from the operator. As a backup, all the men would be carrying a gas mask, which they picked up from the surplus store.

They opened the pallets of fireworks and separated them into three groups. Kats was planning on taking one load with him on the surfboard so he could ignite it somewhere within the Lanza compound. The other two would be used as a diversion outside. As they looked over the box of Roman candles, Kats asked if they could be mounted in some way.

"Yeah, like a rocket launcher," Heckman mused. Two hours later they'd built a two-level steel frame that had forty Roman candles mounted on it. Using some detonation cord, they fashioned a fuse that, lit once, would successively light each candle within seconds.

Late that afternoon, Kats said to Heckman and Baker, "You should head back to Chinatown to pick up our special surprise." Baker gave a shudder, and Heckman grabbed the truck keys.

"C'mon," he said. "Let's get this over with."

Kats and Molly turned to Harry, who had been making bombs along with his men. "We need to call Lanza. You ready?"

"Yeah, let's get this operation going," Harry replied as they walked to his office.

There was a discrete knock on the door from Jimmy Lanza's secretary. She poked her head into the room, saying, "There's a Mr. Charles on the phone for you, sir."

Jimmy Lanza, impeccably dressed as always, smiled at the three men who sat across the office playing cards. One of them, Lanza's newest man, looked momentarily startled.

"Put him through, Gina," he said as he waived the men over to his desk. "Relax, Salvatore, I was expecting this call," he said to the former employee of Harry Charles. The phone rang, and Lanza picked up.

"Hello, Harry. What's new?" he said with a smile that made his men laugh. Franco didn't smile.

"Very fuckin' funny. I know you got Gianni thanks to the fuck Franco."

"Yes, thank you very much for both of them," Lanza said.

"We need to meet. We still got business," Harry pressed.

"Why do I need you, Harry? Do you have the other brother?"

"No, but I got the next best thing. I got his girl here, and he's already pissing himself to get her back. You only have half of the land. You kill Gianni, and Anton gets everything. That's how their old man set it up. And Anton is pissed at his brother. Apparently, they had a big blowup about all the gambling. That's why Gianni went to LA."

Sitting around the office, they all had to admit that Harry was a convincing liar. It was a gift. He continued to press Lanza.

"Let's get together. You bring the brother, and I'll bring the girl. We get our leverage together and make the kid sign over the lot. That way we can both get to a payday."

"Yes, I hear you need a payday, Harry. Why don't I just wait you out and pick up your land from the bank?"

"'Cuz you may not get it. I'll make sure to tell some of my country club buddies about a great land deal they could get in on. They got shit-tons of money and no scruples about using it. Besides, that could take months. We can both get paid if we put this shit aside."

Lanza was quiet for a moment. At heart he was a shrewd

businessman, and Harry did make sense. "Alright. Let's bring our leverage together and then make sure that the younger Vello shows up ready to sign, or pieces of his girl and his brother start arriving on his doorstep."

"Sounds good to me. I can get in contact with the kid and let him know the deal. How about my office tomorrow after hours?" Harry said, knowing Lanza wouldn't agree.

"No, you bring her to me. Just you, Harry. I don't want any complications with our men. Bring her to my office on the pier, and have the young man meet us there."

Harry paused for dramatic effect. "Fine. Tomorrow night?

"Yes, after the main pier gets quiet. 9 pm, and don't try anything stupid." The line clicked off.

"We're set for tomorrow night," Harry said with an evil smile.

CHAPTER 28

As men who had fought in battle, Kats, Harry, and his men knew about the wait before the action. It was the quiet time when you checked and re-checked your gear. You thought about your family, but not too much. You thought about your mission, your team, and your job. You rehearsed your job in your head until you did it perfectly. You kept that image in your head because that image was the pathway to survival. They weren't exactly storming the beaches of Normandy—Harry and his guys knew all too well about that—but they were going into danger against real gangsters with real guns.

Kats and Molly arrived at the makeshift headquarters at lunchtime. Kats checked in with Heckman and Baker. "Did you get our specials?" They looked at each other and then at him. Baker spoke first.

"Why didn't you warn us?" he said quietly, swallowing hard as he did.

"You knew we were getting snakes, right?" Kats asked.

"Oh yeah, we knew," Heckman said. "But we had to go

into the whatever they call it, the farm, to get 'em."

"They raise them underground, in the basement of some fucking building," Baker said. "I seen shit in war, man. This was worse."

Heckman continued, "They were everywhere. In baskets, in big wooden crates. Crawling all over each other," he shuddered. "It was the skeeviest thing I've ever seen."

"I'll never be the same," Baker said flatly.

Kats tried hard not to laugh. He nodded appreciatively, "Thanks for doing that."

Baker shuddered again. "Were you able to get the specials?" Kats asked, not wanting to trigger them again.

"Oh, that fucking monster?" Heckman said. "It's in a box next to the barrel. The guy there said sorry that he only had the one, but it's fucking huge."

"Devenomed?"

"Yeah," Baker said. "Still the scariest thing I've ever seen. Took two guys to get it in the box. Must be eight feet long."

"Good work," Kats said. "What about the fireboat?" "Yeah, we scoped that out, too. It's based out of Pier 22 ½ as part of the fire station there," Heckman said.

"How are you going to 'borrow' it?"

"Easy enough. Couple hours before the actual gig, we start a small fire a couple blocks from the firehouse," Heckman replied.

"Yeah, and when they respond, we slide onto the dock, cut the boat loose, and she's ours," continued Baker. "We were River Rats in the army. Worked on boats, so driving that tug ain't a problem. We sail her out into the bay and come back to Pier 23 on schedule. You should see them water cannons mounted up there like a couple of fifty calibers."

"Except these **pump over 6,000 gallons of water per min-**

ute at 150 pounds per square inch of pressure. Easily enough to knock in a door or windows. Take a man clean off his feet. Like getting hit with a sledgehammer," Heckman said.

"That's what I'm counting on," Kats said as he saw Anton walk in. "You all set?" he asked.

"Yep. I docked her in the municipal pier for the day. Your launch is on board and painted black for night work. We just need to load your supplies onto her." Kats gave him a thumbs up. Anton looked around at the makeshift devices, nodding appreciatively. "Hey, is that bulldozer on the flatbed out front part of this operation?"

"Yeah," Kats said. "Armored transport."

By late afternoon Shig had joined them, and they went over the plans once more. Kats wanted to tell Harry and his men to leave their guns, but he knew that wasn't going to happen. Instead, he drilled into them to use the other tools they'd prepared and leave the guns as a last resort. They reluctantly agreed. The afternoon waned, and the teams made their last-minute preparations. Kats rounded up Shig and Molly, the two least experienced in all of this and the two he cared the most about.

"Shig, I'm counting on you to get Molly clear once the diversion starts. You have one job. Got it?"

Shig looked at his friend, then Molly, and then back to Kats. "I got it, man. I promise."

Kats thumped him on the chest, and the two old friends smiled at each other. Turning to Molly, he wasn't as sure what to say. Seeing his trouble, she spoke for him.

"I promise, as soon as the action starts, I'm out of there. Nothing crazy." Kats looked at her and started to speak but felt a lump in his throat, and his face got hot.

"If anything happened to you..." he began.

"I know," she said pulling him close. "I know." She kissed him fiercely. "You get Gianni and get both your asses out of there, soldier."

"Yes, sir," he said and kissed her again.

Turning to the team, "Time to go."

The sun had set some thirty minutes before, and Anton and one of his men pushed the sailboat away from its mooring at the municipal pier. On board, Kats prepped the waterproof bin that held his equipment for the mission. A small black satchel contained a gas mask, his wooden *tonfa* weapon, two smoke bombs, a section of det cord, a lighter, and a length of silk rope. A thick army-green canvas bag lay next to it and occasionally moved as its reptilian occupant silently voiced its displeasure. Kats had placed his boots into the bin as well. And at the center of the bin lay a bushel-sized box with 100 vertical tubes spread upward in an array. Known as a "cake," this box of fireworks could be lit with a single fuse and then would proceed to sequentially launch its rockets skyward. On the Fourth of July, it would provide quite a show. On a dock in the bay, he hoped it would provide a suitable diversion.

Kats hefted the ten-foot surfboard that Anton had painted black and equipped with a small platform to hold a bit of cargo. The bay was relatively calm this evening, and he was confident he could paddle the board and his equipment right up to the Lanza docks. They're not expecting an amphibious assault, he'd said to his friends, and he hoped that was true.

As they sailed out into the bay, the sky blackened into night. Anton knew the area well. They circled the boat around, and Anton pointed to a distinctive set of twin lights back along the city. "Follow those twin lights," he said to Kats. "That's the nose of Pier 23. Go to the left of those, and you end up on the Lanza side."

Checking their watches, Kats said, "I should go now. Gives me plenty of time to get into position."

Together they lowered the surfboard into the water, followed by Kats. They lowered the bin down, careful to not get the "cake" wet. Kats tied it to the platform and checked the stability of the board. Satisfied, he gave a thumbs up to Anton, who proceeded to hand down the other bags that were placed forward of Kats in the bin. "World's smallest amphibious assault vehicle," Kats said.

Anton nodded and said, "Good luck. Bring everyone back home." Kats nodded and set off, laying forward on the board and paddling with his arms.

At Pier 22 ½, Heckman, Baker, and a younger man named Jackson watched as the station house emptied due to the fire a few blocks away. As the fire truck pulled away, Baker said, "Guys are right on time." The firehouse's front gate was locked, but they'd brought a set of bolt cutters that made short work of the chain. Once inside, they moved quickly to the dock side of the firehouse and began to push the fireboat into the bay. As they checked the controls, they heard a loud barking, and a Dalmatian came bounding toward them and onto the boat.

"Shit!" Heckman said, drawing his pistol.

"You can't shoot the dog!" yelled Baker. "You guys get her underway. I'll take care of the dog," he said, leaving Heckman and Jackson to stare at each other.

Moments later, the barking stopped and was replaced by "Good boy! There's a good boy!" as Baker and the dog played on the bow of the boat.

"Unbelievable," Heckman smiled as he turned the boat out into the bay and into position.

Molly and Harry sat in Harry's car, an uncomfortable silence between them. They were parked five blocks from Pier 23 on Vallejo Street, waiting for confirmation from Harry's men that everything was in position for the 9 pm meeting with Lanza.

He reached into his front coat pocket and pulled out a tiny pistol, a two-shot Derringer, and offered it to Molly. "I know your boyfriend there doesn't like guns, but in case things go bad, you should have this."

"It's not that he doesn't like guns, Harry. He's trying not to get people killed."

"Yeah, well, sometimes you don't have a choice," he said knowingly. She looked at the tiny gun in his big hand and took it. She slid it into her bra and adjusted her clothes to cover any trace of the weapon. Besides, as far as anybody else knew, she was there as Harry's prisoner, not accomplice. She sat back. Harry looked at her, and she worried what he was going to say.

"So, you wanna come back to work for me?" That wasn't what she'd expected.

"Are you kidding, Harry?"

"Nope. You was the best office manager we ever had. Seriously. I know we got a little sideways here..."

"Sideways? You extorted people. You burned businesses to the ground. People ended up in the hospital."

Harry was quiet for moment. Unusually so, thought Molly. She expected him to lash out angrily at her, but instead he quietly said, "Yeah. I'm not too proud of that. I've been fighting for stuff all my life. Usually winning. Shit, when we was in Europe, I was a fucking hero. I got shit done, and the brass rewarded me and my guys. Guess those lessons don't apply back here."

"That was war, Harry."

"Sometimes feels like it's still war over here. Guys like Lanza and the other so-called legit businessmen. They're as dirty and cut-throat as just about anything I saw in war."

Molly couldn't deny that reality and slowly nodded her head.

"C'mon, red. I'm not such a bad guy."

"You're a greedy bastard, Harry."

"Doesn't make me a bad guy." And they both laughed despite it all. Yeah, Harry was a greedy, self-centered bastard, but that was exactly the lessons life had taught him.

"Don't get us killed tonight, and we'll talk," she smiled.

Down the street a truck turned the corner and headed toward them. As it rolled past Harry's car on the opposite side, an arm waved up and down from the driver side of the cab. "That's the signal. You ready, red?"

"Yes," she said more confidently than she felt.

Harry started the car, and they rolled down the dark street toward the pier.

Pier 23 was officially closed until the following morning. Its giant outer doors were closed like the other working piers to its north and south. Streetlights, dimmed by the light fog, tried tepidly to illuminate the city. A tourist might have commented on how dark the city seemed, but locals knew theirs was a city of shadows, islands of light, and with so many cool shades of gray you could write a book about it.[19] As Harry approached the pier and parked his car across the street from the building, he saw four men in overcoats standing outside the door.

"Looks like they're our escort," Harry said.

"Remember to make it look real," she said to him.

He grunted, "Yeah, real it is."

Parking the car, he exited and moved to the passenger side as Lanza's men moved closer, appearing to reach beneath their overcoats. Harry grabbed Molly by the arm and roughly pulled her from the car. He slammed the door, and she twisted angrily in his grasp, staring daggers at the approaching crew.

"Feisty one there," said one of the guards who managed a leer with a cigarette dangling from his mouth.

"You have no idea," Harry said truthfully.

Cigarette man, apparently the leader, said, "We gotta check you, Charles."

Harry grunted, and with his left hand he pulled back his jacket front, revealing his .45 in the shoulder holster. They'd have expected as much. Cigarette man nodded and took the weapon. His partner patted down Harry, and finding nothing waved him inside. Harry held Molly with his right hand, and she walked at his side, clearly angry. Passing through the main entrance, Harry heard the men close the huge gate behind them, like a cell door closing. Harry felt a surge of adrenaline like he hadn't felt since the battlefields of Europe, and he forced his muscles to relax. Molly glanced at him, and he winked at her.

Lanza's men flanked him, and two were behind him, with drawn weapons, Thompson submachine guns, a staple of organized crime since Prohibition. They walked into the pier, closed for the evening. In the near darkness, Harry couldn't see the far end of the pier. To their right, Lanza's compound was bright by comparison. They approached the heavy wooden doors, only open wide enough for two men to walk abreast inside. Harry glanced up and saw a lookout on the gantry above. He, too, held the fearsome submachine gun.

Outside in the narrow inlet on the Lanza side of the compound, Heckman quietly navigated the fireboat into position. Cutting the engines back, he placed the boat in position to quickly reach the dock. He glanced at his watch. Soon.

Molly could feel her heart pounding as they walked the cool, dank pier. She didn't need to act afraid. She was terrified. Not so much for herself, but for Kats, Gianni, Shig, and even Harry. There were a lot of guns, and Lanza's men looked practiced at using them. Passing into the Lanza compound, she saw the wide staircase ahead of them that led to the second-floor offices. She looked left and right, noting at least a dozen more men. When her eyes returned to the staircase, she saw an older, well-dressed man stride forward. Lanza, she thought. Standing just behind him to the side, like a well-trained attack dog, was Franco. She heard a low growl from Harry, as he, too, saw his former right-hand man at the top of the stairs. Lanza smiled at them and rubbed his hands together.

"Welcome, Harry," he said loudly, with the confidence of a man who thought he held all the cards. "And this must be the girlfriend, Miss Hayes." She jerked her arm at that, staring daggers at Lanza. "You both know my newest associate, Mr. Francona," he said, rubbing it in Harry's face.

Harry flushed, and Molly thought he might charge Franco right there. Instead, he managed to snort, "This what you meant by an Italian thing?"

"It's a money thing, Harry," Franco said coolly. "A whole lot a money."

"Mercenary piece of shit," replied Harry.

"Gentlemen, we're here to do business," Lanza interrupted.

"Yeah, we are. I brought the girl. Where's Gianni?"

Lanza made a gesture to someone behind him, and a moment later, two men pulled Gianni to the top of the stairs. He looked disheveled, unshaven, and tired but otherwise whole. His eyes widened seeing Molly, but he said nothing. Lanza then asked, "Where's the other brother?"

"I told him to be here," Harry said, looking at his watch, "any time now. I thought we should settle our business."

"Yes, I thought as much. I took the liberty of drafting some new documents for the brothers to sign tonight. Selling to me."

"That wasn't our deal," Harry said.

"That was before things shifted. Look around you. See the men? See the guns? That's leverage, Harry. You don't have it." Harry glowered but said nothing. "Don't worry, Harry. We still need a contractor for the work out in Bayview Heights. We'll hire you and your crew. You'll make a good payday. But now you work for me."

Harry was about to tell Lanza to go fuck himself when the world exploded.

Just as anticipated, Kats arrived at low tide, allowing him to slide under the dock attached to Lanza's section of the pier. He saw an expensive Chris-Craft motorboat tied to Lanza's dock but no other boats. He settled underneath the dock and listened. No shouts, no footsteps. He was clear. As he stood on the surfboard, he could reach the dock, and he lifted the bin from the front of the board onto the dock and quickly followed it into the shadows. He unpacked the bin, putting on his boots, slinging the black satchel across his shoulders, and carefully placing the green canvas bag to the side. He lifted the cake of fireworks and checked it for any water. Clear.

He checked his watch, seeing he had time until Harry and the other parts of the plan were in place. He stood, walked in the shadow of the main building, down the length of the dock. He noted the lights inside Lanza's compound, the big glass windows opened outward toward the water. He thought he might be able to jump up and into one of them, but as he neared the end of the dock, he saw a metal ladder attached to the building that led up to the corrugated metal roof. Remembering the skylight inside, he decided that would be his point of entry. He just needed to time everything right.

He measured the det cord and, as Heckman and Baker had taught him, the length of cord would determine the time it took to explode. He figured he needed five minutes to get up onto the roof and over to the skylight. He measured out six minutes to give himself a bit of extra time remembering what the two explosive experts told him, "It ain't exactly precise." He then moved the cake of fireworks to the midpoint of the building, right below an open window. He ran the det cord down the pier and checked his watch. Soon.

At 9:15 pm the engine of the bulldozer kicked over and thundered to life. The driver engaged the set of levers and gears, and the urban tank rumbled backward off of the flatbed trailer on which it had arrived. He raised the blade several feet off the ground, providing a forward shield. As he turned the steel behemoth down the street, Shig jumped onto the back of the machine, where he stood next to a large barrel with a wooden cover, which he checked again to make sure was securely in place. Six of Harry's men fell in line behind the bulldozer, each armed with a rifle. Two other men hung further back with a large cart that was covered with a tarp. The squad rolled down the street. Several cars passed them, slowed to look, and then seeing the guns, sped off. They stopped half a block away from Pier 23, around the corner and out of sight. One of Harry's men moved forward and peered around the corner. He turned back, raising two fingers indicating the number of guards. Then he looked at his watch, which made the rest of the men check theirs. Soon.

After lighting the det cord, Kats moved to the end of the dock and began his ascent up the ladder. He slung the green canvas bag over his shoulder. It was surprisingly heavy, and to his great discomfort, kept shifting as it pressed against his back. Just climb, he thought. His internal clock told him he had about three minutes left if the measurements were accurate. Halfway up the ladder, night turned to day.

Fuck!

Even expecting the explosions, Harry and Molly were dazed by the intensity of the fireworks that seemed to be right outside the windows to their left. Part of him had thought, "Fucking fireworks? Kid stuff." But these were not the kind of fireworks kids played with; these were the big ones that cities set off for special events, and Harry had never stood this close to a display like that. It was like a series of mortar shells going off in the next room. The rockets flashed outside the window, but many of them were shooting through the window and exploding inside. Acrid gray smoke was filling the room, and the noise was deafening, but Harry heard Lanza yell above it all, "Kill them!" he pointed toward Harry. Guns swung in their direction, and Harry tossed Molly behind a wooden crate and dived after her. He heard bullets pass nearby.

As the fireworks started, Heckman flashed the lights and blew the foghorn as Baker swung the water cannon around, hit the "on" valve, and the nozzle came to life. Spewing water through the windows, Baker swept the cannon like the 50-caliber machine guns he used in the Battle of the Bulge. Beside him, barking excitedly, clearly enjoying himself, was the fire station dalmatian.

From their cover, Harry could see the gunmen coming down the stairs toward them. Not good, he thought. Then, from across the building, he saw flashing red lights from outside and heard a foghorn bellow. Suddenly water was streaming through the windows as the high-velocity water cannons from *The Phoenix* began to shatter the windows and flood the building. As the cannons swept through the room, they hit the men on the stairs, knocking them off their feet, and they slid down to the warehouse floor. That was all the opening Harry needed.

Rising from behind the crate, he charged the two floundering men. His massive fist found the face of the first man, and with an audible crunch, Harry dropped him. The second man staggered forward, wrapping Harry in a bear hug. He was strong, but Harry was stronger. Harry wrapped his hands around the back of the man's head and brought his knee up, connecting with the man's chin. The man sank to the floor, and Harry felt a surge of adrenaline unlike anything since the forests of Germany. He turned to look around and saw Franco at the bottom of the stairs. He had just time enough to register that fact when a bullet from Franco's gun slammed into his shoulder. Pain erupted across his vision, but instead of going down, the adrenaline surge pushed him forward, and he charged Franco, whose eyes went wide when the big man didn't go down.

Harry slapped the gun away with one hand and threw a tremendous upper cut that, had it connected fully, would have snapped the other man's neck. Instead, it glanced off his cheek, bringing stars to his eyes but not taking him down. Franco pivoted and slammed an elbow into Harry's exposed side. He kicked him in the leg, causing Harry to drop to one knee. Blood was running down Harry's left arm now, and he felt the wetness on his hand. Instead of trying to rise, he surged forward, low like his days playing football, and tackled Franco around the legs. Together they sprawled across the floor, oblivious to the smoke, explosions, and gunfire around them. They were in a private war that each knew was to the death.

They savagely groped at each other's faces, with Franco's teeth closing on Harry's fingers, causing the man to scream. Harry thrust his huge head forward, catching Franco across the nose, breaking it, and momentarily stunning the man. Harry reached out and grabbed Franco from behind, his thick arms locking around the other man's neck. Then Harry began to apply the squeeze. He could feel Franco writhe and struggle against him, but there was no way Harry was going to let go. Franco began to panic, realizing that he was trapped in two python-like arms. His fingers moved from trying to grasp at Harry to the sheath in the small of his back. He grabbed the concealed knife with his right hand, turned the blade over, and blindly drove it into Harry's exposed right side.

Harry could feel his arms constricting around Franco's neck, and he reveled in that feeling of power and revenge. Then there was a sharp pinch in his right side, then another, and Harry felt a looseness in his side followed by a wave of pain. His arms couldn't hold themselves together any longer, and he felt himself slide to the floor.

"No!" Molly screamed as she watched the frightening tableau unfold in front of her. As the knife flashed, she ran forward, pulling the derringer from her shirt. As Harry slumped to the floor, Molly swung the tiny barrel toward Franco and fired. Franco saw her coming and ducked as the bullet careened past him. He lunged forward, catching her by surprise, and they rolled onto the floor. With one hand, Franco secured the pistol while the other punched her in the stomach, driving all the air from her lungs and leaving her curled in a fetal position on the ground.

He stood up triumphantly over her as Lanza's men, no longer surprised and now prepared for the streams of water that continued to sweep the room, had reorganized in the center of the room. As they prepared to move, two small objects fell from above, bounced on the ground, and a moment later exploded one after another with muffled "thunks" followed by billowing smoke that rapidly filled the building.

As she lay there trying to fill her lungs, Molly saw smoke billowing around her, and from outside she heard a crunching noise like the building was falling down. Machine guns roared. The next thing she saw were the huge wooden doors of Lanza's compound come crashing inward followed by the forward blade of a bulldozer. Shots rang off the metal shield with audible "pings" and flashes of light. She was about to stand up and yell when she felt a hand grab her hair and pull her upward. Franco spat at her and said, "You're coming with me." He dragged her up the stairs toward Lanza's office.

As she staggered up the stairs, Molly heard two whooshing sounds and, turning, saw twin clouds of reddish dust race across the room, covering Lanza's men. The pepper bombs! She could smell the pepper in the air as she entered the second floor, and she knew it was terrible for the men inside that cloud. Franco dragged her through the outer offices and into Lanza's sanctum where the boss stood seething. Gianni was sprawled on the floor nearby, a second guard stood over him. Franco tossed her into the room, and she fell near Gianni.

He turned to her, "What the hell is going on?" he asked through a bloodied lip.

"D-Day," she replied.

Shig rode the giant bulldozer through the main gates of the pier after the two guards, seeing the approaching vehicle, realized a speedy retreat was called for. Once inside the main pier, the team lined up behind the dozer and prepared to breach the wooden gates. Outside, the fireworks continued, and they could hear the jets of water from the fireboat. As the dozer surged forward, a guard above the gate opened fire with his machine gun. The dozer driver moved the blade higher, providing some protection, and behind him, Shig heard Harry's men laying down suppressing fire. Moments later the dozer slammed against the gates, which groaned and cracked but held. The driver threw the rig in reverse, backing up, and once again slammed into the gates. This time they gave way, and the dozer rolled through and the gate collapsed beneath it. From behind him, the mounted roman candle rocket launcher began to blaze away, sending fireballs into the compound.

Harry's men moved quickly inside, and to the left and right of the dozer they ignited two more cakes of fireworks, causing even more smoke and noise. Seeing that Lanza's men were scrambling, they brought forward the two makeshift mortars and fired the pepper bombs inside toward Lanza's men. As the red-brown cloud billowed into the room, the dozer turned to the side and brought Shig toward the center of the room. From his perch, he ripped the lid off the barrel and pushed the open barrel toward Lanza's men. The barrel fell to the ground, and like a giant can of slithering noodles, hundreds of angry snakes sprayed out over the floor. As Shig and the rest of Harry's men donned their gasmasks, they could begin to hear screams from inside the compound.

As the fireworks prematurely lit up the night, Kats quickly climbed to the corrugated rooftop. He reached the roof, and by the light of the nearby buildings he could see the ridges of the roof leading toward a square of light in the middle— the open skylight. Skittering across the ridge, he reached the open skylight and looked down to see men running about, with smoke and columns of water moving through the space. I have to get down there! He looked around the opening, searching for a place to tie off his rope. There! Several pipes formed a sturdy looking anchor to which he tied off and then looped the silk rope through his thick leather belt in a makeshift rappelling harness. He pulled the smoke bombs from his satchel, quickly lit their fuses, and dropped them into the open window. Seconds later he heard the muffled release of smoke. Pulling the gasmask over his head, he strode to the edge and slid down the rope into the center of a dark cloud that momentarily blinded him.

As he landed, he quickly surveyed the ground. Gun shots were all around him in the cloud as men screamed and seemed to be firing at the floor. As he stepped, he felt something slide beneath his foot and, looking down, he saw snakes slithering everywhere. He felt a wave of revulsion surge through him even though he was prepared for it. Lanza's men were not. Suddenly blinded, they opened their eyes to see snakes crawling all over them. Angry snakes, that even though not poisonous, weren't shy about biting. Truly the stuff of nightmares.

Kats realized that the men were paying almost no attention to him. Two of them got close, and Kats dispatched them with well-placed blows from the wooden *tonfa*. Around him he saw that the fireballs had started a dozen small fires, and he knew that in minutes, those small fires would turn into one big one. He turned to see the familiar shape of Shig running toward him in a gas mask. But no sign of Molly!

"Kats!" he yelled through the mask.

"Where's Molly?" demanded Kats. Shig shook his head. They both looked around and spotted Harry laying on the floor, unmoving. They came to his side, and Kats saw that the man was wounded. Badly. His shoulder wasn't too bad, but the wound to his side was bleeding profusely. As they moved him, Harry groaned.

Kats pulled up his mask, "Harry! Harry! Where's Molly?"

Harry's eyes seemed to go in and then out of focus. Blood came from his mouth. "Franco took her," he groaned and pointed up the stairs. Kats grabbed Shig and pulled his jacket off. He wadded it up and pressed it to Harry's side. "Shig, press here, and as soon as it's clear, get him to a medic. The fire's spreading, and you have to get everyone out of here. But keep pressure on that wound."

Shig nodded and looked scared. "And you?" he asked.

"I'm going to get Molly and Gianni." He stood, grabbed his *tonfa* and the green canvas bag, and ran up the stairs.

The second-floor landing was clear, and the doors to the office space hung half open. Kats pulled his mask off to better see and entered the outer room, which was spared the worst of the smoke and pepper cloud. Two desks were situated like guardians, along with tables and chairs. A pair of large, dark-stained doors were visible across the room. From the waist level up, the doors contained large, ornately styled stained glass. As Kats approached the door, his shadow must have been visible on the glass. Bullets shattered the left-hand windowpane, and Kats ducked down beneath the wooden door frame. Time for something special.

He unslung the green canvas bag from his back and set it on the floor. He carefully untied the drawstring and loosened the opening. Then he stood to the side of the broken door window and tossed the heavy bag inside. He heard it land with a thud, and a moment later he heard someone scream, "What the fuck?" and shots began to fire. "Kill it!" came another shout. More shots, and Kats wondered how hard it must be to hit a moving, angry snake. He listened as more shots and screams echoed out of the room. Time to move.

As Kats threw open the door, he almost collided with one man who was fleeing the room. Kats slipped to his right and brought his left arm up and across in a flat arc that caught the man at the base of the neck, clotheslining him to the floor.

He could see Lanza crouching behind his desk as Franco and another guard stood, loading their pistols. At the one guard's feet lay Gianni, seemingly unconscious. Molly was beside Lanza. Kats's eyes locked on Molly's, and he sprinted forward. The guard tried to finish loading his pistol, but Kats was on him in an instant. He closed in on the man hoping that Franco would be reluctant to shoot at his comrade. The man brought the butt of the empty gun down on Kats's back as they grappled. Pain flared across his shoulder, and his right arm went numb, causing him to drop the *tonfa*. Kats took him to the ground, and twisting out of the man's grasp, he brought his foot down in a savage heel stomp to the man's chest. Molly heard ribs crack, and the man curled into a ball and groaned.

Franco finished reloading and swung the barrel of the pistol toward Kats, who was still on the ground defenseless. Molly screamed and launched herself at Franco, her fingers like talons seeking the soft parts of his face. He cried out as her nails raked his once-handsome face. Then, pushing her away, Franko swung the gun toward her. It seemed as if it happened in slow motion as the gun exploded point blank at her, and she crumpled to the floor. Kats heard himself scream "No!" but it was too late.

Kats crossed the room in two panther-like strides as Franco tried to bring the gun back around toward him. Kats caught the gun hand, twisting its lethal end away as another bullet exploded from the chamber. As they grappled for the gun, Franco brought his head forward, smashing into Kats just above his right eye, splitting his brow like a cut boxer. Blood immediately washed down his face, blinding him in his right eye. But still he held onto control of the weapon hand. Kats's years of training took over and he pivoted, holding the bigger man's wrist in place as he flipped him over his hip onto the floor below. Franco landed with a grunt but managed to pull Kats down with him.

As they struggled on the floor, Lanza, seeing an opening, grabbed a heavy wooden chair and swung it at the exposed back of the Japanese man. But Kats saw the blow coming out of his left eye and at the last instant was able to twist Franco into the path of the chair so that he took the brunt of the heavy blow. Kats kicked out at Lanza, hitting the man in the midsection and knocking him backward into the corner. To Lanza's horror, the cobra had taken refuge in that same corner, and upon landing next to it, the snake reared up and bit him upon the face. Lanza screamed and bolted for the door. As that was happening, Franco grabbed Kats from behind, and taking a lesson from Harry, wrapped his arms around the neck of the prone man.

Kats could feel the pressure mounting as he struggled to get his legs underneath him and try to escape. As Franco dragged him forward, Kats found himself staring at Molly, lying on her stomach behind the desk, a circle of blood underneath of her. Kats felt his own vision going red as he gasped for air. But he felt a savage anger well up inside of him, an anger he hadn't felt for years. He felt his hands raise upward and find Franco's eyes, and his fingers began to dig. He heard Franco cry out, and his hold around Kats's neck loosened just enough for Kats to slip free. As he did, the anger roared again, and he welcomed it like an old friend. Kats's father had taught him that anger was the loss of control that opened the door to the darkness. So much of his training, first with his father and then with the army, was all about control. He'd become an expert in control. But there was a flip side to that control. The yin to the yang. It was the rare moment of letting go and giving way to the animal, to the instinctual, to the savage inside. That savage now stood before Franco.

Franco drew his knife from the sheath and held it in a position that told Kats he knew how to use it. Kats stood, blood running down his face, and waved him in like a bullfighter. Franco feinted once, twice. With a lightning-fast backhand motion, he managed to slice the blade across Kats's belly, slicing open his shirt. A moment later Kats felt warm blood seep from the shallow gash. The blood only made him angrier. On Franco's next thrust, Kats kicked his lead leg, shattering the knee. Franco fell forward, blade outstretched. Kats easily avoided the thrust and brought his elbow down on the flailing man's collar bone, breaking it. Franco screamed in pain but managed to switch the knife to his other hand and, rising on his good leg, stabbed at Kats's heart. Kats followed the blade toward his center, shifting just enough to let it slide by. Then, turning Franco's momentum back upon itself, Kats twisted the knife backward, while driving the man to the floor. The blade, now guided by Kats's hand, plunged into the center of Franco's chest. Kats gave a scream of victory and anguish as Franco's eyes went wide and then closed forever. For a moment Kats sat astride the dead man, his own chest heaving, his blood-soaked hands still gripping the knife.

In that moment he was back in that bunker in France in 1944. He was that blood-thirsty savage again, the one who had charged the German bunker with an empty rifle and a bayonet. That savage had killed a dozen German soldiers and saved many of his comrades that day. That savage had saved him. And Kats hated him. He hated the loss of control, the loss of humanity, the loss of self. Kats hated that the savage was him. The savage had saved his life and his company and had killed every German in the bunker. Even the last two, who had thrown their weapons on the ground and raised their hands in surrender. The savage couldn't stop.

That day it had been his friend Tak who had talked him back down. Today it was a different friend. Against orders, Shig ran back into the compound after getting Harry out and to his men. He rushed up into the office where he spotted Kats, covered in blood but victorious over the dead man beneath him. The flames were starting to crawl up the walls in the office, and Shig knew they had to get out.

"Kats!" he shouted, falling to his knees next to his friend. "Hey, man. You OK?" he said, looking for wounds. "C'mon, man. We gotta get out of here." He saw Molly behind the desk, and his heart sank. He rose and went over to her, and though he feared the worst, he rolled her over. She groaned in pain and Shig exclaimed, "She's alive. Kats, she's alive!"

Kats heard the word "alive," and it brought him back into focus. He turned and moved to Molly, seeing the wound high up on her chest but away from her heart and lungs. He picked her up and cradled her to his chest. "Help Gianni," he said to Shig, who pulled the wobbly man to his feet. Together they hobbled to the door and down the stairs. Kats could hear sirens outside and saw flashing red lights. The compound was nearly engulfed in flames, and the fire licked the treads of the bulldozer as they rushed past it and out into the night.

Cold water splashed over the bow of the motorboat, hitting Jimmy Lanza in the face. He welcomed the coolness as his heartbeat was finally slowing down. Fleeing out of his burning office, Lanza's main fear was the bite on his face from the horrible snake. His men got him downstairs and out onto the dock. There they cast off the twenty-eight-foot Chris-craft Runabout and away from the burning warehouse. As they sped away into the night, Lanza thought he was going to die. Had he not been preoccupied with his own impending demise, he might have ordered his men to save certain key documents in the upstairs safe or the hidden suitcase of cash in the floor of his office. By the time he realized he wasn't going to die, he started to realize the enormity of his loss. The whole office, the money, the secret documents, the Vello kid, the whole fucking operation, up in flames! He laughed ruefully. As the wind whipped across the bow of the sleek craft, he took several deep breathes, savoring that sweetness. He was alive! The rest was just business, and business was for another day.[20]

It had been a long, strange night for Fire Company 22. First had been a bit of arson at one of the construction sites near their station. That had been easy enough. But then, just as they were wrapping that up, they got a four-alarm call at Pier 23. That had been a strange one. As they arrived, men were fleeing the burning building, and the captain was fairly certain that many of them were carrying guns. As they entered the building, they were surprised to find a bulldozer in the midst of the flames, and they noticed several snakes slithering about toward the cool night air. Later, one rookie would swear he saw a full-grown cobra. Rookies. They'd managed to control the blaze so that the main pier wasn't damaged, but the shed was a near total loss.

As the firemen returned to their station at Pier 22 ½, they immediately noticed something was wrong. Their state-of-the-art fireboat, *The Phoenix*, wasn't where it was supposed to be. The captain and the chief of the boat walked down the dock to the end where, somehow, *The Phoenix* was moored there, tied up to the end of the pier. And inside the closed cabin, barking, leaping from side to side, tail wagging, was Smudge, the station's ecstatic Dalmatian.

The captain turned to the chief and said, "That damn dog took the boat again."

CHAPTER 29

Two hours later, Kats, Shig, and Anton found themselves in the waiting room at Saint Francis Memorial Hospital. Gianni had been admitted for smoke inhalation and to check his head for a concussion. He was safe and going to be fine, Anton told Lilly over the phone. They settled in for the more serious situation regarding Molly and Harry.

Kats, his brow and stomach freshly stitched, paced the emergency room floor while Shig lay crumpled onto a chair. Sleep had taken him after the fear and adrenaline had worn off. Kats felt it, too, but fought the fatigue. He needed to know Molly would be OK before he could relax. The police had come and gone, and he gave them a brief statement that they were out on a date, walking down a romantic, seemingly deserted pier, when all hell broke loose. He wasn't sure they believed him, but he didn't care.

The door to the waiting room opened, and Kats's head swung around, hoping to see a doctor or a nurse. Instead, Heckman and Baker, looking tired and disheveled, entered.

"Hey, Kats," Heckman said. "They told us to wait in here regarding Harry."

"Yeah," Kats replied, "they both went into surgery a few hours ago."

"Any news?" Baker asked.

Kats shook his head but looked at the two men. "Good work back there tonight."

They both nodded in appreciation. "Except for that damn det cord you gave me," Kats said with a half-smile. "Stuff went off way too fast."

"I did say it was an estimate," replied Baker with a wry smile.

"With all the action down at the pier, we sailed back, tied her off to the nose of their dock, and we were gone," Heckman said.

"Nice. Too bad about your bulldozer, though," Kats said.

"Our bulldozer?" Heckman asked with a smile.

"What makes you think that was our bulldozer?" continued Baker with an even larger grin. "We borrowed it from Brandeis Construction."

"Assholes," finished Heckman with laughter.

Kats couldn't help himself. He burst out laughing as well.

Then the doors swung open again and in walked a nurse. "Are you gentlemen all here regarding the two who came in earlier tonight?" she asked as her eyes moved across the expectant faces.

"Yes!" Kats said, and the rest of the group quickly gathered around her.

"They're both out of surgery and stable."

Baker, Heckman, Anton, and Shig let out a cheer, and Kats felt his knees weaken and he bent forward, covering his face. All the tension and fear released as he felt Shig pounding him on the back in celebration.

"Can we see them?" Shig asked.

"The doctors said no visitors until tomorrow. Go home, get some rest, and let them sleep."

It was the next morning and Molly's eyes fluttered. She felt a hand squeeze hers. Kats said softy, "Molly. I'm here. It's OK. Everyone is OK." Her eyes slowly opened and saw the white confines of what had to be a hospital room. Then she saw Kats's concerned face near hers, and she felt a smile cross her lips. The next thing she noticed, her chest and shoulder felt like they'd been hit by a sledgehammer.

"Ow. So, this is what it's like to get shot?" she asked, her voice hoarse.

"Yeah, it is."

"I don't recommend it," she muttered.

"Neither do I," Kats said and kissed her forehead.

Over the next two days, a steady stream of visitors came to Molly's room. Shig and Anton, of course, but also Mrs. Harada and Emiko. Heckman and Baker brought her flowers and, to her surprise, Harry came in, attached to an IV, and sat with her for a few hours. They all quietly got their stories straight, and much to the frustration of the police, no one officially knew anything.

Kats had a final job for Harry. They brought a phone into his room, and he dialed a familiar number. A woman's voice answered, the usual service. "Yeah, it's Harry Charles. Tell Sand I need to meet with him. Tomorrow night, my office in the Russ Building, 9 pm. Tell him it's very important." As he hung up, Harry looked at Kats. "You think he'll come?"

"I'm pretty sure he knows the operation has gone sideways. He'll need to come to try to salvage something with you."

"You want my guys as backup?" Harry offered.

"Sand is dangerous but not that kind of dangerous. I'll be alright."

"So, what are you gonna do?" Harry said, grimacing as he shifted in bed.

"I'm going to scare Sand into doing the right thing."

Harry smiled wolfishly. "Smack that bastard around for me."

"Roger that."

Kats sat in Harry's nearly dark office. The light of a single lamp on the desk illuminated his face as he heard the outer door open and close. Right on time, he thought. A brief knock came on the office door, and without waiting for a response, Sand opened the door. He stood there for a moment, silhouetted in the doorframe, staring at Kats. He entered, taking off his hat, and sat down quietly in front of Harry's big desk.

They stared across the desktop, taking the measure of each other. Finally, Sand sat back, lacing his fingers together, "Mr. Takemoto, still tilting at windmills?"

"No, I'm going after sea monsters these days."

"Sea monsters?"

"Yes, giant, black, poison fish."

Sand looked momentarily confused.

"Inside joke. Never mind."

"I really don't have time for jokes, and I thought I made it clear the last time that we were done. The public isn't going to care about a little environmental issue. They care about security and jobs."

"Yes, the whole chamber of commerce argument. But I also know that you made assurances to the city that there would be no more nuclear materials in Hunters Point and that you would clean up the area. The city would care a lot if that promise wasn't being kept."

Sand eyed him coldly, and Kats continued.

"I think they might be interested in the submarine pens hidden in Hunters Point."

Sand had an excellent poker face, but Kats could tell he wasn't expecting that revelation. Time to hit him again.

"They might also be interested in the nuclear submarine that's berthed there in clear violation of the agreement you all made with the city to keep nuclear elements out of Hunters Point."

Sand's eyes narrowed dangerously. *May as well go for broke,* thought Kats with an internal chuckle.

"They'd also be interested in the nuclear missiles being housed there."

"You're guessing Mr. Takemoto."

"And I know they'd be very interested—no, not interested; they'd be outraged—at the nuclear accident from 1953."

"You can't prove anything."

"Can't I?" It was Kats's turn to bluff. "I have photos. A lot of them. Submarines. Missiles. I even have photos of you, Sand. With Admiral Rickover. And Harry Charles," he lied.

Kats continued, "That incident out on the base you talked about—someone entered through a ventilation shaft, didn't they? Then they somehow eluded your security."

Sands looked at the brim of his hat and appeared to dust something off it.

"I know you're thinking about how to make me disappear. I'm a problem, and men like you make problems go away. But if I go away, those photos will get sent to the *Chronicle*. And the *LA Times, Washington Post,* and *New York Times.*"

"What do you want?" Sand said icily, still looking at his hat.

"I want you to pay a fair market price for the Vellos' land.

Fair based on our shared knowledge that the stadium is coming. I want you to move their business to wherever they deem a suitable replacement space. I hear Sausalito is very nice. And any of the other businesses that want to move as well. You're even going to pay Harry Charles for his land, and you did promise him that contract for the stadium. He might be very upset if he didn't get that as well."

Now the hard part, thought Kats.

"I want you to make sure that any other folks in the basin who get sick will have access to proper medical care. Free medical care. Moving forward, you can't let people live in the basin until you clean it up, and you must clean all of it up."

Sand slowly nodded his head as if he were doing a complex math problem.

"Oh, yeah. And throw in season tickets for the Giants."

At that, Sand let a small smile cross his lips. "Believe it or not, Mr. Takemoto, we're trying to protect people."

"Funny ways of showing it. Arson, extortion, kidnapping, cover-ups..."

"That's the problem with power, Mr. Takemoto. Even when it tries to do the right thing, it's also concerned with appearances. Powerful people aren't afraid of making mistakes. They're afraid of those mistakes becoming public. Power goes to extraordinary lengths to preserve its façade. Even when it's trying to do the right thing."

"Then you'll go to those extraordinary lengths for the people of Bayview Heights and the basin."

Sand and Kats locked eyes across the desk. Sand broke the tableau with a raised eyebrow and a brief nod. "Agreed," he said as he stood. As he opened the door to leave, he turned. "You understand that your people must maintain their silence in this, too. Please impress that upon them, Mr. Takemoto," and Kats understood what wasn't being said.

The door closed, and Kats sat in the quiet office. He took a deep breath and found stillness for a moment. Then he allowed himself a smile at the thought of seeing his friends and telling them they'd won.

Epilogue

"Opening Day! How did you get these tickets again?" Shig asked as they found their way to the third base side of the lower section in Seals Stadium.

"Payment for a job," smiled Kats as he sat down next to Molly and Anton. Good seats, he thought, and four of them. His overall impression of Sand improved. In the three months since he'd last seen the man, the Vellos and almost every other business in the basin had moved out of the area. Anton and Gianni had been very well paid for the land, and somehow the local government found some economic development funds to relocate theirs and the other businesses. Anton had quadrupled Kats's fee.

Harry Charles was also pleased to sell his land and somehow land the no-bid contract to build the stadium.[21] It wasn't as big of a score as he'd hoped, but it was mostly legitimate. Enough for the hard-driving Charles, who despite his injuries, had decided to return to the field and supervise the stadium project in a hard hat instead of sitting behind a desk in an office.

Molly had thought about going back to work for Harry but decided it was best not to return. She was welcomed back to Ann's after fully recovering and had been asked to take on some of the management duties for the club. Her left arm still wasn't one hundred percent, as the shot to her upper chest had damaged some of the nerves. Her arm muscles twitched and felt weak, but the doctors told her that with exercise it should fade over time. The scar, however, was significant. Kats had worried she'd be self-conscious about it, but once the bandages had come off and she was looking at the discolored, rough skin, she put her hand on Kats's upper-left side and said, "Now we match."

Anton had been a busy man. His family and the business had kept him occupied as they moved across the bay to Sausalito, where they found a burgeoning maritime community. He'd helped pay for his workers to relocate, and the whole company had reestablished itself on the friendlier and healthier shore. He'd even found some time to write, and everyone was very pleased when he announced to them outside the stadium that he was part of another poetry event at the Six Gallery the following month. "We'll be there!" Molly said.

"No bar fights this time, Shig," Kats said.

"I make no guarantees," he replied with a grin.

The Giants beat the Dodgers, 8-0.

MAY 9, 1958

Kats pulled at the collar of his shirt. He wasn't used to wearing a suit and tie, but the occasion called for it. He arrived at Molly's apartment early, knowing she'd be stressed about her first Hollywood movie premier. She answered the door with her hair still up in curlers and in a robe. He smiled, said nothing, and patiently waited while she finished getting ready. The result was worth the wait. She stepped into the living room in a long, emerald-green dress that exposed her right shoulder. It was cut high on the leg, and it accentuated her tall curves. Her red hair was swept up, revealing her long neck. Kats gently applauded, which earned him a kiss. As they headed out the door, Kats realized she was a bit taller than him in her high heels. He made a mental note to stand up straight all evening.

The cab got them within one block of the Stage Door Theater on Mason and Geary. The marquee read "World Premier—Alfred Hitchcock's VERTIGO." There was a sizable crowd gathered around the entrance, hoping to get a look at the cast and the famed director. Jimmy Stewart had sent Kats the invitation the week before, which in turn had sent Molly into a spin, searching for just the right dress. This had elicited a tour of downtown department stores: City of Paris, Magnin, Roos Brothers, the Emporium, Liebes, and finally back to City of Paris. Kats just had to press his suit, but he, too, was excited to be in attendance.

They presented their invitation to the attendants, who ushered them inside the ropes and into the theater. Standing in the lobby, they watched the press crowd around Hitchcock and his wife. Kats noticed several actors from the movie and gave them familiar nods. Some photographers approached them and took Molly's picture. She smiled but whispered to Kats, "What are they doing?"

"They think you're a movie star. That's how beautiful you are," he said and squeezed her hand. At that, he could see the flush on her pale skin, and she smiled radiantly. Just then a murmur ran through the crowd, and the photographers headed toward the door. Outside they heard a cheer erupt and the sound of flashbulbs. Moments later, in walked Jimmy Stewart with his co-star, Kim Novak, on his arm. They looked like Hollywood royalty, and the pop of flash photography was momentarily blinding. Stewart shook hands with several people, waved affably, and strode into the crowded lobby. He greeted Hitchcock, and the two exchanged a few words. As he turned from the director, Stewart's eyes found Kats. He smiled and walked over.

"Hello, Kats," he smiled and extended his hand.

"Hello, Jim. Good to see you again."

"And you," he said honestly. "And this lovely lady?"

"Jim, this is Molly Hayes, my girlfriend. Molly, this is…"

"Jimmy Stewart!" she finished for him. "Wow, a pleasure to meet you," and he shook her hand.

"A pleasure to meet you as well. Kats, you've done well for yourself," he said to his friend. It was Kats's turn to blush as he smiled in agreement.

"How do you two know each other?" Molly asked.

"Your fella here taught me how to be a private detective in the movie. He was also my bodyguard, tour guide…"

"Driver mostly," Kats said, and they all laughed.

Stewart nodded and looked seriously at Kats for a moment. "Did that other thing get resolved properly? Everyone OK?"

Kats looked at Molly, who was now beginning to connect the dots. He nodded, "Yes, there was a bit of drama, but it worked out, and we are all OK."

Molly looked back and forth at the two men who were trying to talk about something without talking about it.

"Well, I got shot," she said matter of factly, and Kats noted Stewart's shocked expression. "But in the end, I think the good guys won," she smiled.

"A story for another day then?" Stewart said as he was being waved into the theater.

"Absolutely," Kats replied, and the two men shook hands again. Stewart gave a nod to Molly and was escorted to his seat next to Hitchcock.

Molly turned to Kats "So how is it a movie star was involved in this whole thing?"

He pulled her close and kissed her. "I promise to tell you. Later. Let's go enjoy the movie." Taking her by the hand, they entered the theater.

It was a very good movie.

-              -   -

Kats, Molly, and Shig will return.

AUTHOR'S NOTE

While this is a work of fiction, much of the surrounding people and events are real. Hunters Point and the Bayview Heights community have suffered greatly over the decades. The navy and the NRDL left behind a contaminated wasteland that remains a huge challenge today. Through the efforts of activists, community leaders, artists, and entrepreneurs, that neighborhood continues to show its underlying strength and resilience, and I hope it can transcend its history.

I loved writing about and researching the many real people that appear in this book: Jimmy Stewart, Dorothea Lange, Jack Kerouac, Jimmy "the Hat" Lanza, and especially Shig Murao. Of all the characters, he seemed to come to life the more I read about him. He's a somewhat forgotten, somewhat overlooked character in the San Francisco Renaissance. I hope that my homage to him spurs more to look back at this time in our cultural history and recognize the important role that people like Shig play in making and shaping cultural movements by being anchor points and connectors in an overall creative ecosystem.

As the son of a Nisei man from San Francisco and a red-headed Irish woman from Ohio, Kats and Molly hold a special place in my heart. They're both my parents and my creative children. Their journey draws upon my parents and their experience. I marvel at my parents' bravery for choosing each other in a time when so many forces would try to keep them apart. Heroes come in many forms. Sometimes they're decorated for bravery on the battlefield. Sometimes they simply choose love over fear.

Recommended Reading

Facing the Mountain—Daniel James Brown
Nonfiction account of the Japanese American experience during World War II. From life before the war to the battlefields of Europe, these incredible stories spurred my imagination and inspired this book.

Clark and Division—Naomi Hirahara
Fictional account of a Japanese American family who relocates out of an internment camp to Chicago. My own family also left the Topaz Relocation Camp in Utah for Chicago. I can imagine them walking the streets of Clark and Division like the heroine of this outstanding book.

Cool Grey City of Love—Gary Kamiya
Gary Kamiya has been writing about San Francisco for decades, and his outstanding books have been a cornerstone of my own understanding of the city. His description of Bayview Heights and Hunters Point as the "Mordor" of San Francisco really resonated with me. Gary loves San Francisco, and his writings are insightful love letters to the city.

They Called Us Enemy—George Takei, Justin Eisinger
I grew up with Mr. Sulu on *Star Trek*. Seeing an Asian face on TV was incredibly important to me. This manga-style graphic novel is a memoir that tells the story of Takei's own family's internment, which was emblematic of so many other Japanese American families.

ENDNOTES

1 The term "Beatnik" didn't appear until April 2, 1958, when San Francisco's famed newspaper man, Herb Caen, used the term, unflatteringly, in a column about the Beat art scene. It appeared in the *San Francisco Chronicle*. Reportedly, Allen Ginsberg hated the term.

2 In 1958, Rickover was named to the position of chief of the nuclear power division of ships. He was a life-long advocate for the nuclear navy.

3 Shig was more than just a translator. He was part of the Military Intelligence Service, which was the language training school during World War 2. The MIS played a critical role in code-breaking, communications interception, prisoner interrogation, and negotiations. They also were in danger from their own side as there were numerous incidents where Nisei soldiers were shot by fellow Americans.

4 There was a famous coffee and bagel shop in North Beach called Co-Existence Bagels. I'd thought to include that name here, but the legend of the short-lived café was that despite its name, the shop actually didn't serve bagels. For more on the mystery, see https://www.myrecipes.com/extracrispy/the-beat-generation-bagel-shop-that-didnt-sell-bagels.

5   Shig Murao was famous for drinking large amounts of Coca-Cola. He apparently once told a friend that his autobiography was going to be called *Confessions of a Coke-sucker* in honor of the dozen or so he consumed every day. Sadly, this habit probably contributed to his development of diabetes later in life. For more on the history of City Lights, see https://citylights.com/our-story/bookstore-tour/.

6   In conversation, Japanese Americans use the term "hakujin" to refer to White people. It's broadly recognized as a neutral term, not derogatory.

7   The crane image on the book cover is actually historically inaccurate. The crane in 1958 wouldn't have had the trapezoidal tower on top; that was added in the 1960s as part of the testing for the submarine-launched missile systems. However, the crane has become such an iconic image that it doesn't look right without the tower. So please allow for some creative license on this writer's part.

8   Jimmy Stewart was active in the Air Force Reserve for years after World War II and earned his rank. He eventually reached the rank of major general in 1985.

9   True, the ship was scuttled near the Farallon Islands. It was also later discovered to be filled with thousands of barrels of toxic waste. It remains a ticking time bomb off the coast of California.

10   The photo that Dorothea Lange took that day is actually of my father, Paul Kageyama.

San Francisco, California. A young evacuee arrives at 2020 Van Ness Avenue, meeting place of first contingent to be removed from San Francisco to Santa Anita Park Assembly center at Arcadia, California. Evacuees will be transferred to War Relocation Authority centers for the duration. Photo by Dorothea Lange, U.S. National Archives

11   This paraphrases the quote that she made famous. "The camera is an instrument that teaches people how to see without a camera."

12   Peter Matsumoto was one of my father's best friends. They met at camp and were lifelong friends. I am named after him, and so is Kats in a fashion. My father's other best friend from camp was Masa Taketoshi. In coming up with Kats' name, I blended their two names to create "Takemoto."

13   The Ashizawa family still owns the hardware store in Japantown. It's called Soko Hardware. After the war, the

family returned from Topaz and reopened the store. Masao Ashizawa ran the store for decades before retiring. Today his son Phil Ashizawa runs it. I know the Ashizawa family because my father was the spouse of the only Ashizawa daughter, Asaye. They reconnected in 1988 at a Topaz Reunion, and my father spent the remainder of his life with her in Berkeley.

14 The mystery of the Migrant Mother was eventually solved in 1978. She was revealed to be Florence Owens Thompson, who was working in Imperial Valley in Southern California on March 6, 1936, when Lange photographed her.

15 I never saw that photo of my father until after he'd passed away. If I had, I think I would have understood him better. Like most of that generation, my father almost never talked about internment. He might mention "camp," but I never learned the details. When I saw that photo, I realized that he was a scared teenager and that was probably the worst day of his life.

16 Jess Collins, or just "Jess," really was an engineer who worked on the Manhattan Project. The result of that work inspired a change of heart and career for the man. He was a visual artist known for his paintings and collages. The "Robert" he references in conversation is the poet Robert Duncan, his life partner. The two were seminal figures in the San Francisco Renaissance.

17 During the battle to rescue the Lost Battalion, from October 26—30, 1944, the 442nd suffered 800 casualties.

This included future Hawaiian Senator Daniel Inouye, who received a battlefield promotion for his efforts. They rescued 211 Texans. In 1962, Texan Governor John Connally made the veterans of the 442nd "Honorary Texans" in appreciation of their heroics.

18 The Vanguard was the Navy's missile project. It wasn't the program led by Verner Von Braun. His team had been relegated because many feared that the appearance of a former German—some said Nazi—scientist leading the US space program was bad PR. After the failure of the Vanguard, Von Braun's team was reinstated to lead the space program.

19 Gary Kamiya did write a book about it! *Cool Grey City of Love* was invaluable to me in the writing of this book, and I highly recommend it. I was lucky to spend an afternoon with Gary in March 2022, as he gave me and my then fiancé (now wife) Lisa Wannemacher a personal tour of San Francisco.

20 Jimmy Lanza had many more days. He died of natural causes (not a cobra bite) on February 14, 2006, in his California home. He was 103 years old.

21 There really was a no-bid contract given to build what became known as Candlestick Park. Most of the land was owned by a local contractor names Charles Harney. The city purchased the land from him, and he made a profit of more than $2 million in addition to receiving the contract for the stadium. There was a grand jury investigation into the whole affair, but no charges were filed. See https://en.wikipedia.org/wiki/Candlestick_Park.

ABOUT THE AUTHOR

Peter Kageyama is a sansei, a third generation Japanese American. Born in Akron, Ohio, he attended The Ohio State University, receiving a B.A. in Political Science, and Case Western University School of Law for his J.D. He practiced law for a couple of years but describes himself as a 'recovering attorney'.

Peter is the author of four nonfiction books on cities and urban affairs. His first book, *For the Love of Cities*, was recognized as a Top 10 Book in Urban Planning and Development. He speaks all over the world about better placemaking that emphasizes small, inexpensive, and fun approaches to city building. He was a Senior Advisor to the Alliance for Innovation, a national network of city leaders, and is a special advisor to America in Bloom.

In his spare time Peter is an avid board gamer, comic book geek and classic rock nerd. He lives in downtown St. Petersburg, Florida with his wife, award winning architect Lisa Wannemacher and their dog Dobby.

www.peterkageyama.com

Made in the USA
Las Vegas, NV
14 January 2023

65589370R00215